Falling In

The Lakeville Project: Book One

Falling In

By C.S. Robbie

Copyright ©2021 C.S. Robbie

Cover Photo by Rachel Golding

Cover Model: Sawyer Gallup

Published in the United States By 7th Option Press

ISBN: 978-0-578-34459-1

Dedication

To daydreams and imaginary friends. Don't let anyone tell you it's silly. Thank you to my family and friends who believed they could be real.

Acknowledgments

First, thank you BETA readers: Barb and Scott, Christopher, Christine, Michelle, Anna, Olivia, Haley, Sawyer Jamie, Jennifer, Sam, and Joanne. Thank you to my computer expert Jeremy. If I forgot someone, forgive me. So many have helped me along the way. Your feedback was crucial in making this happen. This book would never have been written without the love and support of my husband, Bobby G., my son Camden, and my daughter, Sawyer.

"Dream as if you will live forever;
Live as if you will die today."

~James Dean

CHAPTER 1

My eyes caught the red glow from the celebratory flares and followed it around the lake where thousands of innocent people partied without a care in the world. Music blared. Laughter bellowed. Conversation ebbed and flowed as if tonight was just another ordinary July third on Conesus Lake. But deep down, I knew better. And this angry boy who stood before me–he wanted to make sure I had it right.

Deafening rockets launched from the dock next door, exploded above our heads, and shot ribbons of twinkling color through the dark smoky sky. It was enough to knock me out of my momentary trance only to find his glaring eyes still locked with mine. His eyes bore through me as if he expected me to read his mind.

"You're not listening, Chelsea," he snapped.

"I get it," I confessed. "People always say that nothing bad ever happens in Lakeville. But they're wrong. This town is the perfect cover for all sorts of evil."

Then suddenly, it became crystal clear. I remembered how it all began on that cold and blustery night back in February. All the signs were there. I should have seen them before now.

Every ounce of air in my lungs expelled at once, and with what little breath remained, I managed to utter, "The problem is–I refuse to believe that we are that evil. And something tells me you don't agree."

~ February ~

Lakeville, your quintessential Finger Lakes town, was surrounded by rolling hills, vast farmlands, vineyards, and flowery meadows. There were antique shops on every corner and boutiques filled with

1

one-of-a-kind finds. The town was riddled with craft breweries, farm-to-table restaurants, and restored buildings built in the 1800's. You'd be hard-pressed to find a neighbor who wasn't helpful or a stranger who wasn't kind.

Keeping that overload of charm in mind, it did have its downfalls. For example, when something big happened in town, you were expected to show up. Tonight, it was the grand opening of the Sheer Art Gallery. It was named after one of the biggest benefactors in town. It sounded like a snooze fest to me, but Brent didn't agree.

My boyfriend, Brent Stewart III, insisted on going to the opening so we could "schmooze with the important people". His words, not mine. Schmoozing equaled boring in my book.

When five o'clock rolled around, and Brent called to tell me that he was stuck at the library prepping for his final debate, I dove into my sweat pants and headed for the living room. I skipped down the stairs two steps at a time, snatched the throw blanket from the couch, and sunk into the brown leather recliner with my book. I was free and clear.

"Chelsea! Chelsea, come here please," hollered my mother.

I froze. She had that "I need you to do something for me" tone to her voice. I ignored her and slid deeper under the blanket.

"Chelsea," my mother repeated, stomping down the stairs. I panicked inside. *Please, don't make me do the laundry. I just want to relax.* "Answer me when I call you," she demanded.

"Sorry, Mom. I didn't hear you."

I sat up in the chair. My sister Meggie came down the stairs behind my mom, looking very much like the cat that ate the canary.

"I heard Brent canceled on you. But your sister wants to go to the gallery opening tonight. She needs to go."

I waited for it. I prayed it wasn't going to happen. But deep down, I knew free and clear was too good to be true.

"So you'll be going with her. I don't want her to go alone."

"No way" was the first response that came to mind. *"Oh, hell, no"* followed that. However, one glimpse at Meggie's lost eyes under her mop of asymmetrical black, blonde and purple bobbed hair, and I felt

myself crumbling. Art wasn't my thing, but it was hers. And though Meggie was six years older than me, maturity-wise, you'd never have guessed it. She was on a quest to find herself, and if my parents thought I could help her in the least, then there was no getting out of it. But I opened my mouth to try anyway.

"No," snapped my mother. "Support the community. We've never had an art gallery. I'd go if I could, but I have to confirm details for the trip."

"You and dad aren't leaving for a few days," I reminded her. All that did was generate "the look".

"Fine. I'll go change," I mumbled.

I took my time, hoping Meggie would change her mind. But my sloth-like behavior only irritated her.

"Hurry up. We can't be late," Meggie snapped.

Ten minutes later we were out the door and headed straight to boredom.

The recently renovated town recreation center was less than five minutes up the road, making the blustery snow irrelevant to our drive. It was Meggie's erratic driving that almost killed us. Yet somehow, she managed to get us there in one piece.

"I'm driving us home," I snapped, stepping out of the car.

"There are like six cars here," Meggie said, locking the doors behind her.

"I told you we were too early."

"Or this is going to be completely lame."

"Yup, there's that too," I said, sighing.

As we entered the peach-colored stucco building, we were hit by the smell of newly painted white walls and fresh cut wood from the oak beams that stretched across the ceiling. Artists buzzed about, adding finishing touches to their displays. A string quartet was setting up in the back corner.

Suddenly, we spotted the words "The Artist Connection" eerily floating in front of us in bold black lettering. We stopped dead in our tracks. It didn't take long to figure out that it was painted across a transparent, twenty-five foot long wall. A sign explained that the

3

drawings on the wall were created by each artist displaying their work at the gallery. They depicted each person's "epiphany of artistic ability". However, there were no drawings on the invisible wall yet.

"See, too early," I said, gesturing to the empty wall.

Meggie ignored me, looked around in awe, and said, "This place is unbelievable."

Though Lakeville was on one of the smaller Finger Lakes, it was true what people said about it; when Lakeville did things, they didn't hold back. And by the size of the quickly growing crowd, everyone who was anyone was there to see it. Brent was going to kick himself when he found out what he missed.

Suddenly, a deep voice bellowed behind us.

"Chelsea Hazel Raleigh, what brings *you* here? No boyfriend, no side kick. Wow, that's a first."

Meggie whacked my arm, her mouth hung open. I cringed. She was barreling full speed into boy-crazy mode, and that wasn't even the worst part. Forget about the way Meggie so blatantly gawked at the hot guy that stood before us. Let's talk about the fact that this hot guy was my boss, Jackson, from Trend Boutique. Then top that off with the fact that he threw my middle name out like it was common knowledge. And to think, I left my sweatpants and a book at home for *this*.

I swallowed the urge to run and hide. Then I reminded Jackson that my so-called side kick Paige, my best friend, was at home sick with the flu. Paige also worked at Trend, and yes, we were pretty much inseparable. As for the boyfriend, I ignored that comment. It was weird. It wasn't like I ever talked to Jackson about him anyway. After another whack on the arm, I introduced him to my sister, emphasizing that he was my boss.

Meggie extended her limp and cringeworthy hand.

"Hello," she swooned.

"Nice to meet you," he said, catching only her finger tips. Suddenly, his face lit up when someone behind us caught his eye.

"Mia," Jackson said.

He pulled the curly-haired dirty blonde into his arms. After

4

Meggie sized up Mia in her short, tight, black dress that her boobs barely fit into, her face deflated faster than an untied balloon.

"Chels, this is Mia, my girlfriend." As he went in for a kiss, Mia turned and gave him her cheek. Jackson said to her, "So glad you made it."

She smiled at him and nodded to us. By that time, Meggie had vanished into the crowd.

"So," I said, rocking back on my heels. Awkward silence was nails on a chalkboard to me. "Uh, yeah. This is crazy, right. Five minutes ago, we were the only ones here. Now, this place is jamming.

"So, I promised my mother I wouldn't make Meggie come to this alone. She just graduated from art school and wants to teach but has absolutely no motivation to look for a job. My mom promised me a get out of jail free card if I would do this so, of course, I agreed. I mean, who doesn't want one of those, right?"

Mia raised her eyebrows.

"That was a joke," I seemed obligated to point out. "I was kidding. I mean, I don't foresee needing to get out of jail. You know, because I'm not going to do anything to end up in jail; I was just being funny…or dumb…"

As if on cue, Mia looked at her cell phone and whispered something in Jackson's ear.

"Hey, Chelsea, we're hooking up with some friends here. I guess they're in the back corner waiting for us. Good to see you out and about."

With that, Mia grabbed his hand and dragged him away. He looked back and said with a wink, "See you in the morning."

Standing there alone, I rolled my eyes and mumbled, "God, what is wrong with me?" I needed to leave, and maybe chill in the car until Meggie was done "making connections". I started towards the door and made it as far as the glass wall.

In a matter of minutes, the invisible wall had *completely* transformed, and I was *completely* mesmerized. Water appeared to flow down the wall, over charcoal drawings. I reached out and put a finger on the wall only to discover that the water was inside. The wall was alive with movement. It glowed with a soft white light making the water sparkle and shimmer as it snaked its way through the glass. The drawings and the water seemed to float and move through mid air. Amongst all the colorful paintings, pottery, and abstract metal art pieces in this room, the wall was a beacon in the dark. The simplicity of the water, light, and basic black and white coloring was breathtaking.

I was so engrossed in the wall that I wasn't aware of others who had also been sucked into its beauty until I bumped into a young man beside me. He had dark hair, black dress pants, a plain white button-up shirt, and the funkiest tropical-patterned bow tie.

"Sorry," I mumbled.

He shrugged it off.

I eyed the drawings for several seconds in silence. As I began to move down the wall, studying each picture, the young man scooted along with me. When I had reached the half way point, I came upon a tall burly guy wearing an orange plaid shirt sitting on a stool, his back pressed against the wall. He was talking to a friend whose palm was plastered to the glass. I skirted around them and kept going.

"Rude," I muttered. "Lean on someone's art, why don't you."

Finally, the guy shadowing me said, "All of our artists tonight, regardless of their area of expertise, were asked to submit one drawing that represented their journey to be here."

"These are so amazing," I responded. I shrugged. "And to be honest, I don't even like art. I was never any good at it."

A smile spread across his face. He placed one hand on my elbow and shook my hand with the other. "I'm one of the hosts this evening. Mason Dale. And I can't tell you how happy that makes me."

I chuckled. "It makes you happy that I hate art?"

He shook his head. "It makes me happy that you found something amazing here, especially since you don't even like art. Do you like music?"

"Love it."

"Music is art."

6

"I hadn't thought of it that way." I pointed to the last drawing and said, "That one is my favorite."

At the far end of the glass wall, was a drawing of a fragile-looking girl wearing a tattered primitive dress and carrying a large ornate sphere. The sphere rested on her back as she leaned forward and trekked up a hill to five crosses stuck in the ground.

"I imagine it to be gold or something," I said, pointing to the sphere. "Or maybe carved wood." I looked closer at the drawing. "Are those faces?"

Mason moved in and eyed the piece. "Yes, it seems so."

"The detail is amazing," I said, noticing the weeping willow tree at the top of the hill. Its branches seemed to blow, indicating that the girl was also fighting against the wind. "The poor girl; she looks so tired."

"She *is* tired. It's been a grueling few weeks getting this place ready for tonight."

"Are you talking about this artist?"

"Yes. I opened the gallery with her a few weeks ago." He looked over his shoulder to a crowd around a copper and iron exhibit, and then back at me. He said, "Please come back again. We're going to start having big party events to showcase our local artists in a couple months. There will be multiple bands. More live music; your favorite kind of art."

"Wait," I said, stopping him as he turned to walk away. "Can anyone join? I mean, how would an artist go about getting her work displayed?"

He leaned in, "Megan pointed you out. She saw you leaving. I believe she was working up to asking me that very question."

"Do you know Megan?"

He nodded. "We took some art classes together in college. She was insecure then, and I think she's even more insecure now. I'll talk to her before the end of the night."

"That would be cool."

"Just make sure you come to her first showing."

7

"I promise," I said. Mason scooted off to another exhibit, continuing his rounds as the attentive host.

I looked back up at the drawing. It was almost hypnotic. I felt for the girl in the picture. She carried such a burden, but at the same time, it was so beautiful. I wondered what it all meant. The five crosses on the hill, like graves. The hill so steep that in real life, no one would be able to carry anything up it. Yet, despite her struggles, I believed this girl would do it.

Without thinking, I reached out to touch the drawing. I put my hand on the glass wall just below the drawing of the girl and got the shock of a lifetime.

"Geez," I gasped and jumped back.

I tried to shake the pain from my hand, but it ran up my arm and through my shoulder. On the other side of the glass, there was a girl about my age ferociously rubbing her arm.

"You get shocked too?" I asked.

"Felt more like I got shot," she said with a scowl.

"I know, right?"

The girl continued to glower through the wall. Her bright blue eyes, surrounded by her long dark hair, stayed locked to mine as she turned and marched away. There was something vaguely familiar about her. But in a small town everyone looked familiar, whether it was because you saw them at the grocery store or the coffee shop or you passed on the street.

Despite getting zapped, I couldn't escape the wall. I must have studied the drawings for another ten minutes before tearing myself away. I spotted Meggie across the room in a deep conversation with Mason. It looked like she was making that art connection she had hoped for. I glanced at the wall ironically named "The Artist Connection". And instead of leaving, I joined Meggie. We stayed for two hours before heading home.

"I'm driving," I said, holding my hand out for the keys.

"Fine," she shrugged.

We were standing at the main door of the building. People shuffled around us to leave while Meggie dug through her purse to fish the keys from the bottom of her bag. As she handed them to me, she dropped them. They plunked to the floor, got kicked by a passer-by, and slid a few feet until they stopped under a wingback chair.

"Seriously?" I scoffed at my sister.

For the simple reason that she looked amused, I demanded that she go retrieve them. Meggie crossed her arms and walked out the door where she stood in the cold and waited under the awning.

"This is the thanks I get," I said under my breath.

I zig-zagged through the cluster of people until I reached the chair. Cursing Meggie, I got on my hands and knees, but all I found were dust bunnies dancing in the cold draft from the door.

"Looking for these?"

Keys jingle above me.

I got to my feet and said, "Hey, thanks. I was worried for a second."

A tall muscular guy in an orange plaid shirt held out the keys. As I took them from him our fingers touched, and again, I was shocked. I flinched. He also flinched. His face scrunched up as if I'd shocked him on purpose.

"Sorry," I mumbled and walked away.

Over my shoulder, I caught his icy stare. *Geez, get a grip, dude.* I rushed outside to my sister. We scurried through the snow to Meggie's car and jumped in.

"What are you waiting for? Start the car," she demanded.

But there, at the entrance of the rec center, stood the angry giant. Glaring at me. Scowling at me. My stomach flopped.

"What are you looking at?" Meggie asked.

"Nothing," I said starting the car and cranking the heat.

People were forced to walk around the giant to get out the door. Meggie glanced at the doorway, where my eyes were locked.

"What's with him?" she uttered.

"I shocked him when he handed me the keys. I guess he holds a grudge." I tore myself away from the guy and focused on Meggie. "And thanks for that. Dork."

She flicked my forehead and said, "He's a psycho. Let's go."

Once home, I tried to pick up where I left off, but I couldn't stop thinking about the way the evening had unfolded: my reluctance about going to the gallery, the amazing wall with the drawing that I couldn't get out of my head, the shock from the wall, the blue-eyed girl who was also zapped at the same time, and the kind host who was going to help my sister find herself. And then there was the big, buff guy with the attitude problem. I pictured his angry eyes glaring at me and shuttered.

If only I hadn't ignored the signs that February night. If only I realized that it was much more than just a bad feeling. If only I could have seen the little tells for what they really were. Instead, it would take weeks, months, pain and suffering, and even death in order to realize that my life was nothing but a lie.

CHAPTER 2

~ *May* ~

My parents weren't anti-vaxxers, super religious, or in a cult. The reason behind being homeschooled was far less interesting and somewhat embarrassing. I was homeschooled because the very idea of going to school was literally painful. I hated school from day one.

In kindergarten, every day was a battle that began with crying and refusal to get on the bus. When my mother drove me to school, getting me out of the car required muscle and the principal. Every single time.

I suffered from headaches and stomach aches and sore throats. I demanded that my temperature be taken every single day because I was sure I had a fever, even when the thermometer said otherwise. But I could not help it. I was terrified of school for no good reason, and at the same time, for every reason in the world.

By the end of kindergarten, doctors had diagnosed me with severe anxiety triggered by school. And instead of starting me on medication at the age of six, my parents kept me home, and my mother put a hold on her career so she could school me. Flash forward twelve years: While completing my senior year in high school, I started on meds, and at the same time, aced Spanish 101 at the local college anxiety free. Yesterday, senior year officially became a thing of the past. I was ready. But ready for what?

As the fog tried to smother the morning, I stood on my dock, wondering where my life was headed. My future stretched out before me. But like the rolling hills that spanned beyond my line of sight and the shimmering water of Conesus Lake, with its sharp bend into the fog, my future was a blur.

I shook myself from a good stare, turned my back on the lake, and walked to the house to get the hose. I dragged it back out to the end of the dock and blasted the paddle boat. Since our trusty Crownline kicked the bucket last week, the rickety craft was our only source of lake transportation. It was a pathetic little thing, but it was all we had until our new boat came in at the end of the summer.

For a brief second, I was blinded as the sun sliced through the fog and hit the windshield of a white and blue Sea Ray anchored about half way across the lake. There it was again, as it had been every day and every night for the last couple of weeks. It always went to the same spot and just sat there.

"Hey, Chels. What are you doing?" Beth asked, tapping my shoulder.

She giggled as I jumped.

"Geez. I didn't hear your car," I snapped. I took a few steps back and grabbed the hose that I had absentmindedly dropped. "I was cleaning the paddle boat for us. The seats are gross."

I turned all of my attention back to the slime. My bestie watched me with a skeptical eye.

"I talked to Paige this morning," Beth said. "She loves Duke. We are totally going to lose her."

"Don't say that."

Paige was on a campus visit at Duke University with her parents. Beth, that friend who was honest to a fault and always the pessimist, was convinced that Paige would go off to school and we'd never see her again. The rest of us were staying local. However, I had known Paige longer than anyone. And I knew, no matter where she went, we'd never lose her for good.

"Wow, you look like crap," Beth pointed out. "Another sleepless night?"

"Yeah. Pretty much."

I looked away and poked at the bags under my eyes. I hadn't thought they were that obvious.

"You were staring at something out there." She nodded towards the lake. "Whatcha lookin' at?"

"Nothing." I sprayed the seat and sides of the boat until the green goo disintegrated. I wasn't going to say anything, but I couldn't hold back. So I said, "See that boat way out there, across the lake?"

Beth followed my finger.

"Uh huh," she drawled.

I dropped the hose at my feet and said, "They could be watching us right now? We would have no idea. Or there, up in the hills. Someone could be up there with binoculars or a telescope." I pointed towards Vitale Park at the north end of the lake. "Or down there in the park."

Beth started singing, "Every move you make, every breath you take..."

"Very funny, Sting. I know, I sound paranoid. And no, it's not my anxiety. That boat has been in the same spot for two weeks straight. It launches there." I pointed to the public boat launch directly across the lake from my house and drew an imaginary line to where it was anchored now. "And it only goes to that point. It doesn't cruise around, no one goes tubing or dives off the thing, and they aren't fishing."

"Okay then, let's say we're being watched. Someone would want to watch us because...?"

"Because they're creepy?" I said, rolling my eyes. I shook my head. "Creepy people don't need a good reason to do creepy things."

"Did it occur to you that it could be Brent? Maybe he's trying to see if you have a new boyfriend or something."

"No. It's over. There weren't any tears. It was the easiest break-up in history. Besides, he'd never waste his time watching me everyday," I said, laughing off the idea.

Brent and I had broken up about a month ago. He was three years into college and absorbed in all things related to his future. And rightly so. We had grown apart, and when I brought it up, he hadn't argue with me. It was time.

Glancing over Beth's shoulder, I spotted our friend Jill sneaking down the deck stairs.

I said to Beth, "Seriously though, there are creepers out there

13

who would just watch you because they're nosey or strange or just plain crazy."

Jill nodded at me as she tip-toed several feet behind Beth, holding a finger to her lips.

"Maybe. But we aren't that entertaining." Beth replied with half a smirk. "Well, I mean, you're cute and everything. But watching you hose off the boat and do all those exciting things you do isn't exactly award winning material. I think you're getting paranoid."

Beth started to turn around so I took her by the shoulders and pulled her in, giving Jill a few more seconds to get closer. I needed something juicy to keep her attention.

I lowered my voice and said, "You may think I'm over-reacting, but how would you explain the man on my dock last night?"

"What man?"

"Last night, I was on the porch reading, when I saw someone in the rain, right here, at the end of my dock." I pointed to a spot next to the ladder.

Beth's eyes widened. "Really?" she said. "Are you being serious?"

"Yes," I uttered. She was hooked. "It was pouring rain, and he was just standing there, looking at me. Staring at me. I hollered out to him and asked if he was looking for my dad or something, but he didn't say anything. He just...stared. Then, all of a sudden, lightning flashed and lit up the whole sky. And when I looked around...He disappeared with the thunder. Just like that. Bam!" I smacked my hands together in Beth's face just as Jill grabbed her by the shoulders and shook her. Beth jumped and screamed. Jill and I exploded with laughter.

"Oh. My. God. You guys are pure evil," Beth clutched her chest and snapped, "You almost gave me a heart attack. You suck, Chelsea."

"Payback," I giggled.

Seconds later, when Beth's breathing slowed, she was laughing with us. She grabbed the hose at our feet.

"Divide and conquer!" I yelled to Jill.

We sprinted off the dock and into the yard, then split off in different directions, scurrying in a zig zag pattern to escape Beth's revenge. Jill slid in the wet grass and got blasted in the back of her curly blonde head.

"You can't get away!" Beth hollered at her.

I headed back to the end of the dock as Jill scrambled to her feet and went to find cover on the back porch. Beth was on a mission to blast Jill again. Not even the whicker chairs could shield her. They were hurling with laughter and taunting each other with witty remarks.

When I got to the end of the dock and looked back at my house, the smile dropped from my face. I closed my eyes and remembered the dark figure standing under the light at the end of my dock last night. Right in the very spot where I was standing. Was I paranoid, as Beth said?

My eyes popped open to find the blinding windshield of the Sea Ray swaying in the water. No, I was not paranoid.

The Ivory Dome

I made my way to the stern of the boat, binoculars glued to my eyes, while Subject Number Thirteen laughed and goofed around with her boring, unimportant friends. She was the special one, not those simpletons. But it wasn't the right time to confront her just yet. For now, it didn't matter that she believed the dullards were the most important people in her life. The ridiculous, meaningless, irrelevant teenage drama her annoying friends infected her with had an expiration date. Soon, she'd know the truth.

Learning each subject's potential, the details of each one's special trait, each one's little secret–that was paramount at this stage in the project. I had to watch them in their natural environment a bit longer, especially this one, Subject Number Thirteen. By no means was N13 the beginning; but right now, she was the most crucial.

Her hair waved in the breeze as she hurried to the edge of the still water at the end of her dock. Streaked with light from the fast rising sun, a ribbon of silky caramel trailed behind N13. She smiled. She laughed. She danced about, a butterfly amongst slugs.

From the corner of my eye, the bright white Lakeville water tower grabbed my attention. It jutted high above the trees on the hill with its proud black lettering for all to see. I couldn't hold back the smirk. This sweet, unsuspecting village was weeks away from becoming the most important town on the planet. And they hadn't a clue.

CHAPTER 3

For the first time in days, I didn't see the obnoxious boat across the lake. My parents had gone to Buffalo for an overnight stay with my aunt and uncle. Beth and Jill left after spending a relaxing day doing absolutely nothing. I finally had the evening to myself. It was time to snuggle into my cozy spot and do one of my favorite things–escape to another world in book.

Our house was built on a hill, with the main road in the front of the house and the lake in the back. When you entered our house it was from a side door on the second floor where the bedrooms, laundry, and full bath were located. Downstairs was the main living area, a small bathroom, and a kitchen that opened up to the back porch and yard.

I grabbed my book from my room and headed downstairs. There was a small office nook just as you got to the bottom of the stairs. I snatched a throw blanket from the office chair and my coffee from the kitchen island, then slipped out the sliding glass door to the back porch.

Once the sun dropped behind the hills, and my coffee was gone, I lit a candle. I plugged in the Edison porch lights that were strung from the ceiling and across the yard to a light pole just before the dock. It was time to dive into the second half of my book.

About an hour later, I reached the point in the book where I could not put it down. The answers to all of my questions, all of my suspicions, all of my hunches were about to be revealed. Except there was one problem–I was freezing. Even wrapped in a blanket, my teeth chattered like a wind-up toy as I tried to finish the novel. A frigid wind kicked up from the lake and whipped across the porch, blowing out the candle. It looked as though it was time to call it a night and bring this one-girl party inside.

I stood and stretched my bare legs. Shorts had been a poor choice. I shivered. That was when I first noticed an odd humming sound. It was quiet as it reverberated softly through the brisk night air. The first thing that jumped into my mind was the man at the end of my dock the other night. The Edison lights gave a soft yellow hue to the yard, so I could easily see all the way to the end of the dock. To my relief, no one was there. I glanced around the rest of the yard, and again, found no one.

As I gathered my book, blanket, and coffee mug, the noise continued to grow slightly louder with each passing second. Then a thought stopped me dead in my tracks. I put everything down and stood very still. I listened. What I thought I was hearing would be impossible in this cold temperature.

The humming noise sounded distant, and I couldn't tell where in the world it was coming from. I thought perhaps it was a boat, but when I turned an ear towards the lake, it didn't seem to be coming from that direction. I rotated in a circle, listening. It could have been a heating unit from a neighboring house or a motorcycle up on the road. But again, I couldn't pinpoint the direction of the sound. Whatever it was, it was getting closer.

I edged my way to the sliding glass door. The sound was quickly becoming clearer. It was definitely a buzzing noise. I put my hand on the door handle and stopped.

"Bees?"

My heart skipped a beat as I was brought back to Grandma Fran's farm when I was eight… How high I had climbed into that peach tree in front of her barn… The mesmerizing peach, the color of a late summer sunset… The unfortunate luck to snap a branch that held a massive bee hive.

Not everyone can say they know the sound of so many bees. Not everyone knows the terrifying rush of pain caused by the panic that snaps from neuron to neuron even before the tiny creatures strike. But I knew it all too well. I stood on the porch, listening to the white noise in the distance with a stampede of sharp panic running through my chest. At the same time, I wondered where the heck I had left my EpiPen.

After finding out how terribly allergic I was to bee stings, I became well versed in the nature of bees. I knew it would be unheard of for bees to fly when it was so cold, especially at night. So the noise had to be something else.

The hum. The buzz. The noise unleashed a beast that held back my most terrifying childhood memory. It wasn't simply about a painful bee sting or that I could potentially have a deadly reaction. It was a sound that ran through me like an electrical shock. It was a direct link to an event ten years ago that I would rather forget but knew I never could. The familiar sound I was hearing–I could not deny that it sounded exactly like an entire hive full of pissed off bees.

I tossed all rational explanations aside and tightened my grip on the door handle. A familiar fear momentarily paralyzed me; one that I had acquired the hard way. The truth was that sometimes you just couldn't run fast enough, and sometimes there was nowhere to hide.

"It can't be bees. It can't," I mumbled. I yanked on the door. "Come on. Open. Open!" I yelled.

With two hands on the handle and my foot braced against the house, I pulled as hard as I could. The door refused to budge. Despite the frigid air, I was sweating. My heart raced faster as the buzz got louder. Whatever it was, it couldn't be far away. Dizzy with fear, I realized I had to find a way inside. So I ran up the deck steps to the side door. On the last step, I stumbled onto the deck floor, threw my hands out, and caught myself before almost face-planting into the wooden planks. I jumped to my feet, at the same time pulling several toothpick-sized slivers from my palm and wrist.

Finally, I grabbed the screen door and yanked it with a prayer. The screen door flew wide open and smacked into the house. I dove over the threshold and onto the floor, smudging blood across the light-colored stone tiles. The door came back at me and slammed shut on my ankle. Luckily, the high level of adrenaline zipping through my veins prevented my body from registering the pain.

The buzzing noise continued to grow. If it truly was a swarm of bees that I heard, there had to be hundreds. I sat on the floor frozen. Listening.

Waiting.

"BUZZZZZ..."

The sound was unbearable, and the house began to vibrate. I stared helplessly at the screen door, waiting for something to happen. A swarm of bees? A helicopter above? All I knew for certain was that I wanted it to be over. Then they hit.

Bees. Not hundreds of bees, but thousands of bees struck the house–and didn't stop.

I kicked the heavy mahogany door shut and locked it. Slouched against the door, wide-eyed and trembling, I listened. It was as if a thousand tiny stones were being hurled at my door and windows. The momentary relief of being safe in the house vanished when the windows started to rattle.

"Oh, God. They're going to break," I sputtered.

I stood and dug into my pocket for my cell phone. My first instinct was to call my father. I began to dial his number, then hung up. "9-1-1. I have to call 9-1-1 first."

All of a sudden, I was jolted by an abrupt impact on the house. It knocked me to the floor. My phone broke free from my hand, slid across the tiles, and smacked into the wall. An eight by ten family photo dropped from the wall and shattered. Glass shot out in every direction. I scrambled across the floor, the shards of glass slicing away at my knees and hands, until I reached my phone.

I propped myself against the wall and pulled several quarter-sized pieces of glass from my knee. What began as tossed stones pelting the house was now a machine gun relentlessly plugging away. It hammered louder and stronger with each passing minute. The entire house shook like the earth was moving. If I hadn't seen the bees with my own eyes, I would have sworn it was an earthquake. But then, with my trembling, bloody finger on the nine, something unexplainable happened.

Silence.

Just like that. There was complete silence. I froze. I heard nothing, not even the tiniest buzz. The vibrating windows and shaking house had come to a halt. The earth no longer moved. I crept back to the door and peeked through the window. It was too dark to see anything.

A thousand bees must lay dead on the deck, I thought. I flicked on the flood light and was confused. There was not one single bee. A lonely white moth fluttered around the light next to the door. Nothing else.

I saw them diving into the screen. I heard them crashing into the house. I felt it, I thought. Didn't I?

I cracked the window to listen. Still, there was not even a hum in the distance. I wandered around the house looking out the windows for a sign, evidence that what I saw had really happened. Yet, just the idea, it was absurd. A swarm of thousands of bees at ten o'clock on a cold May night? I had to look around outside. There had to be an explanation.

I wrapped a small towel from the bathroom around my bloody hand and somehow mustered the courage to step outside where bee carcasses should have littered the side deck. Should have–but didn't. I made my way down to the back porch, past the sliding glass door, and walked out to the lawn. At that point, I got nervous being so far away from the house. Without thinking, I hurried to the locked glass door that hadn't budged minutes ago. This time, it slid open.

I hurried inside and slammed the door. I stood statuesque with my forehead pressed against the cold glass door. My eyes stared aimlessly out into the yard. When the window fogged up from my breath, I drew a bee with my finger.

"What the heck was that?" I mumbled.

I took a deep breath, rubbed the dampness from my forehead, and double checked that the door was indeed locked.

After going door to door and window to window checking that everything was secured, I washed my hands and knees. They weren't as bad as I'd originally thought. I bandaged my wounds, then took one last peek out the window. There wasn't a sound in the air except for the hum of the refrigerator downstairs. Just the thought of the bees hitting the house made my hands tremble again.

"What in the world just happened?" I uttered.

My mind raced as I tossed in my bed that night. I decided a couple of things might be true. There was a freak occurrence of killer bees on the loose in Lakeville, and I was lucky to have survived. Or my sleep deprivation was causing me to imagine things.

To sleep or not to sleep? That was the question that lingered as I stared out the window at the full moon. The sleepless nights had become harder to keep track of. I could try to stay up all night so I wouldn't have nightmares or the wild and exhausting dreams created by my unrestful mind. However, I knew without some sleep I was doomed to be exhausted the next day; and now, it looked as if delusional episodes were becoming a common side effect of my insomnia.

Choosing sleep seemed like the lesser of two evils, at the time. But in the end, I was gravely mistaken.

CHAPTER 4

They were vivid and extremely convincing; I would have sworn it was all real. And it was exciting, more exciting than my real life, so I should have known better. I was living it, as if I were the star of my own set of short movies. Mini-trailers made to tantalize, intrigue, and leave you thirsty for more. A thriller, a romance, a horror film all in one continuous stream. That was the only way to describe the madness of my dreams that night.

Trailer one was a heavenly blink of an eye. At the end of a long, dark, and empty room, lit only by the moonlight, sheer white curtains blew in the breeze from the open window. They fluttered like soft, radiant angel's wings. It was beautiful. It was serene. Only when the wind died down did I notice the man standing beyond the window, hidden by the dancing curtains. Then everything disappeared.

Trailer two was mesmerizing, and no longer than the first. It began with the silhouette of a man. An ominous shadow was cast over his face. I could scarcely make out strong shoulders, a simple white t-shirt, and jeans. He was not an older man as I had first thought. He was young, like me; I could tell by his build, the way he moved, and the smoothness of the skin on his hands. His strong shoulders were thrown back confidently, his head tilted, his hands casually at his sides.

It was the hero shot. The slow motion part of the movie that made your heart stop and your breath stall. The directors way of saying "Get a good look girls. He's a hot one." Only I couldn't get a good look at this guy, at least not his face.

With each step he took, the floor boards creaked. Dust billowed up and a musty odor, like that of a basement in an old house, filled the room. And as quickly as it began–it ended.

My patience started to wither in the dark intermission. I willed there to be more and prayed I would see him again. An unusual amount of emotion was building inside of me. Seconds later, the trailers continued.

Trailer three began with his fiery lips on mine. Unsure of what led up to this moment, and not caring, my eyes flew open. His face, as close as it was, was still shadowed. Even as he pulled his lips from mine, he was beclouded.

"I can't see you," I managed to whisper.

He put a finger to my lips, then leaned in to whisper in my ear. His voice was sweet and deep, his breath heavy.

He said, "Ever wonder how something that starts so heavenly could end so horribly?"

Heavenly? That's how I felt when I first saw him. Was he insinuating that things between us would end badly? Afraid and unsure of how to answer the question, I shook my head no.

His breath was hot on my ear. "But you're smarter than that."

"I want to see your face," I said, pulling back to see him.

His hand cupped the back of my head to keep me close.

Thick with disappointment, he said, "Chelsea, Chelsea. The circumstances are grave. Things shouldn't have to be this way. We've made a terrible mistake."

"What mistake?" I asked.

Suddenly, he backed away. That's when the musty odor in the room turned into a putrid stench. Death seemed to crawl through the air. It was too much; I threw my hand over my nose and mouth.

"I'm afraid I've led you in the wrong direction," the boy said, regaining my attention. "The situation has become too dangerous. I will help you find your way back. Just do as I say, and you'll survive. The first thing we have to do is put an end to this. That happens now."

"No. No. I cannot let you go if that's what you're telling me. I can't let that happen."

I looked away to hide the angst in my face. And there it was again, the smell of death. Formaldehyde, rotting flesh. A clear sign

24

of something dangerous, but I pushed that aside.

"Chelsea, promise me. Promise that you will remember when you wake up. And tomorrow. And weeks from now. Promise me that you will never forget," he pleaded.

"Promise to remember what? Just tell me." In desperation, I blurted, " You could be the grim reaper, here to drag me to hell, and I wouldn't care. I'll do anything for you."

With a defeated sigh, he said, "You see? You should care. If you were really yourself, you would. But you just don't care. That's the problem."

I shivered, it was getting colder in the room.

I said, "I don't understand what..."

"Just say it," he snapped. "Say that you promise, and that you will never forget. Please, Chelsea."

"I do! I promise."

Anxiety gripped my chest. Nausea flood my stomach. It was the feeling you got when someone you loved more than anything else in the world died. Tears ran down my cheeks. I wasn't sure what I was promising. To never forget this conversation? To never forget him? It was hard to believe I might ever forget any of it. Even when it vanished.

Everyone enjoys a shocking ending. Trailer four, the finale, did not fall short.

"I love you," he said. "But this is the only way to help you. So–I'm sorry."

"Sorry?"

"Yes."

I shook my head and asked the question, "What are you sorry for?"

"For this…"

With one quick driving force, this faceless boy, who I somehow loved with all of my soul, plunged his hand deep into my chest and ripped my heart from my body. The suction noise, as he withdrew his fist from my chest, reverberated in my ears for mere seconds before my ear drums popped. My hearing was lost.

25

My hands flew to my chest to hold everything else in before it slid out of my body. But there was no wound, no gaping hole, not even a spot of blood on my shirt. Yet, there he stood, holding my throbbing heart in his hand as a bloody pool grew at our feet. Blood gushed and spurted from my heart, right there, in front of my eyes.

My breathing became labored. Of course, I couldn't hear it. I could only feel the struggle, like I'd felt the painful blow. It wasn't a physical blast of pain. It was worse. It was the pain of complete and utter sadness.

Desolation.

Emptiness.

In that moment, I wished to never breathe again. Paralyzed with grief and realizing my wish was coming true, I succumbed to pending death. I loved him, and he broke me. But the cruelty didn't end there. Like a sudden gust of wind, air returned to my lungs with a freezing burn, and sound blew its way back into my head.

"This is the only way I can help you!" he shouted. "Now, listen."

The pressure that had built up in my head exploded with sound. From complete silence shot an excruciating screech and thud. The screech was a shrilling, blood curdling scream that didn't sound human, nor did it seem like it was ever going to end. Then came the thud. It cracked like a jet breaking the sound barrier and jolting the earth. This blaring pattern repeated again, and again, and again.

SCREECH....THUD! SCREECH....THUD! SCREECH... THUD!

"What is that?" I yelled.

In his hand, my heart was beating simultaneously to the insufferable noise. He was yelling at me again. It took me a minute to separate his yelling from the horrid screech and thud of my estranged heart.

"Wake up. Wake up now, Chelsea. Don't forget your promise. Wake up!"

"No, wait. Don't go!" I cried.

"Wake up!"

"Please don't leave me." I fell to my knees. "I can't live without you. The pain–it's killing me."

"Only you can stop the pain, Chelsea. Only you have the power. Now, wake up. Wake! Up!"

SCREECH... THUD! SCREECH... THUD! SCREECH.

CHAPTER 5

I was wide awake and scrubbing the blood off of the floor and walls by five thirty. The last thing I wanted was for my parents to find such a gruesome sight when they returned from their over-night stay in Buffalo. That would be a tough one to explain.

With the amount of blood on the floor, wall, and dish towel, you would have thought my whole hand had been cut off. But this morning, the wound was barely a scratch, and my knees had only a few small scrapes and a couple of black and blue marks. Nothing so much as hurt. I was scrubbing the old mahogany door when I found a bloody hand print. I held my right hand to the stain. It was a perfect match. Lovely. Add thin blood and clotting issues to my list of problems.

Once the foyer was blood-free, I had breakfast and read some of the book I failed to finish last night. RuthAnn Marney, my elderly neighbor, paddled by in her kayak at six-fifteen. I made a mental note to catch her when she got back. Maybe she had a reasonable explanation for the strange noise last night.

A little while later, I stepped out on the back porch for some fresh air. The sun was surprisingly warm already. Most of the pale green buds had popped on the trees that lined the yard. As I watched the water lap against the wooden dock, I spotted an abundance of dead leaves covering the small flower beds along the edge of the lake.

Naturally, I looked for the mystery boat. It looked like day two without the boat creeper; that had to be a good sign. There were a few people fishing in the cove, and several people cruised by on their boats. Some neighbors waved. I waved back. But those dead leaves kept catching my attention; they were an eye sore. My parents were busy getting ready for their dream trip to Europe, so the yard was hardly on their "To Do" list. I needed a distraction. So I got busy.

I didn't have a green thumb, but I enjoyed the time spent in the garden with my mother. Spring planting had always been our thing for as far back as I can remember. It didn't take long to uncover the green sprouts coming up from the dirt. I smiled. Tulips. My favorite.

"Welcome back," I uttered.

After finishing with the first flower bed, I moved to the one closest to my dock where the little, red paddle boat bobbed in the water.

While cleaning out the flower bed, I kept an eye out for Ruthie. She seemed to be out for a long time. She was seventy-eight, and I worried about her more often than not. Ruthie had been on her own since her husband died seven years ago. Sometimes that was enough to slow a person down, but not Ruthie. She bustled about like the energizer bunny.

"Buzz." A bee zipped passed my ear.

I screamed and danced around like a clown, my arms flailed. Flashbacks from Grandma Fran's farm weren't as fresh as last night's close encounter. I regained my composure and looked around for the bee. I found it buzzing off to Ruthie's yard. I glanced around, feeling like an idiot, and hoping no one saw my freakout episode. After I caught my breath, I dropped back to my knees and continued.

A few minutes later, "Buzz... buzz..." Great. Now, there were two. At least today, I was prepared. The EpiPen was ready and waiting on the kitchen counter.

I tried to ignore the bees as they came and went, but every now and then I was forced to run in circles to avoid them. Finally, I'd had enough and needed a break. Frustrated and thirsty, I headed in for a glass of water (and to give the bees time to finish what they were doing and move on to someone else's yard). When I came back out, they were gone.

The relief, however, was short lived. One bee bumped into the side of my head at the same time the other buzzed around in my face taunting me. Once again, I was jumping around and bobbing and weaving to get away from them. I couldn't seem to shake them.

"You will not force me inside, you evil beings. Go!" I yelled, waving my hands around, swatting at them.

You didn't have to be a rocket scientist to know that swatting at a bee was a dumb idea. I knew I should stay still. But seriously, who would sit still and ignore the one thing in this world that could kill them. I hated when people told me to ignore the bees. As if anyone would ignore a serial killer coming at them with a butcher knife.

I got flustered and kept swatting and running erratically in the yard. I stepped back into the flower bed beside the paddle boat and crushed what I hoped was only a weed. But in truth, all I cared about was getting away from those wicked little creatures, even if that meant sacrificing a few tulips. In a clumsy move to jump out of the flower bed, I lost my balance. At that point, there was only one way to fall. And before I knew it–Splash! I was in the lake butt first.

"Oh!" I yelled, darting up from under the frigid water.

The water came up to my shoulders. I pushed the heavy veil of hair out of my face and scurried towards the dock. Unfortunately, I didn't get very far when the bees were back buzzing around my head again.

"You have got to be kidding me."

I ducked, flailed, and splashed water at them in my panic, once again, antagonizing them. Hiding became my only solution. I took a deep breath, plugged my nose, and ducked under water for cover.

The plan was to stay under for as long as I could. Those bees couldn't possibly buzz about up there forever. The slimy, disgusting weeds brushed against my legs. And I didn't dare open my eyes fearing I might see a fish. As long as they didn't touch me, I could make it a little longer. But after a minute, my lungs screamed for air, and I was turning into a green gooey popsicle. I was about ready to surface, when all of a sudden, two large hands wrapped around my waist and pulled me out of the water.

The surprise of being grabbed by some unknown person caused me to inhale the grimy water. I coughed uncontrollably as I was hoisted onto the dock. My mop of hair fell back over my face. Questions were thrown at me all at once by a guy with a deep, earnest voice.

"Are you okay? Talk to me. Can you breathe?"

At first, he sounded familiar, and I thought maybe, somehow, it was Brent. But when I pushed the tangled mess out of my eyes, I discovered it was someone I didn't know. Crouched next to me, with his red-hot burning hand patting me on the back, was a gorgeous, shaggy-haired Adonis. I buried my face in my hands and continued to cough lake water from my lungs.

After a few seconds, I managed to nod my head "yes" to answer the "Can you breathe?" question. I choked out, "I'm fine," then continued to cough for another minute while his fiery hand patted my back. My body temperature must have been subzero for his hand to feel that hot.

"Maybe you should learn to swim since you live on the lake," he said.

Super. He thought I was drowning. I was flopping around in the lake like a goof ball, hiding from bees, and he thought I was drowning. I wanted to crawl under the dead leaves in the flower bed and disappear.

Then, to make matters worse, I hacked out, "I can swim. I was hiding..."

"Oh, well, now I get it. Hide and seek," he said, as if he understood. "Did I blow your cover?"

From the corner of my eyes, I could see that he was looking around for my seeker. Hiding. Why did I tell him that? How dumb.

"Um, no. There were bees, and I'm severely allergic, and..."

Crap! I looked directly at him. My train of thought vanished. His bright green eyes frazzled me. I looked down at the dock.

What was I saying? Think, Chelsea.

Bees.

"Yeah, and there were two bees that wouldn't leave me alone. I lost my footing, fell in, and figured I'd wait them out," I explained.

This time, I forced myself to look at him. Large droplets of water slipped from his wet hair. Water streamed from his forehead, wriggled its way along his cheek bone to his full lips and just sat there. I wanted to be that drop of water. I snapped back to reality

31

and shook the thought from my head. What on earth was the matter with me?

"Here, let me help you up," he said, taking my elbow and helping me to my feet. "So I was thinking, swimming in Conesus the first week in May isn't the smartest thing. Pneumonia. Hypothermia and all that."

Normally, I wasn't a superficial person, yet I was so easily distracted by his looks. His face, his hair. He was tall. He towered above my meager five-foot-four. His wet, white t-shirt clung to him, accentuating every muscle in his six pack and the width of his strong shoulders. A strand of small, brown stones rested against the tan skin of his neck.

"Thanks," I replied still mesmerized "I'm sorry."

"For what?"

"You're all wet. You jumped in for nothing." I wondered if I would have been embarrassed if he weren't so good looking. "Where were you, anyway?"

My fingers were crossed that he was a new neighbor. This was the time of year when the summer renters began their migration to the lake. If I was lucky, he'd be around for a while.

"Over there." He pointed to a modest fishing boat drifting at the mouth of the cove. "I was going by when you fell in. I saw you come up, but then you went right back under. I assumed you needed help."

"My hero," I joked. Flustered, I said, "I'll get you a towel."

Despite his protest, I ran off to the porch as fast as I could. I grabbed two towels from the storage bench under the side deck stairs when I happened to catch a glimpse of myself in the sliding glass door. I noticed the unthinkable. You could clearly see my gray lacy bra through my pastel pink t-shirt. As a matter of fact, with the shirt wet, it look almost the same color as my skin. It looked like I had no shirt on at all. I smacked the towels against my chest. There wasn't much there to hide, and I wasn't the most conservative person in town, but geez, I just met the guy. Could I embarrass myself more?

When I got back, he was standing on the lawn near the dock. His hands were in his pockets, and he was watching his boat drift. I handed him a towel, keeping the other stuck to my chest. Our fingers barely touched, and I swear an electrical shock ran up my arm. Since he didn't flinch, I knew it was my daft imagination igniting flames.

"Thanks," he said.

"You were fishing?" I asked.

"I was done and on my way back to the launch. Got to get back for Sunday brunch. I'd like to say this takes care of the shower part, but I think it only made matters worse."

He rubbed his head with the towel. When he dried his torso, his shirt came up a few inches, and that six pack that had been hiding beneath his shirt teased me for about ten seconds.

"So you don't live on the lake then?" I said.

"No. I live across the lake." He pointed to the hills south east of the lake.

"On Vineyard Hill?" I asked.

He nodded. "About half way up."

"Oh," I said.

I was not one who usually struggled to make conversation, yet I found my brain scrambling for something interesting to say to him.

Then he said, "So, you must have just moved in. I fish in Willow Cove all the time, and I've never seen you. Unless you're renting?"

My cheeks got hot, and that meant my face was bright red. I hoped I wasn't the only one feeling the electricity between us. Something made me want to grab him and not let him leave. It was the strangest feeling. He ran his hand through his damp hair and pushed it out of his eyes.

"Are you?" he asked.

"Renting? Oh, no. We've lived here forever."

"Hmm. Weird." He shifted from one foot to the other and glanced out at his boat. "Anyway, maybe we could..."

"Hey there, girlfriend!" cried Ruthie as she paddled by. "The water is too cold to go swimming. What's the matter with you two?"

I glanced at my hero and smiled. Darn it. What was he going to say?

Ruthie hollered, "Chelsea, get over here and help an old lady out of her kayak. I think I twisted my ankle at my boyfriend's house."

"Yeah. Go help her out. I'll catch you later," my hero said. He jabbed his thumb in the direction of his boat. It was at least three houses away. "I better get it before it drifts any further."

"I can take you to it." I gestured to the paddle boat. "The water is so cold."

"No, thanks. I'm already wet. Help the little lady out," he said, smiling at Ruthie. He turned and walked away. My heart sank.

"Hey, thanks for saving me," I called after him, attempting to be flirty. Something I had very little practice with.

"Anytime," he said with a wink.

By the time he reached the end of my dock, Ruthie was pulling up to hers. My hero waved and dove in. Coming up a short distance away, he looked back at me as I reached Ruthie in her kayak.

"I didn't mean to scare your boyfriend away, honey," Ruthie said.

"He's not my boyfriend. He stopped to help me. That's all." I tied the kayak to Ruthie's dock, then took a hold of her long skinny fingers. "Be careful," I said, helping her out of the kayak.

"I got it. I got it. He's a cutie pie, that one. And those buns. Whew!"

"Ruthie!"

"Hey. I'm old, not dead. What's that cutie's name?"

"Oh…" I sighed. "I never asked. I was so flustered. I'm so bad at that kind of stuff."

"Nice job, sugar. No wonder you're single. At least he knows where you live. Maybe he'll be back. You better hope anyway; those green eyes are enough to kill a girl."

"I can't believe you noticed that from the water."

"This old girl? Her senses are sharper than a Samurai sword."

"Hey, speaking of that, did you hear anything strange last night? There was a loud buzzing noise. It was weird."

"I heard your friends leave, then I drifted off shortly after that. It could have been a boat or maybe a helicopter."

34

"Yeah, right. That must be it," I said. Neither suggestion made sense, though.

But I had the answer I was looking for. Thanks to whatever caused my insomnia, I was delusional. I couldn't tell my parents. I didn't want to jeopardize the trip they had been planning for so long. The last thing they needed to worry about was me. Tomorrow, I would buy something over-the-counter to help me sleep.

I looked out at the water and saw my hero climbing aboard his boat. He started the engine, looked back at me, and waved once more. I returned the wave and giggled. Giggled like a child to be exact. I caught myself and stopped, but not before Ruthie noticed.

"Someone's smitten," she said.

I shook my head at Ruthie trying to think of a comeback when I was blinded by the sun reflecting off of a boat out in the lake. It was back.

The Ivory Dome

By virtue of the Ivory Dome, each subject had their own story. Their truth. Their reality. As for my latest subjects, there would be nothing vanilla about their saga. Take N13 for example. Where life began lackluster and pallid, it was, at this very moment, on the brink of blossoming into a palette of blinding colors that would far exceeded any of Leonid Afremov's famously colorful works of art. Though her gift remained clouded, or maybe because of this vexatious fact, I knew she would fuse the gap in the countdown to tales of greatness. For she was not the beginning, and she was not the end. But she was needed almost more than anyone. She was the corpus callosum of our new beginning.

Just thinking about my subjects caused my heart to speed up. I paced the deck with excitement as I thought about my latest act of generous benevolence. I gave this group more than they ever could have imagined. Yes, I gave them a tremendous amount of responsibility, but I also gave them an incredible gift. In many respects, I gave them immortality; even if they didn't live forever, their name surely would. Their story would. The feats they would accomplish with my help would forever change the world as we knew it. I did that for them. More importantly, I did that for the survival and the empowerment of mankind.

One might call me boastful, full of myself, cocky…I'd heard it all. Heck, I'd even been called several versions of insane, if you could imagine that. I could only laugh at the accusations. No matter, though.

As my eyes closed to gather my reeling thoughts, I pictured them all together. Soon the doubters and bitter peons will learn of my accomplishments. They will be eating their words by the fall, choking on their snide comments by the winter, and bragging to all their friends that they know me the minute the Lakeville Project hits the media.

I opened my eyes, smiled, and blew N13 a kiss. After years of waiting and watching, the curtain was drawing. There were still a few hurdles to jump, but I could see everything falling into place just as it was supposed to, just as I had planned. It was only a matter of time now. The amalgamative process was finally beginning.

CHAPTER 6

The next morning, I was out of the house by eight o'clock and driving to the neighboring town of Geneseo to meet Jill and Beth at Main Street Coffee. When they weren't working there, it was our go-to hang out place.

With the windows down and the sunroof open, I cruised towards town in my black Honda civic. The wind whipped through my hair, and the sun beat down on my arms and head. When I got closer to town, small drops of rain hit my forehead forcing me to given up on the sunroof. There was a lone dark cloud above me. It was small, but up ahead, towards Main Street, there was nothing but a promising blue sky. Soon, the few drops on my windshield turned into several, and after a minute, my wipers were on full speed. The rain cloud and I seemed to be headed in the same direction.

While passing a large farmers field before the village, I happened to glance into the freshly plowed dirt, which was pretty much mud now. That's when I saw him. I pulled hard to the right and slammed on my breaks on the shoulder of the road. I stopped so abruptly that the angry drivers behind me started to honk and yell obscenities. With the move I had just made, who could blame them. But as far as I was concerned, they could honk and yell all they wanted. The fact was, I had spotted my dog, Barney, running through the field.

Barney was hard to miss with his long, snow white fur. He ran away a few weeks ago, and suddenly, there he was, trotting through the middle of the field. I jumped out of the car, dodging traffic, and screamed, "Barney! Barney, come!"

He stopped and looked at me, then he turned away and started running again. The poor frightened thing. I didn't want to scare him any more than he already was, so I started a slow jog after him. But he kept going. He gave me no choice but to pick up the pace or I was going to lose him. I took off as fast as I could.

"Barney! Stop!" I yelled. "Heel!"

The light rain grew into a downpour, and the whole sky turned black with storm clouds. A steady stream of manure-enriched mud launched from my shoes and landed on my back. So much for coffee with the girls. But at the moment, nothing was more important than bringing Barney home.

I was running hard just to keep him in my sight. I could barely breathe. I kept yelling to him and commanding him to stop, but he ran as if he was chasing something. I gave another stern command, "Barney. Stop." And bam! Barney did exactly that. He stopped running, turned around to face me, and sat down. Exhausted and thankful, I stopped running next to some bushes.

"Good boy. Stay," I said, kneading the piercing cramp in my side.

I almost had him, I just needed one more second to catch my breath. I didn't dare take my eyes off of him in case he decided to take off again. As those few seconds passed, his strange behavior began to trouble me. He sat there, no tail wagging, no panting with his tongue hanging out. He just sat there, staring at me as if in a trance. I cocked my head to the side and squinted my eyes to get a better look at him.

From behind me, a voice declared, "Thank God the rain stopped."

I literally jumped, and my heart dropped to my feet. When I saw who it was, my heart shot directly into my throat.

"You scared me to death," I said to yesterday's rescuer.

"That would be a tragedy. And considering where we are, it would also be spooky," he said, gesturing to a headstone.

Barney and I had managed to run the length of the field. Having been so focused on Barney in the torrential rain, I missed the fact that we'd run into the cemetery. My hero had been standing at the bushy, overgrown entrance when I came in and stopped.

"Yeah, right. I was getting Barney, my dog," I explained.

"Your dog?"

"Yes..."

I pointed to Barney. But this time, when I looked at him, I knew there was something very wrong. He still hadn't moved. It was bazar, to say the least. Panic set in.

"Come, Barney!" I yelled, patting my legs.

For one second, a thought flashed through my head. It was my legs, muddy and wet. Barney's beautiful fur–still as white as snow.

"Are you talking about the..."

My hero's voice faded out. My heart began to pound hard in my ears.

"Barney?" I uttered.

That was when the light went on in my head; and with the rain tapering off, I could see much clearer. Once again, I was running. My short sprint at warp-speed ended with a base slide through the wet grass and face to face with what I'd thought was Barney. My grass-stained hand flew up over my mouth in shock.

What I had thought was my lost dog, wasn't Barney, at all. In fact, it wasn't even alive. It was beautiful and white, just like him, but this dog was cold and hard. I was staring at a white marble statue that looked strikingly like Barney.

My eyes teared up as the memory flooded back to me. The memory of how heartbroken I was when I was seven, and Barney ran away from home. We never saw him again. How in my right mind could I have thought I just saw him alive and well? Here it was, eleven years later, and I was chasing some kind of a ghost, or a memory, through a muddy field in the pouring rain.

Suddenly, I was aware that my handsome hero was standing by my side speaking to me. At first, he sounded garbled and far away. By the time he repeated himself, I had snapped out of my daze.

"I'm sorry about your dog. You had quite a slide. Are you hurt?"

"Uh. No. Just a little confused. I thought this was my dog. I know that sounds weird, but I was chasing my dog. Finally, he–he stopped running and sat down. I thought he looked odd, not moving or anything..."

I shook my head in disbelief, then it dawned on me. I was spewing a bunch of nonsense and sounding crazy. I looked up at the bewildered expression on his face then back at the statue.

"The dog I was chasing must have taken off in another direction. He looked exactly like my dog." I said. I couldn't tear my eyes from the stone dog. "So does this statue. Yeah, that must be what happened."

"I guess from far away this could look real. Except it doesn't move. Or bark. Or fetch," he teased.

"In memory of Chip," I read aloud. "Chip. This is in memory of somebody's dog."

"So this isn't where your dog is buried?"

"No. I...I guess I made a mistake." I shook my head. "Right?"

"I don't think you can bury dogs in a human cemetery. But I could be wrong." He held his hand out to me and said with a crooked grin, "Take my hand. And I'll take a name, if that's alright."

"Chelsea," I said, placing my grass stained hand in his. "Chelsea Raleigh."

He helped me up and said, "I'm Cole. I love your name. It's pretty."

"Thanks. I used to hated it. I guess I don't mind it so much now. I'm sorry if I interrupted you. This is the second time I've been a pest. First, I interrupt your fishing trip, now I plow in here and..." I glanced at Chip. "Anyway. I'm sorry."

My mind was still racing, and I realized I needed to make a conscious effort not to ramble. I brushed off my pants as much as I could, but that only smudged the mud and grass.

"You didn't interrupt me. I was passing through on my way to Main Street for coffee."

"Same," I said. I scowled at the awful smell of my mud-caked jeans. "I was supposed to meet friends."

"A little manure never killed anyone," he said.

Cole reached out and wiped the dirt and grass from my cheek. His touch was magic. The stress from my Barney sighting and tarnished appearance seemed to vanish.

"But maybe you'll want to change your clothes before meeting them, Chelsea."

My heart skipped a beat when he said my name.

"Yeah. I'll let them know that I'm going to be late." I glanced down at myself. Grass stained, muddy, smelly. I looked as if I'd just completed a Tough Mudder. "Oh man, I'm gross."

"An impossible feat for you."

"Hmm." Words failed me.

Cole said, "I'm a little soggy myself. It wasn't supposed to rain today."

"I know, right? That rain came on fast. It took us both by surprise, I guess."

"Yes. That makes two surprises today. You're the better one, of course. I was afraid I'd have to stalk you from the lake to ask you out. Maybe send in the bees and start over." He paused. "It's just that I never got to finish what I wanted to say."

He looked at me for a response.

"Oh..."

His ability to make me speechless was rare skill that not many people had besides my mother. I wasn't sure what was worse: being rendered speechless or blathering like a fool.

"Can I call you?" Cole asked.

"Yeah! I mean, sure. That would be cool."

He pulled his phone from his pocket and added my cell number to his contact list.

"Where's your car?" he asked, looking around.

"My car! Oh, my God. I left it on the side of the road. My keys are in it and everything. I'd better go get it." I did not want to walk away from him.

"Do you want me to walk you to your car?"

"No, thank you. It's muddy back there," I said, gesturing to my clothes.

I looked down at Chip and frowned. Cole laughed. His smile warmed me from the inside out but made me shiver just the same.

"Call me," I said.

"How about tonight?"

"Sure. I'll be home."

"Good. I'm glad we ran into each other again."

"Me too," I said. "See ya."

I turned and ran off towards my car. To play it cool, I didn't look back until I'd almost gotten there. By the time I got to my car, he was gone. I let out a deep sigh.

Cole. His name was Cole.

CHAPTER 7

I got a blanket from the trunk, threw it down on the seat, and slid in. Next, I called Beth and told her I was running late. I didn't attempt to explain that I had been busy chasing the ghost of Barney through a field and into the cemetery, only to find his likeness in Chip, the statue. Considering my latest obsession with feeling like I'm being watched, dead dog sightings would not fly.

I couldn't take my mind off of Cole.

"Cole. Cole. Cole," I repeated over and over.

My mother often referred to me as an old soul and said that I was far more mature than Meggie. Boy, would she have been disappointed in me right now. I was beaming like a love-struck little girl. There was no maturity happening inside my car as I blasted the radio, sang at the top of my lungs, and bopped around in the car like an infatuated adolescent. Nope–no maturity whatsoever. I was hooked on a mysterious boy, and there was no escape.

A few miles down County Road Thirty, my love struck high took a nose dive thanks to a huge cloud of dirt wafting along the side of the road. I slowed up to see what it was and saw tires spinning. They were attached to a hunk of green metal, upside down amidst the corn sprouts. Once again, I pulled over and found myself running through a field.

When I reached the car, it wreaked of gasoline and burning rubber. A young, dark-haired girl stretched unconscious from the driver side window with her face down in a shallow puddle of mucky water. Without hesitation, I grabbed her under the arms and pulled the rest of her body through the window. I stumbled, and she fell on top of me, but I managed to crawl out from under her and flip her over. I gasped at the amount of blood all over her face. Then I wedged my hands back under her arms and dragged her limp body as far away from the car as possible.

I struggled to pull her about forty feet when, out of nowhere, an elderly man, missing most of his front teeth, scooped her up. I followed as he carried her towards a crooked pine tree, where he set her down.

The girl regained consciousness for a few moments. I asked her what happened, but she was disoriented and confused. That's when we heard the explosion. Further into the field, a van was wrapped around a tree and engulfed in flames.

I started towards the van when the man stopped me and said, "Stay away, missy. That there's a bomb just waitin' to blow. And not the only one."

He nodded towards the dark-haired girl's car that was now ablaze.

I told the injured girl that help was on the way, but she kept babbling about someone being dead. Then she went unconscious. By the look of the van across the street, I couldn't imagine anyone would survive that hellish fire.

Within minutes, the fire department and emergency rescuers from neighboring towns arrived on the scene to battle the raging fires. An ambulance pulled down a dirt path close to where we sat under the pine tree. The girl was still unconscious. I moved out of the way while the EMT's worked on her. When I heard an EMT say that she was stable, I sighed and headed to my car.

Along the way, a police officer caught up with me and asked for a statement. I explained what little I had seen as I hadn't witnesses the accident happened.

"Thank you for being brave enough to stop and help. She would have died if you hadn't come along and pulled her from the car," the officer said. "You're a hero."

Suddenly, it hit me. I saved someone's life. Me. Some dumb country girl who was going gaga over a boy just minutes ago. All I had on my mind that morning was Cole, what I would tell my friends about him, and what kind of mocha chino I would get. And now this… But it was a no-brainer, really. I did what anyone would have done in the same situation.

I nodded at the officer and continued to my car, but again, when I tried to slip away, I was stopped. A towering fireman was worried that I had been hurt.

"You're bleeding," he said.

"I'm fine. It's not my blood," I explained. I looked at him closer. "You look so familiar. Do you work at The Green?"

He scowled and shook his head.

"I bartend at The Green a few nights a week. You don't look old enough to know that. Listen, let the EMT's take a look at you before you go anywhere. Let's make sure none of that belongs to you," he said, pointing to the blood on my arms and shirt.

"It doesn't. I have to go..."

"Your wrist, it's cut," he grumbled, taking my hand and flipping it palm side up.

"Ow!" I yelped.

"I need an EMT over here!" he hollered over his shoulder.

I hadn't noticed the cut or the pain until he touched my hand. It was a strange pain, a lightning bolt blast that came and went just as fast.

"I must have done this when I pulled her from the window," I said. He poked the skin around the gash and stung me. Then it dawned on me why he looked so familiar. I forced a smile and said, "There you go again, shocking me."

"Sit down," he commanded. "Someone is coming to clean that up."

The ornery fireman pointed to a clear place in the grass on the side of the road and told me to wait for the EMT. He glanced down at me, then looked around the dry field.

He snapped, "Why are you soaked and covered in mud?"

"There was a pop-up shower a few miles down the road... Why are you glaring at me like that?"

He shook the scowl from his face, as if he hadn't realized he was doing it. But he stared at me with such intensity that it made me uneasy. It was a glare I remembered well. My nerves surged, I began babbling.

"You were at the art gallery a few months back when they opened. You were leaning on the glass wall with your friend. I would've been afraid that I would break it, but I guess you weren't.

"Remember, you found my keys and shocked me when you handed them to me? You must drag your feet a lot. Or one of us does. Anyway, that's why I must look familiar to you. I mean, why else would you be staring at me like that..."

He continued to glare at me. I wondered if he knew his facial expressions were so unfriendly.

He said, "Tall people slouch, they don't drag their feet."

"Oh, I wasn't referring to your height."

"Alrighty then. What do we have here?" said a sweaty EMT, rushing to my side. He threw open his bag and snapped on medical gloves.

"Her wrist is cut. It's a nasty gash," the fireman said. "Some of the blood on her shirt belongs to the girl in the car. At least, that's what she said." He turned to me and said, "Good luck. Jack will take good care of you."

Then he smiled. But it wasn't a "have a nice day" smile. It was a "Thank God, I'm done with you" grin.

By the time the EMT (who was a hundred times friendlier than the giant) was done wrapping my arm, an hour had passed, and I was even more late for meeting my friends. After what just happened, I honestly didn't even feel like going for coffee. But then I thought of Cole and realized that two amazing things had already happened today, and it wasn't even noon yet. I met my hero from yesterday, and I saved a girl from burning, or dying, or both. That put a smile on my face, and I was back to feeling pretty good. Not even a grumpy fireman could bring me down.

When I got home, I took a record breaking shower and threw on some fresh clothes. I was back in town to meet the girls at Main Street Coffee just as I got their seventh text shaming me for being late.

47

The grin never left my face. When I got to the cafe, I scanned the room for Cole, but he wasn't there.

An attractive boy, working behind the counter said, "Welcome back, sunshine."

"Thanks."

His warm welcome puzzled me. He acted as if he knew me, and while I have seen him in here a couple of times, we had never spoken until now.

"Your friends told me to expect a beautiful girl with long, golden brown hair to walk in any minute. And here you are." He pushed a tall mocha chino towards me, pointed to the back corner, and said, "It's on them."

"Thanks," I said, taking the drink.

"Hey," the boy said, before I stepped away. "They tried to give me your number, but I told them that I would get it myself." The over-confident barista slid a pen and a napkin across the counter. He turned on a deadly set of puppy dog eyes, leaned over the counter, and said, "If you will?"

I took a second to think of a kind alternative to "You're pretty arrogant, man." Then I laughed and said, "That's sweet." I leaned in and whispered, "But I'm not exactly available." It wasn't a fib that my heart had been stolen by someone else.

"Acceptable. For now," he said with a slow nod and a wily smile.

It didn't take a genius to figure out which busy body initiated that ridiculous exchange. Jill and Beth were too engrossed in gossip to notice me at first. I took the seat across from them.

"Thanks for the mocha chino," I said, taking a sip. "Ah. You have no idea how much I needed this. Unlike your match-making attempt, Beth."

"I'm not sure what you mean by that. But for God's sake, it's about time you got here," Beth responded. She pointed to her forehead. "Look at me. You took so long I have a wrinkle."

"I can't believe you'd consider giving my number to a stranger."

"He's not a stranger. He's worked here for at least a week now. And his sister is super cool."

48

I shook my head. "Never mind."

"His family owns this place. And he's a hottie. Look at him," Beth said.

She looked down at my wrapped wrist. Blood had seeped through the bandage and dried leaving a big brown blotch.

"Holy crap! What happened?" Beth hissed.

She shot a concerned look at Jill. Jill demanded answers. I told them all about the car accident and the poor girl who was hurt. And of course, there was the lady in the other vehicle who died.

"I overheard the cops talking about how the lady in the van hit the girl head-on. They think the lady may have been drunk," I said.

"Drunk? It's not even noon," Jill said.

"Let me see your cut," demanded Beth.

"You're gross," Jill said to her.

"Come on. Is it bad?" Beth asked.

I pried back a corner of the bandage to check for myself. It didn't look very bad. I wondered why they made such a fuss over it. I pulled the bandage all the way off.

"Look, it's fine," I said.

"It's not too bad. Actually, it's already scabbing up," Jill said. "Did they glue it or something?"

"I don't think so. But maybe they did." I shrugged and poked at my wrist. "Huh–well, whatever they did, it worked like a charm, because it doesn't hurt either."

"Were they cute?" Beth asked, her eyes flashing like a Maglite.

"Who?" I asked.

"The fireman? The EMT?"

"I'll tell you one thing, the fireman's attitude sure wasn't cute. Picture an angry Jason Momoa with short hair." The girls winced. "Now, try to think of something besides boys for a change." I pinched Beth, and turned to Jill who was giggling. I said, "I think my parents are having second thoughts about Europe. They don't want me to be lonely."

"Lonely? They don't want you to party the house into the ground," Jill said.

"I doubt they're worried about that. She's got Ruthie keeping an eye on me."

"I just love Ruthie," Jill said.

"Okay—for the record, I would take Jason Momoa angry, bald, cross-eyed...only a robot wouldn't find him sexy. Are you a robot?" Beth asked.

"Stop," I giggled as she flicked my cheek.

"But moving on, old people can't hear. Duh," Beth said. "We can just have quiet parties..." Beth ignored Jill rolling her eyes, gave her a stern glare, and pressed on. "Anyway, we'll talk to Ruthie. We'll become her best buds so she won't tell. One or two epic parties won't be a big deal."

"Yeah, in case you haven't noticed, I'm not a party animal. My mom said she might have my sister move in for a few weeks to keep an eye on me. But my dad boycotted that. He said Meggie moving back could be even worse than leaving me alone. Her history of "epic" parties is what has my mother all worried in the first place."

"You're not a baby," Jill said. "You'll be fine on your own."

"I'm eighteen. So yes, that means technically I'm an adult."

"When do they leave?" Beth asked.

"Tonight. My sister is meeting some guy in the city, so she offered to drive them to the airport."

"What guy?"

I shrugged. "That's top secret information. My parents don't even know about him yet."

"Tell us," Jill demanded.

"He's five years older than her. He's in a rock band. And that's all I've got."

"Awesome. That's how he makes a living?" said Beth. "He must be amazing. I bet he's hot."

"Don't know. I told you, he's a secret. I heard her on the phone with him last week and confronted her. His band is called Public Executioner. Sounds scary."

I pretended to cower. We giggled. Then there was about three seconds of silence, which was entirely too much for Beth.

"Okaaaay…so that story is dead. You just missed Brent," Beth spilled. "By about ten seconds. Did you see him leave?"

I shook my head no.

"Way to ease into that," Jill said to Beth.

I looked at them somewhat disbelieving. Brent didn't drink coffee.

"Did he say anything to you guys?" I asked.

"Evil eye contact, yes. Exchange of pleasantries, no," Beth said. "Why is he acting like such a freak? People break up every day. And you two were way over due."

"It was his fault," said Jill. "He treated you like garbage."

Jill reached over and rubbed my arm. She was the friend you could count on for advice and a shoulder to cry on. She always knew the right thing to say.

And then there was Beth who added, "Or even if the ass hat had just shown up half the time." She stuck a gagging finger in her mouth.

"It is what it is. And it's over," I said.

Jill and Beth exchanged doubting glances.

"Hmm, suddenly you're good with this. Yesterday morning, on the phone, you were a ball of soggy tissues. Today, not so much," Beth said.

"I never cried," I protested.

Jill, my cheerleader, said, "Nice recovery. He was a jerk. Now, let's talk about the hottie behind the counter. He asked about you. Not me. Not Beth."

I shook my head then downed some of my mocha chino before it got cold.

I said, "I'm not looking for anyone. But I'm pretty sure when the time comes I can find someone on my own."

"Yeah, right. Except you don't have the greatest track record. You need a little guidance," Beth said.

"Everyone needs to worry about themselves, please. Chug up. I need new Vans," I said.

On our way to the shoe store, I stopped at the pharmacy and grabbed a bottle of melatonin. The insomnia was going to end.

Later that night, Meggie came to pick up my parents and take them to the airport.

"If you get lonely or scared, you can join us any time," my mother said, sniffling. "Meggie isn't far away, and Ruthie said she will stop in."

"I'll be fine, Mom. I don't need the neighbor to babysit me. I'll probably work a lot, hang with the girls..."

"Do I have to tell you no parties?" my mother asked. I shook my head no. She said, "You can have friends over, but no craziness. No drinking."

"I know, Mom."

My father was getting impatient.

"Let's go, Ashley. She's going to be fine. Some freedom and independence will do her good." He turned to me and kissed my cheek. "Be smart. We'll call you when we land in Italy."

After several last minute "by the way" mini-lectures, when they had finally left, I headed to the kitchen to make myself some herbal peach tea and wash down the melatonin pill. In the back of my head, a little voice was saying, "I hope he calls."

At seven-thirty my cell phone rang.

"Hello?"

"Hi, Chelsea. It's Cole."

"Hi," I said, slamming my book shut without marking my page. Butterflies ravaged my stomach.

"Were you able to have coffee with your friends today?"

"Yes. Did you?"

"Yeah. I was soaked. Nothing a hot coffee couldn't cure. I met a friend at Main Coffee for about a half an hour."

"Oh."

Jealousy made a childish appearance. Was this friend a girl?

"His family owns the place. I stopped by to catch up," Cole said.

"Cool," I said with a mental sigh of relief. "I'm pretty sure I met him. You must have left right before I got there."

"I didn't stay long," Cole said. "I had a million things to do. But enough about today. Let's talk about tomorrow."

"Yes. Let's do that," I said.

"I have the day off, and the weather is supposed to be killer. I was thinking about taking a hike or a boat ride. I would love for you to join me."

"A hike sounds great. I used to hike a lot, but I haven't been on a trail in months. I was hoping to squeeze in a hike at Letchworth before the end of the summer."

"Letchworth then?" he asked.

"My favorite place to hike," I responded.

Alone in the woods with Cole. Who sprinkled me with fairy dust?

"Great. Do you want to meet at the north entrance at nine? Or is that too early for you? I wouldn't want to disturb your beauty rest. Not that you need any."

"I'm an early riser," I said, thinking of how it was more like I hardly ever slept. "I'll meet you at nine."

"Great. Tomorrow then."

"Yes, tomorrow."

"So, I won't keep you."

"No, wait," I said hastily. "I was only reading a book. A little conversation with someone besides my family would be nice. Although, I'm actually here on my own, with no one to talk to. I mean, I'm sure I could find something to do, like laundry, or call one of my friends. I could bake something, I suppose. But...well...anyway. I guess I'm free to talk longer if you are."

Smooth, Chelsea, I thought. Tragically smooth. Ugh. Sometimes I was pathetic.

"Oh," he said with a snicker and followed by several painfully quiet seconds. I wanted to die of stupidity. Then he said, "I was hoping you'd say that. I like talking to you. A lot."

With those alleviating words, I took dying of stupidity off the table for the time being.

We talked for about two hours. He asked about my family and my job. We talked about my parent's trip and the car accident I stumbled upon after our run in at the cemetery.

53

"You're a hero," he said.

"Just paying it forward. You save me, I save her."

I snickered. I was nothing close to being a hero.

"Except there are no heroics in ruining a game of hide and seek."

"You have to look at the bigger picture," I said.

He laughed. "And what does that look like?"

"Pneumonia, hypothermia and all that. Heck, a few minutes longer under water and there might even have been a hit and run with a kayak," I said. He laughed harder.

When our call ended, I plugged my phone in next to my bed and stared at it with a grin until my eyes got heavy. The melatonin pill was starting to work. I set my alarm for the first time in days. Tomorrow would be a bad day to oversleep. The last time I looked at the clock it was 11:11 p.m. I made a wish.

CHAPTER 8

Oh, the magic of one tiny pill. I managed to get eight solid hours of sleep from something smaller than a pea. There was nothing like peaceful rest and zero dreams.

After a hearty breakfast of scrambled eggs, wheat toast, orange juice, and two cups of coffee, I trekked to the closet in search of something to wear. I lost track of how many times I changed my clothes. While it was just a hike in the woods, I didn't want to look too grungy, sleazy, or matronly. Although anything had to be better than the way I looked the last two times I saw him. I ended up in a pair of tan shorts and a black t-shirt. I grabbed a gray sweatshirt in case it was cooler in the woods.

I laced up my hiking boots and loaded my backpack with the necessities, the EpiPen being the most important. When I got in the car, my nerves started to get the best of me. I gave myself a pep talk and a brief lecture to be cool and keep the babbling to a minimum.

As I pulled into the north entrance at nine, Cole was already standing next to his black, F250 pickup truck digging through his backpack. He spotted my car and stopped what he was doing. I parked next to his truck.

My stomach flip flopped. Dang. This guy was way out of my league. He must see me as nothing more than a friend. That had to be it. He said he liked to talk to me, and that didn't necessarily mean he wanted to date me. I had a sinking feeling that I misread the whole thing.

I took a deep breath and stepped out of the car. Cole was casually leaning against his truck, flipping through a park map. We smiled at each other. I got a little dizzy as I took in the person that stood before me: the tousled brown hair, the chiseled jaw, the masculine nose. He wore khaki shorts, a fitting white t-shirt, and brown hiking boots. My blood boiled over. "Hot" was a word that didn't do him justice.

"Hi, Chelsea," he said.

Again, there was something about the way his voice softened when he said my name.

"Hi."

"Whoa. You look..." he ran a hand through his hair, "you look like a really good hiker." His face turned as red as mine, and we laughed.

"I am a good hiker," I said. Now, I was confused. I hadn't the foggiest idea how to read what was going on between us–if anything. I stayed cool and said, "You haven't been waiting long, have you?"

"No. I've only been here for a few minutes. I have a feeling we might have a lot of the same things in our backpacks. Why don't we combine them, and I'll carry it."

"Sure. I can carry it, though. I don't mind. I'm not a wuss," I joked.

"I know. I want to carry it. I insist. Let me see what you have. We'll put your things in my bag if I don't already have it." He took my backpack. "Do you mind?" he asked before unzipping it.

"No. Have at it," I said.

What a gentleman. His sincerity was something I wasn't accustomed to.

Cole pulled my EpiPen from my backpack and wiggled it in his fingers. "We definitely need this. Also, your water bottle and cell phone. Are we ready?"

"I think so."

"Where do you want to start?"

"How about on Trail E. It's a good one. Not too hard," I suggested, taking the lead into the woods. We found the red sign that indicated where the trail started and began our adventure.

"I haven't been on these trails in so long," Cole said.

"Neither have I. Luckily, this one is well marked, so no worries," I said, turning back to look at him.

"Watch that branch. Duck!" He yelled. He threw his arms out to catch me, but I ducked just in time.

"Thanks. I saw it," I lied.

"We can take another trail if this one is too easy for you. I'm not afraid of a little challenge. Unless you are." There was that sarcasm again.

With a playful scowl, I said, "Be careful. I'm quite an experienced hiker."

We walked in silence for another minute. All of a sudden, he stopped.

"Race you to the top of this hill? Off trail," he challenged me.

I glanced up the steep hill and cringed at its rough terrain.

"Off trail? The brush is pretty thick. Are you sure you want to do that?"

"I wouldn't want you to sprain an ankle or break a nail," he teased.

He shrugged with a sly smile, provoking me even more. Far be it for me to back down from a challenge.

"Seriously? Need a head start?" I asked.

"Not a chance."

We eyeballed the ungroomed hillside, exchanged a quick glance, and took off at the same time.

"See you at the top!" he yelled.

I stumbled right off the bat and almost took a dangling limb to the eye. He kept going, and boy, was he fast. I shouldn't have been surprised. He ran solid and strong as he jumped fallen branches and rocks with ease. His stride was fluid. Quarterback was my first thought.

A few seconds later, he came upon a boulder too big to jump over or climb. He was forced around the mossy mound which allowed me a little time to catch up. Now, we ran almost parallel to each other. Still, it was a struggle to stay on my feet. I was like a dog on ice skates. My feet kept falling into hidden holes and catching rocks and sticks buried under leaves. A sprained ankle was undoubtedly in my near future.

Cole made the uphill battle look like a breeze, but I wouldn't give up. I had to continue. How could I let him beat me after I opened my big mouth and blabbed about how experienced I was? Mental note: start thinking before speaking.

A little more than half way up the hill, the ground smoothed out, and I was able to get better footing. Cole was slightly ahead of me now. He looked back and smiled. He didn't look like he had even broken a sweat. So I stepped into high gear, ignored my burning quads, and gave it all I had.

Just as I pulled ahead of him, I yelled, "Don't go easy on me!"

"I'm not," he yelled with a labored voice. Sweat ran down his brow and his cheeks were bright pink.

All this time, I thought for sure he was trying to be nice and not beat me by a mile, but I was wrong. He was struggling as much as I was. I began to think I might have a chance. The end was in sight. Up ahead there was a flat, sunny clearing at the top of the hill. I was so close.

Then, as luck would have it, the ground got more uneven than before. The leaves and tree debris increased as I got closer to the clearing. I was back to stumbling. I looked back and saw that Cole had slowed up and fallen behind; he must have known he wasn't going to win.

Finally, I burst through the bushes and into the clearing. The sun shone brightly. I welcomed the cool breeze that instantly hit my face.

"Yes!" I screamed with what little breath I had left.

I launched my hands into the air with a weak attempt at a victory dance. I didn't want to rub it in too much. Not to mention my lungs were about to explode. I could barely breathe. I huffed and puffed, crouched over with my hands on my knees. When I straightened up to see if Cole had made it to the top, I got dizzy. I leaned on a hickory tree and tried to put my focus on the shaggy bark.

With my vision still fuzzy, I looked around for Cole. I looked down the hill and saw blurry trees and logs. I turned around and searched the clearing. Even though my vision was blurry, I thought I would at least see his silhouette.

"Cole?"

That was when I noticed an outline of a house on the opposite end of the clearing. It had a familiar shape to it. Suddenly, my clear sight snapped back. The old farmhouse was beautiful. It was strange to find a house right there in the middle of the park, so deep in the woods. Then it registered. This was no ordinary house. It was an exact replica of my grandmother's farmhouse.

The big red barn sat to the left of it, and in front of it was the peach tree. There was a small girl in the tree, climbing higher and higher.

"Be careful!" I heard someone holler from the front porch.

I turned my attention to the house and found Barney and Brent standing on the steps.

All at once, the sky darkened, and a soft gray mist rolled in from behind the house. It drifted into the sky where it crept in front of the sun and blocked the bright warm rays. The murky haze floated around the sides of the house, engulfed the peach tree, along with the oblivious little girl, and rolled towards me.

My chest tightened. I shook my head and opened and closed my eyes frantically. Unlike the dream from the other night, everything in me screamed that this could not be real. I whipped around and looked back down the hill.

"Cole!" I hollered. "Cole, where are you?"

He was nowhere to be seen. I was afraid to turn back towards the house in fear of the once peaceful and beautiful clearing that was now transforming into a scene from a horror film.

"Please be gone," I whispered.

However, when I looked down at my feet, I knew what I would find. The cold mist wrapped around my ankles. It slithered its way up my legs with a pricking sensation like pins and needles. When I turned around, not only was the house still there, but Brent waved at me. I didn't return the wave. Brent mouthed something to Barney, causing him to jump off the porch and run towards me. As I watched Barney disappear in the smokey mist, I began to shake.

"This can't be happening," I said.

I dropped my face into my hands and shook my head back and forth again and again. "Wake up. This has to be a dream. This isn't real," I tried to convince myself. "They are not here."

With a deep breath, I pulled my hands away from my face and opened my eyes. And there was Brent, inches from my face, staring at me with an arrogant smile. I caught a glimpse of my hands and arms covered in red swollen dots just like they had been when I was stung so many years ago. The pain now, even worse.

When I looked back at Brent, he held an EpiPen above his head, ready to stab me. "Someone needs a shot," he said softly.

"No!" I screamed and cowered.

He paused, lowered his arm, and said, "The alternative is death. Do you choose death, Chelsea?"

Slowly, he began to transform. His skin turned grayish green and started to sag. He reeked of decaying flesh. Brent was aging in front of me to the point of death–and I was forced to watch.

"Do you choose death?" he yelled.

Too frightened for words, I screamed and turned to run. But Brent grabbed me before I got more than a few feet, then shoved me as hard as he could. Briefly taking flight, I landed a short distance away from him. A sharp rock ripped my shirt and sliced open my right shoulder. I propped myself up. Blood ran down my arm and disappeared with my hand into the damp, rising mist.

Brent squatted in front of me, the EpiPen twirling in his boney, atrophied fingers. He placed the menacing needle next to me and uttered, "Decisions, decisions, babe. Will you make it all better–or die?"

The sky continued to darken, and the temperature plummeted. I shuddered from the cold. Barney came up behind me and licked my bloody arm.

"Go away!" I snapped, shoving him away.

As loud as I could, I yelled for Cole. I slammed my eyes shut. I could hear Barney panting next to me.

"This is not real. They are not here," I repeated. "Cole, please."

I wanted to curl up into a ball and go to sleep, hoping soon I would wake up and this would be over. When I opened my eyes I found the decrepit, noxious man, who I no longer recognized, still hovering. Mustering all the strength I had left in me, I lifted both feet and kicked him in the stomach as hard as I could and called out for Cole.

CHAPTER 9

"Chelsea. I'm here. Open your eyes."

A hand brush my face, and I cowered back. Then recognition set in. My eyes flew open. Cole was kneeling in front of me with his hand on my cheek. The sky was clear and bright. The mist had disappeared, and the air was hot from the blinding sun.

I jumped into his arms, knocking him off his feet, and fell on top of him.

"Thank God, it's you. What happened? Where did you go?"

"I didn't go anywhere. I'm right here," he said. He held me for a second, then pushed me back and sat up. "Let me see you. Are you okay?"

I was suddenly aware of how close his face was to mine.

"Your eyes are dilated. Here, drink some water," he said, handing me a water bottle from his backpack.

I chugged as much as he would let me before taking it away.

"Not so fast. You could be dehydrated. Too much too quickly will make you sick."

"Sorry," I said, trying to catch my breath.

"Don't be sorry. What happened? Didn't you eat this morning?"
"Yes, I ate," I said. "I'm not sure what happened. I got to the top of the hill and then..." I paused to put the pieces together.

"Yeah, then you fainted and dropped to the...oh, man, look at your shoulder. You must have cut it when you fell," he said, eyeing the sharp, bloody rock next to me.

"No. I didn't just drop. I did a stupid victory dance, except then I got dizzy and grabbed the tree to steady myself. That's when I noticed you were gone. Did you go back to the trail or something?"

62

I looked around the clearing and found nothing but bushes, rocks, blue and yellow wild flowers in the meadow, and a dilapidated old cabin. The unpainted house had a crooked porch and boarded up windows. Half of the roof was missing. It was a far cry from my grandmother's farmhouse. But that wasn't all.

"Hey, wait. Where's that huge tree with the shaggy bark?"

Cole shook his head. "No dance. No tree."

He gestured towards where I entered the clearing a couple feet away. He was right. There was no tree close to fitting my description, just overgrown weeds and rocks.

"But..."

"But nothing. You got to the top of the hill and dropped to the ground. You passed out. Instantly."

"First, I saw... I mean there was a... I don't know."

I shook my head, baffled and still shaking from the fear of...well, of whatever had happened to me. Cole already suspected that I chased my dead dog through a muddy field and into a cemetery. I had to be careful with what I told him. What would he have thought if he knew I just saw the same dead dog here, in my grandmother's old farmhouse, with my ex-boyfriend? Yes, crazy was the word.

"Chels, you passed out for a few minutes. I was a couple of feet behind you, but it happened so fast that I couldn't catch you in time," he explained. He dug through his backpack. "Anyway, hike over. Let's get that shoulder bandaged." He dug deeper then sat back on his heels. "Damn. I didn't pack the first aid kit."

"It's no big deal," I said, attempting to stand.

"Don't get up."

He threw the backpack over his shoulder then scooped me up, cradling me in his arms. He carried me towards the trail to head back to the car. I had to make a conscious effort not to run my fingers through his hair; his wavy locks were so tempting.

As my hand reached across his chest, the clean linen smell of his t-shirt blew past my nose. His shoulders and chest were broad and muscular, but not bulky. It was all I could do to keep my eyes off his ruggedly handsome face. I blushed, and an uncontrollable giggle slipped from my mouth. I hid my face in his neck to hide my embarrassment.

"What's funny?" he asked.

"Carrying me. My legs aren't hurt. It's just my shoulder." I removed my face from his neck to notice the growing red splotch on his shirt. "Oops, I'm getting blood all over your shirt. I can walk, you know. I don't want you to get hurt carrying me."

Cole's brief laugh was followed by a serious sigh.

In a stern tone, he said, "I don't care about my shirt. I don't want to risk you passing out again. And to be frank–I'm not a wuss either. So let me carry you."

I stifled a smile. For a spellbinding second, our eyes met. Then Cole's foot hit a rock on the trail. It was big enough to make him stumble. He righted himself before we could fall.

Cole grinned and said, "I should probably watch where I'm going."

"Right. Or else we'll both end up injured. Then who will carry us?"

Cole's eyes locked with mine again. After a few seconds, I cleared my throat and gestured towards the dirt path.

"Eyes. Trail," I said.

"Right." He turned his focus to the trail. "I should have taken the first aid kit. I can't believe I forgot something so important."

"It's not like we knew I'd slice open my shoulder and need a medical lift back to the car. All after beating you to the top of a treacherous hill, I might add. Did I mention that I won? I think I did," I teased.

"You are cute," he said, smirking. "You honestly thought you could beat me."

"Don't even pretend. I won fair and square, mister."

I gave him a few pokes in the chest. Now, the thought of his body was taking over my brain again and driving my hormones into another tizzy. Then I noticed the sudden seriousness on his face.

"What is it?" I asked.

"It's none of my business. But considering the dog in the cemetery thing, and now the fact that you passed out up there, I think you should see a doctor. Right? Don't you think?"

"I suppose. My friend, Paige, said the same thing."

He nodded his head, then picked up on what I had implied.

"Wait. This is not the first time you've passed out?"

"It happened weeks ago at Main Street Coffee. And maybe another time before that," I admitted.

"Chelsea, go to the doctor. People don't hallucinate and pass out for no reason. Maybe you're vitamin deficient or something."

Hallucinate? That was a heavy word, especially when said out loud. I had already explained that Barney was a simple misunderstanding. I mean, hallucinate? I didn't want him to think that, let alone admit it to myself. He was right about one thing, though. I should call my doctor. The last thing I wanted was another embarrassing fainting spell.

"You have a point. I'll call the doctor when I get home," I told him.

"Promise me?"

"Yes, I promise. And I'm having deja vu right now," I confessed.

"Weird. Me too."

Finally, we got to the parking lot. When we reached my car he set me down. I leaned against the car while he got the first aid kit. A chill washed over me as he walked away, taking the heat of his body with him. That's when I saw that his shirt was drenched in blood. It looked as if he'd slaughtered an animal or had been stabbed.

"I think I ruined your shirt," I said. "You have to let me take it home and try to clean it. You'd be amazed at what OxyClean can do."

"Don't worry about the shirt."

I pulled back what was left of my sleeve and examined my shoulder.

"Yuck. This is disgusting. I don't think I'll need stitches, though," I said. I could see Cole approaching in my peripheral vision, so I aimed my shoulder in his direction to show him. "Do you..."

I looked up to find him shirtless.

"Do I what?" he asked.

"Do you…" I gulped down the lump that was stuck in my throat and averted my eyes to the ground. "I forgot what I was going to say. I'm so sorry about your shirt."

Cole stood in front of me. It was hard not to stare. And I did try not to stare. As I looked away, he grabbed my injured shoulder.

"Ouch," I said.

"Oh, man! This is terrible. I think you are going to need stitches." Studying it closer, he decided, "You're definitely going to need stitches."

"No," I said. "It looks gross because it's dirty. I'll butterfly it. There's some in my backpack."

"Be honest. How bad does it hurt?"

"It's not so bad," I said, marveling at my sudden tolerance for pain. "It really doesn't hurt at all. I mean, I can feel it, of course." I poked about the wound to check again. I should have at least felt some amount of pain based on how it looked. The gash was deep and long. "I should keep my mouth shut, and be happy that it doesn't hurt."

Cole shook his head. "I should have brought the first aid kit with us. I hope it doesn't get infected." He dug through the kit and said, "There's no cotton balls in here. They must have fallen out. I'll be right back."

First, he walked to his truck and took a red t-shirt from the back seat. Good idea, I thought. Then he pulled a small bag of cotton balls from the floor and came back to where I stood.

He turned away from me and placed the antiseptic wash and cotton balls on the hood of the car. My eyes wandered along the sculpted lines of his shoulders and down the sides of his spine. His tan, smooth skin screamed "touch me". My hand had a mind of its own as it reached out. Somehow, I found the power to regain control of my rogue hand. Enough of that–I squeezed my eyes shut.

My thoughts grew louder, "Please put the shirt on, Cole. Please put the…"

"Hey, are you dizzy?"

My eyes popped open.

"I'm fine. Just–grossed out. I mean, look at my shoulder," I sputtered.

"Come here," he said, leading me to the back of his pickup. He pulled down the tail gate and helped me up. "Sit here while I clean your cut."

I sat cross-legged on the tail gate and said, "I can clean it myself. I'm fine."

"Don't argue. Are you a doctor?"

"No. But I was a girl scout for about five seconds," I chuckled. "Are you a doctor?"

"No. But I played one on TV."

"For real?"

I would have believed he was an actor with his looks and charm.

"No. I'm kidding. Gullible girl."

"That was the worst line ever. Really. The absolute cheesiest," I said.

"And who doesn't like cheese?" he responded.

While he cleaned my wound, I realized something. Despite our two hour conversation the night before, I knew very little about him. He could have been a doctor or an actor, and I wouldn't know. I hadn't any idea how old he was either. So I asked.

"Guess," he responded. "How old do you think I am?"

"I can't guess. Sometimes I think you're my age, sometimes I think you're older. Much older."

"Guess."

I wanted him to be my age, or at least close. I was almost afraid he'd tell me he's thirty or something. I made a hopeful guess.

"You're twenty-one?"

He grinned.

"Am I right?" I asked.

"Yes, you are," he said with the grin still stuck on his lips.

Then we had one of those awkward silences, and all I could think about was how embarrassing it was that he was elbow deep in my bloody shoulder. I ruined a perfect day by stumbling like a moron and falling down like a toddler just learning to walk.

"You're talented."

"Clearly, you can't mean my hiking skills."

He raise an eyebrow. "I mean, you should be in a carnival; the one who guesses ages and weight. You'd make a fortune," he said, tossing a bloody cotton ball in an old grocery bag.

Once my shoulder was cleaned up, it didn't look so hideous. He placed a few butterfly bandages over the gash then taped a piece of gauze over the wound.

"You're fixed. It doesn't look like you'll need stitches after all, but you're probably going to have a nasty scar."

He stood up and slipped on his shirt.

Goodbye beautiful skin. So long six pack.

He took my things out of his backpack and returned them to me. I threw them in my car. Our short-lived hike was over. At any rate, the day was young, and I wasn't ready to say goodbye.

"Now, what?" I asked.

Cole stared thoughtfully into the woods for a second, then took my hand and held it to his chest.

"Chelsea, will you do me the honor of escorting me to the..."

"Prom?" I blurted out with a nervous smile. He laughed, so I laughed.

"No. The cab of my truck. I'm going to drive you home. I'll grab a friend later and return your car to you. I don't think you should drive."

He led me to the passenger side door of his truck.

"Oh, I'm fine." I said, trying to hide the disappointment. "I can drive myself home. Honestly."

"No. I'll drive you home."

"No. I said I'm fine."

"And stubborn," he said.

"Yes. That too"

"I'm head first into the tundra winds, aren't I?"

I shrugged. "I'm not sure what you mean," I said.

"You seem very strong willed. I'm sensing that arguing with you is like walking directly into treacherous winds. I don't expect to get very far."

I smiled. "You're wrong. I'm a gentle breeze."

"Good. Then how about another idea. We can hang here for a while. I want to be sure you can drive. And after that, if you don't already have plans, I have something else in mind."

"I have no other plans," I said. And to be clear, if I had, I would have cancelled them.

We spent half an hour talking in the parking lot. Cole was easy to talk to. It was like talking to a friend I'd known forever. Much like talking to Paige, Jill, and Beth.

The time flew by, and when he asked again if he could take me home, I'll be honest, I wanted to lie. I wanted to say, "Absolutely you can take me home. I can't drive. I need you." But I wasn't the kind of girl who was comfortable playing the damsel in distress. So I told him the truth and assured him that I was perfectly capable of driving home.

"Then let's talk about later," he said. "May I be so bold as to invite myself to your house? With your shoulder a mess, I thought I'd bring you dinner. I'd offer to cook, but that would be more dangerous than our hike."

"That sounds nice."

"How's six thirty? Maybe a boat ride first."

"I'd love that."

I got in my car, started it up, and rolled down the window. Cole leaned in and reached across to my injured shoulder. He secured the tape that covered the gauze. His face was so close to mine that I was afraid to breathe. Kindness poured from his eyes. Heat wafted from his body.

"When you get home put something stronger on there to hold the bandage. The tape isn't sticking very well," he said, backing out of the window.

"Thanks, I will."

"Call the doctor."

"I will. I promise. See you around six thirty."

I pulled out of the parking lot feeling as if I was leaving something of great magnitude behind. There was pain in the pit of my stomach and an incredible urge to turn around and go back for him. I drove like a sloth to the main road, then waited at the stop sign hoping he'd pull up behind me so I could see him one more time. After a few seconds, I felt silly and pulled away.

About half way home, I started to feel sharp pain in my shoulder. Talk about a delayed reaction. I was so caught up with Cole that I hadn't realized the severity of the cut. He was the best pain killer on the market. And if I had anything to say about it, he wouldn't be on the market much longer.

CHAPTER 10

When I got home, I scheduled an appointment to see my doctor. After that, I rummaged through the medicine cabinet for pain relief, found some generic ibuprofen, and popped three capsules in my mouth. I collapsed on the couch with the intention to rest for a few minutes. Several hours later, I awoke from a deep, peaceful sleep in a panic.

I heard a quiet knock at my upstairs door and was afraid I'd overslept. I hopped up, worried that it was Cole already. It was just shortly after five, but maybe Cole was early.

I didn't see anyone through the window as I approached the door. When I opened it, no one was there. A loose cedar shingle on the side of the house rattled with the wind. Assuming I solved the knocking mystery, I went back in the house to get ready.

After I showered, I searched diligently for something to wear. Again, I changed my clothes several times before finding something adequate. I settled on my favorite comfortable old jeans and an army green tank top. I abided by the KISS plan: keep it simple stupid. At exactly six thirty, Cole pulled up to my dock. I closed the book I was reading and watched him secure the boat. Then, he crossed the lawn and headed towards the house–towards me. His smile lit up his eyes.

"Hi," he said.

"Hello."

"How's your shoulder?"

"Fine," now that you're here.

He sat next to me on the whicker couch; we were knee to knee. Cole put a hand on my leg and said, "You look great."

"Thanks. Showering was fun. I tried not to get my bandage wet."

He chuckled. "It probably would have been fine if you got it wet."

71

"Now you tell me. What kind of doctor are you?"

"The doctor is out, I'm afraid. Tonight I play the ship's captain, and I would love to take you for a boat ride. Are you cool with that?"

"Absolutely. Let me get my sweater. It's supposed to cool off. Come in."

I walked into the house and grabbed my sweater from the counter.

"Wow, this is great," Cole said, taking half a step inside. "It's bigger than it looks from the outside."

"That's what everyone says. It's like an optical illusion."

Cole tapped a picture on the wall. "This must be your sister or something. You guys look like twins."

"That's Meggie. She's six years older. We don't look that much alike anymore. That picture was taken about three years ago when she was normal."

"Sisters are crazy. I have one, and she used to drive me nuts. We get along better now that she has a life. She's settling down a bit."

"Meggie is in full-time party mode and aways mad at me for something. Apparently, I am solely responsible for all of her short-comings."

"You seem too strong of a person to let that bug you. "

He leaned against the door.

"I guess it comes and goes. My strength, that is."

I understood what he was saying. He was right. Why should I worry about her life when I had my own to take care of? Seemed the KISS plan applied to more than just clothes. I walked to the door to leave, but Cole didn't move.

"I have my sweater," I said. "You ready?"

"Yup."

Cole slid the door open but didn't give me much room to pass by him. He gestured for me to go through first. I smiled and slipped by, my hair and back brushed against him. When we reached the dock, he took my hand and led me to the boat.

"Don't count last week against me," I said, smirking. "I really do know how to swim."

Cole raised his eyebrows then cocked half a grin. He eyed a life jacket tucked under a seat.

"Sure," he said. He put his hands on his hips, then ran one through his hair. He pointed to a small door between the two front seats and said, "Listen, I have plenty of life jackets if you'd be more comfortable wearing one."

My smirk grew into a full blown smile. How cute that he was worried about me.

"No, thank you. I'm fine," I replied. "I trust you."

The view of the rolling hillside surrounding the lake was breath-taking. The sun began its descent beyond the hills, and the bright fuchsia sky turned the glassy water a soft shade of pink. The only waves were from Cole's boat.

"Where is everyone?" I asked. "Boats have been out all day, and now no one is watching this incredible sunset."

Cole shrugged his shoulders and mirrored my bewildered look. He slowed the boat just before reaching the widest part of the lake. We were a comfortable distance from shore. Cole cut the engine. He reached below the front seats into a cooler and pulled out two bottled waters and several small, plastic containers of Chinese food from the best place on Main Street.

"My favorite Chinese take-out."

"Isn't it everyone's?" he said.

Cole popped up a small table in between two back seats and placed everything there. I couldn't help but be wonderstruck by this seemingly perfect guy. He caught me in a mystified stare.

"What? Is this a bad idea?" he asked.

I shook my head. "No. Why?"

"You're looking at me funny."

"I am? I don't mean to," I stammered.

He plopped down in the captain's chair and let out an audible breath.

"Did I get this wrong? This was supposed to be a date. Maybe I didn't make that clear. If you don't feel that way, I understand."

"Oh! No, that's not it. I mean, I wasn't sure if this was a date or just friends hanging out. But a date is what I was hoping we were calling it," I said. My ears got warm.

His smile returned. "Phew. I thought I'd just humiliated myself. It was that look you had. It was strange."

I slid into the chair across from him. "I didn't mean to look at you funny. I was lost in thought for a second."

A few seconds of uncomfortable silence went by, then I realized that he was waiting for me to continue. I stared down at my hands in my lap, embarrassed to admit that I'd been in awe of him. I did not want him to think it was anything bad, so I fessed up.

"I was wondering if you were raised by a pack of girls or if you took some kind of class that other guys didn't know about. You're so thoughtful. And romantic. I mean, dinner at sunset in the middle of the lake...it's perfect."

I glanced at him to see if he was listening and found him smiling from ear to ear.

"Yes. Now you know my secret. I took the class. Romance 101. They teach it right here at SUNY Geneseo, but it's underground. Only real men are allowed to take the course." He moved from the captain's chair and stood next to me. "Even telling you is dangerous. Can I trust you to keep my secret?"

"We'll see. It might cost you."

"Blackmail? How scandalous," he said, rubbing his hands together. "Come on, bring it." He squeezed my knee and made me laugh.

"Not so soon," I said, playfully shoving his shoulder. "Don't worry, I'll think of something good."

Cole and I talked for hours. We poked at lettuce rolls, sweet and sour pork, dynamite shrimp, and chicken lo mien. Eventually, the wind picked up, and it was too cold to stay out any longer.

For most of the ride back, I had the internal battle of whether or not to invite him in when we got home. I'm an adult. At least that's what I told my friends and mother the other day. What could be the harm in inviting him in?

For God's sake, look at him! I thought. As much as my body told me there was no decision to be made, my head told me there was no way I was ready to ask him in. It might send the wrong message. On the other hand, he had been nothing but a gentleman so far.

Cole pulled up to my dock and cut the engine. He helped me out of the boat and safely onto the dock. We strolled towards the house.

"Chelsea, I hate to end the night so soon, but I have an early appointment tomorrow, not to mention you look exhausted."

Internal battle–terminated.

I disguised my disappointment and said, "Yes, I am exhausted."

"May I call you tomorrow?" he asked.

"Definitely. Thank you for tonight. I had a lot of fun."

"Yes, it was fun. Sorry about your fall earlier. It was my fault, and I feel awful."

"It was not your fault. Oh, by the way, I called my doctor when I got home. I'm seeing him next week."

"That's good," he said, pushing some loose hair behind my ear. "I'll call you tomorrow. Have a good night," Cole said.

He leaned in and kissed me on the cheek. It was slow and warm and as perfect as every minute I had spent with him since he pulled me from the lake.

"Good night. Be careful," I told him as he turned and walked back towards his boat.

Alone in the dark, with my teeth chattering, I watched Cole pull away. That's when it struck me. Everyone I had dated or had a crush on since I was a little girl passed before my eyes: all the silly young boys, insecure teenagers, and over-confident guys. As I thought about them, I had a revelation.

Deep within me, there had been a vacancy where true love should have lived at some point in my eighteen years of life. I had never been the girl who got butterflies or obsessed over one boy. I had never wanted the next day to come quicker because I missed him. I had never wanted someone to stay so much that it made me queasy. Those typical young love feelings had never consumed me. Until now. I didn't want it to stop. I wondered, why had I never had these feeling for anyone before? And even more pressing–what was I supposed to do with them now?

CHAPTER 11

"Look, Meggie, you can't be a substitute teacher forever. Bite the bullet. The Livonia School District is hiring," I said while shuffling bedroom furniture around. The phone slipped from my shoulder. "Hang on! I dropped you," I hollered and scrambled to pick it up.

"I can't do it. It's too permanent," I caught her responding as I wedged the phone back between my shoulder and ear.

"So? What's wrong with that?"

"It's Reznor. What if he dumps me because I went all mainstream on him."

Typical Meggie; worried about what some guy would think when she should be thinking about herself and her own future.

"You're an edgy art teacher. That's way cool. If Reznor doesn't like it, you guys weren't meant to be."

"You sound like mom."

"Not my intention," I said, pushing the bed against the window. The curtain fluttered in the breeze.

"A steady paycheck would be nice."

"Get a normal job, and tell Mom and Dad about Reznor. You obviously like him a lot. It's not like Mom and Dad will disown you. Do it now, while they're away. Send them an email. It will give them time to think about it before they get back."

"Exactly the problem," she sighed.

I pushed the dresser too hard causing the Tiffany lamp to wobble to a near fall. I raced to the other side just in time.

"Whoa! That was close."

"What are you doing?"

"Moving furniture. I almost smashed Grandma's antique lamp, so I have to go. Plus, I'm starving."

"Sure. Thanks for the talk, sis," Meggie said. "I'll stop by tomorrow."

"I'm not lonely. I'm fine. Call me tomorrow."

By the time the call ended, my stomach was growling. While searching the refrigerator and cupboards for something to eat, my phone dinged with a text message.

"Lunch?" was all it said.

"Why yes, God. I would love some lunch," I said into the air. It was a funny coincidence that I was in the process of searching for exactly that. But the phone number didn't ring a bell.

I texted back, "Who's asking"

A few minutes went by, and I still had no answer. I assumed it was sent to my number by mistake and continued my search for something to eat. What I needed was a trip to Wegman's grocery store to stock up. The cupboards were full of nothing. Maybe an experienced chef could have whipped something together with what little I had, but I was far from qualified.

Then came another ding.

"I'm that forgettable?" It was followed by a winking smiley face, a mountain climber emoji, and a boat Emoji. Cole.

I typed back, "I'm hungry, so I guess it doesn't matter who you are."

"Lol. Be there in a sec. Hope u r hungry," he responded.

Oh, no! What did that mean? I was a mess. I had dust bunnies all over me from moving my bedroom furniture, and my crazy hair was in a knot on the top of my...

Ding, dong.

"Since when did 'I'll be there in a second' actually mean getting there in one second?" I uttered.

I ran up the stairs to answer the door, sneaking a peek in the mirror. I needed more time than I had to fix the disaster I found. However, time was not on my side. Plus, he could see me through the window.

I opened the door to a beautiful, well-dressed, handsome young man and instantly felt like an ugly stepsister.

"Hi. Look at you. You're all dressed up." I looked down at my cut-off shorts and hole riddled shirt and said, "And I'm a cesspool of dust bunnies and furniture polish. Probably some sweat too." I tried to laugh it off, but I was embarrassed. We were polar opposites.

"I shouldn't have popped in on you. I tried calling your cell, but it wouldn't let me leave a message. I sent the text hoping maybe you'd get that before I got here. And by the way, you and the word cesspool shall never be used together again. Understand, pretty lady?"

Cole shimmied by me, planting a kiss on my forehead as he did so. He pulled a bag of food from behind his back. It was from Mr. Dominic's, my favorite Italian restaurant in the city. Seriously? We clearly had the same taste in food.

He hung his sport coat on a hook by the door, then headed downstairs to the kitchen. I walked down the steps behind him and was slapped by an aphrodisiac of clean soapy linens with a subtle hint of musk and clove. His scent had me practically slithering down the stairs behind him.

"I wasn't sure what you'd like," he explained, setting the bag on the counter.

"It smells amazing."

Cole removed container upon container of various pasta, chicken, and salad dishes from the bag. We ate at the breakfast bar that separated the living room from the kitchen. We talked for about an hour. Cole shared a few childhood stories with me. He laughed out loud when I told him I was homeschooled.

"Not funny. I'm already done for the summer. Besides, home-schooled kids are way smarter," I said.

"And way weird," he laughed.

"Unique. We prefer unique," I giggled.

Half way through lunch my cell phone rang. I hit the "ignore" button. There was no way I could have a short conversation with Paige. I'm sure she wanted to talk about her visit to Duke. But I wanted to avoid twenty questions when she figured out I had company. We had plans to go to the art gallery Friday to see Meggie's paintings on display. I would fill her in on Cole then.

When we couldn't even look at food anymore, Cole Said, "Hey, I'm afraid I have to head out. I have a basketball game with some friends. I have some butts to kick."

"I take it you're good at basketball."

He grinned. And catching me off guard, he said, "I like you, Chelsea."

"I like you too." My heart hit fast forward.

He took my hands. "That being said, I hope you and your parents don't mind that I dropped in. I enjoy your company. A lot. If I become too overbearing, let me know. I don't want to scare you away."

I nodded and smiled. I wanted to tell him that I loved his attention, and I loved spending time with him. I wanted to say, "Being in your presence makes me feel alive, and I will ache for you the second you walk out of here." But I didn't say that. Nothing came out. I was terrified that I would say something stupid.

Then he told me, "I have to go out of town for a few days. I leave tomorrow morning for Syracuse to see my grandparents. I'll be back late Saturday or early Sunday. I'll call you then–if you don't mind?"

"Absolutely. You don't have to ask."

I walked him to the door and thanked him for lunch.

"I'll never be hungry for dinner. I think I need a nap after that feast," I said.

He took my hand from my over-stuffed belly and said, "Have a good weekend." Then he ran his fingers up to my shoulder and brushed them across my bandage. "How does it feel?"

"Occasional pain, nothing severe," I said.

He grimaced. I rolled my eyes.

"Get that look off your face. I'm fine. You should see it, it's practically healed already"

"Keep it clean. You don't want it to get infected," he said, peeling back the bandage for a look.

"I'm sure it's not infected. It seriously looks way better today."

"Am I mistaken or was this nasty yesterday?" he said, gawking at my shoulder.

"I know, right? Less swelling makes a big difference, I guess."

He studied it for a few more seconds, then said, "Either way, I'm glad your parents won't see it. They aren't going to like me if I can't keep you safe when we're together."

"Their biggest worry is that I'm going to be lonely while they're away. They had some last minute guilt. I'm sure by now they're focused more on the trip than me."

He held my hand as we stood in the doorway. The way he seemed to search deep into my eyes, I thought for sure he was going to kiss me.

I spotted Ruthie then, coming back from a walk. She was looking at us. She waved and made a strange face. I imagined the questions I'd get from her later.

"Hi, Chelsea!" she hollered.

"Hi, Ruthie!" I hollered back.

Cole waved at her. "She's cute," he said.

"You have no idea how cute."

He clapped his hands together and said, "I have to go. I'll call you Sunday."

Cole placed one hand on my cheek, then slowly kissed my forehead. Why couldn't he have aimed a little lower? My lips were being neglected. The problem was how comfortable I was around him; it was hard to remember the small fact that we'd only met a few days ago.

I watched him walk up the driveway towards the main road where he had parked. When I couldn't see him anymore, I went in the house with my full stomach and flipped on CNN. After a minute, I remembered I had to call Paige.

"Finally," Paige said.

"Hello to you too."

"I called and texted you. How are you?" Paige asked.

"Great. When did you get back?"

"Late last night."

"Still on for Friday?" I asked.

"Of course. I'll pick you up at six. I'm working tonight. Are you?"

"No. Tomorrow."

"Cool. I'm on the schedule tomorrow too," she said. "How are you doing, Chels? For real. I thought I would have gotten a call from you before now."

Paige sounded concerned, and I couldn't imagine why.

"I'm fine. My parents have only been gone for a couple days."

"I'm not talking about them. I'm talking about Brent."

"Oh. That. Yeah, all is good."

"Oookaaaay," she drawled. "I'm supposed to believe you've made a miraculous emotional recovery? Talk to me."

"Seriously, I'm not upset. It's been a month."

Paige was quiet on the other end. I could picture her face in my head. Her crooked mouth and squinting eyes.

I said, "Look, do you want me to lie? I'm over it. You guys were right. He was a jerk."

She cleared her throat and said, "If you mean it, that's great news. It's just that you were a mess when I left. Feeling all guilty and everything," Paige said. Then she ditched the concern so she could mock me with my own pathetic words. "I was so mean to end things like that. What kind of girl does that?" she whined.

"Very funny," I giggled.

"Whatever. Take time to yourself this summer. Be free. Serial date."

"Serial date? There's some good advice."

"Look, I have to run. I'm late for my shift. Wouldn't want to piss off the big dog. He's got some kind of bug up his butt." Paige huffed. "Anyway, just remember, you don't need a guy to have a great summer."

"Wow, you should start a dating blog."

"I should, smart ass," she replied.

The truth was, Paige was right. I didn't need a guy to have a great summer. But when life dumps one into the lake right in front of you, why would you ignore him?

CHAPTER 12

The next morning, I was off to work. On the way, I stopped at Main Street Coffee for a latte and the latest gossip from Beth. Then I headed to open the store where Paige and I worked. Trend was a small indie-punk boutique down the street from the coffee shop. It was dark when I entered, which made me wonder if Jackson was there yet. I didn't often get in before him. I eyeballed the pile of boxes by the cash register that needed to be unpacked and broken down but couldn't find the motivation to start. From seemingly nowhere, someone appeared in the back of the store and startled me.

"Good morning," Jackson mumbled. He raised his coffee mug. "I just made a pot. But I see you come prepared."

His hair was disheveled, and his shirt was wrinkled.

Jackson was a young, successful entrepreneur who owned three Trend boutiques in the Finger Lakes Region. This was his main store. He spent most of his days here, and lately, he'd spent several nights here on his office couch. I knew he and his girlfriend had been having trouble. I tried not to get involved. Although, Paige kept me up to date whether I liked it or not. Her gossip skills far surpassed those of Beth and Jill.

"You're in early. Or maybe you didn't go home."

"Yep. Let's not talk about it," he said.

"I wasn't planning to."

"Intimidating stack of boxes."

I nodded.

"You look exhausted. Are you alright?" Jackson asked.

I shrugged and plunked my butt down on a table of shirts.

"I'm just tired. I haven't been sleeping well."

83

"Try sleeping on my couch," Jackson quipped as he strolled away and closed himself in his office.

Point taken. We all had problems.

I put my head back and rubbed my eyes. I imagined going to sleep right then. Until Brent popped into my head. I hadn't given him much thought in days. Not until Paige brought him up.

"You look like you're in deep thought," Paige said, flicking on the fluorescents and interrupting my rising anxiety. Paige to the psyche-rescue.

"Same old thoughts," I said. "Nothing new."

"Lovely. He's not worth the time you waste thinking about him."

"For the record, I am not thinking about Brent." Denial. Nothing wrong with that.

Paige smirked, then mumbled, "You should have gone to Europe with your parents. A little distance from Brent would have done you good."

"I don't care about Brent. I'm just tired."

"Fine. I'm just saying. No one here will fall apart without you"

"Oh, yeah? No one? That's a shame. I thought it would be cool to throw someone into a nervous breakdown," I teased.

"I guess maybe I would miss you a little," Paige said. "But no biggie, I'd find a fill-in bestie."

"That's bull," I said. "No one will love you like I do, let alone tolerate you for more than five minutes. You're a triple Type A personality."

Paige laughed. "That's not even a real term."

"Riveting conversation and all. But has anyone noticed the stack of boxes?" Jackson asked. He walked past me and muttered, "The technical term for triple Type A personality is know-it-all." Then he disappeared out the front door.

Paige slithered to my side. "See? He likes you. He could be serial dating victim number one."

"Stop. He does not like me." I refolded a beaded Hurley tank top on the shelf and said, "It wouldn't matter anyway. Why don't you go out with him?"

"Please, pansexual scares him," she said.

"So, I win by default?"

"I'm also not into older men." She gave me a shifty grin. "You seem to," she added as I headed to the pile of unpacked boxes.

"Twenty one is not that much older than us. It's hardly a big deal. Unless you're too immature, that is."

A sock whacked me in the back of the head.

"Yeah, that's what it is," Paige said.

She and I eventually tackled the pile of boxes before traffic in the store picked up. For some reason, it got extra busy around noon which made the day zip by. As my shift dragged to an end, I found myself daydreaming about Cole. Naturally, Paige had other suspicions for my quiet mood.

"Have you talked to him?"

"Who?" I asked, startled at first. I thought somehow she knew about Cole.

"Brent, dummy."

"No. Would you get over it, please. Because I have," I said, squinting my eyes at Paige, feigning disgust.

All five-foot-ten inches of Paige now hovered behind me as I sat at the back desk filling out an inventory sheet. Paige had never made it a secret that she loathed Brent. She had a long list of negative characteristics to describe him. Indifferent was the word she had used most often. Rude, obnoxious, and self-centered had been reoccurring favorites, as well. She walked around to the front of my desk with attitude oozing from her pores.

Suddenly light-headed, I rested my head in my hands. Not to mention, I was sick and tired of talking about Brent. But Paige wouldn't let it go.

"He was special, Chels. A real catch. Remember the time you harassed Brent until he finally agreed to take you to his house for dinner to meet his parents. They were so happy to meet the girl their boy had been dating for two whole weeks. Yeah, try a year. But who was counting, right?"

"I didn't harassed him," I said under my breath.

"Then at dinner his charming mother couldn't seem to remember your name. Sharon. Charlene. Whatever." She laughed, clearly amusing herself. "You were so pissed off."

As Paige rambled on, she sounded more and more like she was in a tunnel. I lifted my head from my hands to find that I was practically blinded by dizziness. I thought she was saying my name, but it was garbled. My head seemed to weigh a ton, and I struggled to hold it up. I struggled to see straight. Everything was blurry, and my vision was quickly going black.

It was too late when I realized I was passing out. Again. The last thing I remembered was my head dropping onto the desk with a thump.

CHAPTER 13

I was back, trapped in the dark room again. But this time, I had questions for my mystery boy. The cold wind blew the sheer curtain. Moonlight beamed like a spotlight through the window. I waited for him, all the while reliving the haunting affect he'd had on me.

"Hello? Are you there?" I called out.

Then it happened.

Brown shoes stepped into the light. I saw his faded jeans. His shirt was different this time; it was a long sleeved, button-up Polo shirt. His chin came into view, then his mouth. Fearing I might screw something up, I didn't move.

Suddenly, he stopped. I could not see his eyes, but what I could see looked familiar. I sensed he was someone I knew. But something wasn't right.

It only took another second before I figured out who this stranger was. The need to run to him and be near him–vanished. As the tension from my body dissipated, my shoulders and head dropped in disappointment. He was not the boy from my previous dream. I knew without a doubt.

"Brent," I whispered. It wasn't supposed to be you, I thought.

As if reading my mind, he asked, "Why not?" He stepped into the light, and I could see him as clear as day. "Why isn't it supposed to be me?"

His frown hung low. This reaction surprised me.

I said, "You look sad. I wouldn't think you'd care. It just wasn't you before, that's all. You weren't the one I saw."

"How do you know?"

"I felt something different for him. I've never felt those feelings before. I'm sorry."

Brent lifted his chin for a moment, then looked in my eyes and snarled, "You'd better get on with it then. Death waits for no one. Even you know that."

All of a sudden, Brent's face morphed into an ugly, gargoyle-like creature. His head began to shake in an unnatural, wicked way. His face got dark and contorted, his features took on sharp angles. His pupils grew until his eyes were black. Brent was more hideous than in the weird dream I had when I passed out in Letchworth Park.

"Wake up!" he yelled.

"Wake up. Chelsea. Chelsea. I think she's coming to. Jackson, I think she's waking up."

Paige's words were distant but clear. I peeled open my eyes and tried to focus on the people standing over me. I was lying on the floor next to the desk. Paige had a cold cloth on my head. I brushed it away and sat up with her help. A muscular figure came into focus.

"Chelsea, it's Jackson. Can you see me?"

"Yeah, I can now. My head…" I felt for a lump, and there wasn't one. But man, my head throbbed.

"You hit your head on the desk then slid out of your chair. Paige caught your head before you whacked it on the floor and ended up with a double whammy," he explained.

"That's my girl," I muttered.

"I doubt you have a concussion." he said, checking my pupils. "Paige said you passed out at her house a few weeks ago. You need to see a doctor."

"I have an appointment next week."

I gave Paige the evil eye.

"I know a neurologist you can see. He's at Strong Hospital. I saw him a few times for concussions."

"Concussions? As in more than one?" Paige asked.

Jackson shrugged, and said, "I'm on a rugby team."

"Give me the doctor's number. I'll call for Chelsea," Paige decided. She knew me well enough to know I wasn't going to call on my own.

"Don't blow this thing out of proportion. I'll see my regular doctor," I said.

"Chelsea, you've passed out at least twice now. You told Paige that you have horrible headaches and trouble sleeping. Maybe it's stress, but get it checked out soon. Better safe than sorry. Right?" Jackson said.

"Geez, Paige. How long was I out for? Anything you didn't share with our boss?"

"Only the important things came up. I'll take you home," she said.

"I have to finish the window display before tomorrow. I'll be fine by the time I'm done."

"I'll do it first thing in the morning. Right now, I'm taking you home," Paige insisted, helping me to my feet. Then she whispered to Jackson, "Text me the doctor's number."

Jackson nodded and walked back to his office, shouting behind him, "Go home, Chels!"

Ignoring my glare, Paige helped me into a chair. She wandered to the register and began shuffling papers around. Ugh, she was annoying sometimes.

I chugged a few gulps of water. When I looked over at Paige, she was staring at me. She looked away and went back to shuffling papers.

I said, "I'm fine. Stop putzing around for my sake. Go. You'll be late for softball practice."

"Come with me. We'll come back and get your car later."

"I can't. Meggie and I have a Zoom call with my parents at five."

She glared at me for a second, assessing my stubbornness I presumed.

"Bye," I said, picking up a shirt, a skirt, and a pair of boots. I marched to the front window.

"Whatever." She grimaced at the fast growing lump on my forehead, grabbed her phone, and headed for the door. "Call me if you need me," she said over her shoulder.

With Paige off to practice and Jackson locked away in his office, I had time to myself. It was too quiet, though. The silence was unnerving. I took the AirPods from my pocket, shoved them in my ears, and pulled up some music.

I had always found silence unsettling, never peaceful. For me, it was empty and dark, and I was terrified that I would get lost in it. If I gave way to complete silence, leaving behind all thought and conscious chitchat, what would stop my soul from drifting away from my body? Yes, it was an irrational thought. But it was there. Maybe that was why my dream bothered me so much. The harrowing feeling of emptiness and loneliness, the deafening silence and lack of control–how weak and vulnerable it made me feel.

Worst of all, in silence I would be able to hear the guilty chatter going on in my head. I wondered how I could feel so in love with someone in a dream and, at the same time, have such strong feelings for Cole. I felt like a cheater and a liar. But in the next breath, how could I feel like I was cheating on Cole with someone who wasn't even real? Not to mention, it wasn't as if Cole and I would even be considered a couple at this point. The feelings conjured up by one stupid dream were almost too much to think about at once. Guilt, love, terror, painful sadness, and abandonment. What the heck? Get over it, I thought. It was a DREAM.

After a half an hour of staging and dressing the mannequin in the window, the light-headedness was gone. But my reeling thoughts spun faster, and my heavy chest only continued to weigh me down.

As I stepped down from the window, I thought I saw Cole walking by. I rushed to the door. He hadn't gone to Syracuse after all.

When I got outside, I didn't see him. I peeked into shop windows, checked down the alley, up and down the sidewalk, and across the street. I glanced in the window at Main Street Coffee.

"Yo," Jackson hollered from the doorway of Trend. "You good?"

"Yeah. Sorry," I said, wandering back to the store. "I thought I saw someone I knew. I was wrong."

I shrugged and shuffled past Jackson. He glared at me, his mouth scrunched and eyes narrowed.

"I'm fine." I took my keys from behind the counter, shook them, and said, "I'm going. I'm going."

CHAPTER 14

That evening, my parents had a Zoom call with Meggie and me. After several minutes, during a lull in the conversation, my father randomly asked, "So, anyone find a boyfriend since we've been away? Let's talk about that."

"Seriously?" Meggie snapped. Then she turned to me. "Seriously, Chelsea? I'm supposed to believe that just came out of nowhere?"

"Yeah," I said. "I'm pretty sure it did." I moved my head out of the screen shot and scowled at her. I mouthed, "Shut up!"

"Hmm, did your old Dad pick up on something?" my father said.

Needless to say, it was too late by that point. Meggie had overreacted. My father thought he was teasing, but Meggie continued to take to the defense, which only made matters worse. I painstakingly watched Meggie squirm as she battled our inquisitive parents about whether or not she had a boyfriend. Meggie attempted to hide the truth about her older, alternative rock boyfriend while my parents set about to unravel her circle of lies. I had to say, she crusaded like a champion for her cause, but she never had a chance. In the end, the truth prevailed.

My father took the news surprisingly well. He simply insisted on meeting this man as soon as they returned home; he was willing to give him a shot. My mother, on the other hand, proclaimed that Meggie would dump him, or at the very least, encourage him to find a steady, respectable job by the time they returned home from Europe.

In true Meggie form, she stormed out of the house in a huff before the Zoom call ended (My guess was to find Reznor and have a good cry on his shoulder). To say I got off easy, was an understatement. Thanks to Meggie's conversational collapse, my love life skimmed right under the radar.

91

Later that night, I went through my usual bedtime routine with one person on my mind: Cole. It was foolish that I missed him as much as I did.

I contemplated calling him. I did have an excuse since I thought I saw him earlier. But in the end, I couldn't bring myself to do it. I wasn't that assertive. The next few days would be a struggle, but you know what they say: absence makes the heart grow fonder. A fitting cliche. I got a pen and wrote it on my wrist above the scar. That way if I reached for the phone, it would be the first thing I saw.

My cell phone rang the second I climbed into bed. My hand slapped the empty surface of the night stand. Grr! I'd left it in the kitchen. I made a mad dash downstairs, squealing with excitement. It had to be Cole.

Without thinking, I answered before looking at the caller ID. It was too late when I realized what I'd done. The number was distinctly familiar and definitely not Cole. I wouldn't have answered had I not been so hasty.

"Hey, Meggie. What's up?" I said, out of breath.

"You are such a jerk! I can't believe you let them do that to me. I would never do that to you. Never," she ranted.

"Wait a minute. Calm down. I didn't do anything."

"Exactly."

"Meggie, if you're serious about this guy then it was just a matter of time before they found out. Now, it's out in the open. And what was I supposed to do? When Mom gets going, there's no stopping her."

"I know. Mom's already texted me twice. She asked if I ran off to see Meatloaf after I left. Did you hear me? I said Meatloaf." We both giggled. "She told me that if we are still together when she gets home, she's going to counsel him on a career change." She giggled again. "As if he's anything like Meatloaf. He's more of a cross between Dan Reynolds and Brendon Urie. I mean, seriously. Meatloaf? I had to google him."

We poked fun at my mother's taste in music and her idea of who she considered to be our perfect mates. She was old fashioned in many respects.

Several minutes into our conversation, my phone beeped. I had another call coming in. I knew Cole wasn't supposed to call until Sunday, but maybe he missed me as much as I missed him.

"Meggie, I have to go. I have another call."

"Who is it? Paige?"

"No. I don't know the number."

"Then don't answer it."

"It could be Mom."

"It's not Mom. Wait. Is it a guy? Are you seeing someone?"

"No. I have to get this. I'll call you tomorrow."

"You are such a liar! I cannot believe I went through all that and you..."

I cut her off and clicked over to the mystery caller. Maybe Cole was calling from his grandparents house.

"Hello?"

"Hi," said a male voice.

A fraction of a second later, it registered. Crap.

"Hi, Brent. What's up?" I said in a deflated tone but thinking: What the heck are you calling me for?

"Don't sound so excited."

"Sorry. I'm just tired. I was getting ready for bed." Again, I asked, "What's up?" Get to the point.

"I called to say hello and see how my girlfriend is doing"

"Friend," I corrected. "And she's great."

He laughed at my comment and said, "I didn't mean it like that. I meant friend–who's a girl."

I ignored that and asked, "Did you get a new number?"

"No. It's a second phone for the internship."

It seemed Brent got the internship he wanted at his father's law firm. Shocker.

"Cool. I knew they'd give it to you. Did you start already?"

"I did. Piece of cake stuff. But listen, the real reason I called–I'd love to catch up. Find out what's going on in your life."

I waited for the rest. The punchline. The kicker to his offbeat comment. But he was silent.

"Okay," I said, unsure how to respond.

It was the most shocking thing Brent could have said. As if he was really interested. As if he would care what was going in my life. He never had before. I laughed out loud at the thought. I couldn't help myself.

"Chelsea? Are you coughing or laughing?"

"Laughing... sorry. It's just funny."

"What's so funny?" he asked.

"Really, I'm sorry. I don't mean to be rude..."

"I can tell."

"It's just that I haven't heard from you in weeks. I think it's funny that suddenly you want to chat."

"Why is that funny?"

"I'm sorry. It just doesn't sound like you. I wouldn't think you'd care."

My stomach fluttered. I had said those very words to Brent in the dream I had when I passed out at Trend. I held my breath, waiting for the ominous warning that death waits for no one. I pictured the creepy gargoyle and its beady black eyes.

"I can't believe you said that. I still care about you, Chels."

I unclenched my jaw and exhaled.

"Brent, I didn't intend for that to be mean. It's not that I don't care about you too. I'm just not sure that we're ready to hangout yet."

"I'm free Saturday. I was thinking about stopping by. Maybe taking you to dinner."

That caused me to pause. Really? With my parents out of town, I thought it would be awkward to be here alone with Brent. What in the world would we talk about? And again—really? Why would he want to see me?

I shook my head and said, "That's nice, but I don't think so."

"Come on, for old time sake. No strings. Just friends. You were my best friend for over two years. I miss you."

"I'm not sure it's a good idea."

"Come on. Just two friends having dinner. You know you want to say yes," he stated.

I toyed with the idea for a minute. How interesting that he referred to me as his best friend. It never occurred to me that he felt that way. Somehow, I found myself flattered by his soft-heartedness. What would be the harm in two friends having dinner, after all? Perhaps, the reality of our relationship was exactly that; we were better off as friends. So after two years together, maybe it was worth the try.

"Two friends having dinner. Sound good. Pick me up at eight?"

"I'll be there at six. Then we will go to dinner between seven and seven-thirty," Brent said, needing control as usual.

"Sure. Sounds like a plan. I'll see you Saturday," I agreed.

"Great. We'll go someplace casual. I have a few ideas. Just you and me, Chels. I look forward to it."

I went straight to bed after that call. My mind raced with a plethora of questions about Brent's phone call. He always could turn on the charm when he wanted to, it just wasn't usually directed towards me. The longer I sat there and thought about it, the more I questioned his true intentions. I couldn't figure out why Brent was suddenly interested in how or what I was doing. In all the years I'd known Brent Stewart III, son of a wealthy and popular partner at the Shatzel and Stewart Law Offices, the only time he was concerned with my feelings was in the first few months of our relationship. You know, the honeymoon phase. I should have asked more questions, but the entire phone call threw me off. Brent wasn't often so unpredictable. I continued to ponder Brent's motivation for a while, but in the end, what was the worst that could happen. It was just dinner.

With that put to rest, Cole consumed the last of my consciousness. All I could think about was how exceptional he seemed. But there was a part of me that waited for the inevitable honeymoon phase to end, like it had with Brent. Even so, how far could someone stray from being their true self? Honestly, Brent was always a step away from being a jerk. But not Cole. He couldn't be more different. Which meant–he could be "the one".

I went to bed with that promising thought stuck in my head, a perm-a-grin plastered on my face, and the light of the moon shining through my window. As my head hit the pillow, my heavy lids shut. Happy thoughts equaled peaceful sleep. Or so I thought.

CHAPTER 15

The lightning woke me up at about two in the morning. I couldn't go back to sleep. There was nothing better than the sight of heat lightning flashing from behind the hills and reflecting into the calm lake water. I got up, grabbed my book, and headed for the back porch. Under the glow of soft candlelight, I snuggled up on the wicker couch and set out to finish the last few chapters of James Patterson's latest Women's Murder Club book.

After a bit, I wandered inside to make a mug of herbal tea. When I moseyed back outside, snuggled under the cozy throw, and reached for my book–it was gone.

I distinctly remembered putting the book on top of the throw before going inside, so I searched behind the pillows, under the cushions, and I shook out the throw blanket. Finding nothing but a quarter, I scanned the porch.

"Hmm, no book. Maybe under the table."

As I got down on my knees, it started to rain. Within seconds it was teeming. Thunder rolled in as lightning flashed. A smile grew across my face; a good thunderstorm was even better than heat lightning. Just as a jagged web of light darted across the sky, something caught my attention. Again. There he was, standing in the rain at the end of my dock.

The night was so dark, that if not for the lightning, I wouldn't have been able to see him at all. When the next flash came, he was still there. He stood motionless in the driving rain with no umbrella, no hat, no boat in sight. A normal girl would have been afraid–like I was the last time I saw him. And I should have been afraid, but I wasn't. I was more curious than anything.

The sky lit up, and this time the person waved in my direction.

His wave seemed familiar. I stepped to the edge of the porch to get a better look, but it was impossible to clearly see his face through the rain. Cole was out of town, so I knew it wasn't him. It had to be Brent; though I was surprised that he would allow his hair to get drenched and risk ruining his clothes. Still, he was about the same height, and I couldn't imagine who else it would be. First, the phone call out of the blue, and now, an impulsive visit. Our phone call must have sparked something. Agreeing to dinner was probably a mistake.

"Brent?" I called out.

With the rumbling thunder and the rain crackling on the roof, I wasn't sure if he heard me. Then the lightning flashed again, and this time it looked as if he was waving for me to come to him.

"You have got to be kidding me," I mumbled. I eyed the iron umbrella stand next to the door. Then louder I said, "Brent, just come here."

The storm hovered above the lake. Thunder cracked and lightning struck at the same time. And in the same unexpected manner as he had appeared, he vanished.

"Hello?" I yelled into the downpour. "Hello?"

How had he disappeared into thin air? I sat down and stared at the empty dock. Every time the lightning flashed, my eyes searched for him. He wasn't on the dock or in my yard. He was gone.

I nabbed the extra-large, black and red, golf umbrella from the stand and stepped off the porch. I should find him, I thought to myself. I should help him. Something must be wrong.

I popped open the umbrella and walked directly to the end of the dock in the wicked downpour. The wind whipped so hard that it stripped the umbrella inside out. Using the force of the wind, I turned my body and righted the umbrella. Since I was now soaked anyway, I closed it and stuck it under my arm. The white capped waves pounded the dock causing it to sway. The ladder clapped against the sides with each breaking wave and gust of wind.

For a brief second, I thought that maybe I hadn't actually seen anyone at all. Maybe it was some kind of illusion caused by the rain, wind, and blowing trees.

I shook my head. No. I was certain someone was there. He waved to me. It had to be Brent. Maybe that was him the last time too.

Without warning, the lightning flashed, and something nearby exploded. I raced back to the safety of the porch. As I reached for the door handle, thunder boomed above me. The wet umbrella slipped from under my arm and hit the wood-planked floor. The slope of the porch made it roll away from the house, but something stopped it from tumbling down the steps and into a puddle.

I turned and there was my book in the middle of the porch, half covered by the umbrella. It was the very book I couldn't find minutes ago and didn't notice as I returned to the porch. A straight-faced James Patterson stared up at me with is arms crossed, glasses dangling from his finger tips. I picked up the soaked book and held it at arms length for several seconds. Water poured out of it like a slow running faucet.

When I flipped through the book to see if it was readable (as if finishing the book was the greatest of my worries), a frigid blast of air whipped across the porch. My wet hair snapped at my face and scrambled into my mouth. But what struck me harder than the icy gust was the red ink-bled scribble written in the last chapter: "Death is chasing you. Run!".

Finally, with a chill running down my spine, I slapped the book shut, and scurried into the house. I slammed the sliding glass door, locked it, then shoved the wooden board in the door frame. I snapped the curtains shut and stared at the closed, wet book in my hands for about ten seconds. My hands trembled. Then, slowly, I opened to the last chapter, steadying myself for the words that almost had my brain thinking something might be wrong.

I searched, peeling the wet pages apart one by one. But I found nothing.

"Where is it?" I said, flipping page after page.

There was nothing but printed text in the last chapter or anywhere else in the book. The ominous words had vanished.

So, what? Did I imagine all that just happened? Was this another episode like at the park with Barney? I had read stories about the mental and emotional effects of insomnia, so I knew my tired brain could have made blowing branches look something like a person. Of course, the last person I talked to that night was Brent, so he was fresh on my mind.

"I'm tired. That's all. I need chocolate," I said, heading to the kitchen. My head pounded. "And marshmallows."

I placed my book on the radiator. Then I grabbed a dish towel and squeezed my dripping hair while I made a mug of hot chocolate. I loaded it with mini marshmallows. The wind whistled through the old windows, and the wooden door upstairs rattled. So, I added more marshmallows.

That was my response to the creeper on my dock, the misplaced book, the life threatening message, and the storm that raged outside my door. I didn't call the police. I didn't call Meggie or Ruthie. I did not cry. I was merely annoyed, maybe tired, and assumed chocolate and marshmallows would be my savior.

I sat down at the table with the soggy book and chugged about half the cocoa before starting the last chapter.

"Let's have it, Mr. Patterson."

Several minutes later, I sat in the afterglow of a jaw-dropping and twisted book ending with slightly wrinkled fingers and an empty mug. And with all clues pointing to the fact there was something wrong in my world, I returned the book to the radiator, crawled into bed with a warm belly, and fell fast asleep.

The Ivory Dome

I took a step back and reminded myself that sometimes answers get lost in simplicity. I ran my observations of N13 through my head, both from tonight and the past several weeks. There had to be something I was overlooking. Something obvious. Something simple.

Evidence for my theory of simplicity came from the day I discovered the perfect blend for the project. After years and years of failed batches, it dawned on me one day that the answer was right in front of me. And it couldn't have been more simple.

All it took was a small amount of my time-tested and methodically calculated oil combinations placed under extreme heat and immediately followed by extreme subzero temperatures. Next, came the non life-threatening biological binding agent. Finally, you needed the perfect subjects; they were the true key to the project's success. And that was the kicker. They had to be children; prepubescent, still in the growing phase, and showing clear characteristics of cognitive difference, or what some would call neurodiversity. It's not something that was socially acceptable, politically correct, or ethical. Nor was it legal, by any means. It was what caused the termination of my government funding, after all.

Once the blend was administered and inherent to the child's genetic code, it would react to cortisol then their special traits would emerge. Cortisol, the steroid hormone produced by the adrenal glands, also known as the stress hormone, was nothing uncommon. Everyone knows the stress associated with pre and early teen years. So if not before then, their grueling path towards adulthood would spark the initial trigger. Although, there were a few subjects, like this one, who needed a little push.

I hoped if I frightened her she would show me something. Anything. This was my second attempt. She was an odd little thing; she didn't appear frightened in the least. As a matter of fact, she was less afraid than the first time I showed up on her dock. That time, she ran straight into the house.

Could that be her ability? Bravery. Fearlessness. It didn't seem like much. Although, there could be certain benefits to having no fear. Then again, there could be a problem. Maybe she hadn't sparked yet. Maybe she was damaged.

I had four little matches and one lighter, all of whom couldn't stay away from each other. It would have been impossible. Their paths have been crossing their entire lives, walking in small social circles for ten years, weaving in and out of each others webs without thinking anything of it. At one point, back in February, I was certain that I had seen the spark with my own eyes. Now, I wondered if I was wrong.

I went back to her fearless behavior. The longer I thought about it, the more I wondered if it wasn't a lack of fear she was projecting, but instead, irrational and inconsistent behavior. She never screamed or cried. She ran off the dock when the transformer across the lake was hit by lightning. But we could call that survival, not fear.

When I tossed the book on the porch, she picked it up and went in the house as if it was no big deal. Through the window, I saw her making hot chocolate as if nothing had happened. Had I been a psychologist, her unusual behavior would have intrigued me. But I was not. I was a scientist who needed results and was gifted no more than mayhem.

The importance of N13 sparking was astronomical. It was important to the success of the entire project. She was one of the final stepping stones to modern evolution.

Once N13 demonstrated that her initial trigger had lit, I would be able to guide them all through the most vital trigger. The great physicist, John Wheeler, once said, "Time is what prevents everything from happening at once. Space is what prevents everything from happening to me." At last, the time had come. We had reached that final pivotal milestone towards the shift in humanity. It was at the mercy of time and space. Not space apart–but space converging. And only my five subjects could set that trigger in motion.

Slowly, they were finding each other. Their paths crossed more often, their world was becoming smaller. Soon they would truly connect, and then they would realize that they needed answers. That was when they would need me the most.

But for now–I had to do something I disliked. I needed to bring someone else into the project. It didn't make me happy, but I knew I had to do something to move N13 along. If her blend was a dud in the mix, I would need to scrap the entire project and start again. Oh, Lord, not again. All five were needed in order for their abilities to become permanent. And without that, they were more than just worthless, they were dangerous.

CHAPTER 16

Paige had an incredible knack for promptness. If she said she was picking me up at six, then darn it, she was there at six. As always, I was almost ready.

"Did you tell Meggie that we're coming?" she asked as I slipped on my four inch Titan Steampunk heels.

"We're surprising her."

"I hate surprises," she said.

"You're not the one being surprised," I reminded her.

Paige made her way to the wall in my bedroom and switched two pictures I'd hung next to each other. She moved on to rearrange knick knacks and magazines on my desk.

I walked behind her, took the candle from the book shelf, and put it back on the night table where it had been.

"Help me move this chair," she said. She got behind the chair and got ready to push.

"No. I like it there." I stood in front of the chair so she wouldn't move it on her own. "I'm ready," I announced, shooing her along. "Let's go. I want to be there before it gets crowded."

"If you put the chair over there, your room would have more balance. Help me move it," she commanded. Then she added, "And I doubt some small town art gallery is going to be jamming at six o'clock. Or at all for that matter."

"Paige, stop micromanaging. Everything is fine the way it is. Let's get going."

"Sorry. I can't help myself sometimes." Paige gave me an apologetic smile. "The place looks great."

"Thanks."

"Except for that curtain. It's driving me crazy. Let me pull it back so it's not blocking the view of the lake."

Paige started towards the large picture window, I took her by the hand as she passed.

"Control the urge, Paige. In order to surprise Meggie, we actually have to show up."

She glanced back at the curtain as we headed out the door.

"You can fix it later," I promised.

"Only if you want me to."

"I'll just change it back after you leave."

"Whatever," she quipped with a playful nudge of my shoulder.

Paige drove up the hill to the gallery. From up there, I could see several vineyards across the lake. Thus, the name Vineyard Hill. That was where Cole lived.

"What are you staring at?" Paige asked, walking to my side of the car.

"The view. It's so pretty up here," I said.

She paused to look across the lake at the green hills.

"Yep," she said. "Come on. Let's get this over with." She grabbed my hand and dragged me towards the recreation center. "What door?"

"Any door. They turned the main room into the gallery."

We wandered through the front door and made our way to the main room. The rich smell of oak still hung in the air.

"Sheer Gallery? Why did they name it that," Paige wondered.

"Mason got the loan for the gallery from the Sheer family."

"The ones who live down the street from you?"

"Yes. I guess their daughter-in-law has several paintings here."

"Of course. If your family fronts all the money, you get a free pass; no matter how crappy you paint," Paige snuffed.

We found Meggie right away and yelled "surprise". She was happy to see us. A band was set up in the corner and a bar in the back of the room.

"I'm so glad you guys came!" Meggie cheered.

"Wouldn't have missed it," I said. I reached out and fluffed her jet black bangs. She colored her blonde streaks, leaving only the black and purple. "Sweet color. I love this."

"Thanks," she said, turning her head so her hair swayed at her shoulders. She pinched her fingers together. "I was this close to going with blue. Then yesterday, I saw this old lady sporting blue. She had to be like 40 or something. The elder completely ruined it for me."

Meggie was in her element, she absolutely glowed.

"Blue would have looked go on you too. Everything does," I said. "Hey, what's with the rock band and bar? Isn't this supposed to be a quiet, sophisticated event?"

Meggie responded, "This isn't the library. It's called Paint and Party for a reason. There are four bands tonight."

"Cool," said Paige. "This might be fun after all. Meet me at the bar," she said, walking away.

"I have a few things to do before more people get here," Meggie told me. "I'll catch up with you in a minute. Ali Sheer's work is up front, Drew Casey's stuff is by the band, mine's over there," she said, pointing to the middle of the room. "And there are a few other pieces by the kitchen door. Those are Mason's"

"I could probably use a map, but I think I got it. Find me when you get free. Go."

Meggie raced off to help organize tables and chairs as more and more people arrived. One minute I was enjoying a beautiful sunset painted by Drew Casey, and the next, I was being swallowed by a sea of people pouring into the gallery.

In search of Paige, I knew the bar was a good place to start. I headed to the back of the room and soon found her listening to the band. She held a glass of clear liquid with a wedge of lime. We strolled through the gallery looking at the art work.

"Circles, birds, more flowers," Paige commented.

"Trees, flowers. Ooh, here's something different. A lake," I giggled. "Wow, this one is beautiful. It must be Conesus."

"Oh, my God. I have info. I can't believe I forgot to tell you."

106

"Do tell," I requested as we continued to eye the paintings.

"So, Jackson has been miserable for the past few weeks?" she began.

"Yeah. What's going on?"

"He told me everything," she whispered.

"Which is…"

"Apparently, his girlfriend, Mia, had this new best friend, Kelly, who she'd been spending tons of time with for the last couple of months. Mia failed to mention one very important thing. Kelly is a guy." I gasped. Paige didn't lose a beat. "Jackson stopped by Mia's work to see if she could do lunch, and he found Mia and Kelly in a lip lock at an outdoor picnic table. She was already having a tasty lunch."

"Stop! Right out in the open for everyone to see? Poor Jackson. How's he handling this?"

"He's pissed. He was suspecting something for a while. I don't think this is what he expected. But he's happy that the truth came out so he can move on." She sighed. "Anyway, that's why he's been sleeping on the couch at work."

"That sucks. I can't imagine how devastated he must feel."

"Jackson told me something else."

Paige waited for me to bite. I never knew where Paige would go when she started one of her stories. Since she insisted that Jackson should be my serial dating victim number one, I knew I was taking a risk. I bit anyway.

"Since when did you two get so chummy?" I asked.

"When he started asking about you."

"Me? That's funny. All of a sudden I'm the topic of choice?"

I had a growing suspicion that Paige was working overtime on one of her unsolicited love connections.

"The other night, during my dinner break, he sent the new hottie to straighten up the shelves so he could interrogate me. Alone."

"So, it's you he's wanted all along," I said, snickering.

"Zip it. I'm not done. Anyway, he asked what was up with you. Like what the chances are that you would work at Trend in the fall and do school at the same time. Or at least holiday hours and stuff. I said not a chance." Paige glared at me. She said, "He looked disappointed. Very disappointed. I think he's in a panic because you'll be quitting to do school full-time."

"I doubt that he's disappointed. He knows I'm done at Trend the end of August."

"Oh, don't doubt me. He's had a thing for you. Jackson's one of those nice guys who would never hit on a girl with a boyfriend. But he knows what went down with you and Brent. And now his relationship is an epic fail, so there's nothing holding him back. Although, college starts in the fall, so you'll be quitting and screwing it all up."

"Paige..."

"Just kidding. Seriously, it can't hurt to go on a date with the guy. Unless incredibly gorgeous isn't your type."

Ugh, this entire discussion was mute with Cole in the picture. Of course, she didn't know that yet. Yes, Jackson was a hottie. But my emotional and physical attraction to Cole was something I didn't have for Jackson. I had to tell Paige. It would end her obsession with finding my Mr. Perfect. I'd already found him..

Paige spoke first. "Listen. I don't want you to get mad."

"Paige, I should tell you something."

"No, let me finish. Don't get mad, but I sort of encouraged him to call you and said you might be interested." She winced, anticipating my response.

"Paige! You didn't!"

"Yes, I did. And I said don't get mad. He asked if anything with Brent had changed, and I told him that relationship died like roadkill. He doesn't like that you're quitting Trend at the end of the summer. So when he asked if I thought you'd mind if he called you on a personal basis, I told him you would not mind at all."

"Paige, you shouldn't have. I'm not interested. And now, when he calls, I'll feel like a jerk. I'll feel like a bigger jerk when I see him at work."

I couldn't believe how easily Paige forgot her own advice. She looked disappointed by my lack of enthusiasm for what most girls would think was great news.

She said, "You should be jumping for joy and thanking me. I refuse to believe you are not interested."

"Oh, Paige. He just got out of a bad relationship. And I'm not really- available."

"Emotionally? Look, I may have told you to focus on yourself, but forget that. Jackson is one of the most eligible bachelors in all of New York State. And he's interested in you. You'd be crazy not to go for him."

"I think I'm seeing someone," I blurted out.

People at the painting next to us glanced our way. Paige's jaw dropped and she managed to be silent for about five seconds before exploding.

"What!? You think you're seeing someone. Who do you think you're seeing? And what do you mean by seeing?"

"Calm down. Everyone is looking at us."

"Speak. Details, you secretive little thing. I was at Duke for three days, and suddenly you have a new boyfriend? Is it a neighbor? Ooh, I know. He's one of those nephews Ruthie wanted you to meet? I can't believe you waited until now to tell me."

"Shh. Shut up for five seconds, and I will tell you."

I took a deep breath and started from the not-so-long-ago beginning. A pining knot formed in my gut as I told her about Cole.

When I finished filling in Paige, leaving out no details, she reluctantly agreed to tell Jackson that there was a misunderstanding in regards to my availability. And although she held strong that I should at least go on one date with him, she couldn't wait to meet Cole. She was disappointed when I told her he was out of town until Sunday.

With that conversation behind us, we made our way to Meggie's display. But we didn't get far. Something amazing captured my interest. I soon realized it hadn't only caught my attention but Paige's as well. Her eyes were already glued to the painting.

"Do you see this?" she asked. "This is your grandma's farm."

I studied the painting from top to bottom. The Raleigh Family Homestead was where my father grew up and Paige and I had spent many summer days. My grandparents still farmed ninety of the two hundred and fifty acres. This artist must have known the farm somehow. As I looked closer, the details struck a chord.

I pointed to the tree in the picture. "That's me," I said. "In the peach tree. I'm reaching for the peach. And look at the branch."

"It's cracked," Paige noticed.

"It is. There's the hive," I gawked at her. "This is creepy."

Her brows scrunched. "How is this creepy?" she asked.

From behind me, an angelic-sounding voice squeaks, "It's called The Angry Peach." A skinny girl with mousy brown hair pointed her finger at the peach and said, "It doesn't want you to eat it."

"Excuse me?" I said to her strange comment. "It doesn't want me to eat it?"

She laughed. "No. I said it doesn't want to be eaten."

Paige laughed too. "That's not really you, Chelsea."

I looked at the girl, then back at Paige. They were mocking me. But something weird was going on.

"Sorry if I don't find this funny," I said. "But that farmhouse, that tree, that girl in the tree." I looked at the skinny, brown-haired girl, then at the signature on the bottom of the painting. "Are you Ali Sheer?"

"Yes. Thanks for coming tonight. What brings you in?"

"Do you know this farm?" I asked, ignoring her warm welcome.

"I do." She hesitated for a second, then continued. "I lived by this farm growing up. I often sat at the edge of our property and wondered about the people who lived there. Children would come to play, and they would laugh and climb that tree. They always seemed so happy and carefree."

My mouth hung open as she talked. I was sure I was one of those children. I was that child in the tree. I sized up the angle that the artist, Ali, would have been looking at the scene.

"There was a freaky commune, or something, that owned the property right next to my grandparents farm. A wacky religious group," I blurted out.

Ali looked away and took a step back. "I know," she said.

"Oh, I'm...I'm sorry. That was just a mean rumor. I didn't mean to offend you."

Paige whacked my hand and scolded me with her eyes.

"It's fine. I'm not a member of that religious group."

Paige said, "You must have seen Chelsea in the tree that day. Right?"

Ali shook her head. "I don't remember that. My paintings just sort of come to me. This is my most recent painting. I drove by the farm last week and became inspired."

I pointed to the child in the tree and said, "But there I am. I had those exact clothes. And there's the cracked branch that moments later broke. And that's the hive before it erupted and sent a hundred bees into defensive mode and me to the hospital."

"I suppose that does look like a hive. I assumed it was some kind of nest."

"You don't know what you painted?" Paige asked.

"Sometimes I start painting with no plan in mind, and when I'm finished I have a painting that seems to have come from nowhere. Other times, like with this painting, I see a specific picture in my head, and until I paint it I can't stop thinking about it. I don't always understand all the details."

"You know what, Chelsea," Paige decided. "This is pretty cool if you think about it."

"It's amazing," I sighed.

It was true, the painting was amazing for so many reasons, and had I not been faced with the recent bee scares, I may have found it even more incredible. However, the feeling I got when I looked at the picture made me very uneasy. It was as if the painting spoke to me, reminding me that at any minute such a tiny creature, such an ordinary event to most people, could end my life in an instant. It made me feel small and fragile. And I didn't like that one bit.

Paige put her hand on my shoulder. "Chels? Hey, you don't look well." Then she leaned in and whispered, "You're not going to pass out, are you?"

111

Ali frowned, her nose scrunched. She shook her head, and with no explanation for the accuracy of The Angry Peach, she turned to me and said, "Take it. It's yours."

"What? No."

"Yes. This painting means something to you. I would be happy if you would take it. For free. It's yours."

"Really, thank you. But I don't want a reminder of that day. I was just surprised to see this." I turned to Paige and said, "I'm fine. But I forgot, I have to go. I have a Zoom call with my parents in fifteen minutes."

"Didn't you talk to them last night?" she asked.

"They wanted to talk again. This is a beautiful painting, Ali. You're very talented," I mumbled. I turned on my heels and stormed out to the parking lot. Paige was close behind.

"Chels! Chels! Wait up. What's going on?"

"I have to go. If you can't take me, I'll take Meggie's car and come back to get her later."

She rolled her eyes, then pointed to the passenger side door. "Get in," she said.

I glanced at the plastic cup in one hand and her keys in the other. "I'll drive," I responded, taking her keys.

I got in and started the car. She tossed the remainder of her drink and slid in next to me. We sat in silence for a second. I broke it with, "I have a headache. That's all. Sorry."

"You didn't say goodbye to Meggie. She's going to be mad."

"She must have seen that painting," I said. "I wonder what she thought."

"I don't get why that painting bothers you. It's just a painting of the farm. And yes, there's a kid in a tree. Kids climb trees. Branches break. Maybe you're reading your own story into it."

"Oh, yeah? Did you see the little yellow bottle on the porch? That bottle had some smelly ointment in it. After I was attacked, my mom put it on my sting marks, and the next day they were gone. It was as if I was never stung."

"But how do you..."

"The bottle was very distinct. I still have it. It was shiny yellow glass with intricate details etched in it. It was identical to the one she painted in the picture. Exactly. How would she know about that?"

"I remember now. We played with the empty bottle for years. We used to pretend it was perfume. But I didn't notice it in the painting." Paige opened the door and got out. "Let's go back in and say goodbye to Meggie. I want to see that painting again."

She didn't wait for me. She was going back in with or without me. I dragged myself from the car and followed her.

More people were arriving, and the gallery was getting packed. Paige and I weaved our way to the middle of the room where Meggie's oil paintings, jewelry, and pottery were set up in a neat circular display.

"What do you mean you're leaving already?" Meggie asked.

"Hey, did you see the painting by Ali Sheer? The one of the Raleigh Homestead."

"Yes. I'm thinking of buying it for dad for his birthday. It's awesome, isn't it?"
"Sure. Anyway, like I said, I'm not feeling so great. So I'm going to go. It looks like these paint and party shows are going to be a big success."

We hugged Meggie, then made our way in the direction of The Angry Peach. Ali was occupied talking with Mason, the gallery founder. I was hoping she wouldn't see us go back to the painting. I felt bad for the way I left and the way I acted earlier. It wasn't her fault that she painted a picture that I found disturbing.

We snaked our way through large clusters of people until we got to The Angry Peach. This time, Paige noticed the bottle right away.

"Yup. Officially weird," she agreed.

"I don't like it here. There's an uncomfortable vibe about this place." I said to Paige, "Have you felt it too? Lakeville has somehow gotten weird."

"Must be the water from the ancient glaciers that made the Finger Lakes."

"The water? What?"

She laughed. "Seriously. The only weird thing here is you." She glanced at the painting and added, "And that too."

I sighed. "Can we go now?" I asked.

"Absolutely."

We drove home in silence. I didn't want to talk about anything. Not the painting. Not my hiking incident. Definitely not Barney. I had even kept the recent bee encounters from Paige. I didn't want her to worry about me.

When I was getting ready for bed that night, it dawned on me that I hadn't even told Paige that I was having dinner with Brent tomorrow. I picked up the phone to call her. Just as quickly, I put the phone down. It was probably a good thing that I had forgotten to tell her. She would have raked me over the coals for agreeing to go to dinner with him in the first place. And with further thought, I wasn't sure that I would ever tell her.

CHAPTER 17

Brent always said, "My greatest motivation is a guaranteed bonus." That bonus could come in the form of cash, the promise of a big money-making job, a free trip, or front row tickets to a hot sporting event. Keeping all that in mind, it was hard to imagine what was motivating him to spend a Saturday night visiting little ol' me.

When we began dating, it was clear that school and his future in his father's law firm came above all else. What at first I assumed was a strong and admirable work ethic, would later prove to be an obsession–a ruthless obsession with winning at almost any cost. Whether big or small, important or menial, as long as he got his way and the recognition he thrived on, he was happy.

Towards the end of our relationship, his mood swings were drastic: calm and aloof one minute then enraged over something silly the next. I had blamed it on the pressures of school. My guess was that things had been running smoothly these days. Maybe his internship was the "no brainer" he said it would be. Why else would he bother with me? Whatever his motivation, he was here, and he was early.

I went upstairs to answer the soft knock at the door, my chest tight with angst. However, I was spared a few more minutes of ease when I opened the door to Ruthie's cheerful face.

"Hi, Ruthie. Come in. How are you?"

"Fine, sweetie. I don't want to bother you." She looked down at my sundress and heels, and her eyes lit up. "Oh! You look so pretty. You must be going out."

"Yes. I'm going to dinner with a friend."

"Lovely. I won't keep you. You have fun," Ruthie said, then turned to walk away.

"Wait. Is everything okay?"

"Oh, yes, yes, yes. I was coming by with an invite. That's all. It can wait for another day." She waved a dismissive hand at me, then tried to walk away again.

"Hold on, Ruthie. Brent shouldn't be here for a while. What's the invitation for?"

"Brent? Ooh, a date," she said bug-eyed.

"No. Not a date. He's an old friend."

"I'll make it quick. I wondered if you would care to join me on my deck in the morning for breakfast. Unless you'll be occupied."

Ruthie winked at me.

"I will not be busy in the morning. He's not going to be an overnight guest. My parents wouldn't like that," I assured her while my face burned red. "I'd love to come for breakfast. What can I bring?"

"Not a thing. It's nothing fancy. How about seven?"

"Sounds like a plan."

"Just call if you're too tired. Or if you have unexpected company and can't make it. I understand."

Again, she winked.

"Great. I'll see you at seven, Ruthie. Have a good night."

"Have fun on your date."

"Ruthie, it's not a date."

"Whatever you say, dear."

Ruthie strolled across the lawn to her house. Upon reaching her front step, Brent zipped down the narrow shared driveway in what appeared to be a new car. He screeched to a stop and parked smack in the middle of the driveway. He pulled his usual obnoxious move and parked crooked to prevent anyone else from parking next to him. Ruthie stood on her stoop, in a not so subtle manner, waiting for a glimpse of Brent.

"Hey, babe!" Brent said, sauntering towards me.

Ick! I never realized how much I hated the pretentious way he called me babe.

"Hi. Did you get a new car?"

"You are kidding, right?" he scoffed. "As if I would buy a Toyota. It's all the rental place had. My Beamer is in the shop. Look at you! Lookin' good, Chels."

He captured me in a hug that seemed endless. Eventually, I pried myself away and invited him in.

He looked great as usual. Brent had always taken good care of himself. Although there were times when I thought he was too concerned with how he looked: taking longer than me to get ready to go out, every hair in place, his jeans always pressed and his shirt perfectly starched, like now.

As soon as we walked in the door, he was inspecting his hair in the mirror.

"I think you're good," I mumbled. "I'll get my jacket."

"I never noticed how tiny your house is. I guess it's only you and your parents though, so it doesn't matter." He shrugged his shoulders. "It's got a certain kind of bohemian charm, I guess."

"Yeah. Thanks, I think," I responded dryly.

"Oh, come on. It's not an insult. Don't be so sensitive," he said, tousling my hair as if I was a child.

I swatted his hand away, and he rolled his eyes. Boy, he was a jerk. I was already asking myself why I had agreed to go to dinner with him. I could hear Paige now, "You always give him the benefit of the doubt." I had to stop doing that.

"Are your parents here?" he asked.

"No. They're in Europe."

"Right. Right. That's what I thought. It's just me and you then, huh?"

I nodded my head and took my jacket from the hook.

"I hear you guys renovated the kitchen. Show me," he commanded.

"They renovated last month. I guess you haven't been here in a while," I said, placing my jacket back on the hook. "They also did the back porch. You have to see it. It's beautiful."

As I passed him on my way to the stairs, he grabbed my elbow. I glanced up at him, waiting for him to either let go or tell me some-

117

thing. When neither happened I ask, "What are you doing?"

"This," he said, bending to kiss me.

I jerked back, dodging his lips.

He laughed.

I scowled.

"What are you doing?" I snapped.

"I've missed you, Chels. And you look irresistible. So I'm not resisting."

Again, he bent towards me, and I moved my head away.

"Resist, Brent. And let go."

Brent held my arm. I tried to pull away, but his grip was strong. He didn't seem to be considering my demand, so I reiterated, "Let go."

"You don't miss me?"

I didn't say anything. We just stared at each other for a few uncomfortable seconds. Finally, Brent let go of my arm and sauntered to the stairs. He stopped to glance back at me. I glared at him. He snickered in amusement and headed down the stairs without looking back.

"Better colors. Nice marble and stainless steel. What contractor did your parents use?" he asked.

Apparently, what just happened didn't phase him.

"They did their own remodel," I replied, hoping he could feel the holes that my eyes were burning into the back of his head.

"Cherry cabinets. Classic," he commented.

He began to open the cabinet doors like he was on a mission.

"Looking for something?" I asked.

"Ah ha! Not anymore," he said. He reached into the liquor cabinet and pulled out a bottle. "Pff, Dewars?"

"You seem like maybe you've already had a few."

"Maybe one. But I guarantee you, it was higher end scotch than this," he snorted.

Once again, I had fallen short. In the past, it was my choice of clothing, food, friends, and even my college preference. This time, it was my parent's choice of alcohol. What would it be next? I had a feeling this dinner was more than a mistake. It was a disaster in the making.

He held the bottle out to me. I shook my head no.

After he slammed his drink back, Brent took me to The Green. It was a casual but pricey restaurant in the village of Geneseo. The only one near Lakeville that was up-scale enough for Brent. He dropped me off at the front door so I could put our name in for seating while he parked the car.

When he came in, I asked, "Do you want to wait at the bar? They said it's a forty-five minute wait."

"No. It's not," he scoffed.

"Yes. The hostess said..." Brent breezed by me and sauntered to the hostess stand. "Brent?" I called after him, trailing behind.

For the first time, I was witnessing Brent in action through completely different eyes. From pissy and self-importance came sweet and charming persuasion, along with a fifty dollar bribe.

Brent's subtle slip of the fifty dollar bill into the hostesses manicured hand was graciously accepted. This was followed by a confident smile and his fingers brushing her shoulder. Miraculously, his name appeared on the reservation list, and we were whisked off to the coziest table for two right next to the fireplace. It was too cozy for me. The roaring fire and candlelight screamed romance. That was not the deal.

"Isn't this nice?" Brent asked, sprouting a Cheshire Cat grin.

"Yes. Very much like a date," I pointed out.

"Yup."

"What do you mean 'yup'? This is two friends eating. Remember?"

Why, why, why did I agree to this dinner? I thought.

He cleared his throat, and before the hostess could get away, he said, "Perfect table. Now, I'll need our waitress to bring a diet coke, and a Macallan 18 on the rocks."

He rudely waved her away, but she smiled at him just the same.

"Where were we?" he asked. "Oh yeah, two friends having dinner. About that–I changed my mind." He winked at me, picked up the menu, and said, "A man's entitled."

A man's entitled? What era was he living in?

"I'm sure I didn't hear you right."

"I'm sure you did," he responded dryly.

"Well, I didn't change my mind," I snapped. "What is the matter with you tonight? This isn't a date. Maybe you should take me home."

"No."

I waited for some kind of explanation for his sudden change of mind, maybe even an apology. Instead, Brent said, "The sweet potato ravioli sounds good. Have you had it?"

"Take me home," I said.

"Maybe the filet mignon. I love filet. No one makes it like your dad, though," he said, ogling me over the top of the menu. Ick!

"Take. Me. Home."

He ignored me.

"You should try the lobster fra diavolo. You like spicy food."

I sprung from my chair, tossed my napkin on the table, and grabbed my purse.

"Goodbye," I said.

He caught my hand as I walked away from the table.

"I don't think so." He nodded to my vacated chair and said, "You're making a scene. Now, have a little decorum, babe. Sit down."

Brent shamed me like a parent scolding their defiant child. With various eyes now watching me, I suddenly felt like that child. So I sat down and tried to reason with him.

"Look, this was a bad idea. I'm sorry if you went through any trouble. I think you misunderstood. We're over, Brent. And I..."

"Wow, relax," he snickered. "I know we're over. I was joking. A little playful teasing. I guess I really got under your skin. Sorry, babe."

He snickered and winked again. Brent shook out my napkin and handed it to me. And while I might have felt foolish, I wasn't ready to believe him. I took the napkin and placed it on my lap.

Our waitress came over with my soda and said to Brent, "I'm sorry sir. We don't carry Macallan here. The best scotch we can offer is Johnny Walker Gold. May I get you a glass of that?"

"My mistake. I should have known better. Johnny Walker Gold on the rocks will suffice."

The waitress scurried off to the bar. Had Brent always been so obnoxious or was he getting worse?

I closed my gaping mouth and said, "Can't we just have dinner and some normal conversation?"

"I can, if you can find your sense of humor."

"When did you find one?" I said under my breath.

"Excuse me?"

"Just wondering when you became so playful?" I said louder.

"Maybe I've lightened up a little since you dumped me."

"Don't say it like that. Our break up was mutual."

"Speak for yourself," he mumbled as the waitress approached.

She put Brent's drink on the table, and he immediately began to order.

First, he ordered my dinner. Next, he ordered his own. I never appreciated the old fashioned gesture when we dated, and I didn't appreciate it tonight. So while the lobster fra diavolo sounded great, I changed my order to make a point (or out of spite, depending on how you looked at it). If that irritated Brent, it didn't show.

The rest of dinner was uneventful. Brent talked about his internship, his car, his hair, his accomplishments. It was a typical Brent conversation. After a bit, he graced me with a few minutes to fill him in on my work and college plans. I left out the best part–Cole. He didn't need to know about him.

After dinner, Brent directed me towards two empty stools at the bar for a night cap. I didn't think he needed another drink, especially since his behavior was already questionable. But it didn't seem to matter what I thought. Brent pulled out a stool for me.

The bartender was leaning on the bar talking to customers when he spotted me and said, "Hey. It's my 'first on the scene' girl. How's the arm?"

As it turned out, the bartender was the grumpy fireman from the car accident the other day. This time, his demeanor was more relaxed; serving liquor was clearly less stressful than fighting fires and saving lives.

I held up my arm to show him my wrist. I could see by the look on his face that he was taken aback by how quickly it had healed.

"It's way better," I said.

Brent's head snapped in my direction.

"You were in an accident? What happened?"

"I wasn't in the accident," I explained. "I pulled a girl from her car and cut my wrist on broken glass."

I glanced at the bartender and smiled. He nodded.

"Your wrist was bad. I can't believe how much better it is. Let me see it closer," the bartender said, reaching for my arm.

"You don't need to touch her," Brent snarled. He shot up from the barstool.

"He's a fireman," I explained. "He helped me that day."

"He's not a doctor. Did he stitch you up or even give you a bandaid?" Brent snapped. "He doesn't need to touch you."

The bartender looked Brent in the eyes, stood to his full height, and said, "If she doesn't have a problem with me looking at her wrist, I'd like to see it."

I raised my arm for the bartender to get a better look. Brent grabbed my wrist and covered my scar. He pulled it towards him.

"Why are you making a big deal out of this?" I said to Brent.

Brent gawked at me and held onto my arm. I glanced at the bartender who glared at Brent.

"Let go," I said under my breath. "Stop acting this way."

As the bartender strolled around to our side of the bar, Brent's hostile eyes followed him. I tapped his hand and urged him to calm down, but he shook my fingers away without even looking at me. The crowd parted for the bartender until he was toe to toe with Brent. This guy towered over him. He towered over everyone. I hadn't realized how enormous he was until now.

The bartender took an unquestionable tone with Brent. He said, "I just want to make something clear. With her permission, I'm going to take a look at her wrist. Now, if you want to–you can try to stop me."

For a brief, unsettling moment, Brent glared up at him. While Brent was not the kind of guy who was easily intimidated, he wasn't suicidal either. Brent released my arm but continued to scowl.

The bartender took my wrist and shocked me. That was the third time he'd done that. Once, when we first saw each other at the art gallery in February, again at the scene of the car accident, and now. I didn't flinch, though. I didn't want Brent to flip out. The bartender studied my fresh scar. He ran his finger along the line. It felt as if he were burning the line himself.

He asked, "Does that hurt?"

"No," I lied, wanting to scream. My eyes watered from the pain.

"It looks perfect, like a doctor glued it. You didn't get it glued, did you?"

"Didn't the EMT glue it?" I asked.

I rubbed hard at the scar when he let go, trying to ease the pain.

"No. He wouldn't have done that on site. If he thought you needed stitches or glue, he would have sent you to the hospital. I thought maybe your doctor fixed this. That's unbelievable," he said.

I nodded in agreement and asked about the girl from the accident. He assured me that though her injuries were severe, she was going to be fine.

"She was lucky you came along when you did," he said. Then he turned to Brent with a smirk and said in a condescending tone, "Nice to meet you. My name is Adam, and I will be your bartender tonight." Adam crushed Brent's fingers in a handshake. "What are you two drinking?"

A half an hour later, the bar was cranking. Brent finally decided it was time to go.

The super moon lit up the parking lot. Brent threw his arm around me as we stepped out into the chilly air, but I shrugged his hand off my shoulder under the pretense of putting on my sweater.

That was when I spotted Cole. He got out of a white Ford Platinum and walked around to the passenger side. He opened the door for a a skinny, red-headed girl. She looked about my age.

My eyes flashed at Brent in panic. I tried not to be too obvious as I stepped up my pace and rushed to the car. I didn't want Cole to see me with Brent. What would he think? But damn! He was here with some other girl, and he wasn't even supposed to be in town.

Brent opened the car door for me. I jumped in and slammed the door. I glanced at Brent and caught a scowl. But I couldn't take my eyes off Cole and the red-head. I was glued to them.

I tried to see my competition better, but they were walking away, towards the restaurant. There were no signs of intimacy. He didn't hold her hand, nor did he put his arm around her. But when she got to the restaurant door, he held it open for her like a gentleman.

The driver side door opened as Cole disappeared into the restaurant. Brent slid into the driver's seat. I glanced at him and then rummaged through my purse. Nothing like some good old fashioned avoidance. I prayed he hadn't seen me staring at Cole and his date, because for those few seconds, it was as if Brent didn't exist.

"Do you know them?" he asked. He didn't start the car, he waited for an answer.

I kept digging through my purse. Again, he asked if I knew them.

"What? Who?" I said.

Playing dumb with Brent never worked. But my mind was racing with questions (mostly for Cole), and I couldn't think straight.

"Those people who just walked into The Green. You were staring at them."

"I thought I knew them. But now I don't think so. I'm cold. Can you start the car, please."

Brent started the car and said, "I have to let it warm up." He cleared his throat. His eyes shifted from The Green, to me, and back again. "You looked like you knew them. You looked bothered."

He was so darn perceptive.

"No. Not at all. She looked like one of my sister's friends."

"Why would that bother you?"

"It doesn't. Can we just go?" I snapped. I had lost all patience with Brent's cross-examination and complacent attitude. So without thinking I barked, "Why are you harping on this? Why are you acting so jealous tonight?"

"And once again, I've hit a nerve. You seem uptight, babe. What's up?" he asked. I stared out the window and ignored his question. Seconds later, he said, "Since I have to guess, I'm going to say it's the lumberjack. Because the firefighting bartender isn't your type."

Brent flexed his uncanny ability to read people as he dug for more information. I fell right into his trap.

"He's hardly a lumberjack," I said defensively.

"Right," he smirked. "Not a lumberjack. Then what? A butcher, a baker? Ooh, I know. A candlestick-maker."

"Cute. I didn't know you knew any nursery rhymes."

"I know everything. Including the fact that the grunge look died with Cobain. Maybe you should tell him the next time you see him."

He winked at me. I wanted to slap him.

"Let's just go, please."

Brent pulled out of the parking lot. Turtles moved faster.

"I wonder if the poor redhead knows about you. You obviously didn't have a clue about her. Did you want to go back in and confront him? That would put the cherry on top of tonight."

"It's not like that. I don't even know him that well."

"Of course. And if that's true, it doesn't look like you stand a chance now. His girlfriend is pretty hot," he said.

Now, I was fuming. He was asking for much more than a slap.

CHAPTER 18

It seemed as though we were crawling. We caught every red light. Brent lingered at every stop sign. I swear, he was doing it on purpose. I leaned over to check the speedometer.

"In a hurry?" he asked.

I shook my head no.

When we finally arrived at my house and pulled down the driveway, a gut wrenching weight began to lift. Now, all I needed was to get inside. Alone. The car stopped, and before I could say good night, he was out of the car and on his way to open my door.

I hopped out before he got there and announced, "You don't have to walk me in."

Ignoring me, Brent headed towards my house. I had a sinking feeling this night wasn't going to end well.

"I'll get the door. Give me your key," he said, opening the screen door and holding out his hand.

I fished through my purse, knowing exactly where the key was but trying to buy time to come up with an easy out. Nothing came to me, and he was waiting patiently. I handed him the key and attempted to wrap up the night with a concluding speech.

"Thanks for dinner. Sorry about the confusion; I know you were kidding earlier. I've been a little sensitive lately, like you said."

"That's unusual for you," he mumbled.

He opened the door and walked inside. I stood on the deck and continued my spiel.

"It's just stress. Chores around the house with my parents away, work. All that stuff," I explained. He motioned for me to come in. I took a deep breath, inched myself across the threshold, and said, "So, it's late…"

He closed the door behind me, surely aware that I wanted him to leave. Something told me that he did not care one bit. I had been numbed by his indifference for so long that I didn't know how to deal with this overly-attentive side of Brent.

All I wanted was to be alone so I could figure out what I had seen at The Green; Cole was in town and currently out with some gorgeous redhead. I needed to think. My tolerance was diminishing, and I was running out of refined ways to make Brent leave.

Finally, I asked, "Don't you have to work tomorrow?"

"Tomorrow is Sunday. Not to mention, I had to quit my job to take the internship at the firm."

"Oh. The firm must be open," I said, averting my eyes to the wall and away from his intense stare.

Brent took a step towards me and closed what used to be a generous gap.

"Honestly," he said, "I figured I'd be busy tomorrow, especially after a late night."

The kiss came hard and fast. He pinned me against the wall with his hands and body. Despite my best efforts, I could not move. A slap and a punch would be minor offenses now. A beating was in order if I could get free. When he tried to stick his tongue in my mouth, I seized the opportunity and bit down–hard.

"Ahh! What the... Are you kidding me? I can't believe you just did that!" he howled. Then he let out a sinister laugh and said, "Crazy little witch. You know you still love me."

I hurled myself towards the door and yanked it open so hard that it hit the wall.

"Get out!" I roared.

Again–he laughed. He'd become such a stranger. I barely recognized him.

"Get out before I call the cops."

"Chelsea, babe, calm down." He dabbed his fingers on his tongue to check for blood. "I'm going. It seems I'm not good at this kind of stuff. I guess that's pretty obvious."

"Just go, please."

There was a moment of silence where Brent's feet shuffled about, and he seemed to be studying the cracks on the ceiling. His face was serious. His eyes were sad. He looked to be what I could only describe as pathetic.

"I'm sorry," Brent said. "I'm going. I promise. First, hear me out. I'm an idiot. I don't know how to do this. I tried the romantic dinner and the spontaneous kiss; girls like that, I thought. And I tried not to get jealous of that bartender and the guy in the parking lot. But this sucks, Chels. I miss you. I love you, and I want you back."

My eyes widened. That was the last thing I expected to come from Brent's pouting mouth.

"No," I uttered.

I shook my head and looked back at the door. Then I caught his eye and was struck by what I saw. Brent's head was tilted to the side, he looked fragile and broken. A tear almost fell before he caught it with his palm. In all the years I'd known him, I had never seen him cry. The thought that I brought this strong guy to this point sickened me. Maybe I was the one responsible for turning Brent into this irrational and impulsive alien who I didn't recognize. How could I have been so blindly hurtful? I was so close to apologizing, but something in me kept my mouth shut.

"Okay. Anyway. I'm sorry," he said after a minute. "I want you to be happy. I'd like you to be happy with me, but if it's rednecks you're into, I won't stop you." His budding smile seemed in conflict with his sad eyes. "It was nice to see you. Good luck with everything."

"Thanks for dinner," I said.

I reached out and put a comforting hand on his arm. A peace offering gesture. Peace for who, I'm not sure. I was the one consumed with guilt for my insensitivity.

"Bye, Chels."

"Goodbye, Brent."

He walked out the door and shuffled up the deck stairs with his head hanging low. Brent got into his car and backed out of the driveway without even a wave goodbye.

When he was gone, I was left alone with my ever-present doubts and insecurities; the ones that typically surfaced around Brent. I closed the door, went straight to my room, and collapsed from exhaustion. Earlier, I wanted to give Brent a beating he wouldn't soon forget. Now, I was the one suffering the blows.

I sat on my bed, staring out the window at the moon. The guilt and remorse for the cold manner in which I dealt with Brent trickled into jealousy and confusion about Cole and the redhead.

I refused to call Cole. Clearly, I misread his intentions the previous week. Why else would he be out with another girl? He'd never even taken me out to dinner. Was having dinner alone in the middle of the lake considered a date? I was doubting the memory of him telling me it was.

But to be fair, there hadn't been any talk of us being exclusive. Technically, I had no right to be angry. So Cole took some other girl on a date. Big deal, right?

"Yes!" I said, vigorously rubbing the scowl off my face. "It is a big freaking deal."

Maybe he didn't want to be seen with me. More than likely, he just saw me as a buddy. After seconds of deep thought, I'd had enough. My brain was tired. I was on an emotional roller coaster that needed to stop.

Just before I fell asleep, a thunder and lightning storm cruised in from the west. I wanted very much to go out on the back porch and watch it pass over the lake. But I was too tired. It didn't take more than a few seconds to doze off. That night I had a dream about Cole.

I dreamt that he was sitting on the edge of my bed. I reached out to hug him, and he backed away with empty, beady black eyes. My heart sank.

"What's wrong," I asked.

"It's over."

"It's barely started. Give us a chance," I pleaded.

His words were cold and harsh. "I've found someone else. She's the one for me. Move on, Chelsea."

"What? No."

"Go to Brent. He's your soul mate. You have known that all along. You've been cruel to him."

"I don't love him. I've never had these kinds of feelings for anyone. Only you."

"You don't even know me. Don't be a stupid girl," he said. He looked over his shoulder. "Go away," he whispered into the shadows.

"Who are you talking to? Who's here?"

"No one. Just do what I say." Cole stood up and stormed to the door. He stopped before leaving and said into the shadow, "Go. Don't confuse her." Cole puckered his brow at me once more and left.

In the dream, I sat very still, staring into the shadowy corner. I sensed someone watching me. I pulled the covers up to my neck and leaned against the headboard.

"Hello? Is someone there?" My voice trembled. Then faintly, I heard a familiar, frightening sound come from the corner.

Screech. Thud. Screech. Thud! SCREECH, THUD!! SCREECH, THUD!!! The noise grew louder with every passing second until it flooded the room.

My eyes popped open to a cloudy dreary morning; the perfect match for my mood.

CHAPTER 19

Ruthie left a message on my cell phone last night, canceling our breakfast. The weather looked glum, and as it turned out, she was the one who ended up with unexpected company. I wasn't up for socializing anyway.

I was drinking my first cup of coffee, and feeling sorry for myself, when the phone rang. I didn't jump up to get it. I let it ring while I debated whether or not I wanted to use any energy to get off the couch. I didn't feel like having a conversation with Paige or Beth, and I wasn't interested in listening to Meggie's drama this early in the morning.

Then Cole's face popped into my head. His big smile. Those green eyes. I had to get the phone. On the third ring, I jumped up and raced to the counter. Having learned from past mistakes, I paused long enough to find out that it was someone I didn't want to talk to.

"Brent. You narcissistic jerk," I mumbled.

I threw the phone across the room. It landed somewhere on the couch with a "Thwack".

"In two years, you never paid this much attention to me," I growled.

It was clear that Brent possessed the same maladaptive personality trait that a vast number of other guys had suffered from in history: wanting what they couldn't have. Why did the guys in my life have to make things complicated? Brent and Cole needed to stop hijacking my emotions.

I paced the floor, trying to think of something to do that would otherwise occupy the space between my ears. I needed a distraction.

Finally, the rain let up, and I thought of the perfect task. Cleaning out the shed.

Old, rusty metal shelves, rotted wood palettes, and moldy boxes (holding who knew what) muddled the entire space for as long as I could remember. My gardening tools had half a shelf in the corner. My father was planning to tackle the chore when they came back from Europe, but there was no time like the present.

I swapped out my sweats for work clothes, shoved my hair under my black camouflage baseball hat, and laced up my boots. I grimaced at the dreaded project that stood before me and swung the door open before I had time to change my mind.

"Cole," I gasped.

"Sorry. I didn't mean to scare you. I was about to knock. Were you leaving?"

"No. I was going to clean out the shed."

"Cool. I like a girl who knows how to live on the edge," he joked. "I'll help. Come on."

"No. It can wait. Come in and tell me about your trip." And the redhead, I thought.

I waved him in, and he followed me downstairs.

"I took my grandparents to dinner Friday. But it turned out they had plans last night, so I came back early."

"It's great that you got to spend some time with them," I simply replied.

"Yeah. I don't get to see them too much. Once or twice a month maybe." He touched my shoulder and said, "Wow. It's almost completely healed. What are you putting on it, some kind of miracle cream?"

I rubbed my shoulder; I had almost forgotten about it.

"I must heal fast," I responded with a shrug.

He nodded in agreement, then asked, "How was your weekend?"

"It was fine." Or not.

"Just fine, huh? That's because you missed me," he teased.

I responded with a smile. Cole parked himself on the couch. Unsure of how close a "buddy" was supposed to sit, I sat on a stool at the breakfast bar. In the distance, my phone began to ring. Cole heard it too.

"You can get that," he said.

"I don't know where I put it. I'll find it later."

"You should look for it while it's ringing. It sounds close."

Oh no. The couch. I threw it on the couch after Brent called. I was quite certain Cole was sitting on my phone. Brent calling could provoke questions, and the last thing I wanted to do was talk about Brent.

"Don't worry about the phone. Tell me more about your trip," I said.

"It was quick," he said, searching behind a pillow. "I got back around nine thirty. I was going to call. But since you get up early, I didn't think you'd be awake for company."

"I was up."

Now, I was treading in dangerous territory. I almost didn't tell him that I saw him at The Green. But I wanted to hear about the girl.

Cole stuck his hand in the couch, feeling under the cushions. Stop ringing, I thought. My phone was on the fifth ring, and the voicemail typically picked up after four. I must have done something to it when I threw it.

"I knew I should have called you last night. Next time, I'll listen to my instincts. I could have been hanging with you instead of my crazy sister. We went to The Green for a late dinner."

Sister. Yes. Despite the hair color, they did look alike. I suppressed a rising grin. I also failed to notice Cole pull my phone out of the couch until it was too late.

"Brent," Cole said, holding it out to me.

Gag! I hopped off the stool, took the phone from Cole, and hit ignore.

"Thanks."

"Poor Brent gets the cold shoulder. Who is he?"

"He's a friend. It's kind of funny actually. Brent and I went to The Green last night, and I thought I might have seen you when we were leaving. But I wasn't sure because I thought you were out of town."

"He's a friend? Do you know him from work or something?"

Was that a hint of jealousy? Before he misunderstood, I said, "We dated a while back. We're just friends now."

"Did you break up with him?" He picked at a thread on the couch, then said, "I don't mean to pry, I'm just curious."

"It was mutual," I said.

And I thought it was, until last night. When a guy didn't feel the need to spend any time with you, and he didn't argue with you when you suggested a break up, I considered that mutual.

"It's rarely mutual," he said. "My guess would be that you broke up with him, and he came here trying to get you back. That's what I would have done if you dumped me. I wouldn't have given up that easily."

His cheeks turned pink, and he grinned. I melted like butter on a scorching fire. I sat down on the edge of the couch, as far away from him as possible.

"Perhaps it was more me than him. But there won't be any getting back together. It's over."

Cue the blaring beep alerting me that Brent had left a message.

"It might not be over for him," Cole said.

"I made it clear last night. He's probably calling to apologize for his wacky behavior."

Cole's tone changed. "Wacky behavior?"

"He's…just…never mind."

"Explain wacky."

"I didn't mean anything by that."

"I could interpret wacky behavior a thousand different ways. Or you could tell me." Cole scooted closer.

"Brent might have been hoping for dinner to be–more. But it wasn't. He gets that now."

"You'd tell me if he needed someone to remind him of that, right?" Cole, my knight in shining armor.

"It's fine. Honestly, I think I was too hard on him."

"I'm serious," he said. He slid even closer to me and took my hand.

"You're sweet; I'm not used to that. You know what they say about chivalry."

"You should be used to that. You deserve better than Brent," he said. "You deserve better than me."

He leaned in as if he was going to kiss me. I bit my lip. Then he dropped my hand and walked to the sliding glass door. I stood up. I wanted to go to him, but my feet were cemented to the floor. He ran both hands through his hair and sighed as he stared out the window. Something in me came alive.

"I'm not sure what I deserve," I said. "But what I want is you."

He turned and saw my blushing cheeks.

"Whoa," I gasped. "Well, whatever–it's the truth."

Cole didn't say a thing. His eyes locked onto mine as he walked towards me. He took my hands. I was unable to look away. Cole pulled me towards him, our bodies collided. I could feel the stifling heat through his shirt.

Cole's hands slid up my arms to my shoulders. He hesitated for a brief second and took a deep breath. In an instant, he pulled my hat off and tossed it to the floor. My hair tumbled down around my shoulders and along my face. Cole pushed the hair from my eyes.

My eyes shifted from his face to his chest. I could no longer resist the urges I'd had since first laying eyes on him. I traced my fingers down his chest to his stomach. I rested my head against his chest where I could feel his heart pounding away.

With his hands entangled in my hair, he tilted my head back, and suddenly his mouth was on mine. I closed my eyes and fell into the moment. It was like falling into another world. Heaven. Paradise. Nirvana.

My hands slid to his shoulders. Cole took my waist and drew me back until he hit the wall. The next thing I knew, I was dizzy. The room began to spin and grow dark. I was about to pass out. The timing could not have been worse. I dropped my head back to catch my breath.

He buried his lips in my collar bone, then asked, "Are you alright?"

"No," I said, struggling to slow my breathing. "I'm dizzy. I'm sorry."

I held on to him so I wouldn't fall. I was seeing stars.

Don't pass out, I thought. You've already ruined the moment. Don't make it worse!

Cole stole a quick kiss then picked me up. He wrapped my legs around his waist and carried me to the kitchen.

"This," I gulped, "this isn't helping."

With a wide grin, he sat me on the counter. "Stay," he commanded.

He pulled two water bottles from the fridge, grabbed my legs, and pulled me towards him.

"Well, I can honestly say this is a first. I've never made a girl dizzy before." He flashed a smile. "You make me crazy, lady."

He put the water down and cradled my face with his hands. His lips caressed my cheek then moved to my mouth where he lingered, teasing me. He stopped abruptly and shook his head.

"Crazy. Why do you make me so crazy?" Cole uncapped a water bottle and handed it to me. "I don't want to rush anything with you. It's going to be impossible to control my thoughts, so play nice. Now, drink your water."

"Play nice?" I mustered. "Sometimes naughty is more fun."

He laughed at my ridiculous attempt at sexy-voice and said, "That's exactly what I mean. Now, play nice."

Oh, come on. Everyone knows the "nice" girl didn't get the promotion, the award, the last piece of cake, or the corner office. And most assuredly, she didn't get the guy.

I smiled at him and nodded. But let me be clear, "nice girl" status didn't stand a chance.

CHAPTER 20

My doctor instantly dismissed my shoulder injury. For something that had looked gruesome last week, it was barely noticeable now. The same with my wrist. The doctor argued with me at first. He insisted the wounds had to be from injuries that occurred several months ago, not days ago. He even became annoyed with me when I swore he had the time frame all wrong.

The doctor suggested that my anxiety meds could be contributing to my problems. But I blew that theory out of the water when I confessed to not taking them in over a month. I wasn't in school, so what was the point. He disagreed with my choice, then went on to explain the next step would be to send me to some specialists.

I asked for a referral to Doctor Armstrong, the doctor Jackson recommended for neurology. When I called his office to schedule an appointment, they didn't seem to think my situation was a priority. Their first opening wasn't until the first week of July. Cole was upset when I told him.

"How can they say it's not a priority? You pass out and have horrible migraines. That sounds pretty significant, Chelsea."

"I'm fine. And the headaches aren't as bad lately," I assured him.

"You down-played the symptoms, didn't you? Chelsea, that's not smart. You need to call back and explain the urgency. And you need to tell your parents."

"No way. I'm not going to worry them. Not to mention, bad dreams and insomnia are not exactly urgent problems. Other people have far more serious problems than this."

"I'm not worried about other people. I'm worried about you. Don't pretend there's nothing wrong. You may think insomnia and dreams aren't dangerous, but what about the rest? What about the big picture when you put all the symptoms together?"

Now he had me thinking. "I'll keep track of my symptoms for the next few weeks and go from there. I'm not sure all these things are related, anyway. If I get worse, I'll call back," I promised. "And honestly, sometimes I think it's not me. I think it's Lakeville."

He scrunched up his eyes and said, "You think Lakeville's haunted?"

I laughed because it sounded ridiculous when he said it out loud. But in reality, it was a gut feeling, and it was hard to describe. The bee situation, the strange sighting of Barney, the guy on the dock, and the unshakable feeling of being watched had done a number on me.

"No," I responded. I shook my head and confessed. "I get a weird feeling in some places in town. Such as the gallery, sometimes at The Green, the gas station."

"Cool. Maybe you're one of those people who can sense when there's going to be an earthquake. If we're lucky, you'll start seeing dead people."

We had a good laugh, and he dismissed my discomfort with Lakeville as yet another symptom of my questionable health.

For the next several days, I paid special attention to my episodes. I even tried to keep a health journal, but it was senseless. I felt great. I had a couple of minor headaches and a touch of insomnia, but that was it. I started to wonder if my problems were psychosomatic. Maybe everything was as simple as an overactive imagination. It was also possible that my anxiety had stretched beyond school. Either way, being with Cole made my health take a turn for the better.

Cole and I began to fall into a comfortable routine. We were always together. Even when I had to work, I'd find him waiting for me on the dock when I got home. He'd be kicked back with his fishing pole in the water or reading a book. It was as if he belonged there.

I was surprised that Ruthie hadn't made more of a point to come over and meet Cole. However, she'd been very busy with her boyfriend lately. He was spending more time at her house. Perhaps her boyfriend was keeping her from being overly nosey. That wasn't a bad thing.

I tried introducing Cole to Paige several times, but the timing never worked out. One day, I decided they were going to meet no matter what I had to do. I got home from work and found Cole sitting on the dock in his usual spot, taking in the sun. I sat down next to him. He didn't look at me; he stared straight ahead at the water. Something was wrong.

"I missed you," he finally said. There was sadness in his voice

"I missed you too. Are you alright?"

"Yes. Fine. Just thinking."

"Care to share?"

"Not now. But soon," he said.

He released a deep breath and looked at me. His eyes looked tired.

I would have been lying to say his ominous tone didn't bother me. The honest to God truth was that it terrified me. But I didn't push. If there was one thing I learned from Brent, it was never push a guy to share his feelings. I gathered my thoughts and moved ahead.

"I'm meeting Paige for dinner Friday. You're going to join us."

"I won't be around. I have to go back to Syracuse Thursday to see my grandparents. I should be back Saturday night." He sighed. "I'm glad you're going out with Paige. You should spend more time with your friends."

"Yeah. You should too." I disguised a pout with a smile and said, "Maybe we could get together with our friends. You know, all together. We could have them here. I'd love to meet them."

"I haven't seen the guys for a while. I should catch up with them soon. They're going to wonder what happened to me."

He ignored the most pivotal words–"all together". Suddenly, I was feeling guilty. Perhaps his suggestion that I spend more time with my friends was a hint that he needed space.

"You should go out with your friends more. I'm sorry that I take up all of your time," I said.

"Don't be sorry. Never be sorry. I'm lucky that you want to spend time with me." He picked up my hand and kissed it. "I'm sorry I can't have dinner with you and Paige. Next time."

Again, I asked, "Is everything alright? You seem sad."

"Everything is fine. I just have a few things on my mind. I'll stop being a baby."

I wasn't sure what to think about his somber mood. And like every time I was near him, thinking straight became increasingly difficult.

I leaned in closer and rested my head against his arm. After a few seconds, I pulled my feet from the water and threw a leg over him. We were face to face, eye to eye. The waiting game was going to end. I kissed him with purpose. There would be no more throwing on the brakes. Not a chance.

He took a hold of my hips and kissed me.

"Hmm?" he said through a mischievous grin. "It's hot."

"You're hot," I said.

"No. You're hot. Time to cool off."

Before I knew what was happening, he was on his feet throwing me through the air, and into the lake.

"Cole!" I screamed mid-flight.

Even though the water was warm, there was a shocking difference between that and the temperature of the air. By the time I popped my head out of the water, he was nowhere to be found. The coward. He couldn't have had time to run into the house and he wasn't on his boat. But he was hiding somewhere.

Suddenly, there was a tug at my leg. I yelped. Cole emerged in front of me, choking on laughter.

"You jerk!" I lunged at him. He dodged me.

"Come on, be a sport. It's hot today."

I sprang again. He slipped away, and I went flying past him. He grabbed my waist, capturing me. I laughed and playfully struggled to get free. It didn't take me long to give up. Being held captive by this resplendent boy was every girl's dream. I wrapped my arms around him, and we held each other silently.

"Now I'm cold," I confessed through chattering teeth.

"It's your fault. You started it," he said.

"Am I delusional, or did you throw me in?"

"I was defending myself. It was either throw you in or... well, you know. What happened to being nice?" He shoved my shoulder and smirked.

"I never agreed to be nice. You just assumed that."

"Then I'll just have to keep you in check."

He made his way to the ladder and beckoned me with a wave. When I got there, I reached for the ladder but grabbed his hand in the process. He leaned in and kissed my fingers. I wiggled away and up the ladder. He followed me and stung my butt with a friendly tap.

"See, there you go again," I said. "If you don't knock that off, your goody-two-shoes waiting game will be over!" I wasn't joking about that one. Fun is fun, but a girl has her limits.

"Ooh. You're such a bad girl," he taunted me. He laughed and threw me a towel.

After we changed into dry clothes, we grilled some burgers and veggies on the back porch. Cole left after dinner with a kiss goodnight and a promise to call me the next day.

I hated when he left. But I wouldn't dream of asking him to stay after he made things perfectly clear. And he never acted like he wanted to stay, either. Of course, that added to my worries about his somber mood on the dock earlier. Something was bothering him, and I needed to find out what it was. The situation with Jackson and his girlfriend sneaked into my head, then there was the redhead from The Green who he claimed was his sister. I had no reason to doubt him, yet I couldn't shake it.

There was another possibility. He could be worried that I was sick. Seriously sick. He might not want to deal with the baggage that comes with a serious illness. I wouldn't want to burden him either. Maybe keeping his distance from me until I had the facts wasn't a bad idea.

The next morning before work, I called Dr. Armstrong's office. Kathy, the receptionist, informed me that she could put me on a

141

waiting list in case an earlier appointment should become available. That was the best she could do. So I asked her to have the doctor call me back at his convenience. She sounded annoyed by my request, but she took down the message and curtly explained that the doctor would be too busy to return calls until after six o'clock that evening. Thirty minutes later my phone rang.

"Chelsea, this is Dr. Armstrong."

"Hi, Dr. Armstrong. Thanks for getting back to me so quickly. I don't mean to be a bother."

"It's no bother at all. Jackson called several weeks back specifically to talk about you. I see you're on the schedule for July."

"Jackson called you–about me?"

"Yes, of course. My son is very concerned for your health."

His son?

"Jackson didn't tell me you were his father," I said with a hard swallow. "Yes, I have an appointment for July. I keep hoping it's nothing, but I'm afraid I may be getting worse," I explained.

"I'm happy that you called. Talk to me."

"I want to see if maybe I can get in to see you a little sooner. I've been fainting and having other episodes for quite some time now. I start school at SUNY Geneseo this fall, and I currently have a job in the village–with Jackson. I have to drive about ten miles to get there, and I'm worried that I could accidentally hurt someone."

"Of course. Jackson explained some of your episodes to me. It sounds like you have some people worried about you. Look, next week I can stay late on Wednesday. Can you do an evening visit? Say, seven o'clock?"

"Absolutely. I hope you're not staying late on my account, though," I said, now feeling foolish for calling.

"It's not a problem, Chelsea. I look forward to seeing you. We'll get this figured out."

"Thank you. I appreciate this."

Landing an after hours appointment with the doctor just because I was friends with his son, who may or may not have feelings for me, ate away at my gut. There were so many other people out there with greater problems than mine.

"I'll see you next Wednesday. If something happens between now and then, call the office and we'll get you in sooner."

"Thanks again, Dr. Armstrong."

The rest of the day flew by. Cole had called and said he wouldn't be over until after dinner. Just before six o'clock, I heard a single knock at the door and someone enter the house.

"Hey there! I'm downstairs," I said.

"You alone?" Brent hollered down the stairs.

Brent. What nerve he had to waltz into my house like he owned the place. I was furious. It was time to give him a piece of my mind.

CHAPTER 21

"What are you doing here?" I demanded. I glared at Brent from the bottom of the stairs.

"Hello to you too. You haven't been returning my calls. Have you gotten my messages?"

He closed the door and made his way down to me. I glanced at the clock; Cole could be here any minute.

"Yes. I accept your apology. But like I said before, I don't think it's a good idea that we hang out. You shouldn't be here."

I had to be blunt. He left me no choice. The clock was literally ticking, Brent had to leave.

"That's your opinion. Not mine. We should talk about this, babe."

He started in with the sad eyes.

"Brent, I'm not interested in talking about it. Do you understand what I'm saying? Don't make me spell it out."

"I hate to tell you this, but you're going to have to. I'm just not buying it, babe."

He continued closing in on me. I inched back and soon found myself cornered in the kitchen.

"I don't have the same feelings for you anymore," I said. "We've grown up. We've grown apart."

"It's that other guy. Right? I've got two years on him. Doesn't that mean anything to you? I love you."

Brent took another step towards me. I was backed against the sink with nowhere to go. He was on the verge of stepping over the line. I had to do something before Cole walked in and found Brent hovering over me.

"You have no right to walk into my house uninvited. And…and I don't love you, Brent," I blurted out.

He moved his head in closer. He was more than invading my personal space, he was smothering it. I looked away.

He said quietly, "You love me, and you know it. Forget this new guy. I'll change." Brent took my chin in his fingers and turned my face back to meet his. He shrugged his shoulders and said, "We can start over, pretend like nothing ever happened. Whatever you want. I'd do that for you, babe."

"It's not about another guy. I don't have the same feelings for you anymore. Things are different now. Please go."

Brent closed the sliver of space left between us and put his hands on my hips.

"Don't," I uttered.

I tried to slip by him, but his hands jolted to the counter, blocking me in. His face contorted with anger. Brent's eyes closed and his teeth clenched. My instincts screamed to get as far away from him as possible, so I elbowed my way past his arm.

I scurried around Brent and over to the stairs. He didn't say anything. He didn't even move. He stood facing the sink with his back to me. I crossed my arms and waited for several painstaking seconds. With his behavior becoming more erratic, I wasn't sure what kind of reaction to expect.

Come on, Cole. Hurry, I thought. Maybe Cole was exactly what Brent needed to stop this unwelcome pursuit.

When Brent turned around, his brows were furrowed and his jaw tensed. In a brutish voice he snapped, "If that's the way you want it. Fine! I'm not going to beg."

The handsome, smooth talking, classy guy that I once knew now reminded me of nothing more than a monster. He stomped in my direction. I stepped away from the stairs to give him room to leave. Suddenly, he reached out and clamped onto my arm. Brent yanked me towards him. I gasped and swung my free arm at his face. He ducked out of the way, and my punch landed weakly on his shoulder. He laughed at me but didn't let go.

I tried to rip my arm away, but that just made Brent tighten his grasp. He grabbed a hold of my other arm and pulled me up to his face. It was as if someone had flicked a switch, instantly turning his amusement into wrath. I wasn't sure which was scarier.

"Listen to me, Chelsea. This isn't over. He will never love you like I do. No one will. He can't possibly give you the life I can. He's nothing but a redneck loser. You're simply a new, hot piece of ass that he's going to use up and throw away," he spewed.

I kept my mouth shut for as long as I could. No matter what I said, it would anger him.

Brent shook me. "Do you hear me? Don't you have anything to say?" he raged.

I said nothing and wouldn't look him in the eyes. He shook me again and snapped, "Answer me. Do not ignore me!"

I finally snapped, "I hear you! STOP yelling at me and get out!"

He snarled then dropped my arms. Not until then had I realized that he had jacked me up against the wall. When he released my arms, I dropped down from my toes. My knees buckled, but I quickly regained my balance and stood up.

"Stop being overdramatic," he said.

He whipped around and pounded up the stairs, only looking back when he reached the door.

"You'll be sorry one day. Don't come running to me when your boyfriend dumps you. He'll figure out how cold-hearted you are. Or maybe someone should tell him and spare him your pathetic drama."

With that, he left, slamming the door behind him and knocking the mirror off the wall. It shattered into pieces. Good. Seven years of bad luck; he deserved it.

My head throbbed, and my hands shook. I slipped on a pair of flip flops and went to sweep up the glass. When I was done and back downstairs sitting at the counter, I was still shaking.

Then I had a thought. What if Brent was up on the main road waiting to confront Cole? I didn't remember mentioning that Cole was coming over, but that didn't mean Brent wouldn't hang around considering the possibility. He did say someone should tell Cole how cold-hearted I was. I knew little about this new and unimproved Brent, so I couldn't take any chances.

I ran out to the driveway and didn't see him. I continued up to the main road. Brent was nowhere in sight. Satisfied that he was gone, I went in the house and sat down with a throbbing headache and a new outlook on the situation with Brent.

I had never seen the scary side of Brent. But he was a guy who always got what he wanted; and now, I was seeing what he was like when he didn't.

I buried my face in my hands and willed myself not to cry. I successfully held back tears, but my eyes were red and weary. Cole would be here soon, and I didn't want to ruin the evening. After I threw some cold water on my face, I took several calming breaths and began to think the rest of the evening through. What, if anything, would I tell Cole?

By seven o'clock, my head was feeling better. I calmed down and decided not to tell Cole about Brent until the end of the night. I wasn't about to let Brent's stupidity spoil our evening.

I was folding laundry in the living room when Cole knocked on the sliding glass door. I waved him in. The true definition of ruggedly handsome slid the door open and stepped in. He brushed his hair from his forehead, his jaw was scruffy, and he was wearing a pair of tattered jeans and a navy blue, vintage t-shirt.

"Hi," I purred. A smile spread across my face.

He raised an eyebrow and said, "I don't want to know what you're thinking. Stay back."

"Very funny." I dropped the shirt I was folding and walked towards my captivating prey.

"You have that look." He took a step backwards. "That devilish look."

"So?" I asked.

"So, get over here."

Cole began a playful chase as I became the hunted. I turned and ran towards the stairs, but he caught me by the belt loop and pulled me into his arms. He lifted me off the ground and tried to kiss me. I played hard to get, dodging his lips as much as possible, yet his lips still managed to catch me behind the ear. I could feel Cole's fiery breath when he whispered, "Just give up."

So I did. He was impossible to deny. It was impossible to ignore his hypnotic voice. A few minutes of kissing went by before I gathered the strength to push him away. It was a taste of his own medicine. But also, I didn't want to throw myself at him, like yesterday on the dock. Cole made it clear that slow was exactly how things were going to run–not that he made it easy. I walked out onto the porch to compose myself before I opened my big mouth.

"Hey! Come back," he said, following me.

"Let's get some air. It's a nice night. I'll start a fire."

We gazed at the twinkling sky and talked for hours. There was no moon that night. At one point, I thought I heard someone talking close by. Cole didn't seem to hear it. At first, I assumed it was the neighbors enjoying the tranquil night just as we were. Then, as Cole headed in to grab another soda, I clearly heard a voice. It was almost a whisper.

"Go. Leave her alone," it said.

Cole hesitated at the doorway just long enough to glance back at me. He heard it, I could tell. I waited for him to say something. Poker-faced, he attempted to go in the house, but I called him out.

"Cole, did you hear that?"

I got up and scampered to where he stood on the porch.

"What?"

"That voice. I think someone's on the side deck." I latched onto his arm and looked up at him. Then came the instant death of a perfect night. "Cole, Brent was here earlier. That could be him."

"Why did it take this long to tell me about Brent?" he asked.

"I didn't want it to ruin the night. I'm sorry." I put my head on his shoulder. He caressed my hair and sighed.

"What happened?" he asked.

"He was mad when he left. He made a comment about telling you how cold-hearted I am."

"That's ridiculous. Did that worry you, Chelsea? Did you think I might believe him?"

"Brent can be very convincing. Plus, I didn't want him to confront you. I don't want some nagging ex-boyfriend to drive you away."

"He would never drive me away." Then looking towards the side deck, he added, "As long as it's up to me, nothing will ever take me away from you. Nothing." He kissed me on the forehead, and said, "I'm going to get that soda, then you're going to tell me what happened with Brent."

I expected him to be more annoyed, but he was sweet and concerned, and he was eager to hear what happened. I was too afraid to be outside by myself, so I went in with him. Moments later, we were cozied up by the dwindling fire, and I was spilling my guts. Well, some of them, anyway.

"First off, don't even do so much as open the door for him. Don't let him in no matter what his excuse," Cole started.

"He let himself in. I had the door unlocked for you."

"Living in a small town doesn't mean there's no crime. Always keep the door locked. I can knock, and I know there's a key under the turtle rock. I wish you would trust me enough to tell me when he bothers you. You can tell me anything, Chels."

"I'm sorry. I never dreamed he would come here again. He's been different since we broke up."

"You left him. Something tells me he's not the kind of guy who takes rejection with a smile. Now, go on. What else did he have to say?"

I chose my words carefully. Cole wanted me to tell him everything. Except telling him how aggressive Brent was before he left could make a bad thing worse. So I skipped that and went directly to the things Brent said. I also told him that he had slammed the door as he left and broke the mirror.

"He's a jerk. How did you date him for so long?"

"That's a popular question."

"Let's go finish this conversation in the house. It's getting cold. I'll get the blanket and the drinks," he said.

I went in the house and plopped down on the couch. My head dropped into my hands, and my chest ached. My anxiety was rising

149

fast. Cole was going to think I was the kind of girl with secrets, someone he couldn't trust. He was going to think Brent still meant something to me.

Cole placed the cans on the counter and dropped the blankets by the door.

"Hey, no worries," he said, walking towards me. "Brent sounds like a complete moron. I'll have a talk with him."

My stomach flopped.

"I don't think you have to do that. This time, he got the picture. I made it very clear."

"Don't assume that. He's persistent and now this is a game. Since losing is probably not in his DNA, I'd be surprised if you didn't hear from him again in the next few weeks."

Cole plunked down on the couch next to me. It was warm in the house, so I pulled off my hoodie and tossed it on the coffee table. Cole darted up and pointed to the dark purple bruises on my arms. He exploded.

"Chelsea, what happened?"

My gulp was audible. My arms had bruised sooner than expected. I ran my hand over the arm that Brent had first latched onto; it was far worse than the other.

"Oh, um, Brent. He kind of..."

"Kind of nothing, Chelsea. Tell me what happened."

"He grabbed my arms before he left. He was really mad. I told you that."

"You told me he was mad. You did not tell me he did that." He pointed at the bruises I tried to hide with my hands.

Cole paced the floor, sending me an occasional glance. His hands danced from his hair, to his pockets, and back to his hair.

I didn't blame Cole for being mad at me. He deserved to know the whole story when he first got here. If I were smart I would have told him, given him Brent's number and address, and let him deal with Brent however he wanted. Even if it meant Brent got the ass-whooping he asked for. The problem was, I wasn't smart, and I wasn't that girl.

150

I was the girl who thought she could take care of everything on her own. I didn't need a man to fight my battles, but then again, I had never had any battles to speak of–until now. The more I thought about it, the more angry I became with Brent for bringing this kind of drama into my life.

Finally, Cole turned to me and said, "Look, I can't let him do this to you. I cannot let him get away with this, Chelsea. You have to file a report with the police. Look at you, look at your arms." He stared at my arms and shook his head. "I'm going to talk to him. This is going to end."

"No, I don't want you to get in a fight with him," I said, jumping to my feet. "His father is a very aggressive lawyer, and if you lay one finger on Brent, he won't hesitate to go after you. Please. I think he's done with me. Let's forget about him."

"I can't."

"Yes. Please, Cole. Just forget about him. I promise if Brent ever comes back I'll drive you straight to his house if you want. Seriously, he was so disgusted with me when he left tonight, I'm sure he never wants to see me again."

"Chelsea, it's naive for you to think Brent walked out of here tonight and is never coming back. He was highly emotional when he left. So highly emotional that he went to the extent of hurting you. He hurt you. That's not a guy who's over you. If he didn't care about you, he would have left without making a scene. If he didn't care about getting you back, he wouldn't have come here in the first place."

"His ego was bent."

"It still is. And because of that, he wants you back even more."

Cole stood silent for a moment. I wanted him to drop it. I didn't want him to get hurt. There wasn't a doubt in my mind that Cole could physically destroy Brent in a heartbeat. It was the repercussions I had to explain to Cole.

Brent's father would dig something up on Cole. And if he couldn't find anything, he would make something out of nothing and destroy Cole's future. I had seen it first hand about a year into my relationship with Brent.

There was a rumor that Brent wasn't going to make the final cut on the basketball team. Two days before the cut, a huge team scandal exploded in the news and wiped out the entire coaching staff. All three coaches walked away silently. One lost everything, another ended up an assistant coach for Syracuse University. And the other coach, he disappeared. Needless to say, Brent made the team.

"He's not going to touch me. There's nothing for them to find and nothing for them to come after," Cole said.

"Please." I walked up behind him, wrapped my arms around his torso, and rested my cheek on his back. "I'm sorry. I can take care of this on my own. I doubt he'll come back. I'll call the police and have him arrested if he does. Please, don't worry," I begged.

Brent had said, "This isn't over." I pushed those words out of my head because I couldn't have them fall out of my mouth. At this point, I had said too much already.

"Where's your tundra wind when it comes to Brent, Chelsea? Why are you soft about him instead of standing your ground and pushing back? Think about it. You're afraid of him. And you should be."

"I'm not afraid of him. He doesn't scare me. He's not..." I shook my head. It was time I stopped trying to convince myself that he wasn't dangerous.

"Watch out for Brent. I'm going to," Cole said.

My chest was heavy with regret. I knew I could have avoided this mess by refusing to go to dinner with Brent in the first place. He played me- completely. He knew I would feel sorry for him. I was as naive as Brent was manipulative.

Cole turned around. "This isn't your fault. But if he comes back, even if it's to apologize, you need to tell me immediately. Because it will be the last time he shows up. Understand? And start locking the doors," he said, throwing me into a mock headlock. At last, he smiled.

"I will," I mustered.

"Anything else you want to share? Now's the time," he added.

"Nope. That would be all."

He let go of me and said, "Good. Let's get back to what little time we have left." He turned on the television and took a seat on the couch.

He seemed satisfied that the conversation was over, but his last comment struck me like a dagger. It could have been the way he said it, or maybe I was reading into his words, but it paralyzed me. What little time we had left? What was that supposed to mean?

After a few seconds, he must have realized how that sounded because he dropped the remote and said, "Tonight, Chelsea. What little time we have left tonight. I have to leave in about an hour. That's all." He tilted his head to the side and looked at me quizzically.

"Right," I said. "It just sounded so final. I'm a little over-emotional right now." Then for the heck of it, and since he wanted me to be honest, I said, "Sometimes I get this feeling that one day you won't show up. That you'll leave me. I feel almost like I have to hold on for dear life. Maybe it's because no one ever mattered as much. Ugh, now I sound like a whack job…"

"I hate to tell you this, but you are sort of a whack job." He grinned. "Isn't that what makes you so perfect?"
"That doesn't make sense," I snickered.

"Come on. Sit with me, weirdo." He patted the empty space next to him. I sat down and snuggled under his arm.

"Who do you think we heard outside?" I asked.

"It was probably a voice carrying from a boat or something. Or maybe a neighbor. There was no one in the yard, so don't worry."

Don't worry. Easier said than done. I wanted to believe no one was there, but I knew something weird was going on. And then, later that night, the dreams started again. They were all very short but disturbing.

In one dream, Brent punched me in the face repeatedly. When Cole tried to stop him, Brent shot and killed Cole.

In another dream, Cole told me that he didn't want anything to do with me because of Brent. He said I came with too much baggage, and he was in love with someone else. He took the hand of a beautiful woman and walked away, leaving me standing next to cold-faced Brent.

And in yet another, Cole stood screaming my name, unable to move. He was forced to watch as a dark shadow overtook me. It sucked the breath out of my lungs through my mouth and almost killed me. As I collapsed onto the cold ground, gasping for air, the shadow slithered towards Cole and whispered something to him. Finally, it slipped into Cole through his eyes and disappeared, leaving his green eyes black and empty. I woke up fighting to breathe.

By then, it was three o'clock in the morning, and I could no longer endure the nightmares. The thought of going back to sleep was frightening. I got out of bed and started my day. I would suffer later, but that would be easier to deal with than another heart-wrenching dream of Cole leaving me.

CHAPTER 22

The next evening, after a long day, I was welcomed home by Cole and his peculiar knack for delivering my favorite meal. That night it was Thai food. As happy as I was to see him, I was exhausted from the previous sleepless night. I couldn't even think about eating.

"Go to bed. I'll call you in the morning before I leave for Syracuse." Cole kissed my head and shuffled me to the stairs. "You need sleep."

"There's no point. I don't want to dream. It's awful. I need you to stay with me," I said, clutching his hand.

"Of course. Come on."

We went to my room, where I kicked off my shoes and sank into my cool sheets. He sat on the bed and played with my hair.

"I wish you would tell me about the nightmares. Maybe it would help."

"I can't. I don't remember them," I mumbled.

I was too embarrassed to tell him that my nightmares all revolved around him leaving me. I didn't want to sound like a needy whiner afraid of abandonment. But wasn't that what I had become?

"I'm sorry about dinner," I said.

"Shh, go to sleep."

"Wake me before you leave."

"I will," he said.

There were no dreams for those few hours. Just undisturbed sleep. I awoke just before ten. Cole was sound asleep next to me with his arm draped across my stomach. He didn't stir when I pushed his hair away from his eyes.

I lifted his arm, slid out of bed, and went downstairs for a glass of water. When I came back upstairs and walked into my room, the curtain was billowing in the warm breeze above Cole's head. The

155

moonlight was shining on his peaceful face. I sat on the edge of the bed and watched him.

I studied the shape of his face, his cheek bones, the five o'clock shadow on his defined jaw, and the shaggy brown hair that had fallen back over his eyes. That was when it dawned on me. He was the boy from my dream. There was no doubt, this was him. He was the boy I loved unconditionally and so completely. The one I made a promise to; a promise I couldn't remember.

He was also the boy who ripped my heart out.

There he was, asleep in my bed. The feelings I'd had in my dream so many weeks ago came rushing to the surface. Had I been able to see his eyes in my dream, the identity of my mystery boy would have been revealed the minute Cole pulled me from the lake. However, in the dream, his eyes were shadowed, like now, while he slept.

I reached out to touch his face then stopped myself. I didn't want to wake him.

As I watched him sleep, it occurred to me that the boy in my dream was not specifically Cole. After all, I had the dream before I met him. My dream must not have been about the boy himself, it was about the way I felt about him. It was about finding someone who I would love enough to fear a broken heart. And now that I found Cole, and had allowed myself to fall so in love with him, he fit the picture. Finally, the dream that had tortured me for so many weeks made sense.

Whatever the reason behind Cole finding his way into that dream, there was still something that would never be true. Yes, I had no doubt that he was a boy I loved with such intensity that the mere thought of him leaving caused me tremendous fear and anxiety. And I did fear Cole breaking my heart, or as in my dream, ripping my heart out. The difference was, in my dream, I survived. I was crushed and disheartened, but I survived. Yet I knew, with no uncertainty, that I could never survive if Cole broke my heart and left. Without him, I was nothing. Without him, I would die.

"I have this eerie feeling that I'm being watched," uttered Cole. He cracked open one eye.

"You look so peaceful. And I like looking at you; you're kind of cute," I said.

He opened his arms, and I crawled in.

"Do you have to go?" I asked.

"No, not yet."

"Good. I sleep better with you here."

"Then sleep. I'll probably be gone before you wake up, though. I'll lock up," he mumbled.

He gave me a squeeze and kissed my head. That was the best night of sleep I ever had, and the first night we spent together. In the morning, he was gone. I vaguely recalled a kiss and Cole saying he would call me from Syracuse later that night.

I wanted to sleep in, but once I woke up the next morning, it was hard to get back to sleep. All I could think about was Cole and the dream I had several weeks back. Lying in bed, I tried to picture Cole in that dream, but it was foggy. It had been much easier to remember last night while Cole slept under the billowing curtain, with the moon illuminating his face.

I shot out of bed aggravated. I wanted to savor the dream and see it all over again, this time with Cole front and center. I had spent weeks trying to interpret that troublesome dream, being haunted by it and frustrated that I couldn't see the face of the boy I loved. Now, I could only hope that the next time I slept I would have the very same dream. I would suffer all its consequences as long as Cole's face was free from darkness.

That morning, I didn't have to work until eleven o'clock. That gave me a chance to get a few things done. I talked to Paige and confirmed our dinner date at The Green tomorrow night. We had a reservation for seven o'clock. This time, I might try the lobster fra diavolo.

After that, I called my sister, who didn't answer, and left her a message telling her I was thinking about her. Next, I emailed my parents and assured them all was good back home. Of course, I didn't forget to check in with Jill and Beth. After my calls were made, I gathered my things and headed out the door.

I pulled out of the driveway and headed north. I turned left onto Gray Road, then right onto Townline Road. Ten minutes later, I was at work for my four hour shift. Avoiding Jackson today was going to be a challenge, but it had to be done. Any conversation with him would be awkward and fake.

On the way to work, I had been followed by a tan Envoy. I assumed someone was headed to the village like I was. I didn't think much of it, even when it drove by the store the second time; the town was small and most businesses were located in this area. But when I left work and almost immediately spotted the Envoy two cars back, I got suspicious.

Why on earth would anyone want to follow me? Brent's face popped in my head. I couldn't imagine that he would give up a day interning to follow me around. And he would never be caught dead in an Envoy.

At three fifteen, I found a note on my door from Cole. I cracked a smile. It said he missed me and would call around six. Then I heard horns honking up on the main road and saw the tan SUV crawling by the house. I tried to get a glimpse of who was driving, but it was too far away, and there were trees in the way.

I waited for a few minutes to see if the Envoy came back. When it didn't, I went inside to make my dinner; a bagel with cream cheese and a side of strawberries. As I ate on the back porch, I couldn't shake the thought that someone had been following me. But the idea was so absurd that I ended up having a good laugh at myself.

After dinner, I was hit with the worst headache I had ever had. I doubled up on the ibuprofen, which didn't put a dent in the pain, then parked myself on the couch. It was after six o'clock, and I hadn't heard from Cole. Incessantly, I began checking the phone for the time, to be sure it wasn't on vibrate, and to see how many reception bars it had.

At twenty after six, the phone rang. "This is ridiculous," I said to myself. I hit the answer and snapped, "Don't call me anymore." With a smidge of guilt, I hung up on Brent without waiting for a response.

Cole would have said I did the right thing, that I was being strong and sticking up for myself. I didn't relish the thought that when I told him about Brent calling, he would be paying him a visit. But since Cole hadn't called me yet, I wasn't that concerned about an impending confrontation. Either way, my doubts about how I responded to Brent faded as the night went on.

Around ten o'clock, and still feeling miserable, I somehow managed to doze off on the couch. Twenty minutes later, I woke up and shuffled to bed. I slipped under the covers with some residual head pain and was worrying about the dreams I might have if I managed to fall asleep for longer than twenty minutes. But what was truly agonizing was that Cole had never called. And that sad fact only added to the events of what was about to be the longest night of my life.

CHAPTER 23

Every ten minutes, I was checking the clock. This went on for hours. At two-thirty, I reached for the sleeping pills on my bedside table. During my struggle with the child proof cap, I realized that if I took a pill now, I might not be able to wake up in time for work. I tossed the bottle on the table and threw on a hoodie.

With few options left, I went to the kitchen and poured myself a glass of bourbon. My father always said it made him sleepy. I checked out the new People magazine and turned on the television. There was always the local twenty-four hour news station to bore me to sleep.

While perusing the magazine and trying to suck down the ounce of heinous liquor, something on the news caught my attention. A reporter was at the scene of a murder on the campus of Syracuse University. I put down the magazine and focused my attention on the news report. A young female student had been found brutally beaten to death.

That was when my heart went dark, and I discovered the truth; what I should have known all along. After all, when something was too good to be true, it would eventually prove itself to be just that.

Behind the reporter, a small crowd of people gathered. I couldn't believe my eyes when I saw Cole standing there with his arm around a gorgeous girl. The young woman was obviously not his grandmother. His arm was draped around her shoulder, and she was holding his hand. She had her other arm around his waist.

"Is that a ring?" I didn't dare try to walk. I slid to the floor. Then I crawled closer to the television, snatched the remote control from the coffee table, and hit pause. "Holy crap—it is a wedding ring. They're wearing wedding rings. He's... he's married?"

160

Stomach acid stung my throat. I sat in shock for about thirty seconds as I processed what I was seeing. Was that truly Cole? But no matter how I tried to convince myself it wasn't him, the picture was very clear. He spent so much time with me, I couldn't understand how he could possibly be married. Yet the evidence was right in front of me.

I rewound the report to the beginning and learned that it was recorded earlier in the day. It had been a live report at six-thirty. I scoured the background, no longer paying attention to what the reporter was saying; that became insignificant. They came into view after showing pictures of the campus.

There they were, standing to the right, behind the woman reporter. There were about five other people standing in the small crowd. Cole had his arm around the painfully stunning girl. He buried his face in her long dark hair and whispered something in her ear. She nodded her head and frowned, then they turned their attention to the reporter.

The reporter turned to the crowd and stepped back towards Cole. She held the microphone up to the girl, and said, "Thank you for speaking with us. Now am I correct, you found the student?"

"No," she replied. "My husband did." Dagger straight to my heart. She continued in her light hispanic accent, "We were walking back to my dorm, and he saw a bloody shoe lying next to those bushes. When he went to check it out, he saw an arm sticking out from behind the dumpster." She hugged Cole. "He is very upset by what he saw."

"Did you see her?" the reporter asked the dark-haired beauty with the pink cherub lips.

"No. He came right back to me, and we called 9-1-1. He said it was horrific. He did not want me to live with seeing such a sight. That poor girl."

"Thank you for talking to us," said the reporter to both Cole and the woman.

Then they were gone. The camera zoomed in on the reporter, who promised more details as they came in.

I guess I had the answer now. He could be married and spend

so much time with me because she went to school at Syracuse University. That's who he was visiting. Again, I rewound the segment and watched it from the beginning, pausing to study the frames with Cole and his wife. I was not sure how many times I watched before I started to cry. I was broken. Shattered into a thousand pieces. Irreparable damage to say the least.

I left the television frozen on the girl and Cole, then I ran to the bathroom and threw up. When there was nothing left, I sat silently on the bathroom floor with my chin resting on my knees. I refused to believe it. That couldn't have been him. It must have been someone who looked remarkably similar. That was all.

I stood up to get my phone. I was going to call him to clear things up. Except it was almost four in the morning, and I couldn't bring myself to make the call–especially if he wasn't alone. I didn't know how to handle what I had seen. I could only hope that somehow I was dead wrong. Unfortunately, my gut told me I had just witnessed the end of my relationship with Cole.

Suddenly, I heard the volume on the television and the report start to play. Too much time must have passed because the pause button no longer worked. I was going to lose the report.

"Maybe it's online," I said, running to my laptop.

Then I remembered that these stories looped several times on the local news channel. I abandoned my laptop and hit the "live" button on the remote. As luck would have it (if you could call it that) the report played a few minutes later, and I was able to record it. Why I recorded it, I'm not sure. Evidence to present to Cole? A means to torture myself for the rest of my life?

I shot back the bourbon, and for what must have been hours, I stared at the frozen image of Cole and his wife until I finally went unconscious. Regardless of whether or not I had actually fallen asleep, my mind was black for a short time. For once, emptiness felt good.

The ringing brought me out of the dark. It rang and rang. It was a struggle to open my eyes, let alone answer the phone. I didn't care who was calling. I didn't care what time it was. I didn't care about work or if Jackson was mad when I didn't show up. I didn't care if my friends were mad that I was ignoring their calls. Whatever… Wallowing in self-pity was the only thing I was capable of. My life was smack in the middle of an emotional overdose.

At one point, the sun tried to peek through the living room blinds. I couldn't keep it dark enough, so I dragged my weary limbs up the stairs to my room, closed the blackout curtains over the sheers, and climbed into bed.

There was knocking at the door sometime later, and I knew it was most likely Ruthie. I ignored the persistent noise the best I could, but it was nails on a chalkboard for my headache. Before I pulled myself into sitting a position, so I could storm to the door and demand the horrid pounding to stop, the knocking ceased. Whoever it was had finally gone away.

In my head, the same newsreel ran over and over. Cole and his wife, the beautiful, dark-haired Latino girl with the flawless olive skin. I was paralyzed with grief.

Being awake wasn't an option after a while. I needed to go back to sleep. I wanted to sleep for a week if I could. I popped a sleeping pill in my mouth and washed it down with lukewarm water and another splash of bourbon. All I wanted to do was hibernate for as long as I could.

After some time, the ringing began again. There was more knocking. When I heard shouting, a fire lit in my brain. It was a timid flame, but the words began to hit home.

"Chelsea! If you don't open this door now, I'm calling 9-1-1! Open the door! Do you hear me?" hollered the familiar voice.

Everything was hazy. I peeled my eyes open, having heard and understood the threat. It was Paige.

"Hold on," I mustered.

I used the walls for support and teetered to the door.

"Chelsea!" Paige yelled again, pounding on the door and jabbing at the doorbell.

I wondered how long she'd been out there. She sounded worried for some reason.

"Coming," I said with what little force I could gather.

I stopped at the door and looked where the mirror used to be. That was right, Brent had broken it, I remembered. It turned out that I had received the curse of seven years of bad luck. And to top it off, he was right about Cole. That stung. I opened the door and squinted from the sudden rush of daylight. Paige's mouth dropped open.

"Chelsea? What's wrong with you?" she asked.

"Sorry. I overslept," I explained, still groggy and rubbing my eyes.

"Overslept? It's seven o'clock. At night. I've been here since twenty after six."

"Six twenty–at night?" I said. "Wait, it's really not the morning?" Where had the time gone? "Why are you here?" I asked.

"Oh, my God. Let me in," Paige said, taking my arm and guiding me to my room. She sat me on the bed and threw open the curtains, letting the subtle evening glow envelop the room. "What the heck happened?" she asked.

"Nothing. I overslept." Cole and his wife popped into my thoughts. My head dropped into my hands. "Is that why you're here? Did I call you?"

Paige snagged the sleeping pills from the bedside table and read the bottle. "What are these for? Since when do you take sleeping pills? You don't even take aspirin."

"I do now."

My eyes were still trying to adjust to the light. Paige was standing in front of the window, which made it difficult to see her.

She knelt down in front of me and started the quiz.

"Smile," she commanded.

"No," I grumbled.

"Put both hands in the air."

"Stop it," I told her, slapping her hands away.

"Who is the president?" she persisted.

I knew what she was thinking. I had also seen the post shared on Instagram.

"I'm only eighteen. I didn't have a stroke. I'm fine. I took one sleeping pill. One! I don't remember when. It's all natural anyway.

And geez, there are four pills missing from the whole bottle, Paige. This isn't why I called you here."

"Chelsea, look at me. You didn't call me here. You missed work today. We had dinner plans. Don't you remember? This isn't like you. Get a grip."

I looked her in the eyes. She seemed to waver, but maybe it was me.

"I don't want to get a grip. I don't want to do anything except go back to bed."

I attempted to crawl under the covers, but she wouldn't allow it. She ripped the blanket and top sheet off the bed and threw them in the corner.

"Well, you're gonna get up, sister. First tell me what happened. Don't tell me nothing because I know better. Is it Cole?"

I slumped over feeling every bit of torture that came with hearing his name. Paige saw this. She would, of course, because nobody knew me better.

"Yes," I whispered.

"You broke up?" she asked.

"Not yet."

I tried to explain it, but I was all over the place. I started with my trouble getting to sleep last night and backed up to the note on the door. Then I explained Brent calling and my cold-hearted response, Cole not calling, a shot of bourbon, and finally the news report. That one I could show her, it was still paused on the TV.

"Let's go," she said.

"I don't want to see it again."

"Let's go. We'll watch it together."

Paige helped me to my feet and led me downstairs. And there it was, paused at the point where you could first see Cole and his wife. I sat on the couch with my head in my hands, dreading to see him again, and more so, dreading to see her.

I listened as the reporter talked, then Cole's wife made her statement. She got the best of me, and I looked up to see her face. I glanced at Cole with heartache eating away at my soul. I studied the

165

man for a second. Something wasn't right. Was that Cole? Was that him? Last night I was convinced. Without a doubt. And he hadn't called, so it made sense.

"Pause that," I snapped.

"He's married, huh?" Paige said, pausing the picture. "And he doesn't speak English?"

"I don't believe it," I said, snatching the remote from Paige's hand.

I rewound the segment, yet again, and I couldn't believe what I was seeing. The man was the spitting image of Cole. But the man on the screen in front of me was not him.

"Chelsea?"

"That's not him." I laughed. All at once, the reporter's words and Paige's question clicked, and I shrieked, "He doesn't even speak English! That's why his wife spoke for him."

I had been so consumed with the man I thought was Cole, and his alleged wife, that I hadn't listened to the reporter when she prefaced the interview with, "Mr. Salas doesn't speak English. His wife will tell us what happened."

I laughed harder.

"What are you laughing at? You're really worrying me," Paige said.

"He's not Cole. That guy is not Cole! I must have been so tired and thought... or maybe...maybe it was all a dream. I feel so stupid. And relieved. Because holy geez, I almost called him."

Paige looked at me with wide eyes, like I was crazy; and she had every right to believe it. "Let me make sure I understand this," she said. "You couldn't sleep last night, so you turned on the TV, had a shot of your dad's bourbon, and saw this report. You thought that hispanic guy was Cole, but he's not. So you spend all night and all of today in some kind of depressed coma feeling sorry for yourself for no good reason. And somewhere along the way you thought it was smart to take a sleeping pill?"

I slumped back on the couch. I could find only three words in my entire vocabulary that mattered.

"He's not Cole."

"And to top everything off, that moron, Brent, called you?" she asked.

"Yes. I keep hoping he'll leave me alone, but he's so persistent. Cole's going to lose it with him.

"Look, I don't know what's wrong with me. My headaches are excruciating, my dreams are so realistic; they're totally messing with my mind. I'm crazy in love with Cole, like no one ever before. All of a sudden, I'm neurotic and insecure. Every time I turn around, I'm afraid he's going to figure me out and leave me." I threw my hands in the air. "So basically, I'm pathetic and crazy."

Paige grimaced. "When are you going to see the doctor?"

"Wednesday. Want to come?"

"Definitely," she said. "Let's get you dressed. It's too late for The Green, but there's always Charli's Diner."

Paige turned on the shower and helped me out of my clothes. The shower was exactly what I needed. After getting dressed, I felt much better. I was able to function on my own.

Regrettably, the clearer my head got the more idiotic I felt. Imagine the humiliation if I had actually confronted Cole. Yikes. Thankfully, Paige was the only one who knew what happened. But make no mistake, that would come with a price; she would never let it go.

After that, I was done sweeping my problems under the carpet and pretending I was fine. It wasn't stress, medication or a lack thereof, nor was it a vitamin deficiency. And as much as I wanted to blame it on Lakeville turning creepy, I could no longer do that. There was something drastically wrong with me. I had a few ideas, and unless Paige brought it up, I was going to keep those theories to myself.

I spent the rest of the night apologizing to Paige. Even though she acted like things were fine, I could tell she was worried. Paige insisted on going with me to Dr. Armstrong's office Wednesday night. The support was welcomed.

I still didn't have an explanation for why Cole hadn't called. I kept hoping I would get a call or a text message; anything that meant he hadn't forgotten about me. I tried not to think about it because it was agonizing. I had found the boy of my dreams (quite literally) and now, only days later, I was afraid I'd lost him.

My mind raced while we ate at Charli's Diner. I was fairly certain I cut Paige off mid-sentences when I blurted out, "Do you think he's hiding something? Maybe he is married. He could have a girlfriend. It's when he goes to Syracuse that I usually don't hear from him. It's kind of weird. Don't you think?"

"Why would you think he's married. You're sure that wasn't him on TV. Right?"

"Absolutely, not him."

"Could he have a girlfriend? I suppose it's possible. Do you trust him, Chels?"

"Yes. I think. I mean, I have no reason not to." I said. "But that was weird last night. It was like the time I chased Barney through the field to bring him home, right? How could I have thought that was him?"

"What are you talking about? Barney's been gone for..."

"Years. I know."

"When did you see Barney?"

I was rambling, and I forgot I hadn't told Paige about seeing Barney. And with what she had just witnessed, what difference would it make if she knew everything now. "Sorry. I didn't want you to worry."

"Too late. Spill."

I filled her in on the Barney episode.

"I really thought it was him. No thought as to how much time had passed. As if I would just run out to the field, get him, and bring him home."

I shook my head in disbelief.

"You're sure you hadn't fainted or something? Or maybe it was some kind of a dream."

"No. I was definitely driving. How could I drive and dream at the same time? Plus, I ran into Cole. He saw me run into the cemetery. I was muddy and everything. I even had to go home and shower before meeting the girls.

"Now, with the news last night, maybe then I was dreaming; like a lucid dream where you're half awake."

"That would explain how you had recorded the newscast," Paige said.

"Yes. I think I was watching it, except in my head I was positive it was Cole. And if you saw him, you would never confuse him for the guy on the news. They look a lot alike, but when I saw it this morning–there was no doubt. It was not him. When you meet him you'll see." I peeked at my phone, and said, "But at this rate, you may never see him at all."

"Stop it. You said things were cool before he left. Maybe there's something wrong with his phone. There must be a good reason he hasn't called. Since you guys have been together, how many times has he gone away?"

"Twice."

"And that makes you think he's married or has a girlfriend?" she asked, snickering. "Just wait. I bet he calls you tomorrow."

"I hope so. Paige, I'm sorry I didn't tell you everything." I sighed. "And while we're at it, there's a few other things I should tell you."

I told her about the bees, and Brent and Barney when I went for the hike with Cole. I also filled her in on the details of Brent's latest mission, his dauntless pursuit. She was furious with Brent, but she wasn't as surprised as I thought she'd be. Not as surprised as I had been.

Paige leaned over the table, and in all seriousness, she said, "He's a time bomb. All cool and collected, and then one day he doesn't get his way. He can't charm it, buy it, or outsmart it. So what else can he do but take it. After all, he has that wicked sense of entitlement. You watch your back."

"It's funny you say that. He used that exact word: entitled. He said he was entitled to change his mind about us. As if the decision was all his. He thought he could whisk me off to dinner, say a few corny words, and bam, we're back together. He thought I would blindly go with it."

"We should have Jackson talk to him. Plus, the more people that know about this, the better."

"No. Why is that better?" I asked, abashed at the idea anyone else might find out about my Brent issues.

"The more people who know, the less likely Brent is to escalate things. If anything ever happened to you, he would be the first person to suspect. The Ego wouldn't appreciate that kind of notoriety."

"He hates me so much that I'm sure he wants nothing to do with me. Don't stir the pot now."

"I want you to come home with me tonight. We'll watch The Office until you fall asleep. Stay the weekend. I'm worried about you." Paige put her hand on mine. She looked painfully concerned. I hated that I made her feel that way.

"Please," she whined. "We're all meeting at Main for coffee tomorrow anyway. Just come to my house tonight and we'll go together in the morning. It'll be fun."

She waited patiently as I thought about it.

"Fine. I'll stay tonight. Not the whole weekend."

I gave in because if nothing else, it would keep my mind off Cole. For a little while, anyway.

CHAPTER 24

The Office binge was supposed to distract me, but Paige fell asleep half way through episode two of the first season. That left me with no one to talk to and bored. I managed to get through the third episode before I switched to regular television, and that was anything but a distraction. The news updates about the Syracuse incident and commercials for The Green were not helpful. I shut off the television and checked my phone for the hundredth time. Cole never called.

The next morning, I got up and made my way to the kitchen. Paige was at the table scrolling through TikTok when I walked in.

"I didn't hear you get up," I said.

"I got up at five. You were asleep, and I didn't want to wake you."

I shook my head and poured myself a glass of orange juice. I was sure I was awake and checking my emails at five. Could I have dreamed that I was awake? I took a sip of my OJ, then said, "I guess it was just one of those nights. I'll drive separately this morning. I'm going home after coffee."

Paige snapped her head in my direction and threw a hand on her hip. "It's not like he can't reach you when you're here," she said.

"It's not about Cole. I have things to do. That's all."

"Fine. But you know what I'm thinking."

Oh, I knew alright. And I agreed that I was an idiot to dash right home after coffee just in case he showed up, called, whatever. Even so, there wasn't a thing in this world that would have stopped me.

Our visit with Jill and Beth at Main Street Coffee was short but sweet. By twelve-thirty, I was home, pacing the floor and wishing I had stayed with Paige at least for the afternoon. My pathetic need to be at home in case Cole miraculously showed up was eating away at me.

171

The cool morning had turned into a warm afternoon. I considered a hike, but that idea depressed me for obvious reasons. I thought about paddling around the lake for a while, except that sounded lonely. Then I had the perfect idea. There was one person who could take my mind off of Cole. And that was Ruthie.

I had made sugar cookies a few days ago; they were Ruthie's favorite. So I packed a few in a tin and made my way next door. There was a bright red kayak tied to her dock. While it could have been a new toy of hers, I had a feeling it belonged to her boyfriend.

I hesitated before ringing the bell. The last thing I wanted to do was interrupt anything, but I had yet to officially meet William, and I was curious. I had to make sure he was good enough for my Ruthie. My finger wasn't off the doorbell when the door flew open.

"Well, hello there, honey. You must be Chelsea. I'd recognize those games anywhere," said the handsome older man, presumed to be William.

"Excuse me?"

"The legs, my lady. Ruthie tells me all about the beauty next door with the legs to die for. She could only mean you. I'm William, a close friend to Ruthie." He gave me a vivacious hug and said, "Now, come on in. Ruthie is in the kitchen fixin' some tea."

William was as spunky as Ruthie, and surprisingly younger. He had to be in his late sixties. He was handsome with a charming personality. He led me to the kitchen where Ruthie had already set an extra spot at the table.

"Hi, Ruthie. I don't want to intrude. I brought you some sugar cookies. Your favorite. How about you, William? I hope you like them too."

"Thanks, dear," said Ruthie. "They will go perfectly with the tea. Stay. It'll only be another minute."

"Yes, you must stay. Share your youth with us, Chelsea. Tell us something fun," said William.

"Hmm..." I thought for a second. My last few days consisted of nothing fun. "Twister. That's fun. Right? Or...I don't know. Maybe Uno."

"So young, and so serious," said William.

"My mother says I have an old soul," I replied.

Suddenly, William caught Ruthie's eye, and his demeanor changed. He sat down in front of me like he was preparing for an interrogation. It was odd, yet funny. I threw a delighted smirk at Ruthie. She responded with a furrowed brow and nodded her head with great seriousness as she poured tea into three teal ceramic mugs. I took her cue and became more attentive. Things were taking a serious turn. Intrigued, I leaned in with my chin on my hands, elbows on the table.

"Sweet child," said William. "I find there's rarely a point in beating around the bush. Subtlety is not my style. So tell us–are you seeing anyone?"

"Not really. Well, maybe," I responded. It wasn't a question I had anticipated.

"Oh dear. That's a terrible answer!" Ruthie howled.

"Yes, bad answer. Why so unsure? What confuses you about the question?" William asked. Then his eye brows spiked, his finger shot up in the air, and he proclaimed, "Ah! Wrong question for me to ask. It's not what's confusing about my question. It's what's confusing, or shall we say complicated, about your answer. Correct?"

I hesitated, then answered honestly. "Yes. I'm sorry, but I don't have a conclusive answer to that question." To Ruthie I said, "I know you have a lot of nephews, but I don't want to be set up. I don't think I'm in any position to be dating right now. I appreciate the thought, though."

Ruthie and William were silent. They exchanged a glance and a nod of the head. Their eyes moved and their hands gestured, but there was no audible speech other than some hushed sounds. It was the strangest thing. They were mostly communicating through body language and facial expression. Clearly, I had been the topic of an earlier discussion. Finally, William spoke.

"First thing that pops into your head. Yes or no: Do you have a boyfriend?"

"Yes. I think. I mean, if I have to lean one way or the other. I haven't heard from him in a few days." I shrugged. "Which makes me wonder if something is wrong; thus, the confusion. Now, where is all this going?"

Ruthie plunked down our tea and sat next to me. She put her hand on mine.

"Well dear, I don't want to alarm you, but I called the police last night. There was a boy lurking around your house. William spotted him, and we became suspicious," Ruthie said, with fidgety hands and a furrowed brow. It was an unusual look for Ruthie.

"What do you mean by lurking?" I asked.

"He was a young man, and he was poking around for a few hours. I wasn't sure if you were home at first. He wandered around and pulled at a couple of doors, peeked into some windows, and then sat on your back porch for a while," said Ruthie.

Cole? I wondered if the spare key was still under the turtle rock in the garden and why he hadn't used it.

"What happened when you called the police?" I asked.

"He was gone by the time they got here. Any idea who it might have been? Perhaps the questionable boyfriend you were talking about?" Ruthie said.

"I guess it could have been him, except he's supposed to be out of town. What did he look like?"

"About William's height. How tall are you, sweetheart?"

William shot out of his chair, threw his chest out, and straightened his back.

"Five foot ten," he responded. "He had a tight military cut and was dressed to the nines. Fancy collared shirt, shiny shoes. He was just kicking back on the porch like he owned the place. We called the police when he tried to jimmy the lock."

"A collared shirt and short hair? Are you sure?" I asked, feeling nauseous. As much as I didn't want to believe it was Brent, there was the height factor that did him in. Brent was five foot ten exactly. Cole was at least six foot two, if not more. Then I remembered something.

"You've seen Cole, Ruthie. He's the guy who pulled me out of the lake a while back. When you hurt your ankle. Do you remember what he looked like?"

"Oh, yes. I remember him quite well. He was a looker. The boy we saw wasn't him," she said definitively to William. "Come to think of it, he looked a little like that other fella you went on a date with. It was dark last night, and when that boy picked you up the other day he was dressed more casual. Gee dear, I hadn't put that together until now."

"That was Brent. And it wasn't a date. As a matter of fact, dinner hadn't gone well. He's been somewhat overbearing lately."

"He tried to break into your home. I'd call that more than over-bearing," said William as he slid back into the chair across from me. "We think he may have seen us watching him, and that's why he left."

"Lock your doors tonight. William is staying here for a few days. We are a holler away. William and I will be right over if you need us."

"Absolutely," William exclaimed.

The thought of the invincible super-William coming to my rescue with his trusty sidekick made me want to laugh. I imagined them with red capes- the Super Guardian Grandparent duo.

"Thank you," I said. "You guys are the best." I put a hand on William's and the other on Ruthie's back. "I like you William. Ruthie might have to hang on to you for a while."

Ruthie flashed a wide smile and said, "So tell me, you found that boy from the lake?"

"Cole and I bumped into each other the day after we met. He's here all the time. I'm sure you've seen him fishing off the dock."

Ruthie shook her head and glanced at William.

"I haven't noticed anyone fishing on your dock, dear. Sometimes when William is here we get too busy around the house." William's face turned pink, and a grin spread across his face. "William has a dreadful hernia that he's having repaired next week. Soon we'll have plenty of time to be nosey neighbors, but for now, we make the best of it. Just what you wanted to hear. Right?"

William got up with his tea and headed to the back door, smack-ing Ruthie on the behind. She laughed like a schoolgirl, which in turn had me giggling too.

My enchanting afternoon with Ruthie and William stretched into the early evening. After dining with them on their back deck, a boat puttered by the house. I thought for sure it was Cole. When I saw it wasn't him, misery hit me. I excused myself, thanked them for a lovely time, and dragged myself home. I knew myself well enough to know that my misery didn't love company, it preferred solitude.

CHAPTER 25

My phone rang at seven o'clock. Finally, it was Cole. I tried to hold out before answering so he didn't think I was sitting around waiting for his call. But who was I kidding?

"Hello?" I said.

"Hi. How are you?"

There it was, that buttery voice that made my knees slippery every time.

"I'm good. I was wondering when I'd hear from you." Or if I'd hear from you, I thought.

"I'm sorry. My phone died, and I didn't have my charger. I'm ashamed to admit this, but I don't know your number by heart. You are number one on my speed dial, though."

"Oh... Don't worry about it," I managed to sputter out. Was I really number one in his phone, or was he just being nice?

"I found your home number in the phone book and tried to call you from my Gram's landline a bunch of times, but you didn't answer. I missed you."

"You missed me?"

"Is that hard to imagine?"

Ugh! I was an idiot. My head was spinning with all sorts of derogatory names for myself to express my stupidity. Not only was I speed dial number one, but he did call me. I was just in too much of a depressed funk to answer the phone.

"We don't use the land line very much so we never bothered to set up the messaging. I went to dinner with Paige, then stayed at her house last night." After my pointless breakdown.

"I was going to swing by, but I wasn't sure if you were home. May I stop over?" Cole said.

I had a moment of hesitation as the hispanic beauty flashed before my eyes. I shook it off and said, "Yes, of course. Come over."

After we hung up, I ran out the back door as fast as I could. I paced up and down the dock while several things raced through my head.

First, I was going to have to tell Cole about the suspicious boy who Ruthie and William saw, which meant he'd be paying Brent a visit. My stomach churned.

Next, I had acted like an embarrassing crazy lady when I thought he didn't call. But just now, I found out that not only had he called, but he missed me. He missed me!

Last, there was a thought tucked away in a dark corner of my mind. Even though I wanted to believe Cole's reason for not calling, a small part of me questioned the truth. I had no reason for that pin-sized amount of doubt, yet it wouldn't go away. Suspicion pecked at my brain like an incessant chicken pecking at bugs in the dirt. Peck, peck, peck.

Several minutes later, he surprised me when he came down the side steps and crossed the porch.

"Hi!" I squealed.

I ran down the dock and jumped into his arms before he even set foot on the grass. Neither one of us was willing to let go first.

"Were you fishing?" he asked.

"No. But I was hoping to pick up a cute fisherman. No boat tonight?"

"Nope. It would have kept me from you for another five minutes. I wouldn't have survived that."

With each word that fell out of his mouth, my doubts slipped away. For a little while anyway.

Cole and I spent a quiet night on the dock. When conversation found its way to how we spent our weekend, I left out the nervous breakdown and the possibility that Brent might have been here.

By two in the morning, Cole was sound asleep on the couch, and I was nestled under his arm. I kept slipping off the edge, and my arm was falling asleep, so I dragged myself up to bed. You would think I

178

would have been refreshed and happy the next morning. That was not the case. Instead, I was a grumpy jerk.

I went downstairs expecting to find Cole still asleep, but he was gone. Sometime around ten, he showed up with donuts and coffee. That was the day of our first fight.

I told him, "We could have gone out for breakfast."

"I didn't want to wake you," he replied.

"Sure. You probably had to call your girlfriend," I mumbled.

"What?"

"We never go anywhere in public. I don't suppose you've noticed that."

"That's okay. I like having you all to myself," he said.

He reached for my hand. I turned and walked away.

"I like to go out sometimes. Are you afraid to be seen in public with me?"

"No. We are out on the lake all the time."

"That's different. We don't go on real dates, like to the movies and dinner. Maybe we could try that," I suggested, trying to control my temper.

"Sure," he said.

You could hear a pin drop while we ate our donuts and drank our coffee. The pressing questions and doubts in my head made it impossible to think, until finally, I could no longer keep my thoughts to myself.

I slammed my coffee mug on the counter and snapped, "Are you hiding something, Cole? Do you have a girlfriend? Or maybe... maybe you're married?"

I swallowed hard and stared at the remnants of my donut. Out of the corner of my eye, I saw him drop his head and release a shallow sigh. I was afraid.

"Are you sure you want the answer to that?"

"Just tell me the truth." My heart plummeted.

"No. I'm not married."

He went back to his coffee and flipped through a magazine on the counter.

"And?"

I needed him to finish. I had to hear the words for it to be real. I waited to hear him say it.

"Yes, I have a girlfriend. Any other questions?"

"No more questions. I want you to leave, please."

I wanted to run to my room and cry. I wanted to lock him out and never see him again. But I kept my composure. I stood, expecting him to leave. Except he didn't move. He continued to read the magazine.

"Cole? Did you hear me?" I sighed.

"Yes, Chelsea. You have more questions. Ask them."

"No. There are no more questions. Thanks for being honest." I rolled my eyes.

"Can I ask you a question?"

"Go ahead. Then you should go. I don't think I can keep myself together for much longer."

"Do you have a boyfriend?"

"What? No. I thought maybe we were on our way to that point. Seems I was wrong."

My nose started to run, my eyes watered. I turned away from him to wipe my face with my sleeve.

"Chelsea, are you really upset?" he asked, jumping up from his chair. "I thought we were goofing around. Are you being serious? How could you think there's someone else?"

"You just said you have a girlfriend. I would call that someone else."

"Unless that someone is you. You're the only girlfriend I have, Einstein." He wrapped me in a hug.

"You think I'm stupid?" I sobbed.

"What? No! I was joking. Oh boy, let's take a step back, Chels." Cole rubbed my back for a minute, then said, "Talk to me. What's going on?"

I tried to gather my thoughts before answering so I wouldn't sound like an idiot. Finally, I said, "I'm sorry. I had a long weekend.

I'm exhausted. I thought for sure you hadn't called because you were with someone else."

"Why would you think that?"

"You never take me out. You go away and don't call. And–I had a dream. Maybe. Who can tell these days? "

Cole took my shoulders, looked into my eyes, and said, "You need to keep yourself together. You are stronger than this. The most important thing right now is your health." Cole shook his head. "You need to believe that I feel as strongly for you as I think you feel for me. Do you understand?"

I nodded my head, and once again, doubt lingered.

"You need to get better. Stop worrying about us. We'll get through this," he promised.

I wanted to believe what Cole said. Except, the dejected look on his face was back, the same one he had on my dock last week. The look that festered doubt and concern.

He stayed for the rest of the day. We never talked about Brent showing up here Friday night, it hadn't even crossed my mind. After dinner, Cole left with what I thought were promising and comforting words. Little did I realize how prophetic they were.

"You are the only thing I have, Chelsea. You're the only one who matters. Just remember that when you doubt me." He kissed me and said, "While some people search the entire world for the right person, others only have to open their eyes."

CHAPTER 26

By noon on Wednesday, I was done with my short shift and heading to Rochester with Paige. My appointment wasn't until seven, so we set out to make the most of the day: shopping, people watching on Park Avenue, dinner.

All afternoon, I had a feeling that we were being followed. My paranoia seemed to have surpassed the suspicious boat in the lake. Thanks to the all-knowing internet, where mass amounts of information were at your finger tips, self diagnosis was easy. That's where I learned about paranoid schizophrenia. I had the symptoms, including the lucid dreams and now, most importantly, the paranoia. While that would explain many of my issues, I couldn't buy into it until I put a few other theories to rest.

As Paige and I pulled into the hospital parking lot the same tan Envoy that had followed me last week pulled in behind us. I stopped at the gate, grabbed a ticket, and watched the gate drop behind my car. When I saw a hand reach from the Envoy and take a ticket, I proceeded at a crawl. And as the gate closed behind it, I stopped and blocked him in.

I wasn't sure what gave me the courage, maybe it was because I was so angry, but I got out of the car and marched straight to the SUV. A strange looking man sat at the steering wheel glaring at me through thick black-rimmed glasses. With his wild, curly, white hair and black handlebar mustache, he looked like a cartoon character.

I tapped on his window. He rolled it down, and huffed, "Come on. I'm late for an appointment."

"Who are you here to see?"

"That's not your business. Move your car," he said.

"Why are you following me?"

I waited for an answer with my arms crossed.

"I'm not following you."

His over-stuffed jowl wiggled as he shook his head, his mouth hung open.

"I'm calling the cops," I said, pulling my phone from my pocket.

"Go ahead," he replied.

"Hey, Chelsea!" yelled Paige, getting out of the car. "Should we show him the pictures of him following you all over the city? We have that video of him taking pictures of you."

That got the man's attention.

"Look, girlie, it sounds more like you were following me."

That's when I laid it all out for him. "I randomly drove all over the city to see if you would follow me. I went all the way to the east side to get gas and far to the south to get even more gas. Then I came back up north to go to a grocery store. You followed me down every out-of-the-way side street I took. Didn't you think that was a little strange?"

"Ha! Someone frickin' underestimated you, sweetheart. Your bulb isn't quite as dim as I was told."

"Who exactly told you that?" I demanded.

"I ain't telling you who I'm working for. So ya better move your car and let me out."

"Do me a favor. Tell Brent to get a life. Tell him if he comes anywhere near me, I'll have my boyfriend beat the crap out of him before I have him arrested." I turned to walk back to my car.

From behind me, the man snickered and murmured, "Boyfriend?"

I snapped back around.

"Is that what this is all about? It's none of his business who I date."

"I ain't saying nothin', sweetheart."

Just looking at this jerk, with his smug grin peeking out from his greasy lip mop, made my blood boil. I could have laid into him for an hour. But what would be the point?

So all I said was, "Just give him my message. And don't call me sweetheart."

I stormed back to the car, swung into a parking spot, and glared at him as he drove away.

"Well? That guy obviously followed you," Paige said.

"He wouldn't say who hired him, but he didn't deny it was Brent. I don't know what to think–except Brent has completely lost it."

"Maybe you should report this, just in case," she suggested.

"Report what? That Brent may or may not have had some creeper follow me around for a few days?"

"Yes. We have pictures and a video to prove it."

"It doesn't prove that Brent's involved. He'll give him my message. Maybe now Brent will realize I'm not an idiot and leave me alone."

"I'm holding onto these pictures," said Paige. "You should go to the police and at least make a report."

"He's been caught. The game is over. I'm no fun for him anymore." I hugged Paige. "Thanks for your help. You're the best."

"Be careful, Chelsea. This worries me."

Paige and I headed into the hospital and up to Neurology. Dr. Armstrong was handing papers to his secretary when we entered the waiting room.

"Hi, ladies," he said. "Come in and sit down."

We took a seat across from Dr. Armstrong's ornate wooden desk. His office looked down over the city and you could see all the way to Lake Ontario. He must have been someone important to have this view.

"Thank you for squeezing me in. I'm sure you have a million other things you could be doing," I said.

"Anything for you, Chelsea. I get the impression you're important to my son." He folded his hands on the desk. "Tell me what's been going on- from the start, please."

"Your son?" Paige asked.

Oops. I had forgotten to tell Paige. I motioned to Dr. Armstrong, and said, "He's Jackson's father."

"For real? I didn't know," she stammered. "He didn't tell us. His last name..."

"Scott is his middle name. Jackson Scott Armstrong. Coming from a family of doctors seems to tarnish his tough guy image. Plus, he's a private guy. Which is why I was surprised he was sharing you with me at all," he said to me with a chuckle. "Now, back to you."

My face got red. And of course, Paige gave me an "I told you so" grin.

I filled him in on the fainting spells and headaches, leaving out the visions for now. That part was embarrassing. I was sure he'd heard it all before, but I wasn't ready to go there. I had already prepped Paige for that lack of information, and although she disagreed with me, she kept her mouth shut.

"So tell me, what do you think about starting with a psychological evaluation? It's my understanding that you've had a lot of changes going on in your life," he said. "Perhaps the headaches and fainting could be attributed to that."

"I don't think she needs a psychological evaluation, doctor. She needs some medical scans. Right? CAT Scan, MRI and all that," Paige chimed in.

I looked at her with my mouth open, ready to answer the question myself. Dr. Armstrong looked at her then back at me. With a smile, he asked again.

"Chelsea, do you think we need to start with a psych eval? The forms you filled out indicate that you have a history of anxiety, not necessarily depression. But that doesn't rule out other conditions."

"I don't think it's in my head, like a psychological thing. It definitely seems like a medical issue. But you're the doctor. Whatever you think is best."

"I spoke to Dr. Lim about your anxiety, her tests, and your current medications. All that seems to be under control. So based on all you've told me, and the review of your medical and psychological history, I recommend a blood work up and a few scans." He looked at Paige and said, "Are you her sister?"

"No. I'm her best friend."

The doctor raised his eyebrows and asked me, "And what about your family? Your parents? Do they know you're here?"

"Yes," I lied. Something I seemed to be doing more of lately. "They couldn't make it. That's why they sent Paige with me. In case I forgot something you said today. Extra ears."

He looked perplexed; I'm sure he wondered what my parents found more important than their daughter's health. But the fact was, I didn't technically live with my parents at the moment, and therefore, I was responsible for myself. Should he ask, that would be what I told him.

"I'll put in the order for your blood tests. Get to them as soon as you can, please. Also, I'm going to schedule you for the soonest possible CAT and MRI. Kathy will call you in the morning to set that up. Does that sound like a good plan?"

"Yes. Thank you, Dr. Armstrong," I said.

On the way home, I made Paige promise not to say anything to Jackson about the appointment. It wasn't his business. We were supposed to meet Jill and Beth out, but I was tired. After shaming me for acting like a "boring old lady", Paige dropped me off and headed out to meet the girls.

As I waved to Paige, I spotted Cole sitting at the unlit fire pit, staring out at the lake. The reflection from the Edison lights twinkled in the water. I kicked my shoes off before descending the steps and sneaked up behind him.

"Hello, beautiful," he said.

"How did you hear me? I was so quiet."

I knelt behind him, draped my arms over his shoulders, and rested my head against his.

"I smelled your sweet scent," Cole said.

He lifted his arms over his head. His fingers sifted through my hair.

"Is that your subtle way of telling me I need a shower?" I asked.

"It's my way of telling you that you smell amazing."

"Don't flirt with me. That could lead to bad things."

"The only bad thing right now is that I can't see you." He tugged me around the chair to sit on his lap. "How'd it go tonight?"

"Fine. He's sending me for tests, like I figured."

He seemed to study my eyes, but it felt like he was diving into my soul. My heart fluttered.

"Good," he said. "Get things going as soon as you can, even if that means cutting back your work hours. You're no good to them if you're sick. If you need me to go with you, tell me. I want to be there for you."

I didn't say so, but his offer confused me. It seemed he could take me for a CAT scan but not to a movie.

"I would have had Paige come down if I knew you were here."

"I didn't mean to surprise you. I wanted to hear all about the appointment."

After filling him in on the appointment, he started a fire, and we sat outside under the starlit sky and talked. Then Cole asked the dreaded question.

"Any word from Brent?"

Darn it. "Not really," I said.

"I'm a guy. I know guys. He came here?"

"Maybe?"

"Is that a question or just a crappy answer?"

"Truthfully..." I began.

"That's how I like it."

"Ruthie and her boyfriend, William, saw someone walking around the house last Friday night. They called the police, but whoever it was left before they got here. The description sounded like Brent. But I'm not certain, so don't worry."

I held my breath.

I waited.

I waited longer.

Minutes went by; I got nervous.

Then, "Is that it?" he asked in an unruffled voice.

"I haven't seen him. He hasn't approached me."

"That doesn't answer my question."

"I haven't had any direct contact with him, if that helps."

"No, it doesn't help. I'd like a clear answer. So I'll rephrase. Is there something you're not telling me?"

187

"What are you, the FBI? I think you missed your calling."

Telling him about the guy who followed me could take things to the next level. I did not want to go there, but Cole was making it hard to avoid.

Cole got up from his chair. Afraid that he was getting up to leave, I sat forward and got ready to jump up and stop him. Instead, he knelt down in front of me. Cole took my hands and plummeted back into my soul with those green eyes of his.

"Chelsea, I'm worried about you. I won't kill him. I won't break any laws and end up in jail. So tell me what you're keeping from me. I may simply have to spend more time here in case he does come back."

"I hate to see you so worried. I'm okay."

He waited. He was far more patient than I would have been.

"I don't want you to be mad. I don't want Brent to get in the way of what we have," I said, holding back tears. Again with the tears. I couldn't remember a time in my life when I cried as much as I had in the last few weeks.

"I told you, you are all I have, and nothing will take me away from you. Especially not some little jack-ass like Brent," he said with half a smile.

With that, I told him everything. Keeping things from him only made matters worse.

Cole wrung his hands–a lot. He paced back and forth in front of the fire–a lot. And he muttered unintelligible obscenities directed at Brent under his breath–a lot. When I was done talking, he was quiet. Too quiet.

"I want this all to stop. To just go away. I want Brent out of my life with as little confrontation as possible, without dragging you into this. I thought I could deal with it on my own. Chaos like this doesn't happen in my life. Not until now, that is. I'm not accustomed to drama and chaos. It's uncomfortable and embarrassing." I put my head down in shame.

Cole snapped out of deep thought and squatted down to my eye level. He said, "Thank you for telling me everything. I'm sorry for what you've had to endure without me. I'm sure this is all crazy for you."

"It's kind of childish," I said. My hand skimmed his cheek bone, stopping at his mouth. I traced his lips then kissed him.

"You have greater things to worry about. I guess I'll just have to stay here more often. Is that okay?" he asked. I nodded my head in agreement. "The alternative is going to Brent. But I have a strong feeling he'll be visiting us in the not-so-distant future. And to be honest, that will be one satisfying visit."

"No broken jaws?" I asked.

"No promises. But I'll try," he responded.

Cole hugged me for what felt like an eternity. I knew he hated Brent and wanted nothing more than for him to leave me alone. No one has ever made me feel so safe.

"What about your parents? Will they be angry if I stay?"

"I don't plan on telling them. They don't know about you yet."

That sparked the conversation about meeting one another's families.

"I feel bad about being dishonest. But I can't leave you here alone anymore. So until you're ready to tell them…"

"I was thinking maybe starting with my sister."

Cole nodded his head. I continued.

"I'm meeting Meggie Saturday night at CJ's Pub. Her boyfriend's band is playing at nine. It will be my first time meeting him."

"Cool," Cole said.

And now for the hail Mary. "Come with me?"

His face momentarily dropped into his hands. He looked up and said, "I already made plans. I'm meeting some of the guys out; an annual Memorial Day thing. We go to the fireworks on campus, then there's a party."

"Right. You should go out with your friends."

"I don't mean to keep disappointing you."

He was right, I was disappointed. However, it was hard to argue the point. He rarely talked about spending time with his friends. I was responsible for that. Since it sounded as if he's going to be spending even more time here, I owed him, at the very least, a night out with the guys. Without me and my problems.

"I haven't seen the guys for a while. But I won't be out late. I'll meet you back here afterwards. I won't leave you alone all night."

"Please, go out with your friends. That's a great idea. I shouldn't be so selfish, using up all your time with my silly drama. And don't worry about coming here afterwards. I'll be fine."

"Chels, I could stay here with you for the rest of eternity and be happy. You could get sick of me, and my friends could get pissed off that I ditched them, but I could do that easily," he said.

"I would never ask you to do that."

"But I would do it."

"And that's why..." I stopped short. I caught myself before I told him that I loved him. It was milliseconds from popping out of my mouth. My face turned bright red.

"What?" he asked.

"I think you're sweet. And I'm beat. I'm heading up."

"I'm following."

"No funny business, mister," I joked.

"I'll stay in the spare room."

"Oh, no. You're staying with me. You're way better than any sleeping pill."

Surprisingly, that night I had a nightmare. I dreamt that Cole was married and I confronted him about his wife, the woman from the newscast. He explained that he loved her and went on to tell me that he kept all sorts of unimaginable secrets.

The dream was so real that I was furious when I woke up in the middle of the night. He was not in bed, but the bathroom light was on. I was stewing; I wanted to confront him when he came back to bed. Lucky for him, I fell back to sleep.

I was still angry when I woke up in the morning, and despite my best effort, I could not shake it. I couldn't understand the level of irritation I was experiencing. I loved him so much, yet I was furious over an absurd dream. I jumped out of bed and hurried to catch him before he left. I was just in time as he headed out the door.

CHAPTER 27

"Good morning," Cole said, kissing me on the cheek. "You look crabby. Didn't you sleep well?"

"No. Bad dreams," I said, trying to control my growing anger.

"I'm late," he said. "I'll see you tonight."

He kissed me again and walked out the door. I told myself everything was fine; I was overreacting. But I couldn't stop thinking about the part of my dream where Cole told me he loved his wife. Then the red-head I saw him with at The Green popped into my head, and I lost it. I rushed out onto the deck after him.

"Cole!"

"Yes?"

His smile beamed. He was innocent. And yet, all I wanted to do was attack.

"They were just dreams, Chelsea," Cole said. "Bad dreams, I know. But dreams, nonetheless. Go have some coffee, and you'll feel better."

He blew me a kiss and headed up the driveway.

Please come back, I thought. Then I hollered after him, "See you later!"

He was right. I had had nightmares before, and this feeling would pass.

All day I tried to talk myself out of being mad at Cole. Except, as the day went on, my anger only fueled. My thoughts became obsessive. After a month of dating, I hadn't met his family or friends, and he hadn't met mine. The time we spent together was always on his terms. He was hiding something. He wasn't who I thought he was. He was a liar, I just knew it.

191

As my day spiraled into hell, my tolerance grew short for just about everything including customers at Trend and my boss. Other than conversations that revolved around work, I pretty much avoided contact with Jackson. When he asked me how I was feeling, I ignored him and walked away. When my mother called, I dumped it. And when Meggie called to discuss our plans Saturday night, I told her I had no interest in listening to Reznor's stupid band.

On the way home, I stopped for gas. That's when I became more than merely grumpy. I became a colossal hellion.

After I filled the tank, I went into the adjoining mini mart to buy gum and discovered that there were three people in line in front of me. Outraged, I snatched a pack of gum off the rack. Several boxes of candy, gum, and mints crashed to the floor. I kicked them out of my way and stormed to the counter. Having zero patience, I threw a crumpled twenty dollar bill in the cashier's face as she cashed someone out.

"You are the slowest person on the planet," I snapped at her. The people in line scowled at me and made angry comments. They were staring at me. They were judging me. "Shut up!" I screamed at them.

As I made my way to the exit, someone grabbed my elbow. A shock zipped through me like I was being electrocuted. I let out a gasp and shook my arm free.

"Don't touch me," I barked.

A giant stood before me with a grin on his face and my crumbled twenty in his hand.

"What?" I snapped, instantly recognizing the giant.

"Here," he said, handing me the money. "The gum is on me. Try to have a better day."

He tilted his head. His grin faded, and he glared at me. Everyone was staring at us.

A filthy mechanic peeked out from the garage and said, "Adam, what's going on?"

Adam ignored the mechanic and said to me, "We just can't get away from each other. Can we?"

I glared at him, then said, "Man, what's up with you? Fireman, bartender, gas station attendant. Is there anywhere that you don't work?" I asked.

"I don't work here," Adam snapped back. The bogus grin made its way back to his face. "Why don't you take your money and gum, and call it a day? Come on, let me buy you lunch. You seem hangry."

"Hey, don't try to pull some reverse psychological crap on me. And since you don't work here, this is none of your business," I said, waving my hands towards the scattered gum and the agitated cashier. I shoved the money into Adam's shirt pocket and chirped, "Keep it."

His lips pursed, and he shook his head. "Such an angry girl," he said. "Come on, let's talk it out."

My blood was boiling. My fists were balled and ready to go. This guy must have a death wish. Could he not see that I was ready to blow? I opened my mouth to scream something at him, but I couldn't think of anything to say. I couldn't think straight at all.

I whipped around and headed for the exit door, almost pummeling a small child as he entered with his mother.

"Hey, watch where you're going" she exclaimed.

I marched to my car, hopped in, and ripped open the gum. I shoved a piece in my mouth. When I looked up, I saw Adam storming towards my car. I threw him the finger, revved the engine, and peeled out of the parking lot.

Moments later, it all hit me. I almost hurt a small child, and I could have been beaten up by his irate mother. Adam sure as hell could have killed me with his pinky finger. And the way I treated that cashier... Cole had once referred to me as the tundra winds. But heck, the tundra winds were nothing compared to the category five hurricane I had become.

I called Paige on my way home and told her I was loosing it. It was obvious that I needed help.

"At least you're aware of what's happening," she said. "You say you're upset because of a dream? You understand that's irrational. Right?"

"Yes, but it's uncontrollable. Completely. What should I do?"

"Go straight home. And stay away from Cole. Wait for this to blow over."

"He's coming by after work. I need to talk this through with him. Something's not right. That must be why I feel this way."

"Not necessarily. I've been thinking that maybe a psychological evaluation wouldn't be such a bad idea."

Again, I lost it. "Just spit it out, Paige. Tell me you think I'm crazy. I don't have time for this kind of crap."

"Yeah. That's what I mean. Your emotions are unpredictable; they're all over the place, Chelsea."

"No kidding, genius. How does your head feel with that inflated brain in it? As if a tumor isn't number one on the short list of what's killing me," I blurted out.

"Tumor? Is that what you think? Chelsea, I'm coming over. I'll be there in half an hour."

"Don't bother. Cole doesn't care to meet any of my friends. That would ruin the charade. His girlfriend might find out."

I couldn't control my displaced anger or the words that were coming out of my mouth. I knew I was being nasty, but there was a part of me that felt I was completely justified. My next thought was that I needed to call Brent and give him a piece of my mind.

"I gotta go," I said and hung up on Paige.

Before I knew it, I was home. Assuming Cole was already there, my call to Brent was put on hold. I tore through the door and down the stairs. Cole stood in front of the sliding glass door. His face was serious, his stance looked ready for the tirade that I was about to unleash. Paige... had she called the house to warn him?

"Well?" I said. "You have some things that you need to explain. Why won't you meet any of my friends or family? Why don't you take me out on dates like normal boyfriends do?"

"Whoa. Did you have a bad day?" he said, holding his hands up as if surrendering.

"No. More like a bad month. Admit it, Cole. You're married. Either that, or you have a girlfriend."

"I thought we talked about this."

"We did. And you lied. So tell me. No. You know what, just leave. There's no point in having this conversation because you've done nothing but lie so far."

His eyes were wide and full of concern.

"Stop thinking and go. I'll survive without you. I have for the last eighteen years," I steamed.

He took a step towards me, slowly, with his palms facing me.

"Enough with the theatrics," I said. "What? Do you think I'm going to hit you or something? Leave!"

My face contorted, and my fists clenched at my sides. I had never experienced such rage. I wanted to hit him.

"Do it!" he yelled at me. "Hit me! Come on, let it out, Chelsea. You're mad? Then do it. Hit me."

"Leave!" I screamed.

"Fine," he bellowed back, startling me. He took a deep breath and let it out. Then with a quiet, controlled voice, he said, "But understand something. I won't turn my back on you. No matter what's wrong with you."

Lies. I didn't want to hear it. I squeezed my eyes shut and yelled, "Get out!"

And just like that, he was gone. When I opened my eyes, he had vanished out the sliding glass door.

I collapsed in tears. By the time Paige got there, I was nothing but a puddle of salt water on the kitchen floor. She got me into bed, begrudgingly gave me a melatonin pill, then stayed the night.

In the morning, Paige left a note saying that she had to open Trend by nine. She demanded that I call her as soon as I woke up or she would be back by noon. By ten thirty, I had texted my mom to see how her trip was going, apologized to Paige, and begged forgiveness from my sister. My behavior yesterday was atrocious. I had no real excuse for anyone. All I could do was move forward with today.

I didn't call Cole. I couldn't. He was better off without me. I loved him too much to do that to him ever again. And if I was being honest, I loved him too much to let him watch me die.

CHAPTER 28

CJ's Pub was packed. It turned out that Public Executioner was quite popular. And frankly, it was because Reznor knew how to rock the crowd; he was an incredible performer with a sick voice. By the end of the third song, I was hooked.

Of course, Reznor wasn't his given name. He legally changed his name at the age of twenty in honor of the lead singer in his favorite band. There was no denying that he was super cool. I could see Meggie's attraction to him.

I stayed a little longer than I had expected. Then after the first set, despite wanting to stay, my emotions began to surge. Maybe it was how sweet and affectionate Reznor was to Meggie in public. He wasn't trying to hide her or the fact that he was crazy about her. Whatever the case, I wanted to end the night on a happy note. I hugged them goodbye before Reznor started his second set.

Controlling my emotions had become quite effortful in the last few days. It was all I could do to keep from bursting into tears for no reason or unjustly lashing out at someone. Everyday it became more clear that something was wrong with me. Nonetheless, Cole hadn't deserved my imprudent and cruel outburst the other day.

Two days had gone by, and I still hadn't talked to Cole. I was sure he was furious about our last conversation (if you could call it that). I hadn't meant to be so accusatory or obnoxious, but that's precisely what I had been.

As a result of Public Executioner's popularity, I had to park half a mile down the street. As I approached my car, I saw someone in a SUNY Geneseo baseball hat walking towards me with his head down and his hands in his pockets. His build and gait reminded me of Cole. I'd never known him to wear a hat; but the closer he got, the more I became convinced that it was him.

He glanced up and seemed to look right through me as he passed under the street light. But those eyes, I'd know them anywhere. It was him. Finally, we could talk, and I could get rid of my guilt and self-loathing.

Please don't hate me, I thought.

Cole ran his eyes over me once more. His face lit up for a brief instant, then his gaze went back to the sidewalk. My heart sank. He was still angry. He kept his head down and walked past me. Yes, I had been mean, but I couldn't believe he would blatantly ignore me. I turned to say something to him and found that he had stopped and turned around. Cole eyeballed me with a smile plastered on his face.

"Hi there," he said.

"Hi." I looked to the ground. "You were going to ignore me?"

Cole took a few steps in my direction. He opened his mouth to speak, but I said, "That's okay. I deserve it. I'm sorry."

He shook his head and squinted his eyes. "What are you sorry for? I'm still dry," he said.

"What?" I giggled at his cryptic comment.

"I came by. I figured either you're never home, or you were avoiding me."

Cole took another step towards me. The hat gave him a whole different look, a boyishly cute one that I adored. He didn't seem very mad anymore, but I wanted to be sure. I needed to get past the awkwardness.

"Look, I have something to say, so just listen. Okay?"

"Sure," he said.

Cole's face turned serious. He closed in until we were about two feet apart. I had to look way up at him, even in my heels. For some reason he seemed taller, maybe it was the hat.

"The other day, I was stupid. Sometimes I say things that I don't mean. Or I think things that aren't...accurate. I don't get a lot of sleep lately, for whatever reason, but I don't mean to upset you and..."

"I don't think you..."

"Please, just listen. Let me finish," I said, cutting him off.

197

I couldn't tell if the look on his face was one of trepidation or amusement. But I had to get everything I'd been thinking off my chest. So I cut to the chase and spit it out.

"I like you. A lot. You are amazing. I get weird, I know."

He snickered at my choice of words. I rolled my eyes and persevered.

"I've never been very good at talking about how I feel. Things either spill out all at once or they never come out at all. So I'm choosing to spill." I paused, but only for a second, before I lost my nerve. "From the minute you pulled me from the lake, I knew you were different. And to think that now you were going to walk by me and not stop..."

I shook my head and took a deep breath.

"But I did stop," he said. "I couldn't keep walking. I'm drawn to you like...like a bee to a flower, or to you, for that matter."

Neither one of us could control our burst of laughter at his corny reference to our first meeting.

Then with a straight face, he leaned in and said, "Seriously, I do think you're a little crazy. I guess I dig crazy."

I had to tell him I was in love with him. I could no longer hold back.

"I want you to understand, I mean, I want you to know... I think that...I..."

The words were a tangled mess on the tip of my tongue; unruly knots of syllables and phrases. I cleared my throat, shook out my hands, and took a breath.

"Let me put it like this. You make my heart beat too fast, it makes me dizzy. I can't think straight around you. I have to keep my hands clenched or in my pockets so I won't be tempted to–lose control."

I sucked more air into my lungs on the off chance that I needed a gallon of it to get the darn words out. But then he stepped forward and took my hands. With a calculating grin, he held my hands to his chest; something sparked. I cringed and expelled every ounce of that gallon of air on three words.

"See. That's bad."

"How bad?" he asked.

"Very bad."

The energy between us detonated. All of the control I'd been holding on to was lost. I knew the second my hands gripped his sweatshirt, and I yanked his head down to kiss him, that he must have felt the fire as much as I did. There was no confusion as he backed me into the narrow alleyway between the coffee shop and the college store. My back hit the brick wall of the building. We kissed like we'd never kissed before.

My hands found the hot skin under his shirt. His hands found my hips. When I made my way to his shaggy locks, he slid his hands up my back and pulled me against him tighter.

Before I had time to process what was happening, everything came to a screeching halt. He practically threw himself off me, leaving me speechless, breathless, and wanting more. He backed against the opposite wall, and threw a hand over his mouth.

"Whoa," Cole said, trying to catch his breath. "I'm so sorry."

"I'm pretty sure I started that," I said.

He released a noisy sigh and nodded his head. The calculating grin returned. "Right. You started that."

Cole stepped towards me, his eyes locked on mine. Every move he made was slow and deliberate. He placed his hands against the wall, next to my head. My heart pounded like a tribal drum. His gaze moved from my eyes to my lips.

He whispered, "You taste like strawberries. My favorite fruit."

Then he kissed me again.

I could have stayed lost in that kiss forever, but all good things have to come to an end. When the kiss ended, he wrapped his arms around me and lifted me off the ground. Suddenly, fireworks blasted through the cool night sky. For a brief moment, I worried that maybe I was on the verge of passing out. Then I remembered the Memorial Day fireworks had been scheduled to go off at the college.

He said, "Appropriate, don't you think? Although I'm pretty sure I saw fireworks before they started."

He put me down and kissed my forehead. I nodded in agreement, then pointed out that his hat was missing.

"It fell off when you dragged me into the alley," he said with a wink.

He poked his head around the corner. I came up behind him and smoothed down the back of his shirt. People were walking around his hat on the sidewalk, under the light. We stepped out from the alley. Cole plucked his hat from the sidewalk, shook it out, and re-positioned it on his head.

"I like you in a hat," I confessed.

A block away, a man standing in a small crowd of guys waved his hand in our direction. He wore the same SUNY Geneseo hat that Cole was wearing.

The guy yelled, "Hey, man! We're leaving. Come on, let's go."

"I'll meet you there," Cole yelled in return.

"Dude, come on," the guy said.

"I have to get home anyway. Go with your friends" I said, high-tailing it to my car. The last thing I wanted to do was interrupt a guys night out.

"No, wait. Don't go," Cole said, rushing after me.

"You comin'?" asked his friend.

Cole rolled his eyes, turned, and glared at his buddy, who was much closer now.

"Hold on," Cole snapped at him.

I slipped into the car and called out, "I'll see you later."

Cole leaned in and put his hand on the steering wheel.

"Don't leave. Come out with me."

What poor timing; now he wanted to take me out. But how could I crash a guys night and steal him from his friends? No way. What would they think? Besides, I was satisfied that he was no longer mad and giddy thinking about the encounter in the alley. The quality of time far surpassed the quantity.

"I can't go out. I need to get home," I said, starting the car.

Cole removed his hand from the wheel, so I closed the door. He leaned on the open window.

"Please wait. I have to ask. Did you feel that back there? The spark between us?"

I blushed and replied, "Of course, I did. I kind of wanted to talk about that."

"Me too."

Cole's friend was now standing directly behind him. Cole huffed when the guy cleared his throat to make his presence known. He took his hands off the car and turned around. I thought it would be best to end the tension between Cole and his friend, so I took the opportunity and made a quick exit.

I pulled out of the parking space, and said, "I'll catch you later. Now's not the best time for that conversation. Have fun with your friends."

"No wait!" he yelled.

I waved and kept going. In the rear view mirror, I found Cole shrugging his shoulders and throwing his hands in the air as I drove away. His face was full of questions and a dreamy smirk.

Cole was at my house two hours later. From then on, he spent almost every night with me. He was often gone before I woke up. Sometimes I would feel a kiss goodbye or his hand brushing the hair from my face before he left.

My love for Cole remained unspoken for several days after that. The manner in which I would confess my undying love for him? Well, it certainly didn't come out during the most romantic encounter. It was drawn out of me in a moment of dark, cold horror. Sucked from me–like life itself.

CHAPTER 29

~ June ~

At the end of a long tiring day, I pulled down my driveway and into the carport. I was stepping out of my car when I spotted Brent's black BMW coming down the driveway behind me. I grabbed my phone and marched to the front door. In my peripheral vision, I saw Brent closing in.

"Wait!" he yelled. "I want to talk to you for a minute."

I opened the door and hurried inside, but not before Brent had his foot in the door. I held firm and tried to push the door closed.

"I don't want to talk to you," I said, pushing harder.

"Chelsea, come on. Don't be like this. I just need one minute. Is that so much to ask?"

"Go away, Brent."

"I'm not leaving until we talk about something. I have something to show you."

"There's nothing to talk about."

When he couldn't convince me to let him in, the fruitless battle ended. He shoved the door open and stepped inside.

"Leave," I demanded.

"Why? Expecting company? A boyfriend maybe?"

"Yes. He's going to be here any minute," I warned.

"Really? Good. He's the one I want to talk about anyway. And now I get to meet him too. Must be my lucky day."

"I'm not interested in anything you have to say. Get out. Now."

Brent flashed an arrogant smile as if he was enjoying my panic.

"Be honest. You don't have a boyfriend, do you? You just made that up to hurt me."

"If you stay much longer, he'll hurt you. He won't be happy when he finds you here."

"Oh, is that so?" Brent snickered.

"I don't want this to get ugly. I'm asking you to please leave."

"I've had a guy tailing you for weeks." Brent reached into his pocket and pulled out some pictures. "And with the exception of this one time, you've never been seen with anyone."

I snatched the pictures from his hand. They were pictures from last Saturday night when I ran into Cole on the street. There were some of Cole leaning into my car talking to me, and others of Cole and his friend as I drove away. I gasped at the pictures of me going into work, leaving the house, at the grocery store, the gas station, the coffee shop...

Brent had skipped pursuing me and jumped right into stalking. Even though I knew he'd had me followed once or twice, finding out that he had gone to the extent of having my every move photographed changed the game. I was astounded. Brent continued his rant while I studied the pictures.

"Just because you talk to a guy a few times, that doesn't make him your boyfriend, Chelsea. You've been lying. And I'm sick of it."

Brent had his chest pumped out and a smug look on his face.

"What about before these pictures were taken?" I asked. I held up the picture of Cole leaning into my car last Saturday night. "Minutes before this, we were making out. Your guy didn't catch that? That's a shame. Would've made a great Christmas card," I growled.

"He's followed you to work, out with friends, and shopping. He's watched you come and go for weeks. You didn't take your alleged boyfriend to the gallery, and he doesn't take you to dinner or the movies. Nothing. What kind of boyfriend is that? My guy has a lot of hours in, Chels. He came up with nothing. If you were trying to get me jealous, you can stop. Your disturbing game of pretend is straight-up stupid, and it's over."

"You're a joke. I'm embarrassed for you."

"For me? You're the one who is pretending to have a boyfriend. You're pathetic!" he shouted in my face.

"Sorry, but you got scammed. Something tells me your investigator didn't give you my message."

Brent said nothing. He raised his eyebrows and smirked, but only for a second.

"That's what I thought," I said. "I caught your private investigator. He didn't tell you?Maybe because he sucks. Sad that he was busted by your dim little bulb. I'm pretty sure that was the description you gave him."

He crossed his arms and said, "You're a liar."

"Goofy white hair and black rimmed glasses. Handlebar mustache right out of 1975. I saw him twice. My guess would be that he took you for a lot of money, Brent. Money he didn't work for or he would have had some pretty steamy pictures. So, what do you think now? Worth the money?" I said, waving the pictures at Brent.

He grabbed the photos from my hand and shoved them in his jacket pocket. Part of me worried for the investigator's safety when Brent left. But first, I had to get him to leave.

"Doesn't matter. Where's your boyfriend now? Funny how he's not here since you said he's here all the time. Does the poor redneck know you're telling everyone he's your boyfriend?"

I scowled at him but said nothing.

"That's okay. Don't answer. I know where he lives. I can go get some real answers myself."

"You know where he lives?"

"Yes. Why don't we go visit him together? Come on," he said, gesturing towards the door.

"He's here almost every night. He will be here any minute."

"Fine. I'll wait."

"Leave, Brent. I don't want a fight."

He ignored me and leaned against the door with his arms crossed. Brent stared at me, fully prepared to wait.

"Why are you doing this? Just get out!" I screamed, losing my patience.

I pulled my phone from my pocket and started to dial 9-1-1. Brent snatched the phone before I could finish and hung it up. I tried to reach for it, but he shoved me away and stuck the phone in his pocket.

"What, you can't wait now? Is that because no one is coming?" he said.

"I can't wait to see that obnoxious grin get knocked off your face."

Suddenly, he grabbed my arms like he had the last time he was here. He lifted me onto my toes and said through clenched teeth, "You're a lying whore. Just admit that you did this to get me jealous. Then maybe I'll leave." He shook me. "Say it."

Admitting to his accusation wasn't going to make him leave. So I said nothing. I wouldn't deny Cole.

He shook me again. "Don't ignore me!"

Angry that I wouldn't engage in his tirade, he threw me towards the wall. I tried to turn my body to break the impact with my hands, but he threw me with such force that my forehead bounced off the wall. The pain ran directly down my body to my feet. I slid to my knees.

It took a second to get my balance back and stand up. When I did, I scrambled into my room, slammed the door, and locked it. Through cloudy vision, I picked up the phone next to my bed to call for help, but there was no dial tone.

"Sorry, babe. Guess you'll have to wait to make any calls," I heard Brent say on the other end of the line. "Come out and we'll talk."

He had gotten to the spare bedroom phone first and took it off the hook. It prevented me from making an outgoing call. He pounded his fists on the wall that separated us and yelled my name. I slammed the phone down and checked for Cole through the window. My dock was still empty. But Ruthie's wasn't.

"William! William!" I yelled out the window. "Help! Call 9-1-1. There's someone in my house."

"Pardon?" William hollered back.

"Help! Someone's in my house. Call 9-1-1."

William had just had his hernia repaired last week. But that didn't stop him. He jumped up from his chair and hobbled into the house with his cane faster than most men on a good day.

"Damn it, Chelsea. Stop being so stupid," Brent grumbled from the other side of the door. Before I knew what was happening, he smashed open the door with his shoulder. Splinters of wood and chunks of molding went flying through the air. I fell back into the corner and dropped to the floor. Dead weight would be harder for him to lift. Despite my best effort, he yanked me to my feet. I fought as hard as I could. I kicked and thrashed about but to no avail. Brent wrapped me in a bear hug, dragged me out of my room, through the house, and onto the side deck.

"Where are you taking me? Let me go. Let go."

"Shut up, Chelsea. Stop fighting me."

"Where are you taking me?"

"We're going somewhere quiet, where there aren't any nosy neighbors. We need to have a little talk."

Just then, I saw someone out of the corner of my eye and stopped fighting Brent.

"Good girl," he said.

But it wasn't Brent who made me stop fighting. It was Ruthie.

"Let her go," she commanded. "I'm an expert shot, young man. And you're on private property."

There stood Ruthie, no longer the frail, sweet, seventy-eight year old neighbor; but instead, an amazingly strong and powerful woman equipped with a gun that she was clearly ready to use if necessary.

Brent put me down and straightened his back. I scurried out of his reach. He was sizing Ruthie up and undoubtedly trying to figure out how serious she was. She answered that unasked question by cocking her gun and aiming it at his chest.

"I could shoot you in the leg just to keep you here, but I was taught to aim at the center mass. I do as I'm taught, just so you understand. Now, sit and wait for the authorities. Nobody's kidnapping my Chelsea."

"I wasn't kidnapping her," Brent hissed. "I'm her friend. Tell her, Chelsea."

"You're not my friend, and I didn't invite you in. And I sure as hell wasn't leaving with you willingly."

"Come on," he said. "Chels, don't do this. You'll regret this."

"On your knees. Hands on your head," she said to Brent. He didn't move. "You hard of hearing?" she asked, taking a step closer to him.

Though angry, Brent did as he was told.

"Do you have any weapons?" she asked him.

"No," he grumbled.

"Is he armed?" she asked me.

"No. No, I don't think so," I said.

Ruthie gave him a quick frisk and said. "I recognize you from the other night."

"Doubt that, grannie," Brent said.

"Shut your mouth, and sit against the wall. Now!" bellowed Ruthie.

Her stern, deep voice was so commanding, it almost made me sit. Brent backed up against the house and sat against the wall.

Ruthie glanced at me. "Oh honey, I'm sorry if I scared you. Are you alright? Did he hurt you?" she asked.

Brent mumbled threats of a lawsuit under his breath. We ignored him.

"No, I'm fine. You didn't scare me." Then I whispered to her, "When did you get a gun?"

"Got myself a small arsenal, dear. I'm an ex-sharp shooter, retired from the DC police department for twenty-five years now," she said, each word seeped with pride.

"Seriously?" I asked.

"Seriously?" Brent repeated.

Ruthie ignored Brent. "Yes, dear. These days, it's not something that comes up in everyday conversation."

"Ha," I laughed, still considering she might be joking. But she wasn't laughing with me, and the look on her face told me she was quite serious. "Wow," I said. "You're amazing, Ruthie."

All at once, both the county and state police were swarming.

"What's going on, Ruth?" asked the first officer to reach us. He was a tall lanky State Trooper with a scowl directed at Brent. He seemed to know Ruthie well.

"Intruder, Grady," she said, motioning towards Brent. "She knows the perp. Ex-boyfriend gone stalker. No weapon."

"Give me a break," Brent said. "I'm not an intruder or a stalker. Chelsea and I go way back. Tell them, Chels."

Grady's partner was Mitchell. He stepped up and said, "Let's go. If you have something to say, say it to me."

The officer escorted Brent to the police car for questioning. After that, Grady walked Ruthie and I to her house for a statement. William welcomed Grady with a friendly handshake.

I told Grady what happened and why Brent was there. I explained how he'd been having me followed and that the pictures taken by the investigator were in Brent's jacket pocket. I was regretting that I hadn't listened to Paige when she told me to report Brent and the private investigator to the police. But then again, I never imagined things would escalate to such an embarrassing level.

After several minutes, Officer Mitchell came to ask me a few questions and to verify the statements Brent had given him.

"Are you being treated for mental illness, miss?" asked Mitchell.

I may have had my doubts about my mental health lately, but I wasn't being treated for anything at the moment. So I said, "No."

Mitchell scribbled a note on his paper and continued. "Mr. Stewart said he came to see you because he was concerned for your well-being. He stated that you have been pretending to have a boyfriend, and he was concerned that this was a part of your mental illness."

The officer rolled his eyes and continued with a smirk on his face. Ruthie and I gawked at each other.

"Then he said he was having someone 'keep an eye on you', as he put it, in case you were in danger. Would you care to comment on any of that, or do you feel that it's an accurate statement, ma'am?"

My jaw dropped open. I was shocked by Brent's mouthful of lies.

Finally, I said, "None of that is true. It's a bunch of garbage. I have a boyfriend, and he's having him followed too."

"Right. A man named..." Mitchell flipped through his notes. "Caleb Maxwell. Mr. Stewart claims that he might be dangerous. Said he might try to take advantage of you due to your illness and all."

"That's ridiculous. I don't even know anyone by that name. My boyfriend's name is Cole. I don't have a mental illness. And like I told Officer Grady, Brent forced his way into my house and took my cell phone so I couldn't call for help. Then he threw me against the wall, busted my bedroom door down, and dragged me out of the house to take me God knows where."

"He said he broke your door down because he heard you calling for help."

"Wow, he's unbelievable. I called for help so someone would save me from him."

"Listen, Brent's full of it," Ruthie told the officers. "He's the moron we looked for the other night when I called you here. William and I can attest to that."

"You're going to press charges, miss?" Mitchell said, more as a statement than a question.

I hadn't thought of that. Brent was becoming more and more dangerous as time went by, and Cole would want me to press charges.

"Yes, I suppose I should."

"We need to take a picture of your head injury," Grady said. I rubbed the lump on my head and wondered how bad it looked.

"I'm fine, though," I murmured.

"Chelsea, he threw you against a wall and hurt you," Ruthie reminded me.

"I kind of fell when he let go of me," I attempted to explain.

But the more I thought about it, the severity of Brent's actions were simply impossible to deny. I had to stop defending him. I had to stop protecting my pride.

"You're right, Ruthie. He did throw me against the wall. He hasn't been very nice to me lately."

"Honey, he was very aggressive with you. Abusive."

"Yes, he was," I agreed. "Take the pictures."

"May I see your arms, honey?" Ruthie asked with a tender smile.

My arms were tender under my sleeves. So I knew we would find the same damage Brent left a few weeks ago. I removed my sweater and sat silently in my tank top while the female technician took pictures of red and purple chaos scattered up my arms, across my shoulders, and down my back.

Ruthie lifted the hair from my forehead. "Don't forget this one," she said to the technician.

I was embarrassed. Mortified. I was the girl in the Lifetime Movie. The one who allowed someone to hurt them time and time again. You couldn't possibly imagine anyone was that dumb. But now I got it. Because today that someone was me. Those girls were naive, and they'd been manipulated. They were blinded by that manipulation and ashamed to admit that someone they once loved could be so horrible. And now, I was in their shoes.

"What does this say about me and my judgment of character? How long would I have put up with this if not for you and Cole?"

"Listen to me," Ruthie said. "Things could have been far worse. You got this under control before things went very wrong. You're doing the right thing. You're being smart."

She put her arm around me. William handed me a sugar cookie. After the police left, taking Brent with them, Ruthie walked me back to my house. She hesitated at the door before she left.

"What is it, Ruthie?"

"I wish you would have let the medics take you in. I'm worried about your head," Ruthie said.

"I'm fine. It's black and blue, but the swelling is already going down." I pushed my hair forward to cover my forehead and hide the bruise.

"I'm just curious about something," she said.

"Go ahead," I said. Ruthie had been so wonderful through all this, I would tell her whatever she needed to know.

"Your boyfriend, he never showed up tonight. I'm wondering if we should send someone to check on him. I mean, you don't think Brent went to his house first. Do you?"

210

"No. If he had, Brent wouldn't have made it here at all. I'll call Cole when you leave. I need to figure out what I'm going to tell him about tonight."

"How about the truth?"

I shook my head and crossed my arms. "Even though you're right, I'm not sure I can do that. Brent–this situation–it's the kind of thing that scares the good ones away."

Ruthie smiled in a knowing way, and said, "I'll stay for a bit. And by the way Chelsea, this isn't the kind of thing that scares the good ones away–it shows you who the good ones are."

"Ruthie, you need to go home to William."

"William is fine. I'll wait. It's about time someone met this boy anyway."

"He's been a little shy about that."

"I get it. But life is much better when everyone you love can be together."

"I'd love for everyone to meet Cole. It's not me preventing that," I said.

Ruthie nodded her head and said, "Whatever the case. I'll let you be. But only because that crazy Brent is locked up at least for the night. I can't believe he told the police that you're mentally ill. That's a pot calling the kettle black."

I hadn't intended to talk to Ruthie about this, but she brought it up, and it was time.

"Brent knows I've been to a doctor. I have headaches, and I've passed out a handful of times. I'm having some tests done next week to figure out what's going on. But honestly, as far as Brent goes, I don't think he considered my doctor appointments. He made all that up to cover his tracks. He's trying to be seen as the concerned good-guy instead of the crazy stalker."

Ruthie hugged me. I think she could tell that I didn't want to talk anymore.

"Please, Ruthie. Go home to William."

"If you're sure."

"I am." I think.

When she left, I locked the door and went to assess the damage in my room. After a second, I remembered the downstairs door might be locked. I shuffled down the stairs to unlock it for Cole. When I got down there, he was standing in my living room.

CHAPTER 30

"I didn't mean to frighten you," he said somberly.

"I didn't hear you come in." He looked upset. "What's the matter? Are you okay?"

"Things aren't good," he said.

It wasn't the answer I'd hoped for. He didn't say that he wasn't okay. He said that things are not okay. Like between us, I thought.

I did not want to have the conversation that was coming; it wasn't going to be pretty. But it had to happen. I hurried over to him and threw my arms around his neck. He smiled with dull, forlorn eyes and slid his arms around my waist. The only thing I needed was for him to hold me and all would be right in the world again. He rested his cheek on the top of my head and squeezed me, almost too tight. I was afraid that he'd seen the police leave with Brent.

"Cole," I said, looking up at him. "I have to tell you something."

"We need to talk," he barked, taking a step back. His brow scrunched, and he said, "I'm sorry. I didn't mean to snap at you. But there's something you need to know, and it's very, very important."

"I have to tell you something first."

"No. I haven't been honest with you. It's time you understand what's going on."

He was quiet for a second. He wouldn't look at me. Cole had a look about him that was difficult to put into words. It was guilt and anger and sadness all in one.

"What is this about?" I uttered.

"This isn't the way I had planned to tell you. But something has happened. The truth is too important now."

In the blink of an eye, I went from feeling safe and happy to being sick and afraid. If this was the moment where he confessed his sins, I was not ready to hear it. I didn't want him to tell me that he had a girlfriend, or worse yet, that we were over because he had chosen her. I couldn't swallow the thought that this could be the end. I needed him more than ever, at whatever price. For the moment, Brent completely disappeared from my thoughts. Fear of Brent was nothing compared to the heartbreak that I was about to suffer.

"Is it–bad?" I choked out.

"Yes. You should sit."

"No. I'll stand."

He disregarded my words and led me to the couch to sit. Then he knelt in front of me and played with my fingers. He didn't look well; he looked as bad as I was feeling. Bile churned its way up and out of my stomach and burned my esophagus. It took everything in me to swallow it back down.

"Cole, what I don't know, won't hurt me. Please. Let's just hang out tonight. We can talk tomorrow."

"No, Chels. There's something important that I need to tell you. All I can ask is that you listen and know that I never meant to hurt you."

He cradled my face in his big hands, so warm and gentle. I didn't close my eyes, not for one second. I watched him as he kissed me sweetly on the lips with his eyes squeezed shut, as if he were in pain.

"Please don't," I pleaded.

"It's not what you think," he said. "It's worse. I'm so sorry."

"Whatever it is, please, I don't want to know right now." Please stop, my insides screamed. "I mean it, Cole. What I don't know, won't hurt me. Maybe that sounds ignorant, but it's true. Please. Don't do this."

"Chelsea, not knowing will cause you far greater pain," he said.

I shook my head. I didn't want to hear it. I finally closed my eyes, hoping this was a bad dream like so many others I'd had before. In the dream, when Cole ripped my heart out, I had felt only a fraction of the pain that now metastasized in my body. As bad as I thought that was, what was coming was certain to be a million times worse.

"Please, look at me. Open your eyes."

My eyes flew open. I took his face in my hands and said, "I love you. Please, nothing else matters. Please let me be selfish and have one more night with you before I know the truth." I couldn't beg enough. "Please, don't leave me. Don't break up with me. I need you."

"I can never give you what you need."

"Yes, you can. You already do," I said, wiping away blinding tears.

"Let me finish."

"You're all I need. We don't need dates and all that traditional stuff. Things are perfect just the way they are."

"Chelsea, this is far from perfect. Please, I need to tell you." He took my hands in his and lowered his voice. "It's important," he said.

I shook my head in protest. But then I saw something I could not ignore. His tormented face and his sad, strained eyes. His pain. Whatever his secret was, it was eating away at him. If he was trying to make right of something so wrong, who was I to prevent that? If Cole believed that telling me the truth would take away the anguish written all over his face, I had no choice. I would hear it. I would absorb his torture. I would absolve him from his sins. I would do it because I loved him.

I inhaled until my lungs were full. And when I had pushed it all out, I wiped my face and waited. I braced myself for the tidal wave of grief that would follow the evil truth. I didn't want to believe it existed. I didn't want to stop pretending. But it was too much for him. He was in love with someone else.

"Chelsea, I'm not married. I don't have another girlfriend. I haven't been unfaithful in any way. I could never do that. I am solely devoted to you and you alone. The fact is, it would be impossible for me to betray you. Because..." He paused.

"Say it," I muttered.

He brushed the hair from my forehead, exposing my bruise, and kissed it. Then he said the most horrible thing.

"I'm not real."

CHAPTER 31

I stared at him in silence. I searched his face for an explanation but couldn't find one that made sense. I had to ask, "What do you mean?"

"I'm not real, Chelsea."

"You're not who you say you are?"

For a split second, I thought maybe there was a chance that there was no other woman. Maybe he was a fraud, had a fake name, or maybe he was a criminal on the run. Sadly, those thoughts gave me hope.

"No, Chelsea. I'm literally not real. Do you understand? This has all been a lie."

It was as if he were talking in another language. I hadn't a clue what he meant. I said nothing while I waited for him to elaborate.

After a few more seconds, I reiterated, "Cole, I don't understand what you're talking about. Are you in the witness protection program or something? Because I don't care about any of that."

I reached out to him, and he shrunk back.

"Think about it, Chels."

My tolerance began to diminish. An emotional episode was brewing. I did my best to hold it back.

"I heard what you said. I just don't get it. Is Cole not your name?"

"What is my name?"

"Your name is Cole," I barked.

Now, my emotions surged. Impatience and agitation were on the rise. If I had to hear this awful news, I wished he would spit it out.

"What is my last name? Tell me," Cole demanded.

My mouth opened to tell him, and nothing came out. I was shocked that I even had to think about it. I was even more shocked when I came up with nothing. We had been together for over a month now, six and a half weeks to be exact, and I was certain he had told me his last name. But in that moment, I could not think of it.

"Oh, my God! I'm losing my memory," I blurted out.

"No. You don't know my last name because you never gave me one."

"I never gave you one?"

A fleeting thought raced through my head. I pushed it aside. It was impossible.

"Yes, exactly what you think," he said. Cole peered into my eyes.

"You don't know what I think, but let me tell you. I think you should get to the point or drop this. You come here all broody and dramatic with the sudden need to confess something so awful except you're making me guess what it is. Can you be a little more specific, please?"

My temper was hitting the boiling point; I was a volcano on the verge of erupting. How in the world could Cole have turned so malicious?

"I can't be more clear. You made me up." His voice was quiet and calm. His eyes were kind. "I'm sorry. I let you do it, and it was all a lie."

I slapped his hands off my knees. "I made you up? And you lied? Why are you playing head games with me?" I demanded.

He was talking in circles and I couldn't keep up. I couldn't piece together what he was trying to tell me. Frustrated, I jumped up and left him by the couch. I walked to the other side of the room to get away from him and noticed through the sliding glass door that his boat was not at my dock.

"I don't think I need the boat anymore."

"Why are you doing this to me."

"Because it's true. I'm sorry."

"So all of this is a lie? You don't care about me? Then just dump me, don't screw with my head."

I was so angry that it wasn't enough to yell at him. I wanted to be mean back to him, hit him, something to make him feel some of the pain that was ripping through my body. I never imagined he could

217

betray me and be so cruel. Tears swelled in my eyes as rage collided with heartbreak. My hands trembled, and my mind raced.

"I do care about you, Chelsea. The thing is, I'm only real to you."

Cole looked to the floor. I saw remorse. But worse than that, I saw pity.

"Stop it," I snapped. "You expect me to believe that for the last month and a half I have been spending time with a figment of my imagination. Is that seriously what I'm supposed to believe?"

"That's the truth."

"Brent had a picture of us together. Explain that?" I scoffed.

"It wasn't me."

"It was you. I saw it."

"No. It was Caleb Maxwell. Not me. Just like Brent told the police officer."

I marched over to Cole and grabbed his arm. I held it up and declared, "See? I can feel you."

I dropped his arm. And wielding every ounce of anger I had, I released an infuriated howl and punched his chest with both fists. Then I froze.

"What did you say?" I uttered. "How do you know what Brent told the officer?"

You weren't here, I thought.

"Yes, I was here," he said. He ran his hands down my arms. "I am where you are. I know what you know."

I stepped back and shook my head. "No," I said

"I am so sorry that he hurt you. I shouldn't have kept the truth from you for so long. You waited for me to help you, but I can't save you from him. I can only help you save yourself."

"I don't need to be saved. I need to understand why you're trying to make me think I'm crazy?"

"You're not crazy. You're sick. Your medical condition is getting worse. But you already know that. You created me to help you through this. To help you deal with everything: Brent, your illness, symptoms of your illness like the other hallucinations. Everything that's been happening to you, Chelsea."

"Forget about what's happening to me. What's happened to you?"

I was pacing the floor now.

"I am one of those symptoms. Think about it. I'm not the first hallucination you've had." He paused to let it sink in. It seemed too impossible. "You know I'm right, because if I know it, then deep down, Chels, you know it too."

"No. No! You're lying."

I stormed to the counter, and grabbed my phone.

"Go ahead. If that's what it takes for you to believe."

I looked at him puzzled. Did he really know what I was going to do?

"Call Ruthie. But if you don't want her to think you're crazy, and you don't want her to doubt what happened with Brent today, I'd be careful what you say."

It was an easy guess. Ruthie could put an end to this. But what if, by some small fraction of a chance, she didn't see Cole? It would mean he was telling the truth. I couldn't say the word. I could barely think it. Was it possible that Cole could be what he said he was—a hallucination? I thought back to when Ruthie walked by the house and waved to Cole and me with a questioning look on her face. And how she and William had never seen Cole on the dock in all this time. Then I remembered the pictures Brent showed me.

"No," I snapped. "Impossible."

I dialed Ruthie.

"Hello?" she said.

"Ruthie, I need you to come over," I growled.

"Is everything alright, dear?"

I paused to regain control of my voice. "Yes. I forgot to give you something. I'd run it over, but I'm waiting for Cole."

"Sure. I'm on my way."

When I hung up, I eyed Cole standing in the living room. He was as clear as day, and as alive as could be. I couldn't bring myself to consider the fact that he might be a hallucination. How absurd. I had spent hours, days, weeks with him, especially lately.

219

"I told you, you're getting worse. That's why I'm here more," he said.

"That's scary. Don't do that."

I shivered, wondering how he seemed to guess what I was thinking.

"I can't help it. I'm a part of your thoughts."

"If that's true...If you're in my head, how come I don't know what you're thinking too? Shouldn't it go both ways?" I challenged.

He nodded in agreement. "If you listen," he said out loud.

"I'm..." Then I heard him–in my head. He said it once. Then he said it again. Without moving his mouth, I heard him as if he was standing in the middle of my brain. But that's not what bothered me the most. It was what he said.

"I love you, Chelsea."

"Ha," I snorted. He repeated it yet again. "Shut up! Shut. Up."

Suddenly, I was overcome with laughter. I couldn't stop. I was powerless against my incessantly changing emotions.

"You love me? Really? You're trying to make me think I'm crazy, and you think this is the perfect time to tell me you love me. Is this funny to you? I didn't think you were a game player. What should we call this little game? Liar's paradox?" Cole's feeble shake of his head infuriated me.

"Oh, I see. It's part of the master plan. It's not enough to dump me plain and simple; you have to completely devastate me and mess with my head. Where's the speaker? What is it, surround sound or something? Bluetooth? You have gone to an awful lot of trouble to pull this off."

Ruthie knocked at the door.

I ran up to let her in, chuckling along the way. All I had ever hoped for was that Cole would love me as much as I loved him. Now, he tells me that he loves me after trying to convince me that he's not real... after telling me the most preposterous lie and disguising it in a cruel charade.

"Thanks for coming back, Ruthie. Come on down."

When we reached the kitchen, Cole was leaning against the refrigerator. I stopped next to him and turned to face Ruthie. I waited. She didn't acknowledge Cole. I felt a stab in the chest.

"What's up?" she asked. "Have you been crying? Your eyes are all red."

I glanced at Cole. "Well?" he said, as if he'd proven his point.

"I haven't been crying. It's my allergies," I said. I picked up the box of herbal tea from the counter. "Here. I bought this last week. It's too sweet for me. Sorry to make you come all the way back for it."

I walked around to the other side of the refrigerator and positioned myself behind Cole.

She can't miss him, I thought.

I passed the box in front of Cole. Ruthie took it without even a glance in his direction.

"Don't be silly. Maybe Cole will like it. You should keep it for him," she suggested.

"It would be too sweet for me too," Cole said to her. He turned to me. "She doesn't know I'm here. Don't you see that? Look," he said, snapping his fingers in front of her face.

She didn't so much as blink. Not even a flinch because the grim reality was–no one was there.

I ran to the bathroom and threw up.

"Sorry," I hollered to Ruthie. I kicked the bathroom door shut, locked it, and continued throwing up.

After a second, a hand ran down my back; a warm, strong, comforting hand. I sat back on my heels to catch my breath and saw the door still shut and locked. There, next to me, knelt Cole, looking every bit as real as he had the first time I met him, with his shaggy, brown hair and deep green eyes that gazed into the depth of my soul. This time there was no brilliant smile. There was only the same sadness and grief that I, too, felt at that very moment.

"Ruthie, I think I'm sick. You'd better go before you get it," I whimpered through the door.

"I'll stay with you, honey. I hope you don't have a concussion. Do you want me to take you to Urgent Care?"

221

"No, thank you. I have actually been feeling a little sick for the past few days. I'm sure it's a bug. Please, I'd feel awful if you caught this. And I would hate for you to bring this back to William. I'll call you in a bit. I promise."

I knew she would think of William and not want him to get sick while recovering from surgery. She left, promising to check on me later.

My defenseless, exposed heart and desolate soul were beyond repair. It was the feeling you got when someone you loved more than life itself was stolen from you by death. When you realized they were gone forever–or in my case, that they'd never even existed.

As Cole gathered my limp body, I fell into his embrace and rested my head against his chest. It rose and fell as he breathed. Warm air spilled from his lungs and streamed through my hair. I was further punished by the sound of his beating heart; an incongruous noise that drummed beyond all reason for only my ears to hear. How could it be true?

I'm not real. I'm not real. I'm not real.

Over and over that same sentence ran through my head. I tried to find a better interpretation for those words, except one didn't exist. The wretched truth had come out. It had escaped from the depths of my soul to haunt me for the rest of my life. If only he were married, a criminal on the run, anything other than what he had just told me. I never would have believed it was possible, but it was worse than I could ever have imagined.

When my tears ran dry and my mind stopped spinning the same incorrigible sentence, I looked up at Cole. Without speaking, he told me that he was sorry. I didn't just hear it, I felt it. His sorrow and pain were the very same agony I was drowning in. I understood why it happened, why he came to be. He didn't even have to explain, I just knew.

Cole loved me, and I could never deny that I was in love with him. It was irrational, yet true. It was the only thing I knew to be real in that moment. So I wiped the sadness from my face, cleared the despair from my throat, and asked the one question for which I had no answer.

"Now what?"

The Ivory Dome

Subject Number Thirteen had been in the bathroom for a long time. When she emerged, she was a mess. Her eyes were glossy and red. Her face was blotchy. Something had upset her. My guess was that it was the over-bearing ex-boyfriend torturing her again with his obsessive pursuit. While the ex-boyfriend made for interesting drama, I had hoped it would push her into revealing her ability. So far, that wasn't the case. I never dreamed her struggles would bring about such pathetic introversion.

It was frustrating that her ability continued to be in question. Figuring out their gift was usually not this difficult. At least, it hadn't been for Subjects Eleven and Twelve. But this one, Subject Number Thirteen, I had been watching her for over a month, and still, I saw nothing but strangeness. She had gone from having friends and family around almost too much, to becoming a loner.

My plan was to keep monitoring her. But soon, should I not be able to uncover her ability, I would have to intervene as I did for Subject Fourteen. I didn't like what I had to do. Causing such pain was not my idea of fun, it was a necessity. I learned that the greater the pain, the easier it was to discover their ability. I would do whatever it took to make this operation a success. I would not fail again.

When the project began so many years ago (and pre-Lakeville), my calculations had included a lag in development while the subjects matured post-exposure. As it turned out, I myself had never anticipated that the completion of this project would take ten years. Nonetheless, this wait time was unavoidable; the children had to grow into their abilities as their DNA evolved.

Now, here I was, more than just a scientist. I was an organic chemist, a modern biotechnologist, and a certified naturopathic physician in a world obsessed with all natural ingredients, whole foods, and essential and organic products. The timing couldn't be more ideal. I had worked for years to create the perfect process and discover the exact combinations necessary to mask any trace of chemical manipulation–all so I could declare my blend pure. It would satisfy every last tree hugger, every essential oil bandwagon junkie, organic farmer, and every gluten and dairy free PETA member.

This group would be my greatest accomplishment once the process was complete. But in order for that to happen, N13 had to show me what, if anything, she could do.

"Show me something, N13. Show me soon, or another young life may have to be sacrificed."

CHAPTER 32

The situation I found myself in would forever remain unrivaled, though not all bad–at least in my scrambled head. Despite the insanity of having an imaginary boyfriend, my life had become ideal in many ways. I was able to spend every minute with Cole. And he was perfect. Why would I create someone who wasn't?

My CAT scan and MRI were on Tuesday. Cole accompanied me to both. It was hard to pretend he wasn't there. I blurted out questions and commented on things he said. I was even caught by a kind nurse who pretended that she didn't hear me talking to myself.

"Can you help out a little?" I asked Cole when we got back in the car. "Stop talking so much when people are around. I look like a nut job, not that I'm exactly sane, I suppose. But come on, don't ask me questions and expect an answer."

"Sorry. It's hard. At least we are in public. That should make you happy."

"Very funny. Should we go on that date now? I could be the freak sitting at a cozy table for two, making goggly eyes at a chair." I laughed. Then I hated him.

My moods swung like a pendulum. While some of it had to do with whatever was wrong with me, some of my erratic mood swings had to do with Cole himself. I would go from hugging and kissing him and being so crazy in love, to suddenly remembering that I was alone. Alone in my insane, yet perfect, hallucination.

My reality was merciless, and it was taking a toll. Since finding out the truth, my fainting spells and headaches had increased. I had no choice but to take a leave of absence from work until I had an official diagnosis and got the symptoms under control. I told Jackson and Paige I was going to visit with my aunt in Buffalo for a while.

Paige was suspicious but didn't question my alleged family visit. But Jackson, he looked shocked. My guess was that he knew I had gone to see his father. He knew something was wrong with me.

I didn't mind shutting myself away with Cole. As a matter of fact, I would gladly have done it for the rest of my life. I tried not to think about what would happen when the test results came back. What I didn't know wouldn't hurt me, right? Except, before I knew it, I received the phone call that I had been dreading.

I was cleaning up the dishes from dinner when the phone rang. A phone call this soon had to be bad news. It was Dr. Armstrong's secretary calling to schedule an appointment for me to come in for the results. I told her that I would check my work schedule and get back to her later.

Cole put his hand on my back and grumbled, "You aren't even working. What are you doing?"

"I'll call next week to schedule an appointment."

"No. Call her back now."

"Not yet," I said. "I just want to have…"

My phone rang, and it was Dr. Armstrong's office again. I wasn't going to answer, but in hopes of removing the infuriated look on Cole's face, I did. This time it was Dr. Armstrong himself.

"Hi, Chelsea. This is Dr. Armstrong."

"Hi, Dr. Armstrong."

"Look, we need to schedule an appointment with you so I can go over the test results."

His voice was hard to read.

"Sure. When were you thinking?" I replied.

"Tomorrow morning. Ten o'clock?"

"Oh. Tomorrow? It's Saturday."

"Yes. I have morning hours."

"Wow, I can't believe you got the results already. That was fast."

"I picked up the pictures a few hours ago. I didn't want to waste time."

"Oh. Thank you," I stammered. He did that for Jackson, of course.

I took a deep breath before speaking. I was not prepared to get this call already. Cole stood next to me, urging me to take the appointment. I turned my back to him.

"So, tomorrow?" Dr. Armstrong repeated.

"How about after the weekend?"

Cole growled, "Take the appointment tomorrow, Chelsea. I'll be there with you. We can do this together."

I shook my head no in response. I didn't want to deal with it yet.

"The thing is, Chelsea, we have to go over the pictures together, and sooner would be better. I want you to come in tomorrow. Bring your parents."

"My parents are out of town. I don't want to worry them."

Dr. Armstrong became silent. Then in a low voice, he said, "At the very least, bring the friend you brought the last time we met."

"I don't want people to worry. Not yet."

"Tomorrow, Chelsea. It's important," Dr. Armstrong implored.

"I'd rather do this over the phone. What did you find?"

His tone was stern. "I want you to come in. If you won't agree to come in tomorrow, I will call Jackson and have him pick you up. I won't tell him why, but I will ask him to bring you in. Are we clear, young lady?"

The doctor's firmness surprised me, and the threat to get Jackson involved would complicate my plan.

Cole pressed on. "Good for him. If Paige gets involved she'll find out about me sooner than you want. She's relentless. Take the appointment. Please," he urged.

"Fine. I'll see you in the morning on the condition that you let me talk to my family when I'm ready. I have a right to deal with this my own way. Agreed?"

"Yes. I'll see you at ten. And think about bringing someone. It would be a good idea. Just think about it."

I will be bringing someone, I thought. You just won't know that.

CHAPTER 33

The next morning, Cole all but dragged me to meet with Dr. Armstrong. I could already guess what the results would be. He would tell me that I had some type of brain anomaly, most likely a malignant brain tumor, and it would be inoperable. I would be facing months of radiation to shrink the tumor and possibly end up with rigorous rounds of chemotherapy. That's what I read online anyway. I didn't bother looking up the survival rate. Quite honestly, it didn't matter as long as I could be with Cole for whatever time I had left.

"You'll do what you have to do to get better," Cole told me as we pulled into the parking lot.

"There will be too many people around."

"I'll be one of those people," he promised, touching my hair.

"We'll never be alone," I said, glancing in his direction. His brows were furrowed. He suddenly looked worried. "Why are you making that face?"

He shook his head. "I was thinking about something."

"What? About me dying?"

"No, not exactly. We'll talk about it later."

He flashed a forced smile.

"That was fake. Tell me what you're thinking," I said. He shrugged. So I asked, "Do you think I'm going to die?"

"No," he said, this time with absolute certainty in his voice.

"Then what? What if I don't die, right? What if radiation shrinks the tumor? Or they remove the tumor, and I have my sanity back? That's what you're thinking about."

"We'll talk about it later, after your appointment. You don't even know that there is a tumor. It could be something simple."

Cole was purposely avoiding the conversation. He wanted to distract my thoughts so I couldn't hear what was on his mind. I pressed harder.

"What if the reason you're here disappears?" I pondered. That was it. I was shocked that I hadn't thought of this earlier. "The answer is obvious."

"One thing at a time. Okay? There's a spot, park there," Cole said, pointing to the end of the isle.

"You'll be gone, won't you?" I slammed on my brakes in a panic.

"Chelsea, that car is backing out. Move!" Cole yelled.

From the corner of my eye, I spotted reverse lights. I stepped on the gas, jerking my car forward enough for the shiny red sports car to pull out of its space without hitting me. At the same time, I missed hitting an elderly woman walking in front of my car by an inch. She waved her hand at me and scowled. I paid no attention, instead I turned to Cole and asked again.

"You'll be gone when, or if, I get better. I would never see you again." I threw the car in reverse, whipped into the recently vacated spot, and shut off the car. "I can't live without you. I won't."

"Don't say that. Let's see what the doctor has to say before we discuss this any further."

That's when I realized that this wonderful man was living on borrowed time. Time borrowed from me. I needed to figure out how to make him stay. I needed to find a way to be with Cole for as long as I could.

"Alright. Let's go," I said, suddenly impatient to see the doctor.

"I know what you're thinking," Cole said, taking my hand to stop me from exiting the car. "There's nothing you can do. I'm here so you can get better. That's the reason I exist. Don't make this all for nothing."

I ran my hand along his cheek and down to his chin. My fingers wandered to his neck and stopped. I looked into his eyes. I didn't care why he was created. I had feelings I had never had in my entire life. I had a love like I never could have imagined. I was obsessed with it, addicted to it, completely consumed by it. I felt alive because of it. And I wouldn't live without it.

"No," he said. He knew my thoughts as quickly as they formed. "You finally found that those feelings were possible. I want you to hold onto them so you can give them to someone else. There will be someone else. I promise you," he said.

"Enough of this. I don't want to talk about it anymore."

I leaned in and kissed him.

CHAPTER 34

All I had to do was sit patiently, listen to the doctor, and agree to whatever form of treatment he suggested. It didn't matter that I had no intention to follow through with anything. I just needed to let the doctor think I was on board so I could get the information I needed. That was it. I thought for sure I could manage that.

Sitting in the doctor's office, I looked over at the man I had come to love with all my heart. He was everything I had ever wanted. Everything inside me screamed that he was supposed to be "the one".

The problem was that no matter what the doctor said today, it was going to ruin everything. Regardless of what he told me, there could be no good news. To top it off, Cole was hoping for one specific outcome, the one I considered to be the absolute worst. Still, I needed a few details if I was going to prolong the time I had left with Cole.

I was lost in Cole's eyes when Dr. Armstrong walked in and sat down behind his desk. He looked hopeful, positive. I figured it was a cover for what he considered bad news.

"Good morning. How are you feeling today?" Dr. Armstrong asked.

"I'm good." I shifted in my chair. "If we could just rip the bandaid off right away, I'd appreciate that."

"Right," the doctor said.

I glanced at Cole. He squeezed my hand and said, "Think positive. You're going to be fine."

And that was exactly what I was afraid of.

"Here's what we have," started Dr. Armstrong. "It appears you have a brain tumor. It's what is called a sphenoid wing meningioma. It's somewhat rare. Now, news of a tumor is generally bad news. But

231

the good news is that more than ninety percent of the time this type of tumor is benign. Here's the scan we took a few days ago."

Dr. Armstrong took an x-ray picture from a large envelope and placed it on the light board on the wall.

"It's in the temporal lobe," he said, pointing to the mass.

"It looks–not so small." I glanced to my side, Cole was nodding his head.

"No, it's not small. It's quite large, as you can see; almost an inch and a half in diameter. But like I said, it's most likely benign and can be removed. We'd use a minimally invasive surgical procedure through a small incision in the eyebrow area. Radiation is another option. Not the best in my opinion. If we continue to wait, it may grow and put more pressure on your brain, causing a number of symptoms," Dr. Armstrong said.

"Ha," I laughed and sat back in my chair. "Symptoms. Great."

"This is good news, Chelsea," Dr. Armstrong assured me.

A tear escaped my eye. Cole reached over to wipe it away. I swatted his hand and did it myself, shooting him a sinister look. He winked at me and smiled, no doubt pleased with the news.

"What if I decide not to do anything about this tumor and just let it be?" I asked the doctor.

His brows slammed together, and his lips tightened into a stiff line.

"I would say we need to keep a close eye on it. We'd have to watch and see how quickly it's growing. But again, let me point out that it's already very large. That's the greatest danger I see right now." With the clearing of his throat and a hint of frustration in his voice, the doctor continued. "You must be having other symptoms besides fainting and headaches, like memory or vision problems. Let's start by discussing some of these things, then we need to get started with a plan for the best course of action."

I rose from my chair and looked him in the eyes.

"There'll be no action. Thank you for your time."

I turned to walk towards the door. Cole grabbed for my arm.

"Wait. You can't leave!" he yelled.

232

"Chelsea. Wait. Let's talk about this more," said Dr. Armstrong, jumping to his feet.

I turned to both of them.

"No. I have all the information I need. There's nothing more to say."

"I don't think you understand what I'm saying," the doctor said. "The chance that this is cancer is very slim. Not impossible but very unlikely. The prognosis is good."

"It's too much of a risk to consider surgery."

"The risk you face, the one that is most imminent, is the choice to ignore this. That is what will kill you. I don't mean to scare you, but I have to be honest here. The surgery is minimally invasive. You'll barely even have a scar."

"I'm not worried about some stupid scar. What people will see on the outside doesn't matter to me," I said.

It's the scar left on the inside that I won't be able to live with, I thought. Removing the tumor–was removing Cole. The bottom line was that I would be killing the one person in this world I loved the most. And that wasn't going to happen.

Cole shook his head. He knew what I was saying. Dr. Armstrong stared at me, his mouth gaping.

I said to him, "What I meant was, surgery could kill me. It's always a risk. If the tumor isn't growing, why would I consider surgery?"

I opened the office door and stepped out. Then I turned to Dr. Armstrong and reminded him, "I'm eighteen. An adult. You can't call my parents."

"Actually, Chelsea…" he began.

"I'll talk to them myself, when I'm ready."

"Even though your particular tumor is usually benign, there is a ten percent chance it could be cancerous. That's a percentage I wouldn't bet against. This is your life we're talking about. At the very least, we need a biopsy," he threw out in good effort.

I shook my head. "No. No biopsy," I said.

"Please, will you sit down for one more minute. I want to explain what's happening to you. You need to understand what happens as the tumor gets larger and exactly what could happen if you refuse medical intervention. Please, let me explain before you leave," the doctor implored.

That stopped me, at least for the moment. I did want further details on how much time I had left with Cole.

"I would like to know something, what will happen if I don't have the tumor removed?"

Cole and I walked back into the office. I could tell he was relieved. I sat down while Cole stood by the door; as if he could stop me if I tried to leave again.

Dr. Armstrong said, "I would like to take another scan in a few weeks, maybe even next week, to see if it has grown. If we see a measurable growth, it would help to determine how fast the tumor is growing. Radiation could help shrink the tumor if we decide to start there."

"And if it is growing, and I decide to do nothing?"

"If it's still growing, which is what I suspect, it will continue to invade your cranial cavity and cause excessive pressure on your brain. Eventually, it will be fatal. Your brain won't be able to sustain itself with that kind of pressure. You will experience significant pain with severe headaches, along with other increasingly uncomfortable physical and mind altering symptoms."

"I saw my dog," I blurted out. "He's been gone for eleven years. I guess it was a hallucination or something. And sometimes I still see him."

"Yes, that's definitely a symptom. Visual hallucinations are quite common with these types of tumors. And it's dangerous because they can be very realistic."

"That's an epic understatement," I mumbled. I scooted to the edge of the chair and said, "My judgment was impaired. I believed it was him, even though he's been dead for years. Anyone in their right mind would never have made that mistake."

"Yes. Impaired judgment, hallucinations, erratic changes in behavior, and mood swings are also common. Disruptive sleep patterns and insomnia too. But you can do something about it, Chelsea. I'm confident that this is benign. I'm even more confident that if left alone, it will be fatal. We're lucky to have caught this when we did."

"I like seeing my dog."

"You're comparing me to a dog?" Cole asked.

"I love seeing my dog," I said pointedly. "Would I still see him? Would I even remember that I saw him if I had surgery?"

"That's hard to answer. Our brains are so complex. Some people report seeing hallucinations at a smaller level for a few weeks post-op. That's most likely residual pressure that would hopefully subside as swelling decreases and healing begins. With radiation, symptoms should slowly decrease as the tumor shrinks. Some people report their full memory is intact, while others experience short term memory loss. But they are alive. They continue with life and live it to the fullest. Something to think about."

I nodded my head. "Thank you for answering my questions. I'll need some time."

"I appreciate how much you cared for your dog. And maybe seeing him brings back fond memories. But he's not real, Chelsea. He's not real."

Immediately, I loathed him for his repugnant comment. But I forged a smile and acknowledged his contemptible statement with a nod.

"Do me a favor. On the way out, make an appointment with Kathy for a scan on Wednesday. If you decide not to keep it, call and let the office know."

"So you can send in the troops?" I joked. I let him think perhaps he'd changed my mind.

"Right. Will you, please?"

"Yes, I will."

"Great. I'll see you next week. I highly encourage you to reach out to your parents. It might make the decision easier to have someone to discuss this with."

"Thank you, Dr. Armstrong." I walked towards the door that Cole was now allowing me to pass through. To continue with my false pleasantry, I turned back to the doctor and said, "Please say hello to Jackson for me. I haven't seen him in a while, and I know he had some pull with getting me in to see you so soon."

"You may be able to do that yourself. I'm having lunch with him. He might be in the waiting area."

I nodded, knowing the timing of their lunch date wasn't a co-incidence. When I stepped into the waiting area, there he was. He popped up from the chair and marched over to me.

"Chelsea, hey," he said, giving me a hug. When he pulled away, he had my hands in his.

I glanced back towards the door at Cole. I was embarrassed that Jackson, my boss, was holding my hands, and doing so in front of my boyfriend.

"Hey Jack, I'll be ready in a minute," said Dr. Armstrong.

"Sure," he said to his father. "Take your time. I'm going to catch up with Chelsea."

I wanted to run out of there and never look back. The last thing I needed was an uncomfortable pity party with Jackson.

"I feel like it's been forever," he said.

I nodded and said, "I've been meaning to stop by Trend and see how things are going. I… just haven't had time."

Jackson still held my hands. I wiggled them away and put them in my pockets.

"So, you didn't go to your aunt's house?"

"No. I just didn't want to worry Paige. I didn't tell her that I had any tests done. Did you know?"

"Not specifically. My dad was worried when you didn't seem to care about what he referred to as 'certain critical results'. He asked me if you ever talk to me about things. Personal things. I think he was hoping you were talking to someone about whatever it is you're going through."

"I don't need to talk to anyone," I said, looking over at Cole.

Jackson shuffled from one foot to the other and said, "This is none of my business. I know I'm your boss, but I would like to think we're friends too. I'm here for you if you need someone to do something for you or to talk to. And when you get better, who knows where our friendship might go."

He was right about something. This was none of his business. I was angry that he presumed I would want him here. And I was upset that Cole was witnessing this conversation. Jackson seemed to think he could say a few magical words and make everything better. Did he think I would jump into his arms and agree to send Cole to the guillotine and live happily ever after with him?

"You shouldn't have come," I said.

Jackson pulled one of my hands out of my pocket and held it.

"All I know is that you are sick and weren't too keen on coming in this morning. That worried me. I had to see you," Jackson said. "Right now, all I wish is to be your friend. You're going through a tough time. I understand that. But call me if you need me. You have my cell number. Don't hesitate to use it".

Like the flip of a coin, my black and white feelings had my repulsion for this guy turning into adoration for his kindness and willingness to help me. I looked up at him and smiled. He smiled back, maybe thinking he'd gotten through to me on some level. I had never realized how sweet he could be. So thoughtful and caring.

"You're a good guy, Jackson. Under different circumstances, maybe...I don't know." I looked back at Cole, and instantly, the warmth that was growing for Jackson became a chill. "Thank you," I said.

I snapped around and stormed away. I didn't so much as glance at Cole as I breezed by him. But Cole caught my draft and followed.

"Stop, Chels. You have to make an appointment for next week. Stop."

"No."

I hit the elevator button but had no patience to wait for it. I stormed towards the stairwell and smacked open the door.

"Chelsea, wait. I'm not mad about Jackson," Cole said.

"Mad? Don't be ridiculous. Why would I think you're mad?" I snapped.

"Don't worry. I told you. There are other people out there. You're attracted to him. There's nothing wrong with that."

I stopped on the landing, and he crashed into me. Luckily, no one was around.

"I don't want him. I want you. Yes, he's gorgeous, smart, single. Any girl would be insane not to like him. But I'm not any girl. I guess I prefer imaginary friends." I sassed. "I can't help it."

Cole's eyes lit up.

"Of course," he said. "That's the problem. You can't help it. You said it yourself, your judgment is impaired."

"I know how I feel about you. It's very real," I said, insulted.

The slow leak from my tear ducts began again. I rolled my eyes and wiped them with my sleeve. Cole hugged me, stopping just short of squeezing the breath out of me. I wept for a moment as he tried to comfort me. When I heard the door open from the floor above, I pulled away from him and turned my face towards the corner. A moment later, when the nurse was gone, Cole turned me to face him. I couldn't look him in the eyes. My head dropped as he spoke.

"When you fell in love with me, you opened your heart to something you never had and found what you never knew you'd been looking for. You cannot abandon that, Chelsea.

"There is a man out there who wants you and will one day want to have a family with you. You need to give your love to him. Let him sit with you at the fire pit, take you to the middle of the lake for a breathtaking sunset, and in the end, grow old with you."

I shook my head. I couldn't imagine anyone else taking his place.

"Chels, think of your future. You're so young. Imagine this: your children and grandchildren jumping off the dock and playing in the water while you sit with the man of your dreams, rocking on the porch swing. Imagine a real future." Cole lifted my chin, and our eyes met. "Chelsea, that man cannot be me."

I listened to him. I let his words sink in. But there was just one thing I wanted.

"I want to go home, Cole."

While there was a part of me that knew he was right, there was a stronger and more compelling part that knew he was the man he had just described. Maybe our relationship wouldn't be the typical love story, but I loved him so much that there was no way I could turn my back on him now. I wouldn't be greedy and expect it all. Life was perfect just the way it was.

CHAPTER 35

"We can't just go to the park like normal people," Cole said.

"There's no reason we can't go. I'll just have to keep in mind that I'm alone. I can do that."

"Only if I don't talk to you."

"Here," I said, taking my AirPods from the drawer. "I'll wear these. If people see me talking they'll assume I'm on the phone. I see people all the time who look like they are talking to themselves. This will work." I was giddy with excitement.

"Then maybe we should drive," Cole suggested.

"Why? It's a beautiful day and less than a half a mile walk," I insisted.

"Okay. But if anything happened, at least we'd have the car and..."

He trailed off in thought, so I finished for him.

"...you could drive me home?" I laughed.

"Not funny," he said.

"Yes, funny. I'll have my phone. You could call for help," I teased with more laughter.

"This isn't a good idea. Look at you. I think you're delirious." Now, Cole was laughing too.

"Let's go," I said.

I slid the AiPods into my ear, and Cole followed me out the door without much of a choice.

"Hey, I was wondering something," I said, walking up the driveway to the main road.

The sweet smell of Peonies hit my nose. I stopped and sucked in the flowery scent.

"The dark pink ones are your favorite," he commented. He put his arm around me. "Ironic that you have such a passion for the garden. Don't you think? I mean, it's the garden that beckons the one creature that is the deadliest thing in the world to you."

Damn him. I shook off his arm.

"Nice try. I picked up on your satirical commentary days ago," I said with a cautionary glare. "Now, back to my question. Why did you tell me you were going to confront Brent? You never could have done that."

Cole grinned. "I wanted to force you into thinking smarter. I know how you feel about confrontation. That's the last thing you would want."

"True."

"That was why I was forced to tell you when I did; you were in danger. Besides, that's what you would have wanted me to say. Your ideal man would defend you at any cost."

"Right. My knight in shining armor idea. Chivalry really is dead."

"There's one way to find out. Find the man who can kick Brent's butt for you." Cole grinned.

"William?"

"Funny," he said. "At least he's physically capable."

I gave him a playful whack on the arm, and he shrugged.

Cole had a lighthearted smile, but I knew where this conversation was headed; the same place it always went since we left Dr. Armstrong's office. I opted for silence for the rest of our walk.

Within minutes we could see the park. It was bustling with mothers who brought their children to play on the swing sets, couples picnicking, and people fishing. Then there was me.

I spread out a blanket under a willow tree not far from the water and took out a book. Cole sat down and leaned against the tree trunk. The glistening water bounced light off his face, drawing even more attention to his flawless skin, bright eyes, and white smile. A gentle breeze blew his hair. Such a pity–people around me didn't know what they were missing.

"Are you going to read to me?" he asked.

I shook my head and whispered, "It's just for show. I read it three times already."

"I know. It's your favorite book."

"Of course. You're familiar with it."

"The main character is interesting. Some people might argue that he's arrogant," Cole pointed out.

"Paige thought so. But I saw him as passionate. I love the way Cole…"

I stopped. I had named Cole after the main character from my favorite book. Cole smiled at me and winked.

"Now, that's funny," he said.

"What a crazy coincidence."

"No. Probably not."

I pulled a couple of popular magazines from my backpack and started to flip through the pages.

"I guess I named you after a great man, at least in my opinion," I said.

That led me to wonder if my Cole was a reflection of what I thought the character in the book might look like.

"He's blonde and Australian," Cole said.

"There goes that idea," I said, studying a magazine advertisement.

After a minute, Cole asked, "You think you saw someone who looks like me in a magazine? I doubt I was an underwear model."

I giggled. I hadn't realized what I was doing. But it was true, I was searching for his face on the pages of the magazine.

"I guess I have been looking for you. Your image must have come from somewhere familiar. Where else would I get the idea for how you look? I'm not creative enough to make you up on my own."

"Maybe you passed a guy on the street and thought he was cute," he said, twirling a strand of my hair around his finger.

"Probably not because I would have followed you until I 'accidentally' bumped into you. Then I would have given you my number, and we would be dating right now. So I doubt I passed you on the street."

"No way. You never would have had the nerve. And for the record, you keep saying 'you', like that man is me. But it's 'him'. He's someone else, his own person. That's important to remember."

Just then a boy stepped out from behind the tree and stood next to Cole. He startled me, which briefly pushed aside my slow rising annoyance with Cole's goading words.

"Shady tree on a hot day. Best spot in the park. I saw you over here reading. Are you alone?" asked the boy. If he was sixteen that was pushing it.

"Yes. I mean, I'm meeting someone in a bit."

"Oh. Do you come here often?" he asked.

"There's an original pick-up line if I ever heard one," Cole said, hiding the smirk behind his shirt collar.

"I haven't been here since last fall. I came for some quiet time. To relax with a good book."

I held up my book, hoping he could take a hint. But my subtly was lost on him.

"That's a great book. I come here a lot. It's a great place to fly my kite and write poetry," he said.

"Tell him to go fly his kite," Cole snickered.

I couldn't help but laugh. My phone rang, saving me from kite-boy.

"Excuse me. I have to take this, it's important. Nice talking to you," I said.

Kite-boy nodded his head and went back to where he came from. I answered Paige's call.

"Hi. I haven't heard from you in a while," said Paige. "Is everything alright?"

I was getting tired of everyone sounding so concerned.

"Yes. Fine. Can I call you back? I'm right in the middle of something."

"Sure. Make sure you do. I want to talk to you."

"I will. Bye."

Cole's sobering face matched his voice.

"You lied to her," he said.

"I didn't want to talk. I answered the call so that boy would go away."

"You will have to tell her eventually. You can't keep it a secret. If there's anyone you should talk to, it's her," Cole said, beginning a lecture.

"Not today. Please. We're having fun. Let's talk about something else. Like the fact we're finally on a real date."

Cole looked down at his lap.

"We aren't in public. You are in public. It's not a date if there's only you."

"Boy, that's sweet of you to point out."

"It's true. Don't try to fool yourself. That's dangerous."

"Dangerous? How do you figure?" I asked.

I eyeballed kite-boy struggling to get his skull and cross bones kite into the air.

"I don't want you to convince yourself that I'm real in any way. I want to help you get better, not worse," he said. "I want you to call the doctor and get treatment. Get a biopsy. Do something."

"So much for our fun day at the park," I scoffed. "Kite-boy isn't looking like bad company right about now."

Kite-boy snapped the kite free from a branch. And for a heartbeat it flew high and free until it smacked into a pine tree and took a nose dive into the lake. Ugh, I could relate.

"He won't help you," Cole said about kite-boy. "But he won't bug you until you get better like I plan to do." Cole's head snapped to the right. "Heads up. Incoming fisherman. You're popular today."

"Hello, there," said the man with a smile. His hair was so dark that I wondered if he colored it.

"Hi," I said.

"I'm Steve. Do you mind if I join you?" he asked.

"Nice. A retired old guy with nothing to do but fish," Cole joked. "He's old enough to be your father."

I barked at Cole, "Too old, too young, too boring! What are you, some kind of matchmaker? And who asked you anyway?"

"Excuse me?" Steve said.

"Sorry. I'm on the phone," I said, pointing to my AirPods.

"Chelsea, calm down," said Cole. "You'll make a scene."

"Calm down? Really? Has that testosterone infused demand ever worked on any girl? Ever."

"We need to leave," Cole said, standing up. "Get your stuff. Now."

"No. We aren't finished talking."

"People are watching you. Get your stuff."

Steve turned abruptly and scurried away as fast as he could.

"I don't care who's watching. Let them. I have nothing to hide," I said.

Cole got in my face, and through clenched teeth, he said, "Yes. You do have something to hide. Now, get your stuff. We are leaving."

I was stubborn. I refused to leave until he agreed to stop pestering me about treatment. I crossed my arms with no intention to go anywhere.

He shook his head, his brows furrowed. "This was a bad idea. If we do not leave together right now, I will leave you."

Wait. What? I thought. But you can't leave me.

"Yes. I can. And trust me, I will."

Darn him and his threat to abandon me. I glared at him until he turned and marched away. At that point, I stuffed all of my belongings into my backpack, threw it over my shoulder, and stood up.

"You're a jerk," I mumbled when I plowed by him.

I stomped through the park and down the road, towards my house, with Cole trailing behind. He seemed in no hurry to catch up.

"I'm sorry. I just don't want you to think we can live like this forever," he said from a few feet behind me. "Not that this is what anyone would call living. We aren't secret lovers. You are sick. Don't forget that."

"How could I forget when you are constantly reminding me," I snapped.

"Get help and you can come to the park another day and have a real date."

I stopped and challenged, "With you?"

"Chelsea..."

245

He shook his head and reached for my hand. I turned and pounded off again.

When I got home, much like a small child having a tantrum, I threw my backpack down the stairs in a fit of rage and stomped to my room. I slammed my door as hard as I could and yelled, "I thought you were supposed to be perfect!"

CHAPTER 36

While we were out, Dr. Armstrong left a message explaining that he had taken the liberty of scheduling my scan since I had conveniently forgotten. He was expecting to see me next Wednesday at nine o'clock or he would be calling in the proverbial troops.

I wondered if Jackson mentioned something to Paige because her phone calls and text messages doubled over the next few days. I didn't answer her calls or listen to her messages, and I did not respond to her texts. I wasn't ready to deal with her. She would inevitably jump on the "get well" band wagon.

Cole disappeared Monday night after we had another argument about my choice to live with the tumor. He refused to listen to me when I tried to explain how hollow life would be without him. He couldn't understand how much I needed him. At last, I was happy and in love. I could enjoy what life I had left, and for me that outweighed everything.

When Tuesday rolled around, I spent the morning trying to forget about the argument in the park. Cole had threatened to leave me. It was unthinkable. And since I still hadn't seen him today, I was a little on edge.

I'd been hearing soft music since breakfast. It started out a mere drone, I couldn't tell what it was, at first. As time went by, the volume grew ever so slightly into a mellifluous whirr. After a while, I figured out that it was the same tune playing over and over, but I couldn't place it. An hour later, the muted music still played, and it was driving me crazy. I stepped out onto the side deck to investigate.

With the exception of a few birds chirping and the barely audible music, the morning was quiet and peaceful. I tried to figure out which direction the music was coming from, but it seemed to surround me.

I searched the cove to see if there was a boat nearby playing music. My only discovery was William and Ruthie sitting in the sun on her deck with their morning tea and the newspaper.

The music grew infinitesimally louder. If it were country music or the standards, I would think it was coming from Ruthie's house. But it wasn't. It was the kind of alternative rock music that Reznor's band played. The song was beginning to sound familiar.

"Hi, guys," I yelled to Ruthie and William.

"Hey, sweetheart. Come on over," William hollered.

I skipped down the deck steps and walked across my lawn to Ruthie's.

"No cane, William? You must be feeling better."

"They graduated me from that horrid thing. I can even go back to kayaking in another two weeks."

I turned to Ruthie and asked, "Do you hear that music?"

She listened for a second and said, "No, dear." She gestured to a chair. "Sit down."

I sat next to Ruthie, facing the lake.

"I've been hearing it all morning. It's just music, no lyrics. It's getting louder, and it's driving me nuts," I explained.

Ruthie poured me a glass of black tea, and the three of us sat on the deck and witnessed the neighborhood come to life. Soon the music began to rise above the noisy lawnmowers, weed whackers, boats, and cars. It was incredibly distracting. I had trouble keeping up with the conversation.

"Well, has he?" Ruthie said.

"Has who what? I'm sorry, I missed what you said."

"How are you handling everything?"

"Oh. I haven't heard from Brent at all. I have a restraining order against him."

"I know, dear. That's the third time you've told me that this morning. But that's not what I meant. What's going on with you? You seem distracted," Ruthie noted.

"What?" I said, trying to talk over the music. "Don't you hear that?"

William and Ruthie looked at one another; their concern was plain to see. And with the current volume of the music, it was obvious they didn't hear it. Now it was obvious: the music was a hallucination.

"You seem a little off today? Where's that boyfriend of yours? Cole, is it?"

"I'm fine. Cole's out. He'll be back later. Why would you ask about him?" I said, trying not to yell.

"Look, Chelsea. I'm worried about you. First, all this talking to yourself stuff, now you're hearing music. There is no music, and I'm far from hard of hearing. I think you should see your doctor."

I glanced at William who was reading the paper and pretending not to listen to Ruthie's lecture. I was taken aback by her bluntness. It had never occurred to me that she had seen me talking to Cole before I knew the truth about him. In essence, she had caught me talking to myself.

I shrugged. "I just talk to myself to let off steam. That's all," I said.

Ruthie wouldn't let it go.

"No. I've heard you carrying on full-blown, one-sided conversations with yourself. I didn't mean to eavesdrop, but at first, I thought you were talking to me. Soon, I realized you were talking to yourself. Brent has put you under a great deal of stress. Maybe you should see a counselor or a psychiatrist."

For a split second, I thought about telling her the truth. But no, I couldn't. She would just be another person trying to force me to have the tumor removed. I'd have to add her to the list of people trying to kill Cole. This angered me beyond words.

"I have to go. Bye, William," I snapped.

They said nothing as I got up and stomped away.

It was when I reached the edge of my lawn that the music detonated. It hit me like a baseball bat to the face. The pressure in my head erupted as if that bat had hit a watermelon at 90 miles per hour. It was so loud and overpowering that I was thrown back onto the cold dewy grass. As the music grew louder, the pain grew worse.

CHAPTER 37

By the time Ruthie and William reached me, I had curled into a fetal position. My skull throbbed in my hands. I may have been screaming in pain, but I couldn't hear my own voice over the music. It was that same song.

Finally, I realized what the song was and where I'd heard it. And now that I knew the song, I could hear the words. They were loud and clear, and they slapped me with insolence. It was the first song Reznor's band played the night I met him and Meggie at CJ's Pub. It was before I knew the truth about Cole. The song was "Only" by Nine Inch Nails.

At first, the main chorus repeated like a broken record. I was defenseless against the cruelty of those words. They mocked me, worse yet, mocked Cole. They spit in my face that he was nothing but in my head. It worsened as the song continued. The words accused me and mercilessly berated me for the senseless love I had for him. He could never fit into my world, they told me. And yes, I was alone. I would always be alone. When the song was over, it started again.

Through blurred vision, I could see Ruthie was at my side. I couldn't see William, and I was worried that he might be calling for an ambulance. I could not let them take me to the hospital. I tried to talk to Ruthie and convince her that I was okay, but no words came out when I opened my mouth. Only the sounds of torture and agony. If only the music and its wicked words would stop, maybe my head would not burst.

Ruthie seemed to be waving her arms at someone. I prayed it wasn't medics. I couldn't go to the hospital and lose Cole forever. I wouldn't. Please, someone stop the music.

Seconds later, it was as if someone had flicked a switch.

The music stopped. I could hear, I could think, I could see again. And I wasn't where I thought I was. I was back in my living room on the couch- alone. I jumped up and ran to the sliding glass doors. Ruthie and William were on Ruthie's deck, reading the paper and drinking tea, as if nothing had happened. I opened the door and stepped out. I heard no music.

"Hi, Chelsea," yelled Ruthie. "Come on over."

I gave a quick wave and feigned a pleasant face.

"I'll be over a little later," I called back.

I walked in the house and leaned all my weight against the counter. The room rocked like I was on a boat in the middle of a choppy lake. It stopped after a few seconds, allowing me to regain my stability and slide into a chair.

I stared at the clock. What I had thought was at least an hour had been less than five minutes. That meant the music wasn't the only hallucination. I had never gone to Ruthie's and had tea, and she had never lectured me. I ran a hand over my dry clothes and knew I had never collapsed on the damp lawn.

It was all very disconcerting. It was becoming harder to tell what was a hallucination and what wasn't. If only Cole would help me. But I had a grave feeling that he wouldn't be showing up any time soon.

I spent the rest of the day trying to make him come to me. I closed my eyes and wished for him. When that didn't work, I commanded him to appear.

"Cole! I need you. Please. I need you, now," I demanded.

Nothing I did seemed to bring him around. For two nights, I waited outside in my chair by a fire. When he didn't come, I went to bed with the window open so the curtain would blow. I watched it all night. He never came. I couldn't understand why he wasn't there for me. I needed him. He said I created him to help me through this painful time, but now he'd gone AWOL on me. It didn't make sense.

I hardly slept. Once, I cried so hard that I fell asleep for about a half an hour and woke up distraught because I couldn't even dream

251

about him. I feared that he was truly gone. Then it hit me. I figured out what he was doing.

There was just one reason he would abandon me. He thought if he was gone long enough, I would assume he wasn't coming back. He thought I would go for treatment or have the surgery if he left me. But he was wrong, I was stronger than that. I was not going to let him manipulate me. I would wait as long as I had to.

To pass the time, I hung with Ruthie and William. We went into town for dinner and to the beach. When Ruthie inquired about why I wasn't working, I explained that I had taken some time off to enjoy the summer before college started. She assumed my parents were in on the decision, and I wasn't about to correct her. Ruthie also asked if I followed up with my doctor. I assured her that he gave me a clean bill of health. I felt guilty for lying. I felt bad for not confiding in her. It would have been the smart thing to do.

It was a week after getting the test results from Dr. Armstrong when I got the call from Cole. Had I not been so angry with him, I would have found it comical that he called instead of merely showing up.

"Hello," I said. "You've been wasting your time. Our time, I should say."

"I'd like to see you," he said.

And like every other time he opened his mouth, I swooned. My heart sped up, butterflies did laps in my stomach, and an uncontrollable smile spread from ear to ear. Just like that, my anger was gone, and he was forgiven.

"You need to call me on the phone to ask permission for that?" I asked.

"No," he replied from behind me. "I just didn't want to startle you. Plus, I know you're mad at me."

I sighed. A boulder lifted from my chest. I ended the call and slid the phone into my back pocket. Suddenly, his warm breath exhaled onto the back of my neck. His hands slid around my stomach and locked with mine.

"I missed you," I told him.

"You're insanely stubborn. It's unnatural."

"I know."

"You missed your appointment this morning. You should have gone, Chelsea."

"I didn't want to go."

"They are going to come here. They will have an intervention and tell Ruthie everything so she can watch you. Paige will tell Meggie. Your parents will come home. They'll all gang up on you. Is that how you want this to go down?"

"Dr. Armstrong can't tell anyone. It's against the law."

"Jackson will tell Paige something. She'll figure it out. She's already suspicious. How may times has she called this week?"

"I stopped counting."

"How many worried messages?"

I shrugged. "I don't listen to her messages."

"She's probably on her way here now."

"I doubt it. But soon, you're right. We talked about this," I said, turning to face him. "I want to be with you for as long as I can."

"We have talked about this, and you still won't listen to me. There is no choice here. You must have surgery sooner than later. If you love me, you will."

"No. That's so wrong. Surgery means you die."

"I can't die. I'm not alive. Chels, I'm leaving regardless of your decision. You may as well save yourself," he said matter-of-factly.

"Why?" I demanded. "Why would you leave me when I need you?"

"You're not doing anything, that's why. Look, this is all coming to a screeching halt anyway. Maybe you can't feel it, but I can. Don't you understand? I'm obsolete now. I'll disappear because other things will take over as you worsen. You will continue to have more vivid, disturbing hallucinations, fainting spells, confusion, and erratic be-havior. And when you die, because you will, you will leave this world sad, frightened, and alone. I won't be there, Chelsea. Wherever it is you go, I won't be there. I'm not real."

"Stop."

I had heard enough about him not being real. But he pressed on.

"There's a second option. The one I prefer, therefore, so do you, but you're so sick you can't see it. You can get treatment, have the surgery to remove the tumor, and get well. You may stop seeing me every day. And even though you might not hear me, talk to me, and feel me, you will remember me. You will remember how it felt to love me. You will be drawn to finding this love again, and you will be happy. Then all that has happened between us, wouldn't have been for nothing."

Cole kissed me lightly on the lips. I heard what he said, and it made sense. Still, I could not shake the overwhelming need I had for him, it was too strong.

"I can't live without you. That alone will kill me. I'm afraid to be without you."

"You're afraid because you're sick, and you can't think clearly. If you would at least agree to radiation to shrink the tumor, you'd be able to understand the consequences of ignoring treatment. You'd change your mind. You'd think of others."

"I am thinking of others. I'm thinking of you."

"You need to think about the real people in your life who love you. People who would have trouble living without you. Your sister, your parents, your friends, especially Paige."

Just then, there was a knock at the door upstairs.

"That's too loud to be Ruthie," Cole warned.

"It must be William," I said.

I headed for the stairs, but Cole stopped me.

"Ask who it is."

"Who is it?" I hollered, obeying the order.

I hated the interruption now that Cole had come back, but Ruthie and William knew I was home. They worried about Brent coming back, and they might not go away until I'd proven everything was fine. When no one answered my question, the knocking became louder and more urgent.

"Don't get it," Cole warned.

"William doesn't hear as well as Ruthie."

254

I marched upstairs and didn't see anyone through the window. Assuming William had started back to Ruthie's, I unlocked the door and swung it open to catch him. I had to reassure him that I was fine before Ruthie came back with her gun, or worse yet, called the police.

I took one step out the door before I was shoved back inside the house with the force of a bull. It took a moment to register what was happening. By then, it was too late. My ankle twisted, and I lost my balance. I was able to catch the railing with one hand to stop myself from falling down the stairs. Brent caught my other hand.

"Hey, hey, hey. Don't fall," he snickered.

Without thinking, I called for Cole. Brent squinted his eyes and cupped his ear to listen for a response; but we both knew that wasn't going to happen. I snatched my hand from his while still holding onto the railing. I toppled down onto the top step, and sat with my back to the wall.

"Wow. Your boyfriend is here? I guess my timing is perfect," Brent said.

"No, he just left out the back. I was hoping he'd hear me."

I glanced down the stairs, Brent did the same.

"Aw shucks, I just missed him," he said in a snarky tone. Brent glared at me, shook his head and said, "This is pretty sad. Are you losing your mind or something?"

"Yes. As a matter of fact, I am," I snapped. "I have a brain tumor, and I'm dying. So go away. I know that's way too much for you to handle."

"That is bull. You are so full of it, Chelsea. You keep spinning lies, and I can't figure out why." He jabbed his finger in my direction. "Do you think I've never been lied to before? Do you think I can't tell?"

Brent slammed the door behind him. He smacked his hand on the wall, growled, and dropped back against the door with a heavy thud. He drew in a long breath then slowly released it.

Then collectedly, Brent crossed his arms and said, "I deal with liars all day long. Better liars than you."

"I'm not lying. That's why I went to the neurologist. That's why I haven't been to work."

I popped up and attempted to get downstairs and as far away from Brent as I could, but he was too fast. He grabbed my shoulder and yanked me backwards. My spine hit the stairs first, then I bounced down two hardwood steps on my tailbone.

Clutching the back of my shirt, he said, "Where do you think you're going? You're not calling the police again. I have a reputation to uphold."

"Then maybe you should stop stalking me," I spat out.

Reeling with anger, I shoved him hard enough to throw him off balance. It allowed me a few seconds to slip out from his grip and escaped down the stairs. But he recovered quickly and was close behind. I jumped onto the couch and slipped my cell phone in between the folds of the throw blanket that was draped over the side. I didn't want to make the same mistake twice. I grunted as pain shot up my back from my tailbone.

"I have a restraining order against you. You're not supposed to be here," I reminded him.

"That's a joke," he snorted.

"It's not a joke, Brent. But listen, if you came here to say something, you might as well say it. Then go," I demanded.

From the corner of the couch, I watched Brent like a hawk. I made myself aware of his demeanor. I prepared for his next move.

He was mad. His eyes scoured the room, taking in everything. His gaze fell on the landline phone on the wall and the two-by-four on the floor. The board was used as extra security for the sliding glass door, but I had a feeling that I might need it for something else.

"I don't have a speech for you. I just want the truth. You owe me that." He sauntered towards the kitchen and leaned against the counter. His eyes darted from the end table to the coffee table, then landed on my body. "Where's your cell phone?" he asked.

"Why?"

"Where is it? Stand up," he said, lumbering towards me.

I wasn't going to make it easy for him, so I stayed put.

"Fine," he said. "Don't get up. I'll find it myself."

He bent over, reaching for my back pockets. His hands braised the cushions and almost made the blanket fall.

"Don't touch me!" I jumped up, and our heads collided. I endured the pain, threw my hands in the air, and hollered, "Look, no phone. What is the matter with you? It's not on me. I think it's in my room. Go get it if you want it."

He backed away, and asked, "It's in your room?"

Brent's grin was doubtful, but he seemed satisfied that I didn't have it. If I could get him to go upstairs to look for my phone, I would have time to get out of the house.

"Yes, it's in my room," I repeated.

He locked me in a stare. Neither one of us flinched.

After a minute, when he didn't seem like he was going to go look for my phone, I said, "Fine. You're right, Brent. I don't have a boyfriend. I just wanted you to move on. I don't want to get back together. I thought if I told you I had a boyfriend, you would leave me alone. There. I said it."

I crossed my arms and waited.

"I knew it. You couldn't get that loser Caleb to go out with you."

"You don't even know what you're talking about. Your detective was an idiot. He made things up. He scammed you."

Brent's eyes were glued to me as he backed up towards the bathroom, next to the stairs. I prayed he was going to leave. Instead, he started a spiel. It began in a calm and refined manner and went downhill from there.

"You are a very pretty girl, Chelsea. Very 'girl next door'. I always loved that about you. That's why I picked you. You didn't even come with any of that jealousy crap or gossiping girl drama. I did think you were smarter, though."

Brent sat down on the third step of the staircase, breathed in a gallon of air, and released it. I could see that he was trying to control his temper.

"You see, here's the problem. I am struggling." His voice grew, his jaw stiffened. "Struggling to understand why you think you can

257

get away with all the lies and manipulation."

"Brent, I..."

"I'm. Not. Done. I wasted two years of my life on you, prepping you to one day be the perfect law partner's wife. Then, just as I'm heading off to law school, you dump me. You. Dump. Me. That was your first big mistake."

He jolted up. His knuckles went white as he clutched the stairway handrail.

"Second mistake: immediately, you start running around, chasing some loser like a slut when I was about to pop the big question."

Panic jabbed at my gut. I was sure he could smell the fear.

"That's right, I was going to ask you to marry me. My parents knew it, everyone at my dad's law firm knew it. I had it all planned." He lowered his voice and said, "I even had the ring."

Brent released the hand rail. He took a breath and went on without missing a beat.

"Granted, we would have had a long engagement so I could finish school and–refine you. Clearly, you needed it.

"So I kept our silly little break-up a secret because I figured it wouldn't take long for you to realize your mistake. And let me promise you, there was no way I was going to start from scratch with some new little bitch, not after the time I put into you. I was ready to forgive you, Chelsea."

Aghast, I said, "I wasn't a project, Brent. I was your girlfriend."

"Right," he snapped. "You were. Now you're not. So where does that leave me? How do I fix this?"

Brent lingered by the stairs, glaring at me. I swallowed hard. The contorted story didn't scare me as much as the fact that he appeared to believe every word he said. And with each passing word it became more evident that Brent was an unstable and dangerous person. He was quite possibly psychotic.

"Chelsea, I need an answer."

"I don't have an answer that you'll like. Sometimes things don't work out the way you plan."

The nefarious smile was back. He began to pace the floor.

"Right, again. And so rarely are you right. But here we are. I never imagined it would end like this. Then again, I never thought you would be so stupid as to sabotage your future. Our future. My future.

"I don't do well with stupidity; you should know that by now. I find it intolerable. Don't get me wrong, I'm not entirely without empathy. I understand that sometimes smart people are capable of an occasional error in judgment. But you, Chelsea, are just plain stupid."

Brent turned his back to me, so I slid my hand into the folds of the blanket. My phone wasn't there. I reached down into the cushions and dug and dug. I skimmed along the edges and around the back but came up with nothing.

Brent rocked his head back and forth, then sighed.

He turned around to face me and said, "I know what you want to say: you're not the only one to blame. Right? Well, I'm not responsible for your stupidity. I'm one of those smart people whose mere error was poor judgement. You see, I made a big mistake when I chose you." Brent shrugged and said, "I didn't want it to come to this. But things have changed so drastically that there is no going back."

Clunk! Brent dropped my phone on the table by the stairs.

"Thought you were clever? I think we already determined the answer to that question."

"Oh, you found my phone," I said, flustered and playing dumb; that's what he said I was.

An evil glimmer flickered in his eyes. He grinned and whispered, "Funny girl."

That was the moment that changed the whole game. That was the moment that my defiance and fear turned into pure terror.

Brent's nostrils flared with his thinning lips. His chest puffed up as he stormed towards me. I had to act quick. I lunged for the sliding glass door, but he was there in a split-second. He slammed it shut, crushing my fingers. I yanked them out with a howl of pain that came from somewhere seemingly outside of my body. He snapped the lock closed, then grabbed my wrist.

"Let go!" I yelled, trying to free myself from his grip. My bleeding, crooked fingers pulsated.

"Stop fighting with me, Chelsea," he yelled back. "This is your fault. It's all your fault. Stupid bitch!"

Out of the blue, he backhanded me across the cheekbone. I fell to the ground and landed next to the two-by-four by the door. I snagged it with my good hand and jumped to my feet. All I needed was to make contact with any part of his body, and it would buy me a few seconds to make a run for it.

I swung the wooden board as hard as I could. He stopped me mid-swing. With one hand on the two-by-four and the other on my chest, he pushed as hard as he could, sending the wood plank and me flying backwards. My head bounced off the coffee table. The two-by-four flew into the television and sent it crashing to the floor.

My head throbbed and was too heavy to lift. I wasn't knocked completely unconscious, but my body tingled, and the perimeter of my vision was slowly fading into black. I could only compare it to tunnel vision–or maybe what the world looked like when your soul drifted away from your dying body.

"Chelsea. Chelsea. Come on. Get up."

Brent kicked me in the ribs; I felt the bones cracking.

"Come on. Seriously?" He kicked again. "You're a worthless excuse for a human being," he snapped.

As if breaking my ribs wasn't quite enough, he kicked my battered head. I saw the blow coming, but I couldn't move to get out of the way. When his black Nike made contact with my head, I almost didn't feel it. I saw that as a bad sign.

"I didn't expect you to be much of a fighter, but this is embarrass-ing," Brent complained.

He bent down, wrapped a meaty hand around my throat, and glared at my bloody head.

"Looks like I've solved our problem," he said.

As Brent raised his closed fist, I saw Cole outside the sliding glass door. I uttered his name. Brent's fist paused mid-air.

260

"What did you just say?" he spat.

"Cole," slipped from my lips one last time.

When Cole yelled and yanked on the locked door, and Brent turned in response, I knew it was another hallucination. But what was real? Was Brent really there? Was there actually a warm, wet puddle budding next to my head, or had the tumor finally taken over my brain? The truth was, it didn't matter now. I could feel it in every bone in my body that this was the end. This time, I was dying.

Cole yanked again, and the door frame shimmied. Brent released my throat and stood up.

"This is none of your business," he hollered.

Cole yelled back, "Open the door." Then to me, he said, "Hang on! I'm coming in!"

Inside, I smiled at him. I didn't know if that's what he could see on my face, but I hoped he could.

"Get away from her!" Cole shouted at Brent.

This time, he pulled the door handle harder, and it crashed open, taking some of the frame with it. Brent tried to stand his ground but was bowled over by Cole. Brent's body smashed against the counter, knocking the wind out of him. He crumbled to the floor.

Cole rushed to my side and knelt in front of me.

"Can you hear me? Say something," he said.

It brought me back to the first time we met, when he pulled me from the lake. I remembered choking on lake water, and he wanted me to say something so he would know I was okay. But this time, I couldn't.

He brushed the hair from my face. His hand lingered on the side of my head, and he mumbled, "Oh, God." When he lifted his hand, it was covered in my blood.

Suddenly, Brent came up behind Cole and reached for the back of his shirt. Cole instinctively turned and grabbed Brent by the front collar. He shot up and body slammed Brent into the wall.

Brent threw a punch that Cole ducked to avoid. Cole's return punch hit dead-on, breaking Brent's nose and sending him back to the floor. A crimson stream poured down his face, but that didn't stop him from getting back up.

Brent tackled Cole at the waist. They both went flying over the recliner, taking it down with them. I couldn't see what was happening at that point; they were out of my view. I heard a lot of punching, grunts, and groans. Then Brent came sliding past me on his side, his face was bloody and swollen.

Again, he got to his feet. Brent wouldn't give up. He wouldn't stop.

When Cole came back into view, he had a small gash across his cheek. Suddenly, Brent barreled at him. He came from behind and locked his arms around Cole's body, trapping his arms. He tried desperately to wrestle him to the ground. This only enraged Cole further.

"Son of a bitch," Cole grumbled. "You're such a cockroach."

Cole took a quick step back with one foot and placed it behind Brent's knee. Then he grabbed Brent by the front of his legs and dropped to the floor on his back. He landed hard on top of Brent. This time Cole made sure Brent wasn't getting back up. He shuffled on top of Brent's chest and slammed his fist into his face. Brent was out cold.

"Don't move!" Cole snapped at the unconscious jerk. "If you get up again, I'll freaking kill you."

Cole hurried to my side.

"I called 9-1-1. They'll be here any second. I hear the sirens now," he said.

I looked up at Cole, knowing this was it. This was the end that I had been dreading. It was the end of us. Whether I was truly dying or not, the pain was the same either way. My brain had created a grand finale which ended with my death. One final hallucination and the last time I would see Cole. I closed my eyes and a tear trickled down my cheek.

"Don't cry. You'll be okay," he said, wiping my tears.

I wanted to tell him I wasn't crying because I was in pain. I was crying because I wanted to believe he was wrong and that he would be wherever death was taking me.

I heard the sirens and Ruthie's voice just before my world went black.

CHAPTER 38

The bright light burned behind my closed lids. When I opened my eyes, I was back in the living room standing with Cole, just as I was before Brent had arrived. I was the rat in a maze that didn't know what she would find as she ran from one corridor to the next. Or in my case, as I was vaulted from one mind boggling hallucination to another.

"You're still here," I gasped, searching the room for mayhem. "And I'm...I'm alive?"

"See, Chelsea. Time is running out. You can't keep this up forever," Cole said.

The sun was blaring through the windows, and the warm lake air drifted in through the screen door. Cole snapped his head to the side and glared under the stairs where a small wooden table stood next to the leather chair. On the table was a reading lamp and my cell phone.

"What are you looking at?" I asked.

"Reality," replied Cole.

Then I heard a whisper come from under the stairs.

"Times up," it groaned.

Cole shoved me behind him as if shielding me from something. All of a sudden, the room went dark, and the warm breeze turned icy. In a split second, a wicked storm slammed the house.

"Cole, what's happening? Was that Brent?"

My voice wavered and my teeth chattered both from fear and the biting cold. Cole turned his back on the stairs and took my face in his hands.

"That can't be Brent. He's unconscious. It's a warning, and you need to listen. You need help badly."

Though visibly shaken by the crazy hallucination I just had, I was back with him and perfectly safe. Strangely, at that moment, I was feeling healthier than I had in a long time.

Cole said, "You're not healthy. Things are not good, Chelsea. You can't even tell what's real and what's not."

Outside, the wind howled. The eerie voice came from another direction this time. It came from the kitchen, behind me.

"Game's over, Cole," it groaned.

Again, Cole put himself between the voice and me. My hair blew wildly from a gust of wind that ripped through the room. Cole pushed the hair from my eyes and looked around, he seemed to just notice the storm.

Outside, the sky had become other-worldly; it was sinister and frigid. Black, heavy clouds swirled over the lake, yet there was a bright blue sky beyond the hills. Hail, rain, and debris pelted the roof. Boats cut against the docks as the waves slammed into them.

Cole asked, "Do you remember the dream you had a few months back? You were in a dark room with a man whose face you couldn't see. Do you remember?"

"Yes. Of course."

"Do you remember what I told you?"

"I knew that was you."

"Don't focus on that. Answer me. Do you remember what I asked you to do?"

Lightning lit up the room, and thunder cracked above us. The howling wind whipped our hair in all directions.

"The details are foggy," I said. I racked my brain to remember, but memories were so hard to recollect lately. Then it came to me. "I made a promise," I hollered over the wind.

"Yes. You need to keep that promise. Now. Please swear to me that you will keep that promise, Chelsea."

I shook my head, searching for the answer. I couldn't remember what I had promised in the dream. That deja vu feeling revisited me. At the same time, I was realizing that all I had surmised from that dream was wrong. There was nothing mystical or romantic about it.

It wasn't about finding love or discovering a new side of myself. The dream was my future. My heart sped up, my thoughts raced. If Cole was actually the man in the dream, then this moment was headed full speed at becoming that nightmare.

"I should remember," I said. "Why can't I remember what I promised to do?" Suddenly, a memory came flooding back. "Wait." I clutched my chest, remembering how he ripped my heart out of my body. He knew what I was thinking.

"No, not that. I won't hurt you. Chelsea, you promised not to forget. You promised you would remember, and you need to do that now, even though things may seem like they've changed."

"You ripped my heart out. Why did you do that?"

The grotesque and frightening image was burned into my head. He had said then that he didn't want to hurt me. Yet there we were, and it was beginning to play out in an all too familiar way.

"It was done to jog your memory, in case you forgot. It was to help bring you back to this moment. And most importantly, it was to show you what you were capable of," he said. "But I didn't do that to you."

"But it was you. You said so."

"How could you forget something so terrible, right? That was the point. It was a strong message."

"How could something that starts so heavenly end so horribly? That's what you asked me."

"Have you ever wondered that?" he asked.

"Only once," I replied.

"Exactly. Listen to me, there's duplicity here that you're unaware of. Try to understand that I didn't ask you that, and I didn't rip your heart out," Cole said.

"I did it," someone in the room hissed.

I jumped and shrieked. I grabbed onto Cole, and he wrapped me in his arms. The long curtains danced in the wind next to the door and knocked the lamp off the end table. The pictures on the wall swayed, and magazines flew into the corner of the room. I buried my face in his chest.

Cole, unexpectedly calm and composed, lowered his face to mine. He smiled and kissed me. Despite the torrential noise and wrath of mother nature going on around us, he spoke quietly, now. I heard him as if we were alone in a bubble.

"Chels, it's very simple," he said. "You promised one simple thing. Wake up, that's all. All you need to do is wake up. You're stronger than you know. And if you truly want to wake up, you can. I can't shield you from this much longer."

Then in a startling, uneasy instant, the raging arctic winds stopped howling. The room went dead silent and pitch black with the exception of one sheer, white curtain. It blew softly as the moonlight streamed through the window, illuminating one spot on the floor.

And Cole was gone.

CHAPTER 39

I was frozen, paralyzed with fear. I didn't speak, I barely breathed. There had been someone else in the room with Cole and I before he disappeared. I knew I wasn't alone. Someone, or something, lurked in the darkness. Despite its androgynous whisper-like groan with the indistinguishable tone, I still wasn't convinced that the eerie and somewhat familiar voice wasn't Brent's.

I watched the curtain blow in the wind. It had once been a comfort, but that was no longer the case. I waited, not knowing what or who was going to pass in front of the window. How similar would this be to my original dream?

I heard a groan behind me. Then I heard voices, whispers in the dark. There were so many. I could not make out what they were saying; the voices were too low and all muddled together. Time seemed to be moving at a glacial pace.

After a moment, I could no longer stand the feeling of being entombed. I couldn't take the emptiness and deathly cold air. I was overcome by the hideous smell that crawled through the room and the growing fear that I was trapped. The fact that someone was in the room waiting to hurt me became trivial. Hurt me. At the very least, I would feel alive, I decided.

"Cole!" I screamed out. "Cole. Are you there? I can't do this alone. I don't know how to wake up from this!"

There was no response. The whispers picked up; there were more, and they were getting louder. One in particular stood out from the rest. He said, "I won't leave. I'll be here when you come back."

I would have sworn it was Cole.

"It wasn't me, Chelsea," Cole said as he walked into the light of the moon, his face shadowed just as expected. When he passed by the window and stepped out of the moonlight, he disappeared into the darkness.

"But he sounded like you."

"I know. Exactly like me."

"Why do you keep leaving me? I'm scared."

Cole appeared before me now. I could tell first by his warm breath on my face, then his strong hands came to rest on my waist. Instinctually, I pulled him in and hugged him, afraid to let go. I squeezed him with the intention of never letting him slip away. Then he spoke softly in my ear. What he said caused the first gut-wrenching rip in my soul.

"You heard what he said. He's waiting for you."

That's when I realized that in all the time I had spent with Cole, worried that he would leave me, he never intended to stay. He would never be with me forever. I could try to hold on all I wanted, but it wouldn't make any difference because he had always planned to leave me. And if I did wake up from this hell–he wasn't going to be there.

I shook my head, tears slid down my cheeks and onto his shirt.

"No one is waiting for me," I said. "Please don't make me go. I won't go."

"You, and you alone, have the ability to prevent this from getting worse, Chelsea. I need you to do that. You have power deep within you. A strength that you need to find."

"No."

I didn't loosen my hold; I wouldn't let him slip away without a fight. He pulled his head away from mine and took my face in his hands. His face glowed from the soft shadowy light.

"I can see you," I gasped.

"You think I'm everything you've ever wanted," he said. "But you're wrong. I like exactly what you like: the same food, the same books, the same everything. Because that's what you know, that's what you like. But that's not who you need.

"You need someone different who will surprise you, challenge you, push you, open new doors for you. Most importantly, you need someone who will love you and add to your life, not take it away. He's waiting for you."

"No," I uttered. "There's only you."

"You didn't pull me from nowhere," he reminded me. "All of your hallucinations seemed to have come from something familiar. They were things you knew well or felt strongly for. They were the good and the bad."

"I would remember if I'd met someone like you," I told him with unwavering certainty. "What's the difference if I made you up? You exist to me and I'm dying. So let me die happy."

His frustrated scowl made me nervous. I was afraid he would leave. So I ignored the increasing noise of muffled chaos and whispering voices coming from behind me, and I prayed that I could talk some sense into him.

"Cole, I'm in this too deep. I can't even breathe without you. Let me stay here with you, wherever we are right now. Can't we just stay here?" I begged.

"Listen to what you're saying. This isn't you."

"There must be a way that I can be with you."

"You can't live with me. But you can have a lifetime of remembering me and what we had. You're a fighter, Chelsea. You aren't someone who gives up. So fight. And do it now. I know you hear the voices. Chelsea, the end is near."

"The end is here," the sinister whisper groaned directly into my ear.

"Go away!" I screamed over my shoulder. "What is that, Cole? Tell me what that is!"

"It's too low," I heard a woman say behind me. I looked back but could see nothing in the darkness.

"She's crashing!" a man shouted.

"Chelsea. Come on!" another man yelled.

"You must leave her. Leave her, and she'll make it," groaned the whisper.

"She'll die if I don't help her," Cole told the dark voice.

"Cole, who is that?" I asked again.

"Chelsea! Don't do this," yelled a familiar voice.

My arms were locked around Cole's waist, and I had no intention to let go. I said into his chest, "I'm scared. What's happening?"

He stroked my hair, and asked, "If I stay with you right up until the end, will you keep your promise, and wake up when he tells you to?"

"Will you be there when I wake up?"

"Lie to her." It was the faintest whisper.

"You have to tell me what that is," I implored. But I never expected the tornado of truth that ensued.

"It's you," Cole said.

I wrenched my head back. "Me?"

"You never should have created me. That voice is the part of you who knows this was all wrong; a tragic mistake. It's that lost part of you who wants to survive and knows that I am nothing. Chelsea, please," Cole pleaded. "Listen to that terrified voice inside of you who knows that there is a life waiting for you. Your death is imminent; listen to your will to survive, and I'll stay with you as long as possible, if you will please, please promise to wake up."

My head began to spin. Two worlds were colliding inside of me. For so long, I had been focused on doing whatever it took to be with Cole, and that even included dying. But now, something was changing. There was a part of me that wanted to live, even if it meant living alone.

All of a sudden, guilt washed over me. I was betraying myself and Cole. I was evil for wanting to do anything other than what let me have him the longest. All this time, I assumed that meant I would have to die.

It felt as though I was being pulled down into a murky abyss. I couldn't see clear. I couldn't think straight. The fine line that existed between my reality and my hallucinated perfect life was disintegrating beyond my control. My instinct to live was fighting with my inconsolable heart. She was fighting my broken soul for power–and she was winning.

As the fog in my head gradually cleared, an unpropitious vision of my family, standing around my casket before being placed in the cold ground, flashed before me. My parents were there. Meggie. My friends. Paige under Jackson's comforting arm. I saw Jill and Beth, each one torn apart with grief.

Then there was Cole. He stood behind Ruthie and William with his head down and his eyes closed.

I was drawn back to Paige, Meggie, and my parents. The otherwise joyful family that I loved and admired, now shattered by the loss of a friend, sister, and daughter. I wanted what they had when they were happy. I wanted what they had when they were sad. In them, I saw love that could never leave me. By the time I looked back at the man resembling Cole, everything I thought I knew and wanted had changed.

With my thoughts reeling, my legs collapsed. Cole held me up.

"Hold on to me," he said.

He pulled me up and held me tight. Mumbled voices chattered behind me. But it was Cole's words that were the most clear. At last, I truly understood what he was saying.

"You're going to get through this. You've always been the only one who could fix this. You just need to understand how very special you are. More than anyone knows. And now you understand–it's time to get better," Cole said. "Just listen and wake up when they tell you. And remember, you will never be alone. I live deeper than your heart–I'm in your soul."

A tear slid down my face. I nodded my head, rested it against his chest, and wondered how this could all be happening. He felt so warm. The rhythmic breathing as his chest rose and fell, the strong beat of his heart... it was so real. I counted the beats and memorized the pattern. I inhaled his scent, the faint smell of soap and cologne. I took in as much as I could before he was gone.

"I love you. Thank you for letting me fall in love with you," I sobbed.

"Hang in there, Chelsea," a familiar man's voice yelled.

My chest ached with sorrow and loss for this incredible man I knew as Cole. Words would never be able to explain the person he was or what he meant to me. I would forever hold our love in my heart, alone, unable to share the profundity of what we had with any other human being. He would be mine, and mine alone.

"Wake up. Chelsea. Please, wake up," the voices yelled.

I heard them, but I didn't move. I held onto Cole.

"Find him and you will always have a piece of me. He'll help you find the truth," Cole whispered in my ear.

I raised my head to meet his eyes.

"I will never forget you. I will love you until the day I die," I promised with a hard swallow. "But today is not that day."

"Trust me. You have a greater purpose."

I looked deep into his brilliant green eyes and witnessed one last heart-stopping smile.

I kissed him.

There would be no mention of goodbye in that last moment. Never again would I fear being alone knowing that he would always be with me. It was that belief that gave me the courage to keep my promise.

So I woke up.

CHAPTER 40

I had been airlifted to Strong Memorial Hospital, where I remained unconscious and in serious condition for a day and a half. When I woke up, Dr. Armstrong came in to explain my injuries. I had a concussion, twenty seven stitches in the back of my head, a black eye, a severely bruised collar bone, three broken fingers, and four cracked ribs. I was a mess.

He also told me that something unusual had happened. Upon arrival in the ER, they stabilized me, then they prepared to remove the tumor. However, a pre-op scan revealed that the tumor was gone. Completely. He was as shocked and perplexed as everyone. He noted cases of spontaneous recovery, but he had never witnessed it, especially in such a short period of time.

Dr. Armstrong considered that perhaps there was a problem with the initial tests, and maybe there never was a tumor to begin with. But then what would explain my hallucinations, insomnia, fainting? What would explain all the symptoms I had suffered? What on earth would explain Cole?

Either way, the tumor was gone. As if Cole had taken it with him.

My short term memory was now a puzzle. Some pieces were still missing, but the doctor believed it was only a matter of time before it all came flooding back.

Like a blessing, I remembered Cole. I couldn't recall all the details of what had happened that day, but I knew it was something terrible. There was a deep emptiness in my heart that told me, with no uncertainty, that Cole was never coming back. I wasn't sure if I could face that. So when those painful details popped into my spotty memory, I pushed them aside.

My first day of clear thought was the day I left the hospital. Paige was helping me get dressed while my father pulled the car around to take me home. She held me steady while I slipped on my jeans. She was the first of very few people who would ever know the full story behind those tumultuous months.

"So...maybe you could tell me what happened with Brent. No one wants to talk about it," I said.

"Dr. Armstrong told us not to push your memory. Stress and frustration- not good for you. He said your full memory should come back at its own pace."

"Stress?" I said. "What is there to stress about?"

"He's concerned about what may have caused your hallucinations. Maybe stress? Being home alone? Starting school in the fall..." Paige said. "Look, I do have to ask you something."

"It wouldn't be like you to hold back," I said with a smirk.

"The day you woke up, I asked if you wanted me to call anyone for you. Do you remember that?"

"Not really."

"I specifically asked if you wanted me to call Cole."

She waited for an answer before she helped me with my shoes.

"What did I tell you?" How honest had I been?

"You said that he was dead." Paige sighed. Then she said, "What did you mean?"

"I said that?"

It seemed I was very honest. I didn't want to think about the fact that Cole was gone; dead as I had put it. Except, now Paige was asking me to explain. I wasn't sure how to do that, but I had to tell her something. I knew I could tell her the truth; if there was anyone in my life who wouldn't judge me, it was Paige.

"Yes, you said that. Did you mean you guys broke up?"

"No, I meant he's gone, and he's never coming back." I looked into her questioning eyes. "Like he's dead."

"Did he move away?"

"No."

There was no easy way to explain Cole. So I laid it out exactly how it was. Facts only.

"He wasn't real. I made him up, sort of. He was... a hallucination," I murmured.

The words were painful. I looked at the floor, then sat down on the bed. The room rocked as I prepared for a barrage of questions.

Paige was silent. She merely nodded her head as if she understood. She bent down, slid my Vans on my feet, then sat down next to me. Paige's eyes perused the room. I couldn't imagine what she was thinking. Finally, her eyes found mine.

"I'm sorry about that," she said. "I know how much you loved him. When you're ready, you can talk to me. Understand?"

She put her arm around me and squeezed. I didn't have to explain further. Wow, I loved her. To think, I was willing to leave her–my Paige.

"Maybe in a few days," I told her.

Tears swelled in my eyes. Paige squeezed my hand and smiled.

"Whenever and anytime of day, even if it's the middle of the night."

"Thank you."

"Let's go. Your car is waiting, and that driver of yours is probably getting cranky."

Paige helped me into the wheelchair and wheeled me to the lobby door. I gave her a hug and got into my father's car.

"Took you long enough. Your mother is very impatient. She's called twice and even managed to Snap me," he said lightheartedly.

"Sorry, Dad," said Paige.

"Sorry, Dad," I repeated. Paige and I exchanged a knowing smile.

"I'll see you tomorrow," she said.

"Bring me a mocha chino from Main Street Coffee? Decaf."

"You got it."

My father drove me to our beautiful home on the lake. And though I was happy to be going home, it wasn't without an inkling of dread. Cole had been in that house with me for weeks, and now I would be alone. Well, not truly alone. "I live deeper than your heart–I'm in your soul," I could hear him say.

My dad was quiet for most of the drive. Knowing him, he probably wasn't sure what he was allowed to say. My guess was that my mother gave him a list of rules and regulated conversational topics to abide by. She wouldn't want me getting upset.

"Sorry about your trip," I said, breaking the silence.

"Don't be. I hate traveling."

"How many places did you hit before you had to come home?" I asked.

"We made it through Italy and were heading to France when we got the call from Meggie. Paris is too expensive. Anyway, that ended your mother's shopping spree, so you saved me a lot of money," he said.

"I ruined your trip."

"Honey, there is nothing more important than you girls. It wouldn't have mattered where in the world we were; you girls come first," he said, taking my hand. "I wish you would have told us earlier."

"I didn't purposely keep it from you guys. I'm sorry."

When we arrived home, my father helped me out of the car and grabbed my bags. Out of the corner of my eye, I saw a familiar flash on Ruthie's back deck. By the time I turned to look, no one was there. Initially, I thought it was Cole. My heart plummeted, and I reminded myself what Dr. Armstrong had said. It's possible to have further hallucinations since they weren't sure what caused them in the first place.

The whole family, plus Reznor, was there to welcome me home. But for days, everyone acted strange, as if I were fragile. They all seemed so worried and sad. It got to be extremely annoying.

"Why's everyone acting like you have brain damage?" Reznor blurted out one day.

My mother gasped, Meggie smacked his arm. My father was half-listening and didn't bother to look up from his newspaper.

"Technically, she does," my father said. "But it's only temporary."

I laughed until my head pounded. "Thank you, Reznor."

"For what?" he asked.

277

"For making me laugh. It's so depressing around here. Everyone is acting like I died."

The word "died" had barely made its exit when my hand flew up over my mouth. I ran to the bathroom and cried my eyes out for half an hour while my false reality crashed down around me. It was nothing I didn't already know; it just hadn't fully registered yet.

I didn't die, Cole did. I would never see him again. My grief turned to panic. I needed a hallucination. I worried that I would forget what he looked like, sounded like, smelled like. I wanted to touch him and kiss him. I wanted to love him again.

"I just need a minute," I mumbled through a tissue when my mother knocked on the door.

After a while, when I knew no one was standing outside the door, I scooted upstairs to my room. I watched life happen outside my window. Neighbors worked in their yards, people cruised by on their boats, Ruthie and William were getting their kayaks ready for a trip around the lake. Ordinary life happened outside my window. There was a strange emptiness to that observation because all that life once had to offer me–would never be the same.

During that week, I had a few minor headaches and slight dizziness. I thought I saw Cole two more times, always far away and quick, and always at Ruthie's. A few times, I looked for him and tried to make him appear with wishful thinking, but that never worked.

I started to wonder what would happen if I let myself think about the night Cole left me. I would get to the part where Brent knocked on the door, and Cole warned me not to answer. Then I would stop.

Maybe I didn't want to think about Brent's cruelty or my stupidity. Maybe I didn't want to think about my final moments with Cole. But what if I did? What if I could? Would that force my brain into a hallucination?

Ultimately, I couldn't think about the words that were exchanged or the intimate details. For some reason, all I could deal with were the plain, simple facts: I had a tumor that miraculously disappeared, Brent tried to kill me, and Cole was dead.

The end–for now.

CHAPTER 41

~ July~

July 3rd was the biggest night of the year in Lakeville. It was the night of the Ring of Fire. The Conesus Lake Association had been handing out flares for days to get the lake residents prepared. At ten o'clock that night, everyone who lived on the lake would light their flares and torches at the lakeside in celebration of the Fourth of July. My parents decided to have their annual Ring of Fire party since I had made such a quick recovery. I think they were desperate to find something that would cheer me up.

I had been pain-free since coming home from the hospital. My stitches were taken out early, and my broken and bruised body had fully healed. My mother criticized the hospital staff for "splinting me up for nothing"; bones couldn't possibly heal that quickly. Everyone wondered at my speedy recovery. If only my heart could heal as fast.

As it turned out, my parents had been somewhat successful; planning the party had me looking forward to something for a change. Maybe surrounding myself with enough family and friends would mask the anguish I carried in my empty heart, at least for one night.

July third started out a roller coaster ride. Dr. Armstrong had explained that my hallucinations should fade after a few weeks if they were truly caused by the mysteriously vanishing tumor; and they did until today. At first, I was excited to see Cole on Ruthie's dock in the morning. I had raced out the door at top speed, only to find him gone by the time I got there. Instantly, I felt foolish for thinking he would be standing there waiting for me.

Shortly after that, I saw him go by in a kayak, following Ruthie and William. I was standing at my bedroom window when we made eye contact. I waved on impulse. When Cole waved back, I fell to the floor in shock.

Seeing him twice in one day was unusual, and I began to wonder if there was greater meaning to his sudden reappearance. The tumor had grown so quickly the first time, it would be naive to think it couldn't happen again. Or who was to say the last scans I'd had weren't the mistake, and the tumor was still there? Either way, I would keep my new suspicions to myself for now. I'd deal with that next week, openly this time, with family and friends.

As I helped decorate the house for the party, I couldn't escape the thought that no matter how many people I surrounded myself with there would always be someone missing.

For the past couple of weeks, I had been repeating the words Cole had said to me. "I live deeper than your heart–I'm in your soul." Despite my best effort to convince myself that what he said was true, I didn't want him in my soul. I wanted him standing next to me, holding my hand, kissing me. Eventually, I abandoned all hope that he would be with me in any tangible way. The thought that he could only be in my soul was agonizing enough, and despite the painstaking search, I still hadn't found him there.

Even the fruitless seed that Cole planted about someone waiting for me was an impossible joke. For I had nothing to give; I would just be a disappointment. I reached the point where I believed a love like I had with Cole didn't even exist–just like him.

It looked as though I had become what I'd always feared: lonely, empty, and hopeless. Nonetheless, for the people I loved, I surrendered to the idea of simply living each day until I died. Breathe, eat, work, sleep. I could do that. I wouldn't live fully or happily, but I would exist. Cole wanted more for me than half a life, but half was all I was capable of.

Guests were coming at eight. My mother and I munched on hors d'oeuvres as we prepared them. She tried to get me to eat a "decent meal", but I hadn't had much of an appetite lately.

Around seven fifteen, my mother went up to shower and dress for the party. I changed into my bathing suit, slipped on a floral cover-up, and headed for the lake.

Before stepping onto the porch, the two-by-four next to the door caught my attention. My eyes scanned the room, stopping to check out the new flatscreen TV mounted on the wall. I noted the coffee table, freshly sanded and lacquered to remove the stain of my blood. The work of my father, I assumed. I ran my hand down the repaired door frame that surrounded the sliding glass door. A memory of Cole yanking the door handle and yelling to me from the outside crept into my head.

That was the moment. It had been long enough. It was time to remember as much as I could about that night and him.

Mustering all the strength I had, I closed my eyes. I saw him pulling the door open against the will of the frame and the shards and splinters flying through the air. I heard the cracking noise as the wood split from the body of our home. I saw Brent's shock and anger when Cole shoved him aside to get to me.

My eyes popped open. I wondered about the person who really saved me. My mind had turned him into Cole, but Ruthie said he was a neighbor in the right place at the right time. I had so many questions. What was his name? Why was he in my backyard? If not for him, I wouldn't have made it. Brent would have killed me. It was only right that I should reach out to him soon to express my gratitude.

I opened the door and strolled across the grass, all the while reliving the journey towards Cole's demise in my head. I remembered Cole begging me to get help; he knew I was dying. The wretched storm that came and went so fast, the phantom-like voice who turned out to be me; I did want to live after all. Then–my final moments with Cole.

I continued barefoot across the dock until I got to the end. The warm air washed over me. I knelt to feel the water before jumping in. That's when the sky faded into a soft pink. The beautiful reflection in the water, as the sun dipped behind the hills, stripped away every bit of strength I had.

I was torn. I wanted to remember everything, yet I was still afraid.

I crumpled onto my stomach. My arms and head dangled over the edge of the dock. My hair slid into the water and floated around until it hid the pink light from my view, briefly shielding me from my memory of Cole.

After a few seconds, I couldn't take it. It hurt too much. The fleeting satisfaction of not thinking about him began to smother me. It was no longer about what I wanted; I needed to see the pink water again, I needed to remember. So I flung my hair to one side to see the glistening water. It was soft and warm like all of my memories of Cole.

When I successfully gathered my emotions and the urge to cry had passed, I got up to remove my cover-up and froze. A young man was walking across the lawn from Ruthie's yard. The blood drain from my face.

Cole looked more magnificent than I remembered. His hair was a little longer, it curled out from under his hat. He was wearing a white button up shirt half tucked into his jeans. His necklace was almost invisible against his tan skin. I took a deep breath and let it slip out as reality sank in.

What I had suspected earlier was right. I needed him again, and he was back to help with the rough road ahead. I was elated to have him back, but at the same time, I knew how things worked. If I was going to die this time, I prayed that he could stay with me until the end. More than anything, though, I hoped he would end up with me when I left this life.

Cole stopped at the edge of my dock. I glanced around to see if anyone was looking in our direction. No one was close enough to see that I was talking to myself.

"Hi," Cole said.

"Welcome back," I replied.

"I hope you don't mind, but I got tired of watching from afar. I couldn't wait anymore."

"No, I don't mind. I've seen you around and wondered if you'd be coming by."

He nodded his head and put his hands in his pockets. He strolled towards me. I was ready to throw myself into his arms until I saw Ruthie from the corner of my eye. She walked onto her deck and hung a wet towel over the railing. She didn't seem to notice me as she walked back inside.

"I wanted to come by earlier, days ago, but I was forbidden," Cole said.

"Well, I'm glad you're here now. And I know what this means. You don't have to worry about me. I truly believe that if this is the way it's going to end–I wouldn't change it for anything."

He cocked his head to the side and asked, "Do you always talk in riddles?"

By this time, he was an arms length in front of me and looking deep into my eyes. It was as if he had never left.

"You know what I mean," I said.

For a few seconds, time seemed frozen. We were like two people who hadn't seen each other in years and didn't know where to begin the conversation.

I broke the silence with, "I was just going for a swim. Come on."

I pulled my cover-up over my head and jumped in. I expected to see him next to me when I came up, but he was still standing on the dock.

"Come in," I whispered, in case Ruthie was listening.

"I'm not wearing my swim shorts."

"So? You're going to let that stop you?"

Cole glanced over at Ruthie's house in thought, shrugged his shoulders, and kicked off his shoes. Next came his shirt and pants. Until finally, he stood on the dock in his black boxer briefs preparing to dive in.

"Your hat," I said.

"Thanks," he replied, taking it off and throwing it on top of his clothes.

Then he dove in.

That's when several things happened at once.

That's when life as I knew it changed forever.

First, when Cole raised his arms to dive in, I spotted a scripted tattoo on the left side of his rib cage. The Cole I knew, never had a tattoo. Then I heard Ruthie.

"Oh, for heaven's sake. Tell that boy to put some clothes on." A red swimsuit went flying past my head. "Good Lord," Ruthie huffed and stormed into the house.

My jaw dropped, and goose bumps covered my body. He was under the water somewhere. For a split second, I thought the whole thing was a hallucination, and perhaps he would never come up. I waited motionless, holding his swimsuit, scanning the water with wide eyes.

Finally, he emerged in front of me. He pushed his shaggy locks out of his face, giving me a better look at his tattoo. It was like I was seeing him for the first time. I stood there looking dumb.

"What's the matter?" Cole asked with a smirk. "You told me to come in. I couldn't get completely naked."

Unable to think of anything else to say, and trying to comprehend what was happening, I mindlessly asked, "Is it always that easy for a strange girl to get you out of your pants?"

He laugh and said, "Well, you are strange. We agree on that. But no. I was afraid if I left to change my clothes, you would be gone before I got back." His eyes widened. "Hey, are those my swim shorts?"

When he reached for the swimsuit, my fingers grazed his tattoo. He retracted and laughed again.

"How long have you had that?" I asked.

"I got it when I was sixteen. Thought I was being rebellious," he said. "I suppose it's still relevant."

Written in elegant black script was:

"Dream as if you'll live forever.
Live as if you'll die today."

"I agree. It is very relevant," I said. "That's James Dean. Were you a rebel without a cause at sixteen?" I seemed to be asking everything but the obvious.

"I only thought I was a rebel without a cause. Life is proving me wrong lately. Seems I have a cause, after all. Anyway, didn't work out for James in the end."

"I suppose you could say he lived by his words," I said.

"And died by them." He cleared his throat. "Where'd you find my suit?" he asked.

I pointed to Ruthie's house.

"Yikes. That's what I was afraid of. We went kayaking this morning. I must have left it in her bathroom." He leaned in and asked, "She saw me here?"

I nodded yes. He winced.

"Ooh...She's going to kill me. Literally. I bet she's loading her nine millimeter as we speak."

I nodded again. All I could do is wait for the hallucination to end. But what if it didn't? Could it truly be that this wasn't Cole. His face sobered with his next question, which eerily came out of the blue. It was as if he could tell what I was thinking.

"You do know who I am, right? I mean, Ruthie said sometimes you're a little forgetful. Because of what happened."

I studied his eyes. I watched the water trickle down his cheek and settle on his lips as it had the first time we met. A puzzle piece fell into place, and everything around me screamed that this person was not Cole, but in fact, very real.

"You're him," I uttered. "You were here in May when I jumped in the lake."

It was an unbelievable recollection. An incredibly hot boy pulling me from the lake was not a hallucination. More importantly, the boy was real. The person standing in front of me was the inspiration for my heavenly hallucination. He was the dawn of Cole.

"You were hiding from the evil bees. They were trying to kill you, remember?"

My cheeks started to heat up like on that first day.

"Yes. Stalkers actually." Stalkers. Brent! I gasped. "You're him. You're the one who broke down my door and called for help."

"I did. Sorry about the door."

"Don't be. It's already fixed."

"I know. I did that too."

"You did? Thank you. Thank you for everything. You saved my life. There's so much secrecy about my incident."

"That would be Ruthie's fault." With his swimsuit in hand, he turned and swam towards the dock. "Be right back. Don't go away," he said.

When he reached the dock, he wiggled around, then flung his boxer briefs onto the dock. My heart skipped a beat.

"Caleb Maxwell! That's it! What kind of girl do you think she is?" Ruthie snapped from her kitchen window.

Caleb Maxwell, that name sounded familiar.

"I'm getting my swim shorts on," he explained, wiggling more. When he dove under the water to swim back to me, he made sure his swimsuit was clearly visible.

"I think you said you had somewhere to go, young man. Aren't you going out with a friend?" Ruthie declared.

"Oh, I don't know, Ruthie. I might have found something else to do," he said, toying with her. He winked at me.

"Stay," I said. "We're having a party for the Ring of Fire. Stay. Invite your friend. There's going to be a ton of people here."

Caleb glanced at Ruthie, who now stood on her deck glaring at him.

"I'd love to, but I'm not allowed. Orders from the boss." He gestured toward Ruthie with the nod of his head.

"That's silly. I'm inviting you, so stay." I turned to Ruthie, "Caleb is staying. And he's bringing his friend."

"It's Max," he said. "No one calls me Caleb. Just the boss."

"Max is staying," I told Ruthie.

"Then you better get ready because your company is due to arrive any minute. It's almost eight," Ruthie barked and marched into the house.

"Are you sure you don't mind if my friend comes? He's an odd guy."

"If you think he'd want to hang out here. I don't discriminate against weird. I wear a little bit of weird myself."

"That you do," Max said. "We still have fifteen minutes. What were we talking about before we were rudely interrupted?"

"Secrecy. Ruthie is so hesitant to talk about what happened. Do you know why?"

"She worries about you. She says she's following doctor's orders. Plus, she thought you'd be afraid here because of Brent. She wants you to feel safe. And she didn't want me poking around either. But I warned her."

"About what?"

"I told her I made you a promise. And I always keep my promises."

We waded around in the water, getting closer and closer to my dock, and each other.

"Care to elaborate?" I asked.

"I said I'd wait for you. I had already waited months. I mean, I came by a bunch of times, but you weren't here. Then when I finally caught up with you, you were almost unconscious. I wasn't sure if Brent was your boyfriend or some crazy guy who just broke in. Either way, I wasn't going to leave you or let you get away this time. That is—unless you want me to go away."

"No. I told you, I want you to stay for the party. And Brent is not my boyfriend. He is just a psycho jerk."

By this time, I was next to my dock. I pulled myself up the ladder and sat on the top step while Max made his way closer.

"Ruthie filled me in about Brent. I shouldn't have let him off so easily," he said with a scowl.

"Let's not even talk about him."

"Let's not."

"So, you've been hanging around Ruthie's lately?" I asked, thinking about all the times I thought I'd seen Cole.

"Yes. I don't want you to think I'm a crazy stalker. I'm no Brent. I'm sure Ruthie's already done a full background check anyway. I've been hanging out with Will and Ruthie the last couple of weeks. I was worried about you. Plus, they're super cool."

287

He went under water then popped up next to the ladder. He held onto the edge of the dock because the water was too deep to stand.

"Why haven't you talked to me until now?" I asked.

"Ruthie said the doctor wanted you to remember things on your own. Plus, she recognized me from the day I pulled you from the lake, but she thought I was someone else."

"Cole?" I stammered. Saying his name while looking into Max's face wasn't as painful as I thought it would be.

"Yes," Max said. "Another admirer?"

He moved closer. His hand brushed my leg when he reached for the ladder.

I took a deep breath. "No. And that's a long story."

"Got it. But just so you know, we have a lot to talk about. I'm sure we'll get around to him too."

I stood up and wrapped myself in a towel.

"So what you're saying is that you come with an agenda?" I asked with a grin.

"A hefty one, I'm afraid," he said, getting serious.

"I'm sure it will be a fascinating conversation. I look forward to it. I think."

He grimaced and shrugged. I wondered what he could want to talk to me about that would be so important when we'd only met once.

"I should go in and get ready," I said.

He climbed the ladder. I blushed and looked away. Feelings were stirring that I thought were gone forever. In a matter of twenty minutes, I went from feeling hopeless and lost without Cole, to thinking maybe, just maybe, the future did hold something more for me.

I tossed him a towel from the basket my mother left at the end of the dock for guests.

"I'll go get changed and be back in a little bit. It's time for me to go take my beating like a man," he joked.

"Good luck," I told him. "You're going to need it."

I shivered as he walked by. He stopped, rubbed my arms to warm me up, and said something to me. I didn't even care about the sting that pricked me when he touched my arms. I looked up at him as he spoke, and whatever he said disappeared. His words were drowned by his eyes and the smile that made me turn to mush.

"Huh?" I asked.

"William. He's got my back. I'll see you in a bit." He picked up his clothes and handed me the towel. Max jogged next door and caught Ruthie glaring at him out her kitchen window. He hollered up, "Let's go, Ruthie. I'm not afraid of you!"

She shook her head with an adoring smile then waved to me as I walked into my house.

My mother popped her head out of her room when I walked by.

"Are you okay, honey?" she asked.

"Yes. Why?"

"No reason. I'll be on the side deck. Hurry up and get changed."

CHAPTER 42

I threw on a little makeup, camo cut offs, and a loose white t-shirt in record speed. I stepped out on the side deck as my father, Meggie, and Reznor arrived. It was refreshing to see how kind my mother was to Reznor. He was definitely growing on her.

Ruthie, William, and Max arrived next. I introduced Max to everyone, which turned out to be unnecessary. He seemed to be well acquainted with them already. Reznor's "Hey man, good to see you again" completely gave it away. Max did say he repaired our door.

I felt a ping of disappointment that they all thought I was too fragile for them to bring Max around, as if they had to hide him. I was anything but fragile. I almost said something. I wanted to tell them that if they had just let Max talk to me sooner it might have spared me weeks of feeling sorry for myself. Before I could say something, Jackson, Paige, and her parents arrived at the same time, followed by Beth and Jill.

We took the party to the backyard where Reznor connected to my bluetooth speakers with strict instructions from my mother not to play anything "wild". His playlists were bit over the top for some of this crowd.

"Not everyone has your artistic style," I tried to explain. "And my mother has none."

"Train? Van Morrison?" Reznor asked, flipping through the songs on my family playlist, and fully aware that my mother hovered behind him. "Neil Diamond and the Beatles? Really? This is a new millennium. Embrace it."

When my parents walked away, Reznor leaned in and whispered, "Don't tell your mother, but I love the Beatles. As for Van Morrison, Into the Mystic is one of my favorite songs. You should hear my acoustic alternative version. It's killer."

With a playful punch in the arm, I said, "That's my all time favorite song. I'd love to hear you play it. And I have other playlists in case you want to accidentally play something from this century."

"Reznor, the Beatles are icons," my mother announced, sauntering back towards us with her arms crossed in front of her. "I grew up listening to them, and they're still very popular."

"Yeah. Sure," he scoffed, choosing a song from the "safe" playlist.

Reznor turned up the volume on I Want to Hold Your Hand by the Beatles. My mother turned it down.

"You can't fool me," my mother said.

"No fooling, with all due respect Mrs. Raleigh, the Beatles are ancient history. Dare I say...archaic."

My mother stepped closer.

"I know you're going back to school in the fall. Architecture suits you. Your eccentric character is quite inspirational. So you see honey, you're not as badass as you think you are." She patted Reznor on the cheek and flashed him an adoring smile. "You're just a great big teddy bear," she added.

She caught my father's arm as he walked by and off she went, getting the last word, as always. Reznor's cheeks turned bright pink.

"Don't you hate that?" I said.

"Hate it," he growled.

I leaned in and wrapped my arm around his shoulder.

"Just a cute, little, old teddy bear," I mocked.

He laughed and gave me a playful shove.

"Get out of here," he said. "Or I'll blast some gangster rap and shake the hell out of this place."

I wandered off and found Beth. I had a plan for her. I didn't tell her what it was. All I did was ask her to help Jackson find the sparklers in the basement. They had never formally met, other than a wave and a hello when the girls came in to see me at the store. As expected, there was instant chemistry. I excused myself, leaving the rest in their hands.

As the night progressed, I watched Max mingle with my friends and family. He was kind, courteous, witty. He was smart and easy going. He was humble. And the more I watched him, the more nervous I became.

Eventually, Ruthie and Paige cornered me.

I gave them the abbreviated version of Max's connection to Cole. Ruthie finally understood the extent of my hallucinations. And Paige, well, she was surprised to find out what Cole had looked like.

"Man, look at him," Paige said, pointing at Max.

"Stop pointing," I said, grabbing her hand. "Great. Now, he's looking at us."

Max was talking to my mother. He held my eyes for a moment. I waved from across the yard.

Just then, I heard the deep rumble of a motorcycle pull into Ruthie's driveway. Max's friend had arrived.

Seconds later, a tall muscular guy dressed in all black was crossing the yard. It was almost dark, but I could see him remove his jacket and casually toss it on a lawn chair near the stairs. When he turned to look at the lake, I caught a glimpse of his profile against the light of the tiki torches. The guy had a presence you couldn't forget.

Max weaved through the guests, and stood next to me.

"Here comes the crazy train," he said with a crooked smile.

"Crazy sounds about right. Adam and I have already met."

"You mean the night we talked at the Memorial Day fireworks? That wasn't him, that was my friend Mike."

"The Memorial Day fireworks?"

"Okay, I admit it. We did more than talk," he said, getting pink in the cheeks.

That's when it came to me. The hallucination of Cole and I making out in the alley. My mouth dropped open. My face got beet red. I looked up at Max who shifted from one foot to the other.

No. No, no, no, no, no. It couldn't be. I didn't. Did I? I glanced up at Max. Oh, God. I did. I had dragged a stranger into an alley to make-out thinking it was Cole. That was no hallucination. That was Max.

Adam eyed Max in the crowd and headed in our direction.

I cleared my throat. The conversation needed to move elsewhere. Immediately.

"Uh, so… Are all your friends so good looking?" I blurted.

"All but this big ugly one," he said.

"Jealousy. I like it," said Adam as he approached. He turned to me and grinned. "We meet again."

"Hey, you do smile," I said.

Adam reached out to shake my hand.

"Sure you want to do that?" asked Max, pushing down Adam's rising hand. He, too, must have experienced the stinging result from Adam's shuffling feet.

Adam smirked at Max. He looked at me, and responded, "I only smile during the holidays. And when people shove money in my pants." He turned to Max and shrugged. "She thought I was a stripper. Honest mistake."

"Very funny," I giggled. "And it was your shirt pocket, not your pants. But seriously, I'm sorry about how I acted at the gas station. I wasn't quite myself that day."

"None of us are the same anymore," Adam responded.

"Stop," Max said under his breath.

"What? She was having a bad day," Adam said. "That's all I meant."

"I'm not the rude, impatient person you saw. Honestly," I said.

"No worries," he said. "So, I hear Max had the pleasure of pulverizing your twerpy boyfriend."

Max nudged Adam's boulder-like bicep and said, "Leave it alone."

"He was lucky enough to meet Brent at The Green one night," I explained to Max. "Brent tends to rub people the wrong way."

"Small world. Funny how you two know each other," Max said, glancing at Adam.

"Random encounters," I shrugged.

"Doubt that," Adam replied. "I would bet they were one hundred percent not random. What do you think my genius friend?" he said to Max.

"Enough with my eccentric friend here. Let's go for a walk," Max said to me.

"I'm stepping up in your book, man. Yesterday you called me enigmatical. Today I'm eccentric. Look at you flexing your vocabulary to impress the lady."

Adam's jesting shove almost knocked Max over.

"Go eat, Adam. It's been like ten minutes; you must be starved."

Adam rubbed his stomach, and said, "Nah, I'm thirsty. Beer time."

He marched over to the keg where Reznor was pouring a beer.

"What are you doing here, man?" Reznor asked. "Someone call the fire department about our sparklers?" Adam and Reznor shook hands and slapped backs.

"Small world," Adam replied, glancing back at me. "Max and Chelsea invited me."

It wasn't a surprise that they knew each other. Adam, the manager and bartender at one of the few restaurants within twenty miles and a volunteer fireman, probably knew most people in our small town.

Max and I left the two of them to talk and made our way up to the side deck. From there, we stood and watched a barrage of amateur fireworks exploding all around the lake. The town's big show of fireworks weren't going off until ten.

I put my hands behind my back and intertwined my fidgety fingers.

"I bet Ruthie let you have it earlier," I said.

"Nah. I got the cold shoulder for disobedience, but that only lasted about thirty seconds." Max took a step closer. "So tell me," he said. "About Memorial Day...you don't remember. Or do you?"

"That's not it. I do remember."

I looked down at the deck. My face got hot. How could I sum up my experience with Cole in a few words? How could I explain randomly kissing him on the street?

Before I could conjure an explanation, he said, "Don't worry about it. Ruthie told me your memory is spotty. I have a more important question anyway."

"Ask away. I'll answer if I can."

Max stepped forward and hooked his fingers in my belt loop. He pulled me towards him and smiled.

"You're healthy."

"That's not a question," I pointed out.

He leaned in and kissed my forehead. It wasn't just a peck, his lips lingered.

He took a breath and asked, "Have you thought about how or why that is?"

In that moment, thinking was like blindly crossing a freeway of racing emotions and nerves. My nerves made me want to run for the hills while my emotions wanted me to tell him to shut up and kiss me.

"No. I'm just happy to be alive," I said. "But since you asked, I suppose I'd have to go with the misdiagnosis theory."

"We have a better theory," Adam's voice boomed from behind me.

Max took my hand and said to Adam, "I need a minute with Chelsea. Do you mind?"

"A minute is too long. We need to expedite things." Adam held up his phone. "He's coming here. Now."

The Ivory Dome

I watched them from the front porch of my hilltop home, where I could see the entire lake and beyond. I rented the old Victorian for the summer (the perfect perch to watch my subjects with my high powered, government issued telescope when I wasn't out on the water trying to uncover N13's ability).

The three of them huddling together on N13's side deck (most likely discussing their little secret) was proof that the ring members wouldn't be able to stem far from one another in the end. They would be linked forever, and forever they would be drawn together like neodymium magnets. Strangers who had been rotating in the same infinite circles for most of their lives were finally crashing into one another.

Now, it was only a matter of time before they came to me. They needed me, if for nothing else, to help them understand what was happening to them. I was about to provide my most important audience with answers to their growing number of questions that only I could answer.

In the meantime, I gave my secret weapon a few more moments to show before heading to the party that Ashley and Parker Raleigh had kindly invited me to this morning. A closer look at Subject N13, and another conversation with the boys sounded just about right. I knew the boys hadn't been honest with me. So perhaps what they all needed was to be slapped with some reality. Their reality.

At first, I feared N13 was a poor specimen, and the mixture had a flukey effect on her. Yet, there they were. The three of them all together. She was hiding something from me. She left me no choice but to intervene with my alternate plan. The outcome of my next move could devastate her and perhaps even kill her. However, there was a greater chance that she would do as I suspected and rise to the occasion. It was a risky move on my part. It was like playing with a loaded gun; it could undoubtedly backfire. But I was running out of time.

Suddenly, there was a flash of light that could easily be explained away as the blinking of an eye. Ordinarily, I would have thought nothing of it. It was the strong force of swirling pressure behind me that gave it away. The pressure pushed me into the railing. I turned to find my secret weapon standing on the porch with me.

"Brent. Welcome," I said.

"What the...?"

"No worries. You have been doing a wonderful job. I can't say I am completely surprised. Something must be motivating you."

"I thought you were a whack job," Brent gasped, still trying to get his bearings.

"Come on, now. Lean against the railing. It's going to take more than a few flashes before you become accustomed to the head rush." His left arm was in a cast from the elbow down. I took his good arm and settled him against the wooden rail of the porch. "Tell me, how did you learn to control it?"

Brent shook his head.

"Something happened. My dad turned his back on me. Said I was on my own and that I disgraced the family. I got mad. I closed my eyes and wished it were true–what you told me a couple of weeks ago. And now, here I am. Holy crap. Here I am."

I put my hand on his shoulder. He was alone now, and I was all he had. I had to play on that in order to keep him under my control. I had to be the father figure he would need. I thought about my own child and tried to imagine the feelings I might have had–had I been a true father. I channeled what little I knew.

"You're going to be fine, Brent. But I have to tell you, when they discover that you're gone, they will think you escaped your cell. You're a fugitive now. There's still time if you want to go back to that life. However, you should keep in mind that I'm here for you. I could help you to grow your skill, your gift. I could be your family."

He stood silent for a minute, rubbed his forehead in thought, and no doubt in pain. He looked down at his hands and the rest of his body, which seconds ago resided in a jail cell 40 miles away.

"I'm in," he exclaimed. "I can't go back to that life. It's over for me. But tell me, how did I get here?"

"You teleported, my boy."

His excitement gave me a proud smile. I knew this young man would embrace his ability. In time, he would even consider it a power. He just needed to make the right choices in order to live long enough.

He stared at me in awe.

"Can I do that whenever I want?"

"Not frivolously. It will take a lot of work in order to develop it, so that you are safe," I explained, hoping he wouldn't test my advice. "It is very dangerous, especially in the beginning. I will train you."

His eyes grew wide. A smile spread across his face. My pride sunk in that sinister smile. I was quickly reminded of the risk that came with my decision to use him. He was from a failed operation after all, most of whom had all been eliminated. As exciting as this could be, I couldn't forget that despite the strength of his ability, he was fractured, breakable, unpredictable. And that made Brent disposable.

"Are there more people like me?" he asked, bringing his broken wrist to his chest.

"You are the only one who has this particular ability. There are others, though. They have different abilities. Just as amazing as yours, only different."

"You made it seem like you knew of others who could do what I did…teleport."

"I did," I replied. My acting skills were essential here. I looked down at my feet, then deep into his wondering eyes. With a solemn voice, I said, "The ones that were like you didn't make it. They are no longer with us."

He scowled, then puffed out his chest when he realized he was one of a kind.

"What about the other people with different abilities. Where are they?" he asked. "I want to meet them."

"You already have. But you need to practice your skill before reconnecting with them. Plus, we have an important mission. It requires the utmost discretion." I placed my hands on his shoulders and looked him in the eyes. He needed to understand the importance of his role in this mission. "This is a very big deal, Brent. It will be the biggest thing you will ever be a part of. Are you up for the job?"

"Absolutely."

"Good. I shall tell you about them. You will meet them briefly tonight. After that, we train. Now–have a look through here," I said, gesturing to the telescope.

Brent looked through the scope aimed at the group on the Raleigh's side deck.

"Them? No way."

"I am afraid so. Life likes to play silly games. But imagine the fun you're going to have. All things considered."

Brent smirked and said, "If only I had control over this amazing power when I tried to get rid of Chelsea. Wow, life just got a lot more interesting."

"That's the attitude, my boy," I said with a fatherly pat on the back. "But don't be overzealous. Our goal was not to kill Chelsea. You must understand that by now. Correct?"

Brent nodded.

"So listen, dear boy, I have three of them corralled. Your Chelsea just found out she's special. However, I'm not sure of the nature of her ability. I fear they are hiding it from us. But together we will discover what it is.

"In the meantime, we must begin the change. We will start the process necessary for unleashing their true power and finally give the world my gift. It will happen tonight, with this." I showed Brent the yellow gel capsule that held the final blend.

"What is it?" Brent asked.

"It's the beginning of a new world."

The anxious boy said, "Talk to me. Tell me everything."

"Patience, Brent. I understand your thirst for knowledge. And I agree, it's only fair that you learn how it happened. You will want to know who all of my subjects are and what they are truly capable of. But first, we must focus on our immediate goal: to guide them through the next and most important phase. It's time to give them the final oil blend. I believe they have found the final member. I am certain of it. Now, it's time to light the true Ring of Fire."

"There are more than three of them?"

"There are a total of five, my boy."

"Including me?"

"Oh dear," I sighed. "You are special. You are the only one lucky enough to have survived in your group. But I promise, I will tell you everything as soon as we complete the final step to this project." I held up a hand as he was about to speak. "Hold all of your questions. Answers will come," I assured him.

"Fine. But I have one last request before we get started. Can you at least tell me who exactly you are?" Brent said.

It was only natural for Brent to have so many questions, as would the others. And I was the only person who had answers. At long last, people would know me. I nodded and answered him forthright.

"I'm so happy you asked that question. I am the mastermind behind your greatness. I am the creator of pure, imperial, earth-fed superiority," I explained. With an excited sense of pride that I could no longer hold back, I declared, "My boy, I am the Ivory Dome."

CHAPTER 43

I opened my mouth to ask Max who they were talking about, but I was cut off.

"She's not ready," Max said. "It's not fair to do this now. We all had months to figure this out."

Adam frowned. "At the risk of sounding insensitive–screw fairness. There's a lot more at stake than that."

"We don't even know exactly what she went through. It's been more complicated for her. It's all been in her head."

Max's 'in my head' comment threw up a blazing red flag. They acted like they knew things about me, things I had only told Paige and Ruthie. After everything I'd been through, I wasn't about to let this slide by.

"Hey," I interrupted. "Stop pretending that I'm not standing right here. What's going on?"

Adam said, "There's no time to ease into this. You're going to have to trust us. But you already know that. You can feel it. The fact is, we all have something in common."

Adam marched towards me. Max squeezed my hand and dragged me behind him, creating a barrier.

"Stop," Max commanded, slamming his free hand into Adam's chest.

"When I said he's coming, I meant it–literally. He's coming here. He's coming to see her," Adam said, pointing to me. "He doesn't know what she can do yet. We all agreed that keeping it from him is our only advantage. Or am I wrong? Let's not forget that you're the one who said we have no leverage if he knows everything. It's bad enough he knows about our abilities."

"Who are you talking about?" I asked. "And what abilities?"

"We don't know for certain that our theory is even right," Max told Adam.

"Yes, you do, brainiac. You're the one who put the pieces together. I know you like her," Adam said. "I know you don't want this for her. But there is one cold hard fact that is never going to change–she is like us. And we need to prove that before he gets here. Then we need to get the hell out of here."

"How can we possibly prove that?" Max demanded, throwing his hands in the air.

I stepped out from behind Max. I didn't need anyone's protection.

"Look, I have just been to hell and back, so whatever is going on here, I don't want any part of it."

"You don't have a choice," Adam snapped. "Are you going to stand there and tell me you don't know that? Look me in the eyes, and tell me you don't feel how different you are. Something has been going on with you for months. And it's far from over." He snapped his head towards Max and said, "Why don't you go get a beer?"

"I am not leaving her here with you."

Adam softened his posture and said, "I promise to keep my mouth shut. Just take a walk, and think about it. And if you decide to wait–we wait. All I ask is that you seriously consider the consequences we're all facing right now. This isn't only about us."

Just then Adam's cell phone rang. He looked at the caller ID and said, "It's for you."

Max grabbed the phone from Adam's hand. "Yeah?" he said into the phone.

I didn't doubt that Max was trying to protect me from something. But if I was understanding Adam's cryptic words, it meant that whatever their disagreement was about, it was directly linked to the nightmare I had just been through. The last thing I needed was someone stonewalling an explanation. So if Adam knew something, I was going to make him tell me.

While Max was on the phone, I said to Adam, "Well, let's have it."

"I told Max I wouldn't say anything."

"But this is exactly what you wanted; a distraction, time to prove your theory is right. So let's prove it."

"Do you want to hear it first?" he asked.

"It doesn't sound as though we have much time. Isn't that what you said?"

"Good. You trust me. And you're surprisingly brave."

I lowered my voice so Max wouldn't hear me.

"Don't underestimate me," I said. "I have been stalked, beaten, and mentally screwed with. I have survived a hallucination that almost killed me and some kind of brain issue that made me want to hurt people. Including you. So whatever stupid charade this is, it's nothing I can't handle. Nothing."

Adam jumped in with, "You were beaten, almost to death. The bruises, broken bones, the tumor...Look at the scars you have. You call that nothing?"

"So it's true? This theory of yours has something to do with what happened to me?"

Adam began to circle me. Max was still on the phone and heading a few steps down the stairs. When Max was just out of sight, Adam said, "You healed too fast. The tumor disappeared."

"I was misdiagnosed. It was never there."

"You know it was. You know you did it."

My eyes caught the red glow from the celebratory flares and followed it around the lake where thousands of innocent people partied without a care in the world. Music blared. Laughter bellowed. Conversation ebbed and flowed as if tonight was just another ordinary July third on Conesus Lake. But deep down, I knew better. And this angry boy who stood before me–he wanted to make sure I had it right.

Deafening rockets launched from the dock next door, exploded above our heads, and shot ribbons of twinkling color through the dark smoky sky. It was enough to knock me out of my momentary trance only to find his glaring eyes still locked with mine. His eyes bore through me as if he expected me to read his mind.

"You're not listening, Chelsea," he snapped.

"I get it," I confessed. "People always say that nothing bad ever happens in Lakeville. But they're wrong. This town is the perfect cover for all sorts of evil."

Then suddenly, it became crystal clear. I remembered how it all began on that cold and blustery night back in February. All the signs were there. I should have seen them before now.

Every ounce of air in my lungs expelled at once, and with what little breath remained, I managed to utter, "The problem is–I refuse to believe that we are that evil. Something tells me you don't agree."

All at once, the town fireworks began to blast. Our guests and crowds of people from neighboring house parties let out resounding cheers. Down in the backyard, Reznor began his acoustic version of "Into the Mystic".

Without hesitation, Adam grabbed me in a bear hug from behind and sliced my palm open with a pocket knife. I screamed out in pain. Blood spilled everywhere, all over the deck, all over my clothes. My mind raced out of control. This was the last thing I expected to happen.

Adam slapped his hand across my mouth and said into my ear, "I'm sorry. I'm sorry. Listen to me. Shhh.... listen. Close your eyes, and think about your hand. Think about the pain and the cut."

I struggled to free myself from his grasp. He was too strong. I stopped struggling, hoping to catch him off guard and get away. Then suddenly, my palm started to burn. It began as an endless shock that grew into a steady stream of lightning. The pain raced up my arm and through my entire body. I knew instantly it was Adam. The other times we touched, there was a spark, like a nasty shock. Now, the pain was rooted and merciless.

The blood drained from my face, my head tingled. It was all I could do to stay conscious.

Adam said into my ear, "You can make the pain stop. Heal it, Chelsea."

Then he turned and yelled, "Help me. Convince her she can fix this!"

Just before passing out, I heard Adam yell again, "Wait, Max! Stop!"

304

The next thing I knew, I was looking into the ice-blue eyes of the girl from the art gallery so many months ago. We had been shocked at the same time when we touched the glass wall. Now, we were alone in the field where I had pulled the dark-haired girl from her car back in May. The smoke was thick, and the air reeked of burning rubber.

I asked her, "Are you her? Are you the same girl I pulled from the burning car?"

"It seems so," she said. Then with great urgency, she took my shoulders and said, "Listen to me. We aren't going to hurt you. We're trying to show you who you really are. You can heal the wound. Believe you can do it. Want to do it. You're the healer, Chelsea. Do you understand what I'm telling you?"

Suddenly, I heard Max, far off in the distance. Then my eyes opened, and I was on the ground leaning against the house. Max had my hand in his.

With amazement, he said, "You did it, Chels."

Adam was sitting on the ground next to me with a bloody lip.

"Theory proven," he said, out of breath. He winked at me, then said to Max, "Told you so."

I ran my fingers over the vanishing bloody line on my palm. The gash had been replaced by a bright pink line that was fading into a peach colored scar, like the one on my shoulder, the one on my other palm, my wrist, my head... My eyes widened.

"Who was that girl?" I gasped. I looked to Adam. "The one from the car accident. She spoke to me."

Adam and Max exchanged a glance.

"That was Emma," Max said. "We need to get out of here before he gets here."

"Who?" I asked.

"The person responsible for this. The one who did this to us," responded Adam.

Adam stood up. He and Max helped me to my feet. I was wobbly.

Adam said, "You'll get used to that dizzy feeling. Max, take Chelsea to say goodbye. Make something up so we can leave without raising questions. Meet me in front of Ruthie's house. Our tin god could be here any second, so make it fast. Don't let her out of your sight."

My thoughts were reeling, but there was no time to waste.

"Will everyone be safe here?" I asked Max as we hurried down the deck steps.

"Everyone is safer without us."

Max stopped when we got to the bottom of the stairs. He grabbed Adam's jacket from the lawn chair and tossed it to me. My bloody clothes would provoke questions.

"What will you tell everyone?" he asked.

I slipped into the enormous jacket and shook my head. What could I tell everyone? How could I get out of here without a hundred questions? Then it dawned on me.

"Nothing," I said. "All I need is one person with a hundred questions who won't ask them until I'm ready to answer." I spotted my group of friends far out on the dock watching the fireworks. "Paige will cover for us. If there's one thing she's good at, it's telling a believable story."

"Master confabulator, huh?" Max mumbled..

I grinned and remembered Adam calling him a brainiac.

"Sure," I replied. "Whatever that means."

We weaved through the crowd of people, all staring up at the exploding sky, until we reached the end of the dock. I tugged Paige's elbow and whispered, "I'm leaving with Max and Adam. If anyone asks where I went, make something up so no one worries."

"What? Where are you going?" she demanded, taking my hand.

"I can't tell you now. I promise I will later. Trust me."

Paige tilted her head and squinted her curious eyes at Max. I squeezed her hand.

"Please," I implored.

After another second, she sighed. "I've got you covered," she said. "Go. You owe me, though."

"You're the best. I love you."

I hugged her, then turned to walk away. For a split second, my stomach sank. Uncertain of when I'd see her again, I turned and hugged her once more.

"Seriously–is everything alright?" she asked.

"Never better," I replied.

Max grabbed my hand, and we slipped out of the party. My head spun with questions and one unbelievable truth that would become my greatest secret. I couldn't begin to understand how it all happened or what would happen next. And I didn't know what it all meant, like Max and Adam seemed to. But there was one irrefutable reality. I had become the person I was meant to be, the person I am today.

I had become–The Healer.

Made in United States
Orlando, FL
01 July 2022

19339657R00189